Praise for *The Blazing Tree*

"MARY JO ADAMS
with her mid-ninetee
voice and the atmos
into a rewarding rea

—Dianne Day, author of the
Fremont Jones historical mysteries

. . . and the other mysteries of Mary Jo Adamson

"ADAMSON WORKS THE CLASSICAL
WHODUNIT FORMAT WITH GREAT
INGENUITY. She writes like a dream."
—*New York Times Book Review*

"MARY JO ADAMSON OFFERS AN ENGAGING
DETECTIVE STORY peopled with striking
characters." —*Publishers Weekly*

"ADAMSON HAS GIVEN US A GOOD, SOLID
MYSTERY that is satisfying and fun. I highly
recommend her books."
—*The Drood Review of Mystery*

The

BLAZING
TREE

A Michael Merrick Mystery

Mary Jo Adamson

A SIGNET BOOK

SIGNET
Published by New American Library, a division of
Penguin Putnam Inc., 375 Hudson Street,
New York, New York 10014, U.S.A.
Penguin Books Ltd, 27 Wrights Lane,
London W8 5TZ, England
Penguin Books Australia Ltd, Ringwood,
Victoria, Australia
Penguin Books Canada Ltd, 10 Alcorn Avenue,
Toronto, Ontario, Canada M4V 3B2
Penguin Books (N.Z.) Ltd, 182–190 Wairau Road,
Auckland 10, New Zealand

Penguin Books Ltd, Registered Offices:
Harmondsworth, Middlesex, England

First published by Signet, an imprint of New American Library,
a division of Penguin Putnam Inc.

First Printing, June 2000
10 9 8 7 6 5 4 3 2 1

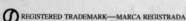
PUBLISHER'S NOTE
This is a work of fiction. Names, characters, places, and incidents either are the
product of the author's imagination or are used fictitiously, and any resemblance to
actual persons, living or dead, business establishments, events, or locales is entirely
coincidental.

For Shannon Jean Schieber

List of Principal Characters

Michael Merrick: narrator, Police News reporter for the *Boston Independent*

Jasper Quincey: owner of the *Boston Independent*, lives in Cambridge, Massachusetts

Trapper: Pequot Indian, occasionally employed by Jasper Quincey

Freegift: manservant to Quincey

Philemon Wells: a trustee of the Hancock Shaker Village

Crispin: a young boy, lame and unable to speak, taken in by the Hancock Shakers

Samuel Grant: former Boston businessman, now a trustee at Hancock

Giles Grant: son of Samuel, has a neurobiological condition now known as Tourette's syndrome

Esther: one of the four trustees at Hancock

Mercy: a young girl taken in by the Hancock Shakers

Thankful: deaconess of the Hancock community

Mother Alma: one of the four elders at Hancock

Jacob: one of the four elders at Hancock

Esau: deacon at Hancock, Jacob's twin

Elijah: artistic brother, shares a room with Giles Grant

Hepzibah: one of the four trustees at Hancock

Seth: the brother who does the veterinary work at Hancock

Amos: the brother who does the blacksmithing at Hancock

Agatha and Ruth: the sisters assigned to nursing duties

Bertha: kitchen overseer at Hancock

Jed: brother in charge of the Boys House

Chapter One

Another young woman drowned. A suicide, no doubt. I was seated at my rolltop desk at the *Boston Independent,* doing another article on it, angry words spurting from the end of my pen as fast as its badly trimmed nib would allow. Once again, no attention had been paid to her death. Like the others, this girl was poor, friendless, and therefore of no interest to society. No one cared. The fisherman who dragged her from the Bay complained that her body had snarled his lines.

When I started writing, the summer evening's light filled the room. Now shadows were waiting in the corners to take over. I was aware of that because I had to squint at the foolscap paper. But I didn't stop.

I was alone. I was sure I was. The offices of the newspaper closed at 6:00 P.M., and the doors were locked. The pressmen, who'd been at work since early morning, hurried out as fast as they could to their supper, their families. The quiet was loud without the uproar of the printing press, the commotion of people. I'd have heard any noise, the slightest tread on the creaky wooden floors. I was familiar with the old building's arthritic complaints since I was often there at that hour. I had nowhere to go.

Although I'd been the Police News reporter for only a few months, the story I was working on was already a familiar one. These dead girls—there were too many of them. This one was with child. That was not unusual, either. Her name would probably never be known. She'd be buried in an unmarked grave long before she was missed, if she ever was. She could have been a servant sent away without a ref-

erence and, without that, she'd have been unable to find another job. Since women only worked as servants, she could
starve or take to the streets. The sole notice taken of her
passing would be in the list of police activities, the account
often followed by the arrest of a pickpocket or the damages
done by a runaway carriage horse. Any injuries suffered by
the horse would be described. Hers wouldn't be.

Death by drowning. I described it as best I could so the
readers could imagine. The desperate lungs swelling in the
need for air, the last frantic gasp, the mouth flying open, and
the choking water pouring in. My own breath became short.
My pen nib slashed at the paper in places.

Writing a longer story on the drownings was all I could
think to do. It might be printed, even if my previous efforts
to do this had been ignored.

To call myself a reporter was not quite accurate. All my job
entailed was the simple noting down, without elaboration, of
the pursuits of the Boston Police, formed only three years ago
as a response to the even less effective constabulary system. I
didn't think of myself as a journalist, an opinion obviously
shared by my editor.

Yet the sight of those young girls, unprotected in life, sav-
aged by death, wouldn't leave me, try as I would to forget
them. I did try. I'd decided that, to live at all, it was best to
sink into a state of emotional lethargy. Some feelings I'd
completely forgotten: joy, love, hope. I was used to the
deadweight of despair, the rat teeth of guilt. But anger
caught you unaware. Lately, it happened a lot.

I felt its flash today at the morgue, looking down at the
girl just pulled from the Bay. She hadn't been in long—her
features weren't bloated. There was a heavy bruise near her
mouth, perhaps caused by a floating log. The water from
her streaming hair dripped down her pale cheeks like tears.
She lived in a city whose numerous churches rang with ser-
mons on Jesus' teachings, which He'd summarized neatly:
Love God and your fellow man.

At Harvard, courses in theology were required, so I'd
taken them. I was not interested, but the campus rang with
debate between the Calvinists (who had control of the uni-

versity) and the Unitarians (who wanted the control). As an undergraduate, I just threw up my hands and closed my ears.

I wanted nothing to do with any God, particularly the Calvinists' fierce, mean-spirited one. He'd sent His son to save us, but only a few of us. Everyone else was damned at birth, not only to the hell that earth could be, but everlasting torment below, no matter how good a life they lived. The trick was to decide whether or not you were one of the saved. In the journals of the early American settlers, there was a story about one young woman. Driven mad by the agony of wondering, she threw her baby down the well, saying, "There, now I know I'm one of the damned!"

The Unitarians' God seemed more benevolent, but no one was sure of His exact address. They didn't believe Jesus was God, even though they thought Jesus' teachings were those of a genius. Their idea on the afterlife was that there was one. Someone remarked that the Unitarians had forgotten everything about religion, except meeting on Sunday. Most of the Unitarians had clean nails and sat in libraries where they pondered the soul of the universe. It was an intellectual religion.

But religion blazed with emotion for every other American. In the revival tents, preachers ignited the audience with the idea of God's infinite love and mercy and, in the same breath, described the exquisite tortures of the fire waiting for most of us if we didn't change our lives to suit Him. Moreover, each day a new sect mushroomed up to tell us how to do that. They all had definite views of the afterlife. It didn't concern me: I knew there wasn't one. I was grateful.

Passing the street-corner preachers, I noted that all this burning zeal didn't seem to melt the hearts of the religious toward their fellow man. It became dangerous when it hardened into law. If believing in God's goodness was difficult for me, seeing any in man was impossible.

Why the fate of these girls weighed so heavily on me, I didn't know. Until very recently, I'd been living on the docks where they'd beat you senseless to steal your sodden handkerchief. Of course, while I was there, I had a way of getting away, so to speak. In some corner of every dark alley, there was an opium den. My own feet had brought me to the edge of the sea. These young women had no choice. Someone should have cared for *them*.

Then, there was what happened on my first day in this position some six months ago. It was a bitter February afternoon. I'd been following an officer with a young recruit in tow. Picking our way down a filthy street where the ramshackle buildings leaned on each other or they would have all fallen, the men were stopped by an angry woman flying toward them, her thin gray hair straggling from a mobcap. She cried out, "Murder! You come and see what she's done!"

Still yelling, she turned into a tall tenement, and we hurried behind her up five flights of rickety stairs. She flung open the door of an unheated attic. An unconscious young woman lay on a bed of blood. She was dressed but her long skirts were above her knees. Between them lay a blue, wrinkled infant, obviously dead. It was so cold in the room that a thin skim of ice had formed on the pooled blood.

Indignantly, the landlady gasped out the story. "Comes here last week and her condition was plain, only I didn't guess she was that far along. Said she'd been a tweeny maid and was turned out because of her belly. Master did it, *she* said." The woman snorted in disbelief. "For the few coins in her pocket, I give her this room and a bit of supper if she'd do the washing up. One week only and that was goodness on my part."

Her skinny hand swept the dirty, low-raftered room. "Could've put two men in here and gotten a bit more, I could. And look what she does to me. She didn't come down last night. Lazy, is what I thought. I come all the way up here this afternoon and find *this*. Wicked girl!"

Because of my height, I was forced to bend my head near that bed. The girl's features still had a childish roundness and I was forcibly reminded of my sister, although Celia had been older, nearly eighteen.

The officer was feeling for a pulse. When he let go of her arm, her hand fell toward me, stretched out in mute appeal.

His face stonily indifferent, he nodded toward the young recruit. "Still alive. Fetch a wagon. We'll take her off to jail."

I burst out, "But she needs to go to a hospital."

"That's as may be," the policeman answered. "But the babe's dead. Got to answer for that, don't she?"

The next day the girl was all but carried into the courtroom. Her skirt was stiff with the brown, dried stains. She couldn't stand in the dock so two policemen held her upright when the conviction of murder was read out.

Remembering that scene, I threw myself against the chair back and sat still. At last, rubbing my strained eyes, I glanced up. There *he* was, standing silently beside my desk. He'd made no sound. That didn't surprise me, nor did it occur to me to wonder how he'd gotten through a locked door. What shocked me was seeing him at all. Always before, when he came to my memory, I thought he was one of the dreams brought on by the tincture of opium to which I'd been addicted. It appeared he was real.

Dressed now in a sack coat, a standing collar, his black hair almost hidden by a flat-crowned hat, he looked only vaguely like the Indian he was. On the street, should he be noticed, he might have passed as a clerk of Mediterranean ancestry. But in the weeks (months?) we had spent in the forest, he'd worn just a loincloth and a headband to hold back long hair.

His face was not remarkable, but his eyes I remembered. They were not dark, more like the color of the hazelnut, and as hard as that shell.

He was my savior and my torturer. He'd force me from the rounded hut with its lung-stopping heat into the bone-cold river. Brought back, I'd be tightly wrapped in soft bark impregnated with herbs. The smell of those herbs—some sweet, some vile—was as much a presence there as he was. When the desire for the opium shrieked through me, he brought a liquid mixture of them in a cup and held it to my lips. This drink, whatever it was, soothed me.

You would expect, if I could recall so much, that I would be sure I had been in that hut and with that man. No. Only another opium-eater would understand. For then you often dwell in a shadowy cave with real dreams. In one I was buried for centuries in the viscous mud of the Nile and could sense its slimy weight on my skin, could taste the brackish water on my lips, could smell the rotting reeds, feel the reptile skin of snakes and crocodiles as they crawled over me.

Then I awoke to trumpets, and the nightmare ended. I saw the faces and forms that were worth all the world to me. My hands were clasped; it was only allowed for a moment. I would never see them again, and I knew it.

But I was not awake.

When I finally came to myself, I was in a clean, bare room on a back street, only the occasional clop of horses on the cobblestones to make me aware that I was in the city. The craving for the drug remained, but I no longer had the desire to satisfy it, quite a different thing. Mrs. Parker, my landlady, was willing to talk—on any topic—but she knew little of the circumstances that brought me there. I'd come in a hansom cab, and the driver gave her an envelope with sufficient funds and a brief note regarding my care. He and her son Abner helped me to bed. Since then, she told me, every week a cab would call, always with a different driver, with another envelope containing money and nothing else. I had no relatives, not even distant ones, and my friends had given up on me long ago. This happening might as well have been part of my dreams. I couldn't imagine who would care for me.

Soon I was well enough to dress and do a few errands for Mrs. Parker. On these outings, I often spied her hulking son somewhere in the background. One day a note came requesting me to call at the office of the *Independent*. The editor who hired me asked a few questions about my previous studies at Harvard, possibly as a way of making sure I could read and write. The job of police reporter was an unimportant one and he seemed only interested in filling it. When I agreed to take it, he gave me a few directions and picked up his pen as a sign that the interview was over.

I asked, "Could you tell me who recommended me for this position?"

He gave me a long look and then returned his attention to the paper on his desk, muttering, "I can't recall."

Trying to find the answer to that question, I asked the reporter at the next desk who owned the newspaper. Although he covered the shipping and financial news, he shook his head, saying that the *Independent* was part of a company called Harmony Holdings but who or what *that* was he hadn't been able to discover. Leaning nearer to my ear, he added that the word was the owner was someone named Jasper Quincey, a rich eccentric, supposedly very unsociable. It was known that he sent notes to the editor, who then became unsociable himself, but no one at the paper had ever seen the man. Rumor had it that Quincey saw no one.

Quincy—without the *e*—was a well-known name in Massachusetts, but I wasn't acquainted with anyone by that name, no matter how it was spelled. I couldn't think of any connection I or my family had had with newspaper people. Soon I gave up wondering about it. My daily routine didn't bring me into contact with old friends, and I made no attempt to call on them.

The break with anything in my past was complete. Then I looked up and saw him.

Before I could speak, he said, "Mr. Quincey wants you."

I kept staring at him. He was real. He'd said what I thought he said. I glanced down at my clothes. It was now late in the evening and my wilted shirt was barely presentable. It had been a hot day and I spent part of it at the morgue, so that penetrating smell still clung to my tan cloth coat. But clearly I was expected to go immediately. I stood up.

In the hansom cab, I remarked to my companion that I didn't know his name. He didn't answer for a long moment, then he replied. "Your people call me Trapper. You speak with Mr. Quincey." He said nothing else during the long ride through the dark streets. Because of his straight-backed silence, I didn't talk either. I wanted to, but I wasn't sure what to say.

In a way, I was well acquainted with him, yet he'd said almost nothing in that time. Of his thoughts and feelings, I had no inkling, and he seemed too different for me to even guess at them. I was sure he'd answer no questions.

As we finally clattered across the West Boston Bridge, it became obvious we were going to Cambridge. I pressed against the seat so I was more in shadow. It was not to keep from being recognized. That was always possible, of course. Although last year Cambridge had pronounced itself a city, its growth spurred on because the bridge had shortened the distance to Boston from eight miles to three, it was still the village it had been, unchanged in its spreading trees and rooted population. Harvard students came and went, but the families who'd settled there had never left and those who taught always stayed, as indeed did some of those who came to study.

I was no longer the fresh-faced youth I'd been then. And I'd kept the beard I'd found myself wearing when I arrived at Mrs. Parker's, although trimming it severely, because I felt it hid the thinness of my face. Unlike my straight dark brown hair, the beard had a touch of curl.

In any case, no one was likely to see me. The heavy carts and clumsy drays that delivered goods to the college during the day—even during the summer holidays—were gone. There were only a few scholars strolling near the Common, deep in conversation, an occasional gentleman on horseback, trotting homeward. No respectable woman would be out on the streets at this hour. It was country-quiet.

I was pulling back, hiding from the memories that inhabited those familiar streets. They were real. I closed my eyes to them.

The layout of Cambridge was not that of the usual town, with the finest houses in symmetrical blocks. There were the palatial residences of "Tory Row" along Brattle Street, but the town's rural origin showed in the scattered country mansions, many now deprived of their surrounding fields. When at last we pulled up in front of a tall fence with iron picket spikes, the outline of the house beyond loomed as large as any of those on Brattle Street. But this was a lonely road, and the murmur of the Charles River was close.

Leafy elms obscured much of the house, which was set

well back from the entrance. The lanterns beside the gate were unlit. The trees and its distance from the road gave the place an air of aloofness, even secretiveness.

Usually I didn't care where I was. One place seemed much like another. But I didn't want to be here. Mr. Quincey didn't sound like anyone I wanted to meet.

Trapper opened the half door of the carriage and gestured that I was to go in alone. The cab was leaving even as I fumbled with the iron latch.

High above me, I could make out a piece of the roof rail and two square chimneys against a pale-mooned sky. The crunch of smoothed gravel beneath my feet was all that kept me on the pathway. As I neared, a little light came from a twelve-paned window to the side of the entrance.

I lifted the heavy knocker and waited.

Chapter Two

The door opened abruptly, but just a crack, and that was filled by a thrust-out candle. It almost blinded me and must have prevented the person holding it from seeing as well. I addressed the candle. "I'm Michael Merrick. I was asked to see Mr. Quincey."

The crack widened barely enough to let me enter. The manservant was thin and small and as well gave the impression of shrinking inside himself to take up the least possible space. His clothing added to his gnome-like look since his brown weskit reached almost to his knees. Under that, he wore a collarless white shirt with rather full sleeves. There was more gray than blond in his thin hair and it was cut oddly—straight across the front, trimmed under the ears and left rather long in back. His colorless lashes blinked constantly.

"I'm to show you to the study." He said it as if he'd had to memorize the instruction or otherwise he would never have considered doing such a thing.

On either side of the wide entrance hall, a graceful banister swept up a curving staircase to an upper story, but the hall itself seemed curiously empty of furniture. There was only a straightback hardwood chair of the kind usually reserved for tradesmen who had to wait. I followed the man, and the candle showed another strange feature. All along the walls, some six feet up, at my eye level, was a narrow board from which protruded spaced wooden pegs. I couldn't imagine the use of so many—there were enough for an entire congregation to hang their coats on.

He preceded me into the room at the end of the long passageway, and when he turned up the oil lamp's wick, I was taken aback. Instead of the cozy, deep-chaired place the word "study" calls up, this was as bare as a Puritan church. There was one leather chair standing at the head of a sizable refectory table. Pine cabinets were built into two long walls. The only touch of color was a thin woven drapery of vivid purple and blue stripes taking up the entire third wall. The fourth one held something I'd never seen before. Ladder-back chairs were hung upside down from pegs identical to the ones I'd noticed in the hallway.

The servant unhooked one, placing it next to me as an invitation to sit. Still staring at this odd system of storing furniture, I did so.

There were two others still hanging on pegs. Gesturing toward them, I asked, "Forgive me, but why are the chairs kept there?"

He blinked at me in surprise, as if the answer were obvious. "It makes the sweeping much easier, sir. Then, they're handy, if needed, but don't take up space when they're not."

"Ah," I answered, then added, feeling more was needed, "very efficient."

He nodded, his lashes moving so rapidly his eyes were obscured, and said, "Mr. Quincey regrets that you had no opportunity to dine. I will bring you a plate."

Having nothing else to do but wait, I did that. The sound of the river was loud; no doubt its bank bordered on the grounds of the house. I decided there were French doors behind the draperies and that the garden came right up to them. There was the intense purple scent of lavender and the Christmas cookie smell of anise seed. My eyes kept returning to all those closed cabinets. The upper ones, given the size of the doors, might have held shelves of books concealed behind them, but the lower drawers were of all sizes, some quite small, all precisely fitted. There were even drawers built into the table, at least on my side. Apparently it served as some sort of four-sided desk as well. I could think of no other reason why a table would have drawers. Given his style in furnishing, Quincey's reputation for eccentricity was deserved.

My friends' houses, and my family home, were decorated very differently. Now that I thought of it, every room was swathed in fabrics. The floors were spread with carpets, the windows shrouded with thick draperies, usually of velvet, and curtains often hung across the entrance to a room. Everything in a room was covered with some material or other. My mother put fringed shawls on side tables and the piano. Scattered about the rooms in étagères, hanging shelves, and on mantelpieces there were all sorts of artworks and pictures: needlepoint, painted china, sculptures and engravings. Every inch of space was filled. The swagged valances above the window drapes were topped with elaborate swirls of brass and cording. Above that was carved molding, and the edges of the ceiling over that were painted with stylized designs. All this was seen as fitting for people of refinement. I was so used to such rooms that I didn't imagine it could be done otherwise.

The servant returned quickly and silently, carrying a tray. He placed before me bread fragrant from the oven, slices of rare roast beef and cream white cheese, a beet salad, crisp greens, and a glass of beer with just the proper head. I hadn't eaten since breakfast but until I saw and smelled that food, I hadn't realized how very hungry and thirsty I was. "That is wonderful," I said fervently. "Thank you."

I'll never forget his expression, one quite rare in my recent experience. His twitching eyelashes stilled to show the mildest of blue eyes. His smile showed how pleased he was that he had contributed in any way to a fellow creature's comfort. "Mr. Quincey is very particular about food, sir. He has a delicate stomach. Mrs. Hingham, the cook, that is, has been with us for years. My name is Freegift and should you require anything, just ring that bell." He gestured toward one hanging on the pegs on the back wall next to the chairs.

Again he left the door open, but my whole attention was devoted to my appetite. When I set aside my napkin and empty plate, I looked again at the room, noticing this time its sense of space and proportion. It seemed to unclutter the mind. Filled with an unaccustomed sense of well-being, I decided that meeting my employer might not be as trying as I'd foreseen.

Then he entered the room. He barely glanced at me, moving to the padded chair, thus putting him too far away for me to offer my hand. I rose. He was a tall man, although under my own six feet three, and quite heavy. His clothing was distinctly old-fashioned, but his straight coat was finely woven and fitted, like his butternut trousers, to hide his bulk. The dark vest was long-waisted and his cravat was tucked into his shirt bosom. Although his wiry gray hair was cut in the same style as his servant Freegift's, it didn't lie neatly on his forehead but curled up with a will and energy of its own. He seemed to be glaring at me but I attributed that to the fact that he had protruding eyes which bulged out beneath half-shut lids.

When he spoke, however, there was an irritated edge to his voice as well. "How do you do, Mr. Merrick. I am Jasper Quincey."

Gesturing to me to be seated, he lowered his substantial weight into the leather chair, causing even that stout piece of furniture to creak. His eyes rested on my cleaned plate.

"My thanks for the excellent supper, sir," I began, "and I'm persuaded that I owe you far more for—"

He interrupted me by placing his palm, not loudly but smartly, on the tabletop. "Since I myself intensely dislike being under obligation to another, I do not wish anyone else to be put in that position. We will not speak any further on this topic." So saying, he drew out a drawer on his side of the table and took out a pair of half-spectacles and a folder of papers.

His first words aroused real skepticism in me. If he did not want me to know that he had any part in my cure, then why send the mysterious Trapper to fetch me? Any hansom cab driver could have done so, and as Jasper Quincey was my employer, I would have assumed I'd been sent for in regard to my work. So I *was* being reminded of an obligation and was to listen with that in mind.

Now, you must understand that I was not grateful. The pleasures of opium are real. I'd first taken it when I'd had an intolerable toothache, and a fellow student pointed at a druggist's shop where I purchased a pennyworth of laudanum, the common name for tincture of opium. My throbbing jaw quieted instantly but, more than that, I felt for the next eight hours a serenity of spirit that was the nearest any human ever comes to happiness. Later, of course, there were those appalling dreams. But, however much I suffered through taking that dusky brown drug, I didn't want to return to the daily anguish that drove me to it.

My immediate past is of no concern here, but I'll set down a few brief sentences about my youth. One night while I and several other students were in a Cambridge tavern debating some philosopher's ideas on the meaning of life, my life lost all its meaning. I returned at dawn to find my home destroyed by fire. Everything was gone—every room familiar from my infancy, my dead father's vast library where I'd sit and feel him near—all was reduced to smoking rubble. That I could have borne. But my mother and sister died in the conflagration.

No doubt men should withstand even dreadful blows with fortitude. I couldn't. At least I didn't. My friends tried to help, but nothing helped. At last, I returned to that druggist's shop. Again and again. Soon I needed a stronger mixture. That was more expensive. Over time I spent my inheritance and abandoned my friends. My once bright prospects for the future were gone.

It must have been Jasper Quincey who, for whatever reason of his own, jerked me back. I didn't want to return. Now I found the man himself wholly unlikable. My attempt at thanks, which had been difficult for me, he'd brushed aside. His manner was rude and arrogant.

But I had to consider something else. He'd provided a way for me to fill my hours. Following in the footsteps of the police takes up the day and much of the night. I traveled all over the city of Boston, by hansom cab and on foot. I came back to Mrs. Parker's so tired that I fell asleep as soon as I finished my cold supper. And, to be honest, seeing the crimes of some of my fellow men made me feel I was not the worst of the worst. The salary was sufficient for my small needs. By getting on the day's treadmill—and staying on it—I could survive. For that, I supposed I owed the man.

Tapping his fingers on the closed folder of paper, he said abruptly, "Most gentlemen would find the work you do repugnant. Do you?"

I considered the question before answering. My plodding round gave form to my days. I had no other reality. I was loath to lose that after so long a time of drifting between illusion and delusion. Whether the work was to my taste or not certainly didn't enter into it. I hedged. "I've learned much that I didn't know."

"Of what nature? Our officers of the law are neither educated nor trained. Shakespeare's Dogberry, who looked for the 'most senseless and fit man for the constable of the watch' might have chosen them. Still, their experience teaches, I suppose. Have you gathered something about their methods?"

I couldn't imagine what lay behind his questions. I answered cautiously, "A few things. Most of their investigations can hardly be termed that. They have little time. A clever criminal will probably not be caught, but most of them are not at all clever."

He took the pages out of the folder. They were in my handwriting, the unpublished articles I had done on the young women who drowned. He looked up; his eyes, even more prominent behind his half-glasses, were fixed intently on me. "You don't say that these deaths were anything but suicides."

Astonished, I said, "I saw nothing that made me think they were."

His reply came. "Yet you might have implied it. You're skilled with words. Had you put forth the suggestion that there was some madman stalking young women, these reports would catch the editor's eye and be published. It would greatly help your career. Didn't that occur to you? The reader would wait for each edition to follow the story."

I clenched my back teeth in an effort to swallow anger. So *this* was why I'd been summoned. He wanted me to invent a trumped-up tale to attract readers. It was hard to control my voice. "Sir, these girls died before they were grown; some could not have been more than twelve. Almost all were without any family. They had no hope of earning any kind of a living. Their choices were the crime of prostitution or death by starvation. They drowned themselves because it's quicker. Society offers them no help at all. Now *that* is a crime. The public should be aware of it. But that can't be done by conjuring up some sort of demented killer creeping after them. To do that to sell newspapers—"

He cleared his throat loudly. "The public *is* aware of it, Mr. Merrick." His dry, sarcastic tone implied that only fools would imagine anything could or would be done by reminding people of these women's situation.

His bulging eyes were fixed on me for a long moment before he went on. "I have no wish to sell newspapers that way either. But I had to dangle a lure in front of you. So, you still retain a concern for the truth and a measure of compassion. It was necessary that I know that."

Then he frowned down at my work. "Of course, these articles are a little . . . too overwritten. Overheated, in fact. You must learn to control your imagination in your writing as well as in your thinking."

Looking up, he asked, "Now, what do you know of a group here in New England called the United Society of Believers in Christ's Second Appearing, commonly referred to as the Shakers?"

I had my eyes on the table so he couldn't see how infuriated I was by his ruse and his comment on my work. I jerked my head up at his abrupt shift. By chance, I'd overheard a quarrel between two women on that very topic the Saturday before. As a way of paying him back, I related it as an answer. The incident took place in the open air market where farmers' wives were setting up their fruit and vegetable stalls. One thin-faced woman was holding forth to her companion about the Shakers. "Our preacher has read a book, a whole book, about *their* goings-on. Written by a man who was one of them. He says they are the spawn of the Devil. They talk folks into signing over their property to them. Even whole farms! They've been taken to court for it. And on Sundays, they don't sit and listen to a preacher like decent folks. They shake and wiggle their bodies, dancing and pretending to call out to the Lord. The worst is," here she'd dropped her voice a little, "they dance at night. Outside. Nekkid! Men and women together." Her listener tittered nervously.

But a red-haired woman at the next stall, in a brogue as thick as the peat in her native Ireland, burst out. "Sure, and I won't be hearin' anythin' bad about Shakers. Not one word. I'll be tellin' you what a Shaker man did. The year, the bad year, we had the drought and then the spring came, drownin' the fields, he came by, sellin' their good seeds. We needed 'em bad, we did. But I had nothin' to buy with. Lookin' around the place, he could see that. He says, 'Take them. As a gift.' An angel he was, not a man."

The first speaker drew herself up. "Are you saying our minister would tell lies? He is God-fearing. And, and . . . a ejicated man. He read these things in a book—a printed book."

The Irish woman waved away the remark with a freckled hand. "There's lies told that way, as well as with mouths. So our priest would say." Then she saw her neighbor's hand close over an egg and she grabbed for a ripe tomato.

I finished, "The policeman I'd been talking to rushed in to stop them."

Quincey shrugged. "That mixture of half-facts and gossip is the extent of the general public's information. What do *you* know?"

He was a hard man to needle. I answered shortly, "Nothing of the Shakers' beliefs. I've heard they do a thriving business in their seeds and medicines and they have a reputation for quality."

"Indeed. Their 'physick gardens'—as they call them—are a wonder to behold, and the syrups and ointments they make from what they grow are exactly concocted each time. The seedhouses where they package them are kept scrupulously clean, and each variety sorted into its proper drawer. All of this is a most time-consuming process. Many herbs are regarded as weeds and yanked out of tidy yards, but to cultivate the best strains is not easy. Others are seen as flowers, the *Crocus sativus,* for example. It takes infinite care to extract a tiny amount of saffron from the stigmas of that plant and—"

He interrupted himself, although his look implied that it was I who'd rudely stopped him. "I do *not* digress. This is to the point. I can vouch that the Shakers' reputation is deserved." Waving a hand in the direction of the bright drapery, he added, "I have a conservatory where I grow herbs year round."

Tapping a finger on the tabletop, he went on. "The group is prosperous. They sell their products in all the American states and in London's Covent Garden. As far away as Australia. Their eighteen communities—each self-sustaining—stretch from Maine to Kentucky and as far inland as Ohio."

Leaning back in my chair, I said dryly, "It seems one of my farmer's wives was wrong. I can't imagine such industrious people capering about under the moon—with or without their clothing—and then rising early to accomplish all that they do."

He puffed his jowly cheeks and then blew out the air. "In *almost* every way, sir, the Shakers live intelligently. That is the correct adverb. I've adopted some of their principles myself. Using the mental capacities to procure the best in meeting the basic needs of life—food, clothing, shelter—is not a widespread practice in this world, odd as that seems for a species endowed with reason. The very rich, who can afford to choose, do not choose as they ought. In the name of fashion, they wear clothing that is neither comfortable nor sensible. The women wear such tight corsets that their organs are displaced. Their houses are not warm since most of the fire's heat escapes up the chimney. They fill their dwellings with stuffed furniture and rugs that collect dust. It makes one sneeze to think of it. Their food may be delicious but is often not nutritious. On the other hand, the vast numbers of the poor lack the very basics. You see them every day, crowding the streets of Boston. Their clothing is rags, their children barefoot in the bitterest weather. Yet every Shaker is well fed, well housed, well dressed."

Not only did Quincey have decided opinions, he rumbled them out in a tone that made you want to argue even if you agreed. However, he was my employer. I asked, "How do they manage to do that?"

"Banding together. Other species, from wolves to ants, have seen the wisdom of this. No one man can use his acreage efficiently if he alone must plow, plant, reap, look after livestock, and keep equipment in repair. No woman can well spin, weave, sew, cook, bear and train children alone. The Shakers pool their skills. Their motto is 'Hands to Work; Hearts to God.' They do work hard. They make everything they use, and each thing is as good as it can be, from the smallest chair peg to the largest building."

"Each family's house is close to the next?"

"No. As a group, they consider themselves a family, united not by blood but a deeper union. The 'brothers and sisters,' as they refer to themselves, inhabit large living quarters with separate entrances, and in some cases, even separate staircases for the two sexes. They lead celibate lives."

"Celibate?" I suppose there was disbelief in my voice. I was startled.

Peering at me over his half-glasses, he replied, "Yes, Mr. Merrick. The Shakers offer both security here and salvation hereafter. For one or the other—or both—many human beings will at least attempt celibacy, which is a strict requirement for staying. Admittedly, the rest of the world finds it hard to believe that it can be done—hence the stories."

"With no children as future converts, however, I imagine this will be a short-lived sect." It wasn't easy to hide my lack of interest.

"On the contrary. Eight of them came to America over seventy years ago, just when the colonies declared themselves free of England. Since then, they have flourished. At every failed harvest at the end of summer, a new crop of converts arrives at Shaker villages. They are called 'bread and butter' Shakers or, perhaps more aptly, 'loaf' Shakers. All are willingly taken in and some of them stay past the winter. And there are children, many of them."

I did not so much as raise an eyebrow, asking only, "And where do they come from?"

"Occasionally a whole family joins, although that is rare. The husband and wife then live in their separate quarters. But there are many, many children. The Shakers take in those orphaned or abandoned. Sometimes desperate parents—who cannot feed or care for their offspring—leave them on their doorstep, knowing they'll be well cared for there." He stared at those handsomely stained cupboards as he spoke.

"Admirable." It was, of course, but I was waiting for him to come to the point. I couldn't imagine that I'd been summoned so he could tell me about the Shakers. He certainly wasn't proselytizing, instead speaking of the sect as a botanist might about a useful herb that was unexpectedly thriving.

Almost musingly, he continued, "They live isolated from what they call 'World People.' It's true that they have again allowed outsiders to observe their Sabbath services, which had been closed for some time. Journalists come, usually to titillate their readers with accounts of the unusual manner of worship. And those that style themselves 'Society' attend as a way of entertaining themselves. There are several spas near the upstate New York villages and the carriages of those there to take the waters line up outside the Meeting-house."

"They do dance then on Sundays?"

His bright gaze was penetrating, despite his half-mast lids. "If, Mr. Merrick, it is considered acceptable to raise one's voice in song in worship, I cannot see why one shouldn't move one's body in dance."

"Nor can I." I certainly had no fixed ideas on religious practices.

A brief silence followed. By now, I was sure he was avoiding the point. I commented, "The public prefers its gossip spicy. So this ritual dancing is reported as taking place, not in the Meetinghouse, but under the stars."

Abruptly, Quincey pressed a hand on his springy hair and stared at the tabletop. "Some odd occurrences have taken place in those quiet villages. It started ten years ago in Watervliet, New York. Some young girls began whirling about dizzily, going into trances, singing songs in unknown languages. They claimed they saw angels. This spread to all the communities. Angel sightings became commonplace. Believers became 'instruments' for spirits, some of them the Indians who once inhabited their lands."

He blew air out noisily. "Even the elders, who seem sensible people, became involved. Each community established a place for outdoor spiritual worship on the highest spot available. These 'Mountain Meetings' are held at night. Sometimes a 'Midnight Cry' rings throughout the living quarters and all excitedly march there for a gathering of the spirits."

At this point, my patience was gone. To avoid any connection with the mainstream religions, I'd go blocks out of my way. As for the religious fanatics—which the Shakers must be—I'd measure the distance in miles.

If my reaction showed, Quincey didn't notice. He went on, "Some of the happenings, if reported correctly, are inexplicable. Some are all too understandable when people express their feelings. The elders closed the services to all outsiders and imposed greater discipline within."

Now he lifted his head and stared at me. For the first time there was a little hesitancy in his voice. "The problem may stem from the original excitement or the recent suppression of it."

When he didn't immediately elaborate, I asked, hoping the end of this discussion could be hurried along, "What problem?"

"Fire, sir. It would be. And too many to regard as accidents. All of them have occurred in just two villages, only three miles apart. One is Hancock on Massachusetts's western border, and the other New Lebanon on New York's eastern side. The latter community houses the central ministry for the entire sect. At first the fires were small and did little damage. The elders assumed it might be mischievous children, or more likely some troubled adolescent who was stirred up by the ferment I described. They took precautions

with the young, as well as carefully checking their stoves.
The fires continued. One night, the entire first floor of the
New Lebanon Herb House was destroyed. It's a huge build-
ing, the size of three barns. No one was hurt. But then in
Hancock, a smaller village of some two hundred, in the
Seedhouse . . ." He stopped and frowned.

"Someone was."

"Yes, an elderly brother, a man in his eighties. He often
didn't sleep well, and when they were behind in their seed
orders, he would take a candle and go over to work. He was
known to do this."

My mouth was dry. Death by fire. Worse than death by
drowning. The smoke would choke and sear the lungs and
the flames claw at the screeching skin. I pushed away that
thought. "Still, an old man, who might have been overtired,
a candle—" I paused before saying, "If this had been the
first—"

"Exactly, sir. But it wasn't. And it hasn't been the last. On
Monday week another. It was caught quickly."

"What actions are they taking now?"

He sighed heavily. "They held a ceremony called, 'Bury-
ing the Devil.' It involves digging a pit, chanting, and
putting large stones over the closed top. They are not able to
deal with a problem like this one. Calling in a rural constable would hardly help. He would need to look at members of
the community first, know their routines, interview them.
Most of them wouldn't want to respond to his questions.
And more than a few of them, even amongst the elders, can't
believe that it is a fellow Shaker who is guilty."

"Do you think an outsider, or outsiders, could be responsible?"

"Yes. Both villages have extensive acreage, filled with
trees, and many outbuildings—barns, schoolhouses, tanner-
ies, laundry buildings, poultry houses. With a little fore-
thought, anyone could find a place of concealment until
after dark. The Shakers sleep soundly. The truth is that they
have many enemies. They are hated for their beliefs, their
withdrawal, for their very success. Then, they have competi-
tors in the seed and physick business. The relatives of those

who, upon becoming Shakers, sign over their properties to the community constantly quarrel with them, in and out of court."

"Motives aren't in short supply: greed, anger, revenge. But wouldn't their dogs alert them to the presence of a stranger?"

"The Shakers keep no dogs. They see them as 'useless' animals. In this case, the fattest laziest cur who would bark at an outsider would be most helpful. His very silence would wake them to the idea they close their eyes to: that one of them may have such a dark place in the soul that only fire can light it. To live suspecting one's 'brothers and sisters' is hard, but denial of suspicion is no easier."

His face, somber as he spoke, became even gloomier. "They have appealed to me for help, which I am bound to give."

Seeing his expression made his remark about how hateful obligations were suddenly very clear.

His eyes fixed on the wall above my head, he added, "Unfortunately, I cannot offer it in the most assured way. I cannot go there myself. I am a recluse." He made it sound like an uncorrectable condition, present from birth. "I never leave my home. And Hancock is across the state, well over a hundred miles away." From his tone, one would have gathered the Gobi Desert stretched between Boston and that village.

Now, I'd had a spurt of fellow feeling over his reaction to the weight of obligation. But his calm assumption that if he were on the scene, the Shakers' troubles would soon be over got my back up again. The man was pompous, abrasive, and puffed up. And my immediate future lay in his hands. My presence here, especially given his question as to whether I had learned anything of police methods, was now explained. He wanted me to go in his stead.

Looking at my hands, I said, "Any non-Believer would be treated exactly as your rural constable. No one in the community would confide in that person either."

"That's true."

"Your plan, then, is that . . . someone . . . would actually join the sect. Gain their trust by pretending to be one of them. Go in disguise. Infiltrate."

Although he winced slightly at my word choices, he nodded, staring straight ahead. "It need only be for a relatively short time."

"It could take months."

"A keen-eyed observer on the scene, someone used to collecting information, someone capable of reporting it accurately, could gather a great deal in a matter of days. His insights could then be analyzed by a person adept at that."

In his mind, that expert analyzer would have to be Jasper Quincey. I was only to be his eyes and ears. I thought it over. Now, there was no suggestion either in what he said or the way he said it that I was being ordered to do this. At the same time there was no assurance that, if I refused, the position of police reporter for the *Independent* would still be mine. I could plead that such an undertaking would be opposed to my own religious beliefs, but I'd already indicated that I was open-minded, at least about practices. Quincey was a clever man.

I continued to stare at my hands. I felt just capable of trudging around Boston with no other thought than the comfort of my solitary supper and mindless sleep at night. I was not experienced in questioning people. Moreover, gathering the information would require me to be someone else. That is best done by a person who is sure of who *he* is.

"They need help," he repeated in a neutral tone.

No doubt they did. But even if I were able to provide it, I wasn't willing. Charitable the Shakers might be in taking in children, but that was to their own advantage. Such a society must be fenced in with rules. Separate staircases. Perfect wooden pegs. How could they be forbearing with others? I was not tolerant of intolerance.

I didn't reply. I was somewhat mollified by his attempt to persuade me to step forward on my own. Then I thought it over. That needn't indicate graciousness on his part. Someone operating from choice was going to be more effective in carrying out the assignment.

"It's a very healthy life," he pointed out. "The food is

good and nutritious as well. The work is hard, but at this time of the year being outside in the fresh air is restoring. Exercise is beneficial. For the young body, that is." He settled his own bulk more comfortably in the padded chair.

I still said nothing. Both refusing and accepting were out. I needed to come up with a way to put Quincey off until I had an alternative plan of my own. Clearly a better candidate would have to be found. One of the police officers might have a recommendation. I was not optimistic, and it wouldn't do to suggest it now, given Quincey's opinion of the men on the force, which might extend to their acquaintances.

He leaned forward, taking off his spectacles to look at me directly. "Now, you'll pardon me for remarking on it, but you are quite pale and just this side of gaunt. It can't be good for you."

With a distinct edge in my voice, I answered too quickly. "On the other hand, my appearance of less than perfect health would make my arrival at the Shakers' door believable."

"True. Your beard should be taken off at once. It will have to be done eventually since the brothers are required to be clean-shaven."

This was not the way I wanted the conversation to go. I temporized. "There will have to be some further discussion. In any case, my affairs would have to be arranged; the editor notified; Mrs. Parker informed. And I would have to have appropriate clothing."

"Yes." He gestured to the peg holding the bell. "Would you please call Freegift?"

The man appeared as quietly as he had before. Quincey rose and said, "Mr. Merrick will be our guest for the night."

Freegift, blinking furiously, was obviously as taken aback as I was. He stammered, "But Brother Philemon is also spending the night."

Quincey's voice held barely contained impatience. "The entire west wing is unoccupied. The rooms are aired regularly, are they not?"

"Oh, yes, yes," Freegift answered. He was apparently trying to get his mind around the unprecedented idea of having not one, but two, guests.

Quincey turned to me. "Philemon Wells is a trustee at the Hancock Community. He will be returning near there, although not directly to that village. He can set you down and you can walk the rest of the distance. He understands the necessity of subterfuge and, as you travel together, he can answer any questions you might have. For that reason, it is best to accompany him rather than go by rail. The train through the state's interior is quite slow in any case, and that form of transportation is full of risks and trials." He shut his eyes to the very thought of it before going on. "He has a system by which you and I can communicate. He leaves early tomorrow morning."

I stood up so quickly that I knocked the chair over. "But arrangements for the matters we spoke of—"

"They've all been seen to," Quincey announced. With that he sailed out of the room.

Chapter Three

Brimming with resentment, my freshly shaved cheeks stinging, I came down to breakfast the next morning. I had to make Quincey see how futile this all was. I had no experience in investigating. To question people, to draw them out, required an understanding of the way they thought. *I* was going to a village of religious zealots. That insistence on perfect wooden pegs was all I needed to know of their narrow, straitened lives.

I had no intention of going, but I planned to show my employer I was ready to go. I'd taken off my beard and put on the clothing Freegift laid out for me when he brought up the basin of hot water. The outfit was well chosen. The straw hat was frayed, but had a stylish planter's brim. The striped collarless shirt was faded, but of good cotton. Someone had clumsily tried to mend a rip, as if the wearer remembered what it was to be respectable. It fit with the kind of story I'd need to tell about an abrupt downturn in fortune. Although the pants just grazed my boot tops, they'd belonged to another tall man. The boots were cracked, but the soles were good.

At the bottom of the stairs, I ran my fingers around the brim of the hat, considering how to handle the conversation during and after the meal. I'd disguise my feelings. My objective was to raise real questions in Quincey's mind about my suitability. As we ate, I would point out problems, express my reservations. He was an intelligent man, if pigheaded. It would soon occur to him that sending a man with absolute doubts on the existence of God to a community of believers was not to be thought of. There could be no meeting of minds.

The Shaker trustee would be at the table as well. Surely a man of decided views, he would reject my candidacy out of hand when he grasped the situation.

Confidently, I put the hat on one of the pegs, knowing I'd not have to wear it. As I turned, Freegift opened a door onto the spacious hall. "Breakfast is served in the morning room, sir." He did an about-face and went down the corridor without meeting my eyes.

He stopped, and stepped back to let me precede him. I took a deep breath and walked in. The early morning sun streamed into a room as open as the study or the bedroom where I'd spent the night, but not as sparsely furnished. A profusion of green plants were on graceful candlestands next to several large and comfortable chairs grouped in one corner.

Then I noticed that the round table in the center was set for only one person.

Unhooking a chair from the wall pegs, Freegift set it down before that place, saying, "Brother Philemon has eaten and gone on to the livery stable. I will give you directions there." He caught my stony expression. Blinking anxiously, he almost gabbled out, "Mrs. Hingham, the cook that is, says that if you do not take pork, there is fresh cod in new cream. The eggs this morning are shirred, but I'm to advise her if you prefer them another way."

"Where is Mr. Quincey?" I bit out the words.

"Working in the conservatory, sir, where he cannot be disturbed. But," he gestured toward a thick envelope beside the place setting, "he left this for you to take with you, instructions as it were." With that, he was gone.

I sat and stared at the wall across from me. Freegift silently came and went, carrying in platters and covered dishes which he spread before me.

At last I stabbed the perfect yolk of a baked egg and began chewing. There was only one thing to do. After breakfast I would stalk upstairs and put on my own suit. I would leave a brief note for Quincey. I pondered the phrasing. I would state the case reasonably and politely, despite the acerbic words that leapt to my mind.

Swallowing the last bite of ham and bit of fish, I put down my napkin. Then the unwelcome thoughts crowded in. After my dignified exit out the front door, what would I do? My editor no doubt had been notified, as Quincey said. Someone else would be occupying my desk. Mrs. Parker would be very surprised to see me return. On my meager salary, I'd managed to save precious little money, and it might be some time before I found another position.

It was the empty day stretching before me that undid me. I closed my eyes in fear at the way I might choose to escape it.

When I shoved myself to my feet, my hand fell on the fat envelope Quincey had left. I could imagine the detailed marching orders someone that self-impressed would give. Without opening it, I jammed it into my coat pocket.

At the scrape of my chair, Freegift appeared immediately and, looking sideways, murmured the way to the livery stable. I only nodded. At the front door, he handed me a small bundle, explaining, "Clean linen." As he gave me my hat, he cleared his throat and brought out, "Brother Philemon will be a most pleasant traveling companion. I promise you, sir." I thought it best not to reply.

The Shaker near the door of the stable was immediately recognizable by his clothing. His broad-brimmed hat, plain collar, and straight coat belonged to a much earlier era. He acknowledged my introduction gravely and repeated his name. A spare, older man, he had the face of a Yankee trader: shrewd eyes, long nose, narrow lips. No wonder the sect is prosperous, I thought. This man would haggle over every penny.

He turned back to his inventorying of the contents of his long wagon. It was loaded with wooden crates, barrels and half-barrels, hampers, stacks of woven lidded baskets, and bags of seeds.

My heart sank as I took in that there was only to be one horse. It would be a long, slow trip. Admittedly, the horse that was being harnessed was strong-shouldered and heavy-rumped without a rib showing in between. Its coat gleamed.

When I asked him why there was only one, he pursed his thin lips. "We make our wagons so they're balanced right. Then one horse is all that's needed. Be wasteful to use two."

Reaching into his right jacket pocket, he drew out a handful of scraps of paper. "Tasks for the day," he said, holding each at arm's length, studying it. A few he put in his left-hand pocket, turning them over to see if the other side was usable before doing so. Then he nodded in satisfaction. "Four miles distance from here is a market day. We'll stop. I've plenty of wares still."

We climbed into the seat, as comfortable and highly polished as a piece of parlor furniture, and he flicked the reins. The animal stepped out smartly, pulling the heavy wagon behind him like an afterthought.

The morning was fresh, and our pace quite fast, but I sat in silence, nursing my ire at Quincey's high-handedness. Nor was Philemon a talkative man. The first miles his only words came as we passed a few cows grazing in a field recently greened by rain. "Every farmer should do as we do and keep one sow for every cow. The sow eats the whey which otherwise would be poured out. And the ham which we then sell is quite good. We get a nice price."

I muttered some reply. I had no interest in farming and knew nothing on the subject. He added, "We must be economical, thrifty. Mother Ann insisted on that."

When I inquired as to who she might be, he launched into what was clearly a favorite story. "Our foundress, Mother Ann Lee. Came from England in 1774. She grew up on Toad Lane in Manchester. It was a filthy place, with human waste running down a ditch in the middle of the street and seeping into the wells. The water was undrinkable and the air was foul. She worked hard at a factory, but many days all she had in the cupboard was a little vinegar to drink to still the hunger pangs."

As I listened to that, the emphasis on cleanliness and good food became quite clear.

"After her marriage, she suffered much, losing four babes

in infancy, and then her body was wracked many times more with those not born alive. At last, she went without sleep night after night, saying she could no more lie down on the bed than she could on hot embers. It was in prison that a vision came to her that proved she was right in her growing belief."

"Prison? Why was she there?"

He shook his head sadly. "For what she preached. She said that in order to be perfect we had to overcome our carnal nature, that we must not join our bodies for self-gratification, even in marriage. It was not a popular belief. She was put in a cell not high enough for her to stand upright and given neither food nor water. But she had already attracted followers, and one gave her sustenance through the keyhole. She sipped milk laced with wine by means of a reed. When the jailer finally opened the door, he expected to find a dead woman. But she walked out without any aid."

Quincey was right. At a Shaker village, it would be fire. Their system denied desire. So then the burst and blaze. The repression in the air of such a place would be thicker than smoke.

I decided I might as well have it all, chapter and verse. I asked, "Mother Ann decided then to come to America?"

"Yes. Her brother, who was always one of her strongest supporters, dreamt of a flourishing tree in a new land, and they gathered a few of their band and embarked. They could afford very little for their passage so their ship was not seaworthy. Condemned, in fact, for its rotted timbers. On board, Mother Ann was appalled at the sailors' behavior. When she spoke to them, they cursed and swore at her. The captain, too, was angry with her and finally, in the midst of a storm, he laid hands on her, threatening to throw her overboard. Just then a plank broke loose on the side of the ship and he and the crew, seeing that, thought all was lost. But Mother Ann gazed up at the masts and saw a bright angel on each one. She told them not to fear. A huge wave rose and slapped the board back in place. The ship arrived safely."

Angels, I thought. Yes. People who saw them invariably believed in them *before* seeing them.

"Now, I myself," Philemon added, raising a finger, "only had the story from Father James Whittaker, who was on the ship. I never met Mother Ann, since she died in 1784. My own mother became a Believer the following year when I was about eight years old."

I was surprised. That meant Philemon was over seventy now. I'd have guessed him more than a decade younger.

"Mother Ann Lee," he went on earnestly, "was soft to her followers. One young woman came to us big with a child conceived out of wedlock. She wouldn't eat and couldn't sleep, just sitting stiff as death on the edge of her bed. Hearing of this the next day, Mother Ann came and sat beside her, saying nothing, just gently stroking her hand. At last the girl burst into hysterical words. She'd been told that, because of her sin, she would suffer terribly for days giving birth and that the child would be horribly disfigured.

"Mother Ann took the girl's face into her hands, brushing away the tears with her thumbs. She looked into her eyes, smiled, and said. 'That will not happen. You will not suffer at all. The babe will come forth quickly and will be as pink and perfect as that rose.' She pointed out the window at the flower. And so it came to pass. I was told this by one who was there.

"But Mother was very strong, too. Never flinched from her duty. She was away from the village with a few of her followers preaching when she was hurt. She always gathered a crowd, but her words angered many. One day a mob broke into the house where she was staying. The men tried to bar the door, but we Believers know that violence breeds. There is no end to it. Jesus went meekly with the Roman soldiers. She was dragged down the steps and out to a sledge by her feet, her poor head hitting every stair and rock. Died a few months later."

Wiping the sweat from his brow, he replaced his hat securely. "The elders could see then that we had to stay apart from World People, our ways being so different. We only leave our villages to visit other communities of Believers, except for the men trustees like me who go out to sell."

He pulled off the road at the next village and began neatly

laying out his wares. His wagon was at the end of a cobble-stone street, choked with weeds, lined with just a few shops and several small houses intermixed. The street itself was filled with women, wandering between the stalls set up by the farmers' wives. Glancing down at the other end of the street, I spied a tavern, which explained where most of the men were.

At first, no one approached us. I'd have said no one was paying any attention to us, except that soon I could see that wasn't true. Instead of moving about, the women were clustered into small groups, and their heads were repeatedly turned our way. Philemon kept busy rearranging his inventory on the wagon's gate.

Then, one older woman, stuffed into a brightly colored cotton dress and wearing a bonnet decorated with new ribbons, sailed directly up to us, followed at a little distance by another, also well dressed. The voice of the first carried. "I'll have some of your cider vinegar since I've a deal of beets and cucumbers to be pickled. Did very well with *my* garden this summer, though some did not."

The Shaker gestured toward one of his boxes. "Have you sufficient dill? Some seed to be used now or to plant in the spring? And the tarragon is good if you're putting up beans." By the end of the transaction, he'd sold her the vinegar, some seed packets and dried herbs, as well as several bottles of sarsaparilla. To occupy myself, I offered to carry the purchases to her wagon. She marched grandly ahead of me, not speaking.

On my return, I was subjected to hard-eyed glares from the women behind their own, now deserted, stalls. One spat out a single word, "Heathen!"

Almost all their customers were gathered around Philemon. One or two with larger orders tried to bargain, but he'd not take a penny less than the asking price, only shaking his head firmly. That filled me with a rising disgust. Everything about the Shaker spoke of the sect's prosperity: the abundance of goods, the solid wagon, the strong horse. Although his clothing was plain and out of date, the material was wonderfully woven and there was not a visible mend. Yet the farms we passed showed the owners were barely subsisting. But I came and went, carrying the heavy half-barrels of fresh cider or vinegar.

Each time I noticed, standing a little distance back, a thin woman and a small girl whose dresses had more patches than original cloth. The child caught my attention because of her silent crying. Both her eyes and nose ran, but there was no sound to her tears. One thumb was being sucked hard, the other hand clasped her mother's, who had her head bent toward the girl, not speaking to her, only nervously and constantly patting her shoulder. The woman's long bonnet, which seemed to have been fashioned from a man's castaway straw hat, hid her face.

Then, as I waited for Philemon to tote up the last order, she glanced up. Her face was badly disfigured, as if from some disease. Her left eye was only a downward slit in the scabrous, wartlike mass around it. There seemed no bone in her cheek below it, although her jaw bulged as if with a permanent toothache. As she saw my look, she bowed her head hurriedly.

I couldn't think what could cause that, although I somehow remembered another face so marred. Someone I'd seen on the dockside. Turning away quickly, I clambered up on the wagon to roll a barrel to the gate's edge.

As I hoisted it on my shoulder, I recalled with a jolt the man whose face was like hers. He was an old boxer, not successful in the ring, and the skin was puffed and thickened from being hit so much and so hard.

By the time I'd delivered the cider, she and the little girl were the only ones there, and the mother was speaking to Philemon. I stood across the street to avoid embarrassing her with my presence, but I could hear his response. "Yes, this elixir with willow bark should help the child's earache." He took up a pretty woven basket and put two bottles in it. One of her hands flew up anxiously at the sight of both bottles. She shook her head and brought out a very tiny purse from her pocket.

"No," Philemon said as firmly as if he were bargaining with her. "I cannot accept any money for these. I cannot be sure they'll work in this case. It would be best if you'd take this syrup as well," he put in a good-sized bottle, "and have the child try it so I'll know if I can recommend it to others with this type of ailment. The syrup is for catarrh and you know how often that accompanies ear problems. When next I'm through here, you might kindly let me know if the medication was effective. We wish to maintain our reputation in physicks, so we value comments and good words from our customers." He handed her the basket and its contents, along with his thanks.

There was no question in my mind that he was giving away the profits on the last several sales, but the way he spoke would have given anyone the impression he was in her debt for her acceptance of the products. I couldn't hear her reply because her low voice trembled.

Just as she was about to turn away, Philemon added, "These can also be obtained at our village at Shirley, north of here. If you find yourself—or the child—taken ill, the two of you could go there and the sisters would care for you. Or you might go just to see how we live. There would be no charge, of course, for your stay."

She'd only moved a few feet from the wagon when I heard the angry bellow clear from the other end of the street. A burly, bearded man coming out of the tavern charged toward us, yelling as he ran. His hat flew off behind him. Everyone scattered out of his way. He was a bull of a man, a half head shorter than I but twice as broad.

The target of his threats and curses was the woman. "Ye damned hussy! Said, din't I? Tole ye to stay away from the ungodly. All the day all ye do is disobey! Ye won't be learnin' your lesson."

The child buried her face in the mother's skirts, but she herself stood where she was, only lowering her head, folding her arms across her chest, hunching her shoulders. The hopelessness in her bent head, the helplessness in her thin shoulders struck me like a blow on the windpipe.

Without even slowing his pace, her husband swept her aside with an outflung arm, sending her and the girl sprawling on the cobblestones in front of me. He roared up to

Philemon, spraying him with spittle as he shouted,
"Damned, dancin' whoreson Shakers! I'll see ye in hell
where ye belong!"

I helped her to her feet, and her only concern seemed that
the precious bottles in the basket had not broken. I moved
slowly toward Philemon, convinced the man was a blusterer,
one to take on only women and children. And I was trying to
swallow the anger, like vomit in my throat, before I reached
him.

The Shaker's face was calm as he faced the bearded man,
now screaming that it was a wife's bounden duty to bed with
her husband. "Ye preach about purity to the silly sluts to git
'em alone in the woods at night." Out of nowhere his fist
came up and clipped Philemon on the jaw. The blow reeled
the old man backward, slamming him into the side of the
wagon.

At that, I launched myself at the bully's thick back. My
height gives me considerable weight. He crashed facedown
beneath me on the rounded rocks of the street.

Clutching the back of his hair, I pulled his head up, intending to pound his face on those stones. If there was ever
a man who deserved it, it was he. But my arm was jerked
backward. "Michael! No. We don't hold with violence."

My eyes were glazed with the bright red of rage. "*I* am
not a Shaker," I gritted out. But Philemon's wiry grip was
surprisingly strong. I let go of the brute's hair abruptly, and
his head bounced on the surface again.

He lay still as I stood up. He was either knocked out or
pretending to be so. Through the thick bottle-glass windows
of the drinking house, he hadn't realized the old Shaker had
me with him.

"We'll have to see to him," Philemon announced. Blood
was seeping from the cut on his own cheek, dribbling from
the corner of his mouth. I looked up and saw two men, almost ambling toward us, passing the women who stood
silently watching. I tensed up. Then I saw both were grin-
ning.

"No," I replied. "They'll do it. We'd best be on our way."

The sprawled figure at our feet was clearly not liked, but the crowd's mood might shift.

The Shaker paused, then nodded. He took a folded handkerchief from his pocket and carefully dabbed at his cheek and lips. Then he inspected his jacket to make sure no blood had splattered there. We climbed up in the wagon and drove off.

Chapter Four

That night we stopped at a friendly farmhouse where Philemon often stayed. After supper, his eyes closed in prayer, he knelt for a long time beside the pile of fragrant hay in the barn where we were to sleep. I was sitting on a bale nearby, staring straight ahead, wondering how few days I could stay with the Shakers before returning to Boston and telling Quincey that it was a hopeless assignment.

As he settled himself, I glanced at the old man. His jaw was swollen and, although the slash on his cheek had closed, the side of his face was huge and purple. It hurt to look at him. He nodded at me and, speaking thickly, said, "At first, I didn't see much resemblance between you and your father, but now I do."

Startled, I replied, "You knew him?"

"Yes. Gilbert Merrick. We Believers are in his debt. I've been a trustee for twenty-some years, and when I met him, we were just expanding our seed business. We had customers, but selling door to door was slow. We didn't know what to do. Your father had a reputation as a good businessman and so one day I went to his office, though he was our competitor, carrying a different line of seeds. Told him right out that ours were much better, that his had too much chaff and that cheated the buyer.

"'Let's see,'" he says. "'I'll pick three bags from your wagon and you choose any three from my warehouse below. We'll spread them out on a cloth and take a look. If you're right, I'll help you establish your line.'"

Philemon swallowed in some pain before he went on. "He was took back when he saw how good-sized our seeds were and how many more per pound there were without hardly any chaff. Said he'd cancel his other orders and carry only our seeds if we kept up our quality. We paid him the same commission as he'd gotten before, but we weren't then able to fill really large orders, so he lost money at first. Used to shake his head at me and say, " 'Only the Shakers have made honesty *pay*.' A good man, your father."

With that, he croaked out a "More love, brother" and closed his eyes. I was wide awake. Philemon's words brought up a vision of my father saying that to him, a rueful smile on his face. That sharpened the sense of the terrible loss of him I always carried with me.

And I was sure I knew now how things had happened. From their contacts in the Boston business world, the Shakers heard my story. Feeling an obligation to my father, they'd asked Quincey to find me and help, and they'd paid the costs. Because he was indebted to them, for whatever reason, he complied, enlisting Trapper. No doubt they'd told him to keep it secret and so he was uncomfortable taking credit. Then when the group approached Quincey again with their current trouble, he saw a neat way of escaping effort on his part—he'd send me to deal with it.

Relieved as I was not to owe anything to Jasper Quincey, this gave me a bigger problem. It meant I *had* to help the Shakers, and I had no faith at all that I could do anything. Quincey, planted in his comfortable chair in Boston, wasn't going to be any help. I hadn't even opened his letter.

At last my gaze rested on the sleeping Philemon. He was a good salesman, which meant he knew people. He must have his suspicions. I would have to try and pry them out of him. I decided a sideways approach would be best.

But in the morning, his face had swelled further and all he could do was mutter a few words. Of course, we still had to stop religiously at every market town.

By the third day, the wagon was almost empty and his jaw was almost normal size.

The fact that Philemon could talk more easily didn't mean that I was hearing what I needed to know. He answered all my questions about Hancock and the routine of the village.

Often at some length. He even proved to have a knack for telling stories. But he said never a word about who might have started those fires.

Waiting for him to do so, I'd circled the question, starting with the presence of outsiders. "Do you have many visitors to the community?"

"Oh, yes. On Sundays sightseers come to observe our services. We do a deal of business at our Office Store then, sell a lot of baskets."

He reached behind him and handed one of these to me. It was oval, made of polished maple, and on the sides had a pattern of swallowtails, each held precisely by a copper tack. "Attractive design," I said.

"That is *useful*," he corrected. "Cutting the maple that way allows the wood to swell when the weather is damp. Trifles make perfection, but perfection is no trifle. As Mother Ann was wont to say. We have our regular customers—and our neighbors—stopping by the Trustees' Building to conduct business during the week."

I considered that. The seedhouses at both Hancock and New Lebanon had been burned, which must have caused inroads into Shaker profits. The Sunday sightseers probably could be ruled out, but the weekday visitors would need a close look. A pattern might emerge if I could get an accurate account of who was there on the days the fires started. "Is there a record of transactions, a sales record perhaps, that gives the names of visitors?"

"Indeed. We're all encouraged to write everything down, but it's mandatory for elders, deacons, and trustees." He touched a notebook in his bulging pocket. I'd noticed him recording in it each evening, taking out the scraps in his left-hand pocket and copying them. "Not only our day's work, but our thoughts to be put down later in our spiritual journal. The four trustees for each village—two men and two women—are expected to keep exact receipts since we hold the property of the community in our names."

"You have women do that as well?" I couldn't imagine a woman in a place of business. I tried to conjure up a vision of my sister Celia, in one of her plainest dresses, blond hair in a bun, seated at a desk totaling up columns of numbers. How we'd have laughed at the idea. She hated arithmetic, saying she couldn't see the plainest bit of use to it. But I could certainly see her in the future she never had, my mother beside her, as they bent delightedly over a frilled cradle, and that vision blurred my eyes.

Philemon was going on, "The women are called office sisters. And what I, and Brother Samuel, would do without Sister Esther I can't imagine, since we often have to be out of the village. She handles everything most efficiently. Why, it was she who, in going over our records, noticed how much higher the bean yield was with the oil fertilizer than it had been with the potash. We therefore changed. And it was her idea to put a picture of the plant on the herb seed package. It's women who buy these for the kitchen gardens and she knew that many who couldn't read could recognize the plant. Her ledgers are perfectly kept. A record of every caller."

I sighed inwardly. Someone said each of us meets ourself coming down the street. We judge everyone by what's inside us. Philemon would always be surprised by cruelty, although he'd seen it often. Here I suspected he was imposing his own competence on that office sister. But she might have some records I could look at. And Sister Esther was undoubtedly one of those sharp-nosed spinsters who might be sharp-eyed as well. If she could recall—

"As for visitors, there are the Iroquois, now that I think of it," Philemon said. "If they need food or medicine, they come to a Shaker village. They know we'll help." He added, "These lands were once their hunting grounds."

With an inward groan, I thought of that as a motive. "Many of them?"

"Not now. And especially not in the summer, not so many of them about. It was different when we first came. One day in the spring when I was a lad, and we were just settling in— we'd but the one building then—a band of braves marched into the kitchen without a greeting. Arms folded on their bare chests, they just stood there for some time. Then they gathered up all the loaves of bread that the sisters had finished baking. The women were heartsore because we'd little enough to eat and that was the last of the flour in the barrel. But the sisters tried to smile, knowing we must share, and nodded to the Indians as they marched out with the loaves. Two, three days went by, and those braves returned, carrying a deer they'd killed. It was the first meat we'd had for months. Thereafter, they always came with food, sometimes plants that we'd not known were edible. Cowslips in the spring, when they're tender, are very tasty. They brought medicinal plants as well. They always wanted bread, since they'd no ovens of their own, and they became quite fond of venison sausage."

He suddenly turned to me with a troubled look. "But, Brother Michael, if you are considering that the Iroquois might have a grudge against us, put the idea from your mind. Our relationship with them has always been good. As for our customers or neighbors, that is not to be thought of, either. So I told Jasper Quincey. Now, he is an astute man, but," he shook his head sadly, "he is most suspicious of *everyone.* I put it down to his way of living. Never venturing forth from his household, just reading of the world's doings in his newspaper, he doesn't see the essential goodness of people, only their failings."

It occurred to me that if Quincey went out more instead of tending his green herbs in the conservatory, he might be even less convinced of mankind's humanity.

The same thought might have been in Philemon's mind because he stirred uneasily on the wagon seat. "Some have a long way to go to realize their inner nature, as you've seen. Mother Ann said that we Shakers had to come back for another life to serve as teachers for others. Last winter, I met a man that—" He paused, his lean face growing longer. "I saw a small boy, a-staggering under a load bigger than he was. He was lame. The man with him carried nothing but a wicked switch. He kept lashing at the boy's bare legs to make him hurry. And the blood was already running down into the holes in the child's boots and leaking onto the snow. I stopped them and said, as calm as I could, 'Friend, I'm in need of a stable boy. Is that your son?'

" 'Naw, but he's mine. Indentured to me.' He takes me in from hat to boots and spits. 'I paid ten dollars for 'im.'

"Looking at him, I knew he'd never had ten dollars in his life and, if he had, he wouldn't have put it out for a herd of donkeys. I wasn't about to leave the boy, but I hadn't near that much. I stepped back and said, 'Hm. No. He's a bit too small to be of much use in a stable.' I made as if to go.

" 'Wait,' he says. 'Small, mebbe, but he's plenty strong enough for muckin' stalls. How much you give me for 'im?'

"After the deal was struck and he pockets my money, he points to the load the boy had and says, 'But he's still gotta carry that to market fer me.'

" 'Your arms were strong enough to beat him hard,' I returned. 'Carry it yourself.' " Philemon sighed. "Later I had to confess the sin of anger to Elder Jacob."

"And where is the boy now?"

"With us, of course. Brother Crispin goes to school and does his work as well. We never strike a child. I'd thought him seven years at most, but he's shot up. We marked his size on a tree trunk when he came, and now he insists I measure him whenever I return from a lengthy trip."

"These children you take in, do they stay as Shakers when grown?"

Philemon pressed his lips together. "Some. But the . . . fleshly affections are hard to overcome. Most choose to follow the flowery path of nature rather than to labor under the cross of denial. We believe that, if one cannot take up the cross, then one should marry and cleave to one's spouse. Lust is for use, not for pleasure. What the World needs is fewer and better children. We teach the ones that come to us to care for themselves and for others. All have learned more than one trade, and we give them the tools for whichever they prefer." He looked away. "Still, it is hard to see them go."

Children, abandoned, abused, and then later—no matter how kindly treated—

He might have been following my thought. "At first, a small blaze near the woods, on the edge of a field. Another sent a haystack up. No one was concerned. We all saw it as boys' mischief. But since then, each child has been under the eye of an adult."

That, I decided, was undoubtedly true. I said, "It's unfortunate, though, that we don't know the precise dates of those small blazes."

"We do." Philemon turned to me. "I'll look them out for you. Sister Esther writes down such things. Recording the happenings of the day proves useful. How she finds the time is a marvel since she is already doing the work of two. Our other office sister is no longer able to do her portion."

"Why?"

"Sister Hepzibah is considerably up in years, although the picture of rosy health. But she has forgotten much, even the names of things. She spends her days in a rocking chair in our shop next to the Office. We have some of the sisters' handmade products there for sale. Not long ago I saw her hold up a strawberry pincushion to show to a customer, calling it a needle. Not that it mattered since the lady bought it anyway," he added hastily, "but you can see Sister Hepzibah cannot keep records."

"Why not appoint a younger woman in her place?"

Philemon's brow furrowed. "The elders have often discussed it, but Sister Esther insists she is able to keep the Office up by herself. I worry since she seems to me to have gotten quite thin. But there is no question of the quality of her work, so the decision has been put off. It would mean moving Sister Hepzibah to the care of the nursing sisters in the Infirmary. That would upset her routine since she likes to go each day to the shop next door to the Office. The younger women there watch her. And she is used to sharing a room with Sister Esther and she always recognizes *her*." He fidgeted a bit with the reins before continuing. "Then, the logical person to appoint would be Sister Thankful."

As if that explained the entire situation, Philemon said no more.

I waited a bit and then prompted, "Sister Thankful doesn't wish to be a trustee?"

"Quite the reverse. But, in any case, we believers always take on whatever duty is assigned. Obedience is required.

It's just that—" He paused, his glance slipping sideways as if the right words were lurking in the roadside daisies. "It would mean that Sister Thankful would then move into the Trustees' Building. You see, we four live above the Office because of the nature of the business. I share the other room with Brother Samuel. Sister Thankful would be right across the hall, and . . . would be as well in the office every day."

He tightened his mouth at the thought. "Now, we men are often out, but Sister Esther would have to . . ."

I guessed what he was trying not to say. The two hundred some Shakers at Hancock probably all had their ways of avoiding this Sister Thankful. I could also see Sister Esther, gimlet eyed, with a freshly sharpened quill pen held like a lance, defending her fief from any intrusion. With the men gone, and Sister Hepzibah happily in her rocking chair next door, the Office was hers.

"Mind you, Brother Michael, Sister Thankful now is deaconess and she is very, very good in the position. It's a most responsible one, since the deaconess must oversee all the physical needs of the community, from coats to candlesticks to soap. Myself, I put her sharpness of temper down to her age. One must be patient with all to live together. Our standard greeting to one another is 'More love, brother,' or 'sister,' as the case may be. With Thankful I try to say it with deep feeling."

"She is elderly, too?"

"No, no. Only at the start of her fifth decade. But I notice that women develop," he cleared his throat, "problems then. It's the course of nature."

It was hard to imagine a woman committing these crimes. Still, one who was very disturbed might be capable of it. And a woman who'd never had children now seeing all possibility end might have very disordered senses.

"*Some* women have problems then," he amended his thought. "Mother Alma, one of four elders, I have known since girlhood and she is nearly my age. Always wise and good. Our elders hear our confessions. The women come to her. She listens, all the while carding wool on the paddle in her lap. They say she never talks much, but when they leave their hearts are as light as the combed wool. And I should say," he held up that cautionary finger again, "Sister Thankful was, for years, at New Lebanon, and I gather that no one there found she was *ever* easy-tempered."

Then he shot me an alarmed look. "Brother Michael, you must not infer from my words that Sister Thankful is unbalanced. Or that she could have— No. No woman could have done this. That's not possible!"

It was now the fourth day we'd been on the road. Philemon had ruled out the children because they were monitored. He'd ruled out the women, the Indians, the neighbors, and the customers, apparently on the grounds that they were women, Indians, neighbors, and customers.

A nasty suspicion began to form in my mind. Jasper Quincey had another good reason for not coming himself. Knowing the Shakers as he did, he realized it was an impossible task. *He* wouldn't fail. I would.

It was several miles before I unclenched my teeth. Then I decided not to fail.

Philemon had not ruled out the brothers. He might be reluctant to bring out a name lest he be wrong.

Trying to get around that, I decided to eliminate some. His fellow trustee, as a salesman, was probably not there on all occasions so perhaps he could be safely excluded from suspicion. "Now Brother Samuel travels, as you do?"

"Well, no, although that is unusual. He spends most of his time advising at the New Lebanon village. He's a very experienced businessman and, for that reason, was appointed a trustee at Hancock after only two years, when he signed the Covenant, giving his property to us. Part of it, at least. I understand he'd made a good deal of it over to his older son before joining us. Still, he's a godsend because of his abilities. For example, before he came, we'd always made our own cloth. Wore like iron, it did. We'd tried buying from the local mills, as a neighborly gesture, but the machine-made material didn't last like ours. Still, he observed that, while more time was needed making new garments more frequently, we saved far more time by not having to do all our own spinning and weaving. It freed us to concentrate on our more profitable endeavors."

"Was he a cloth mill-owner before?"

"He did own several. But he was a man of many affairs. He had timber mills, feed and grain warehouses, and such. A well-known Boston merchant. Perhaps you've heard of him? Samuel Grant?"

Samuel Grant. Indeed I did know him. He was my father's partner. He came to our house now and again. A rock-faced man who never smiled. When I was quite small, he'd insist on my putting out my palm. Sometimes he'd drop a penny in it, sometimes he'd slap it hard. "Let that be a lesson to you, boy," he'd say. What lesson that could have been I've never known.

I was eleven when my father died, and I never saw Grant again. Our lives changed. Most of our servants had to be let go. A good part of the house was shut up, and the rooms we stayed in were never as warm again. We weren't in want but, as I grew older, I took note of my mother's constant economies. Mutton instead of beef on the table, kindling instead of coal in the fireplace. Celia's art and French lessons ended, and the dressmaker came only seldom. Harvard's tuition had risen to over seventy dollars a year, and when it was due, Mother's face looked pinched with worry at such a sum. When I questioned her about the changes in our life, she said that Grant had told her he was giving her more than a fair price for my father's share of the business. Later I learned from a neighbor that, after my father's death, Grant built a mansion on Beacon Hill.

To Philemon, I replied only with a nod, then saying, "So he has become a Shaker. That is amazing. A fervent convert?"

"He is heedful in his religious duties," Philemon answered carefully. "Elder Jacob has repeated that we cannot judge the depth of a man's faith. There was some . . . whispering at first and much doubt that the Grants would stay. Grant is a widower. His younger son Giles came with him, you see. The young man, not above eighteen years now, is much afflicted. Sister Thankful is persuaded that the sole reason the father came was to obtain our help for the boy."

"How is he afflicted?"

"It's difficult to describe what comes over him. One moment he is as you or I. Then of a sudden, his arms jerk and he lunges at the person next to him. He does no harm, of course, although when he throws things about, one must duck down quickly. In these spasms, he speaks gibberish and sometimes even breaks out into obscenities."

"Has he epilepsy?"

"The doctors Brother Samuel consulted, and he saw many, say not. The boy does not lose consciousness, as is usual with epileptics. Apparently many courses of cure were tried, but the medical consensus at last was that he was subject to fits of madness. His father was advised to commit him to an asylum where he could be restrained physically. But he would not. On the whole, having Giles with us has worked well."

I stared at Philemon. "It has?"

"Particularly since the Grants left New Lebanon and come to Hancock. It is smaller and quieter. Brother Giles is a willing and able worker. We leave him to the chairmaking, which he loves. Every leg and back is perfectly turned, every seat meticulously finished. While he is about any kind of carpentry, he does not twitch at all. Moreover, he brings joy to our services, singing and dancing so well."

"So he has been accepted by the community?"

"His oddities are hard for some to overlook. His habit of cursing is much against our principles. We do not utter any exclamations, let alone those dreadful ones that spill from him. But it seems to me that he cannot control his words when these fits come over him. Certainly he doesn't seem able to stop his convulsive movements. Some believers see *those* as a sign of the inner light."

"What 'inner light'?"

"The Spirit in us. Mother Ann began as a Quaker, and she knew their understandings were right. We need no priests or ministers since God speaks directly to the individual. This is often accompanied by a trembling of the body. The site of our first settlement was chosen by an elder holding out a shaking hand and following it."

"The Believers' tolerance of his son's condition must have comforted Samuel Grant." I was still trying to get my mind around the idea of that hardheaded man undergoing any kind of a religious conversion. It was no easier to see him giving up his prosperous life to take care of his boy. What could he be doing there? I'd find out.

Philemon's wide-brimmed hat dipped emphatically as he nodded. "Brother Samuel had been told so often by clerics that this was a case of possession by the Devil that he'd even had the Roman Catholics arrange an exorcism. It didn't stop the problem. Coming to us, it was an enormous relief for him to feel that we did not think his son was inhabited by a demon."

His voice turned gloomy. "When the fires started, many stared sideways at Brother Giles. But he shares a room with Brother Elijah, a young man near his age. And *he* says that on the night the entire Seedhouse went up, the two of them were restless because both had evil dreams and spent the hours awake praying and talking. Elder Jacob examined him closely and is sure of the truth of his statement."

I didn't share the elder's view. Elijah must have been sleeping some time to have had his dreams. I gave up on the subtle approach. "You know these men well, and you are a good judge of character, Brother Philemon. I need your help to help the community. I won't repeat your answer to anyone, except Jasper Quincey if it becomes necessary. Which brother, or brothers, do *you* suspect, for whatever reason?"

Philemon stared at me, aghast. "We are family. I do not think any of my brothers capable of this crime."

It took quite an effort to keep harshness from my tone. I liked the man. In fact, I was surprised how much I liked him. The words I had to say were bad enough. "It is a crime. Arson takes away property. Now a man has died. That makes it murder as well, however unintentional. Now this elderly brother who died in the Seedhouse fire—"

"Brother Zebediah," Philemon interjected. "A very good man. A hard worker."

A thought occurred to me. "Was he well liked by the community?"

"We mourn him deeply."

There was no mistaking the evasion in his answer. I pried as tactfully as I could. "He was up in years. Was he perhaps . . . crotchety?"

"That was it, you see. He was sharp-tongued. Very apt to, as Sister Thankful put it, Make Remarks." Philemon's tone suggested capital letters on those words. "He did have a habit of telling her each time some necessary item hadn't been provided in sufficient quantities in the Living Quarters—soap, candles, or some such. She felt he was implying she was failing in her duties as deaconess and took it very much amiss."

"Did he make these remarks to everyone?"

"I'm afraid he did," Philemon sighed. "Well, I shouldn't think he would have to Mother Alma. No one would, as kind as she is. But he said, more than once to Sister Esther—I mentioned she had us put the pictures of the herbs on the packets so that women who didn't read could identify the plant—that our good seeds didn't need prettifying up with such drawings. She was . . . hurt because that wasn't her intent. And when Samuel Grant asked us to consider how we might increase our profits—to help the poor—Brother Zebediah answered that in order to gain entrance to heaven, Mother Ann wouldn't count the pennies in our purses. Then, to Brother Esau, who's very particular about our keeping to the rules, he—" Philemon interrupted himself. "That sort of thing. Although we saw it was due to age and the pains in his bones."

I thought about that. Was Zebediah an intended victim? Even in such a close-knit community, would extreme irritation be a cause for murder? But there were those other fires. Could the arsonist have known Zebediah was inside?

I asked, "Where did the Seedhouse fire start?"

"In the mud room. That's a large entry space where we store wood to keep the cauldron for rosewater simmering, and there's long shelves on the sides where we chop off the parts of the plants that aren't needed. We hang bunches of herbs there from the ceiling to dry. It was thought that Brother Zeb took in a candle and set it down. Then he lit the kerosene lantern, took it inside, shut the door, and forgot about the candle. A bunch of herbs might have fallen beside it. The real damage was to the mud room. His body wasn't burned, you know. It must have been the smoke seeping under the door and he didn't notice. He might even have worked awhile, gotten sleepy, turned down the lantern, put down his head, and dozed off. We found him once like that." Philemon's voice trailed off. Then he added firmly, "It was an accident."

My tone was sharp. "Elder Jacob doesn't believe that or he wouldn't have sent you to Quincey for help. There've been too many of these fires. Someone has started them and will likely continue. It is someone you know or someone you've seen more than once in the village."

Suddenly Philemon looked all of his seventy years. The reins slackened in his freckled hands. The horse slowed and at last glanced over his shoulder. Then the Shaker tightened his grip once again and looked straight ahead. His face was without expression. "There must be some other explanation."

He said nothing else for an hour or more. The rising road signaled we were nearing Hancock, tucked up in the Berkshire Hills. The sort of farm I had been watching for appeared on the right and I asked Philemon to stop and wait for me. He asked no questions, even when I lifted a half barrel of cider onto my shoulder. All I said was, "Put this on Jasper Quincey's account." Without a word, Philemon duly noted down the amount.

On my return, though, when he saw the cider gone and a yellow dog trotting at my heels, a startled exclamation escaped his lips. "Hallelujah!"

"Good name for him," I replied, gesturing to the dog to jump onto the wagon's back gate. He leapt right in, circled a bit, sniffed, and settled down on a folded burlap bag. He was about a year old, short-haired, medium-sized, and looked as if he'd been put together with spare parts of various breeds. A bit of boxer in the chest, the quick eyes of the border col-

lie. One ear drooped and the other stood up. "Good boy," I
said, shut the gate, and climbed in front.

"But we don't keep dogs, Brother Michael. They aren't
use—"

"This one barked at me when I was but halfway to the
house. Didn't stop until his mistress ordered him quiet. She
had several and was quite pleased to trade this one for
Shaker cider."

Philemon let out his breath. After a moment, he said, "Our
cider is the best. We have all varieties of apple and mix the
sweet with a few of the sour. We don't use windfalls, as is
usual, but pick them from the tree. We start making it right
at the start of the summer with the ones we call June-eaters."
His voice turned mournful. "Every morning when I first step
out in the summer, long before the light comes, I've smelled
three things: apples, roses, and peace. Our name for our village is the City of Peace. Now I only catch the scent of apples and roses. We do need your help. I am sorry I can offer
none to you. So you must do what you think best.

"When you arrive on foot, go directly to Elder Jacob and
tell him you were sent by Jasper Quincey. When Jacob sent
me to Boston for this purpose, he said he had not even talked
this over with the other elders. *That* is unheard of and is the
truest measure of our plight. He lives above the Meetinghouse with the other three. He's not always there since he
often works alongside Esau, his birth brother, to show that
he is not above others as an elder. A very good man, Elder
Jacob. He'll know what to do. Sister Esther at the Trustees'
Office will know where he might be found since she has the
schedules. She'll regard you simply as a newcomer and so
you must appear to her. I'll set you down in one more mile.
I've many stops before I return myself."

Then and only then did I reach in back for the bundle
from Quincey. I pulled out the fat envelope. After opening it,
I stared. It contained a stack of banknotes and a very short
note. The first line referred to the money. "Use as needed." I
didn't see what use it would be among the Shakers. I put it
back in the envelope.

The second lines read: "Trapper will be observing New

Lebanon. Concentrate your own efforts on Hancock. From time to time, he will appear there. Give your letters for me to Philemon Wells and only to him. Report *exactly* to me."

This was followed by: "Freegift grew up at Hancock. I questioned him at length, but his only useful comment was 'I've always been worried about Jacob.' He would not elaborate. I include it for your consideration."

As I tore the note into small pieces, I wondered *how* I was to consider that. Was the one man I planned to trust untrustworthy? If so, why did he ask Quincey for help?

To Philemon, I said, "I'm to give you letters for Jasper Quincey."

He only looked at me, lines of trouble etched on his forehead, as he stopped the horse. Taking off his hat, he patted his fringe of white hair with his handkerchief and bowed his head in prayer. I jumped down, got my bundle, opened the back of the wagon for Hallelujah, and whistled him out. The two of us came around and stood by Philemon.

When he lifted his head, he unexpectedly smiled. "It has come to me, Brother Michael. Over the last years, many of us have been visited by angels. Celestial beings also come in disguise. You are named after the warrior angel. And you have been sent to us. Praise God and Mother Ann."

Replacing his hat, he waved at me cheerfully and drove off. For a moment I stood, speechless. Then I looked down at Hallelujah. "Just remember to bark."

Chapter Five

Hallelujah was trotting purposefully ahead of me as we approached Hancock. I took that as a good sign. Maybe *he* knew what he was doing. His one upright ear stood up even straighter and I could hear the distant shouts of boys at play. Beyond them were men haying in the fields, but the young ones had obviously been given a little time off from their chores. They were gathered in a meadow bordered by a thick stand of trees.

Keeping the dog close at my heels, I slipped into this copse. Most of the boys were at the far end, getting ready for a race. Near me, one paced by what was obviously the finish line. He limped as he walked and waited. I hunched down, pointed at the boy, and whispered in Hallelujah's ear. "See him? He's going to give you the best ear scratch you ever had. Don't look back. Just hightail it straight over to him. Go!" I gave him a slap on the rear. I was relying on the natural connection between boys and dogs.

He raced across the field in the right direction. As soon as the boy caught sight of him, his mouth opened in delighted surprise. He didn't say a word, just crouched down. Hallelujah knew what to do. He licked the smiling face enthusiastically and, of course, got his head scratched. As the other boys ran up, I made my way out of the trees and back to the road unnoticed.

Walking into the Shaker village, it occurred to me that, whatever peace smelled like, it might well look like this. The quiet in the air was that of an eternal Sunday afternoon. Order reigned. Every building looked like it'd just been painted the day before. The crops in the field, the trees in the orchard, the rows in the herb garden, the pathways—all were arrow straight. Even Nature cooperated. The green hills that cupped the settlement seemed designed to hold back any outer chaos.

Philemon said the round brick barn had been built that way for reasons of efficiency. It was set into the side of a hill and the hay wagons climbed that to the back side of the barn and unloaded on the second story. The cows were herded into their pie-shaped stalls on the first floor and the hay was dropped into the open circle in the middle. It *was* practical but, like a Roman rotunda, it pleased the eye.

The severe squareness of the other buildings was softened by the summer trees, the flowering herbs, and the blooming roses. Their deep scarlet blossoms climbed high trellises and low fences. When mentioning these, the trustee had pointed out that rosewater was used for fever poultices, in ointments, and as flavoring for apple pies. Those who gathered the petals were told not to glory in the flowers, that making an idol of anything imperils the soul, and that they should consider instead the usefulness of the flowers. The air was filled with the fragrance of the rosewater, kept simmering in a cauldron in the Seedhouse.

I'd never seen an orchard like this one. The branches were carefully pruned, and every bough was laden with bright fruit. Philemon told me one of the brothers said, "A tree has its wants and wishes, and a man should study them as a teacher watches a child to see what he can do. If you love the plant and take heed of what it likes, you will be well re-paid by it. I don't know if a tree ever comes to love you, and I think it may, but I am sure it feels when you care for it and tend it, as a child does."

The Shakers might think it wrong to cultivate beauty, but they managed to create it.

In every other way, the village exactly reflected their beliefs. What I was seeing filled me with despair. The Shakers imagined they could make a Paradise on earth.

Not only do we see ourselves coming down the street, but when we look upward, the sky becomes a mirror. We make God in our image. The Shakers' God was a woman. A mother. One who knew all about the pain of childbirth and the far worse pain of losing that child. So: Avoid sex. Keep your room neat. Clean your plate. Dress warmly. Be kind. Share what you have. Love your brothers and sisters.

Those who even attempt to follow those last rules are lambs in a wolfish world. At least the Shakers had the good sense to stay as far away as possible from the World.

But all those legions of angels couldn't keep the serpent out of the Garden. He was there when it was planted. The Shakers couldn't help me spot him if they denied he was there. I let out my breath. What could *I* do? Keep an eye on the unwalled boundaries? All one of me. Plus a dog. Talk to the people, Quincey said. At the moment, there wasn't a soul in sight.

Everyone who could—brothers and sisters—must be working in the fields. It'd be first priority at this season. At least it made it a good time to take a careful look at the scene of the last fire. The building to my left, next to huge squares of greens and blooms, had to be the Seedhouse. Surrounded by pink-flowered bilberry shrubs, it was painted brown. Only a very close look showed that the rectangle of the mud room that jutted out from the front of the building was slightly fresher paint. The whole structure looked quiet and solid in the afternoon sunlight.

It wasn't that way the dark night it burned. I could see it. The yellow flames eating up the sides of the entry room. A smoky orange light against the sky. An alarm bell clanging, a sudden frenzy of noise in the predawn silence. Men and women in their nightdress running up, grabbing the pails, frantically passing them from hand to hand, trying desperately to save months of hard, hard work. The fire would have lit their agonized faces. They didn't know the worst. An old man lay slumped inside.

But one person wore a different expression. Satisfaction. Excitement. An outsider watching from a distant vantage point? Or one of those with bent back and aching palms handing a bucket to the next in line. Did Elder Jacob see that look flash out? Was that why he so secretly sent Philemon to Quincey? Or was it simply that there were too many fires?

Whoever had set it might not have known there was someone in the Seedhouse itself. Brother Zebediah could have arrived much earlier, worked awhile, found himself sleepy at last, turned off the lantern, put down his head on folded arms. The very old tend to sleep when and where they can. Or did the fire-setter not care that he was inside?

I stood for some time, intent on my inner vision of this crackle and blaze. An unseen memory of my family home in flames shot up. I began to feel a hotness on my skin, uncomfortable at first. Then it was too much like exposing a fresh burn to any heat. Hurrying toward the door of the mud room, I escaped inside.

The fire was started here. There was no sign there'd ever been one.

The smell of the clumps of drying herbs hung from every inch of ceiling overpowered the other senses. The Shakers made their medicines and ointments from them, but the scents called up in me images of food. Turkey roasted in sweet sage and thyme. Tart pickles in the brine of dill. Apple pie with the light licorice of fennel seed.

As Philemon had said, both sides of the room were lined with waist-high shelves where the plants could be stripped. Baskets to hold seeds and leaves were hung from pegs above the benches. Underneath them were stacks of short logs for the simmering cauldron inside.

Opening that door, I was wrapped with the aroma of roses and the intense warmth of an iron stove in the corner. Although the room was uncluttered, all the space was filled. The pegs on the walls held fine silk sieves with curved handles and all sizes of baskets. Open cupboards had shelves lined with glass bottles, bowls, mortars and pestles. Built-in cabinets on one side had rows and rows of small drawers, each neatly labeled with the kind of seeds it held. Two long heavy oak tables were in the center of the room. On them rested long wooden boxes with curved bottoms like cradles, obviously designed to separate seeds at one end from chaff at the other.

Herbs hung from the ceiling in here, too, and their fine dust danced in the air. But everything was tidy. No blackened walls. The floor was spotless. I backed out into the mud room. Now I could detect here, over the bouquet of the herbs, the clean smell of fresh-cut boards. The Shakers had rebuilt the entry room in the two weeks since it burned. There were no traces anywhere of that disaster.

Shutting the outer door, I prowled the outside, pulling back the leathery leaves of the bilberry bushes to inspect the stone foundation. Even that looked as if it had been scrubbed. I stooped down, hoping to catch a whiff of the coal tar used in paraffin or the pungency of kerosene. But, if either had been used, the smell was gone.

In frustration, I spun on my heel, glancing upward at the windows of the Living Quarters to judge what might be seen from there. A dark outline filled the glass in an upper window. Then it was gone. I kept my eyes on that window for some time.

I didn't like the idea I'd been observed. And I didn't think I was mistaken about what I saw. I'd check to see if a brother or sister hadn't been feeling well.

Stepping back, I took in the Seedhouse again. All that wood inside, that floating dust of chaff. The entire place was an invitation to another fire.

If the rest of the Shakers, like Philemon, insisted the first was an accident, they wouldn't protect the building. Or themselves.

Yet one of them had his doubts. Jacob had sent Philemon to Quincey for help. Why did he keep his suspicions to himself? Because telling the other elders would require a meeting and he thought the arsonist would be sitting in that room, a member of that group?

I was going to find him and ask. Right now.

Chapter Six

Walking fast, I headed for the Meetinghouse, which was unmistakable since it alone was white. There was a gambrel roof with dormer windows jutting out where the sleeping quarters for the elders must be. The front of the building had two separate entrances, presumably one for the brothers and one for the sisters. I took the nearest.

Inside, it seemed more of a theater than a church, with movable benches facing a long, polished floor. Sunlight from surrounding windows bounced off the floor's gleaming surface and onto the high cream-colored ceiling. In contrast, the lower walls were painted a glossy Prussian blue which held the captured light.

I found the offices for the elders, but it seemed there was not an elder there to answer my called-out greeting. Nor could I find anyone outside to direct me. It was late afternoon, but not yet the dinner hour.

As I made my way past the orchard, I could see a woman seated on the step of an official-looking brown building. I cut across the grass, and the climbing roses partially hid me from her view. She was intent on the work in her lap, mending a man's white shirt. All I could see was her profile with pale, even features. Her hair was covered with a transparent cap, like those serene Madonnas of the Dutch School of painting. Without glancing at her sewing basket, she reached in its depths and pulled out what was obviously not what she wanted. A handful of satiny pink ribbons. She entwined them in her fingers, slowly, a little reluctantly.

Then, with eyes tight shut, she raised her face to the sun. The look of pain on her face was so intense that I, some yards away, could feel it twisting my own insides. A tear glinted and then slid down her cheek. I stepped back, without intending it, and my boot heel scrunched in the gravel. Her eyes opened and, startled, she stood up, the shirt on her lap falling at her feet.

Hurriedly I raised an arm as if I were wiping my brow on my shirtsleeve, hoping she'd think I hadn't noticed. I took off my hat, cleared my throat, and came nearer, saying, "Pardon me, ma'am. I'm looking for Sister Esther at the Office of the Trustees' Building."

She looked at me unseeingly for a moment, standing with those bright ribbons clutched against the drab shawl front of her dress. Then she dropped them into the basket, all expression gone from her face. She picked up the shirt and answered in a low voice, "This is the Office. I am Sister Esther."

Now I was the one staring. She couldn't be. The efficient sister that Philemon described keeping track of fertilizer on bean patches had to be a middle-aged spinster, merciless on narrow detail, with features to match. The woman before me had light hair, dark-lashed gray eyes, a straight nose, smooth cheeks, and a most sensual mouth. She was barely out of her twenties, if that.

Standing near, I could see that the shape of her face was too bold for that cap. Her wide cheekbones were pronounced and her otherwise delicate chin hinted at squareness at the corners. I suppose that, tucked in their minds somewhere, most men have the idea that a woman without a husband lacks one because she is plain. Probably I assumed that all Shaker women were so. I was wrong.

This all came to me later that evening. Then, with her before me, I was only able to fumble out the words "I understand you can direct me to Elder Jacob. He's not at the Meetinghouse."

"He and the other elders have just been summoned to the Central Ministry in New Lebanon. It was a matter of some urgency and they may not return until quite late." She paused, then added, "If the meetings carry over until tomorrow, they may well spend the night there. Could I help you?"

Had I my wits about me, I would have thanked her and immediately gone to talk to Jacob at New Lebanon. It was only three miles away. Since he knew Quincey would send someone, he would have given thought to my introduction to the Hancock Community.

I'd been waiting to hear his plan and therefore had not fixed on the details of my background, or even what I should be called. Philemon and I had agreed that, since copies of the *Boston Independent,* which carried my byline over the Police News column, did find their way to Hancock, it might be better if I gave a different surname. If there were any suspicion that I was a journalist, my effectiveness would be gone. Moreover, if the Shakers were to answer any of my questions with openness, I would have to be accepted from the start. And Philemon had pointed out the difficulties with that.

I would certainly stand out. Few men between the ages of twenty and fifty joined the Shakers. Celibacy was too high a hurdle. Those in that age group who came to the village were usually drifters, rural farmhands who could find no work for the winter. Attempts were made to convert them and to integrate them into the community, but to no avail. These men left in the spring, at least in better boots than when they arrived. They stayed at the Newcomers' House in the East Family, a half mile out.

Some rare men, driven only by the intensity of their beliefs, did come. Of these, several were educated. Philemon had mentioned a Boston cleric and the son of a rich Virginia planter. Since my speech put me in that group—and it would be hard to disguise that for any length of time—I would have to be regarded as a convert, a man of religious conviction, which had been strengthened by my obvious ill fortune. Traveling here, I'd had no problem with that, other than a concern that I could carry it off.

Looking at Esther, it seemed shabby to engage in any kind of pretense. I wanted to be who I was, only have her think I was so much better than I was. But there was no help for it. "I'm Michael—" I cleared my throat. "Call me Brother

Michael. I wish to join the community. A good friend of Elder Jacob's suggested I see him about this."

Her face stayed closed, but her quick upward glance betrayed that was not what she expected to hear. She folded the shirt neatly over her arm and replied, "You would need to speak to the elder then. Tomorrow would be the best. Brother Esau, the deacon, will see to your lodging tonight. Since it's the first harvest, everyone is in the fields now, but they'll be coming in to supper soon. You could wait in the Office, if you wish." She turned and opened the door. I nodded and leaned down to brush the dust of the road off my boots. As she went in, I took off my hat and hastily combed my hair with my fingers.

Following her a few seconds later, I heard the wail of a young girl's voice. "Sister Esther, I *kin't* make these figures come out right! And I've blotted the page *agin*."

The speaker was seated at half of a double desk, her side strewn with papers. One of her arms was in a splint spread across her chest. She was ten or eleven, a round-faced girl with a milkmaid complexion. Catching sight of me, she turned an embarrassed pink but her gaze didn't drop.

"Sister Mercy, this is Brother Michael, who has just come to us." As Esther spoke, she gestured to a ladderback chair across the large office and poured me a glass of water from a jug on the counter in the center of the room. The girl kept looking at me as she murmured, "More love, brother."

I bowed, and took the water gratefully, glancing around, noticing how closely Jasper Quincey had modeled his study on Shaker principle. Here were the spaced wooden pegs at eye level, these hung with an extra chair, a long candleholder with the hole at the top, a broom, the two women's outer bonnets. There was the same furniture, elegant in its simplicity. Above the double desk, on each side there were pigeonholes and, over those, bookshelves with neatly stacked ledgers. Shutters, now open, were fitted into the window frames on either side of the desk. There was no carpet on the immaculate floor.

"It's just that your pen needs trimming," Esther said to the girl, "and you can't do that one-handed." Before she reached the desk to help, the outer door burst open. The boy I'd seen in the field almost tumbled into the room. Hallelujah skidded in behind him, his paws slipping on the floor.

Esther was more than surprised at the sight of the dog, but her voice was calm. "More love, Brother Crispin."

As a response, he patted his chest near his heart. Then he swept off his Shaker hat. His tousled brown hair was sunstreaked, his short nose was freckled, and his blue eyes were eager. As he limped nearer the two women, I realized this must be the boy that Philemon had found in Boston, being beaten on the way to market. His eyes were fixed not on Esther but the girl, moving his hands in a sign language. Watching him, Mercy came around the counter, just barely avoiding hitting the bent elbow of her splinted arm on the wood.

I couldn't understand all his gestures, but it was clear what he wanted: to keep the dog. Troubled lines appeared near the corners of Esther's mouth. Mercy turned to her and said, "Cris— Brother Crispin, I mean, says this dog was sent to us." She stopped, a small frown puckering her forehead, and added, "It's queer where he could've come from otherwise. There's no place fer miles and miles. Anyway, Cris says we kin't turn him away. He's a gift."

Before she could answer, I exclaimed, "He is indeed a gift. Hallelujah!" At that, the animal obediently trotted over to me, tail wagging. "Yes," I said, trying to sound as if such expressions always leapt to my lips, "you can see that the sound of God's glory calls to him. His name should be Hallelujah."

Crispin looked at me, nodding vigorously, anxious eyes wide with hope. He kept those eyes on me as I said my name, and his mouth tried to form an *m* in imitation.

I addressed Esther. "I've been told you don't keep dogs. But they do have superior senses of smell and hearing. This one may well have come to you to warn of—" I spread my hands to show that I couldn't think of anything in particular and ended, "anything amiss."

"Ye-es." Esther drew out the word. She thought for a moment. "On the farm I felt safe because of the dogs." Then she glanced at me, adding, "We had a fire recently. Brother Zebediah died in it. Perhaps he'd be with us today if we'd had a dog to warn us at the outset." There was nothing in her face to indicate that she thought it anything but an accident.

Turning to the children, she said, "But the elders will have to make the decision to keep him. Since they are gone, I see no harm in letting him stay until tomorrow. I will speak to the deacon. Brother Crispin, put the dog in the mud room of the Seedhouse and see that he has food and water."

Crispin beamed and Mercy gave a joyous skip. This time she did whack the edge of her splint on the counter. Wincing and rubbing it, she said with a plea in her voice, "It'd be better if I went along to the kitchen, too, 'cuz the sisters won't understand what he wants food fer. They'll be thinkin' he'll eat it himself and ruin his supper." She glanced somewhere near me, adding, "No one but me kin understand his signs. I don't know why, I jes' do. It's a gift."

With some urgency, the boy pulled on her sleeve and made a rapid scribbling gesture. Mercy nodded and explained, "He's learnin' to write though. Then it'll be good 'cuz he kin tell people that way. See, he's not stupid—he just never had no schoolin' before."

Feeling the weight of Crispin's mute look, I answered, "We all have to be taught." The quick hope on his face made me add, "It took me some time. I remember my sister learned much faster."

"Maw taught me when I was real little," Mercy said with some pride. "She'd draw the letters in the dirt with a stick. 'Afore she took sick, that was. Cris don't recolleck his ma at all. Some things I forgit about mine, but I kin see her face plain. I ain't been *here* long, but I was with some other folks quite a time. Maw's comin' fer me when she gets better." Her tone was matter-of-fact, but she looked away as she brought out that last sentence.

Esther stepped forward. "Yes, go with Brother Crispin. It might be best not to mention the dog at all. Simply say I have requested the food." She followed them out the door. I came, too, and we stood on the step, watching them race toward the Seedhouse, quickly reappearing and heading for a tall building of mellow brick. Given its size, it must have been the Living Quarters, which Philemon said housed a hundred brothers and sisters. It was three stories, besides the high attic and a ground floor. The building was solidly Federal in design and wouldn't have been out of place in Harvard Yard, resembling Massachusetts Hall without a spire.

Standing next to Esther, I found that all that was really on my mind was that her dress smelled wonderfully of lavender. She straightened the shawl over the front, and as her white hands moved over it, I imagined the softness of the skin beneath those layers of clothing.

"Perhaps," she said, as much to herself as to me, "even keeping the dog a short time wasn't the right thing."

"It was. Gifts must be accepted." I was putting my faith in Elder Jacob's seeing reason after I talked to him.

"Yes. But there are the rules. The children will be very disappointed if in the end the dog is sent away. Hard for them both, especially given Crispin's—" She didn't finish that sentence. "He came to us only last winter. He still doesn't . . . ," she thought, her teeth catching her full lower lip, "trust. In some ways, he's doing well. His leg is improving."

"Can't he talk at all? Make sounds?"

"No, but there doesn't seem any obvious reason why he can't. We had a doctor from a nearby community examine him. Mercy is the only one that seems to understand his signs and therefore is allowed to spend time with him. We don't encourage particular friendships between any two people, but because of his lameness, he can't join in many of the boys' games. He is often frustrated because he can't be understood. Mother Alma decided that, in this instance, some relaxation of the rule would be allowable. In late afternoons, they both work with Brother Seth. He says Mercy has a sixth and a seventh sense where animals are concerned, and is a great help with the sick ones. In turn, she's learned a great deal about medicines for their various illnesses. Having her in the barn is good in another way. I'm afraid Sister Bertha, who oversees the kitchen, groans inwardly when Mercy is on the list for duties there. She has a tendency to break dishes."

Esther was clearly making conversation, even overcoming a natural reserve to do so. Perhaps it was an effort to ease a new member into the community. But I had the impression that she had something on her mind and that she was edging toward it.

"Do you all take turns, then, doing different tasks?" That wasn't what I wanted to ask. But all the questions I had for her couldn't be asked.

Still watching the kitchen door where Crispin stood sentinel, she answered, "Yes, we do. The sisters, of course, don't work side by side with the brothers, except at harvest. The women have their set responsibilities and the men theirs. Still, we've found that having people do unaccustomed work results in good ideas. One of the brothers who was sweeping the rooms found the round brooms unsatisfactory. He designed a flat one, and now we have more orders for those than we can fill. And a sister, seeing two men pushing a saw back and forth drew a plan for a circular one that she made on her spinning wheel. We use that saw and sell many. I've learned a great deal since I came, particularly from Sister Hepzibah, the other office sister. She taught me so many things before—" She stopped, then finished, "Before she became less able."

"But surely it wouldn't be efficient to keep training people to do detailed office work." I intended to stand on this spot, continuing our talk even if she brought up obscure passages of the Scriptures and asked me to explain them.

"Certain positions require continuity. Elder, trustee, deacon and deaconess. Sister Bertha who oversees the kitchen. We are not rotated, no." For the first time, she smiled, adding, "I looked forward to working in the herb garden and the Seedhouse, but I do *not* miss my turn in the laundry."

That smile undid me. All my thoughts scattered. I grabbed for the nearest one, saying with a gesture toward the office, "It's unfortunate that there aren't enough brothers to take this on. You can't enjoy working with numbers. It must be a terrible strain."

"On my mind?" There was an edge in her voice. "Washing clothes—pulling soaking wet sheets, dresses, and trousers from one tub to another, wringing them out, hanging them up—is quite a strain on the arms and the back. Always and everywhere, laundry is women's work. Luckily, we have strong backs, presumably to make up for our weak minds."

I stared at her, too surprised at her words to make any reply.

Raising clear gray eyes to my face, she went on, but in a more neutral tone. "When I came here, I was ignorant. I was aware of it, but I didn't guess the depths of my ignorance. However, as you said—we all have to be taught. In teaching me, Sister Hepzibah showed she had every confidence that I could learn. Working with figures is satisfying once one grasps the meaning of the numbers and sees how to translate that into running one's business. As well, I now know what our customers are in need of. It means we can plan for that. And, when I talk to them, I sometimes think of what they don't know they're in need of and they buy it, too." She paused and added, this time with passion, "I wish every woman had such opportunities to learn."

"But," I protested uneasily, "you could hardly allow women to go into the workplace in the world! They'd be exposed to such dangers—"

"Think of the dangers they're exposed to in not being allowed to go into the workplace! They can't earn a living."

"They shouldn't have to! They should be cared for, protected—"

"And are they? Any but a privileged few? Besides, those are terms one applies, rightly, to the needs of children. I am not a child."

I simply stood there. I'd never had such a conversation with a woman.

Abruptly, she turned her head, but not before I saw a look of surprise on her face that suggested she was not in the habit of expressing those ideas to a man either. After a moment, she remarked, as if to close the subject, "There's always much to be done here, but I can order my day. It gives one a sense of freedom."

How, I wondered, could she possibly feel free in such a

regimented society? But I recalled the narrow world even
women of means inhabited. Needlework. Making and returning visits. My sister Celia was very bright, excelling at
our French lessons; our tutor would listen to her with approval and then grimace as I tried to get my tongue around
the language. She spent as much time in our father's library
as I did. It had never occurred to me that in many ways she
was as ready a learner as I was.

Gazing into the middle distance, Esther said carefully,
"Many who come here—men particularly—find that our
way of life is too constricting. Our *Millennial Laws* are detailed. There are, however, 'out families.' They are Believers
who do not live communally. The Krugers, for example,
have a farm some ten miles from Hancock. Frederick
Kruger mentioned this week that it was difficult in winter
for his children to attend our school. He is prosperous and
would welcome, I think, a man who could help with the harvest and then tutor during the cold months."

Very tactful. She was saying that if poverty had driven me
to the Shakers, here was an option that might be more acceptable. There was her strong implication that I was unlikely to stay. I needed Elder Jacob to spread a few gentle
words about my extraordinary commitment, brought on perhaps by my past problems. He needn't stray from the truth
on that last part.

I stayed on the straight path in my answer. "Of late, I've
learned a great deal about the Believers, and I admire their
principles. I wish to know more."

Then, down the path on our left came a procession of
Shakers, the sisters in their sugar-scoop bonnets and the men
in their wide-brimmed hats. They were returning from the
fields, walking two by two. They were moving briskly for
people who had spent the afternoon working hard under a
hot sun. Their pace was deliberate and they wheeled so they
turned the corners exactly. All were silent, except for two
men at the end of the line who were talking, their hat brims
almost touching.

As I watched, something so odd happened that my casual
glance turned into an astonished stare.

Chapter Seven

As if enraged, the brother on the nearest side suddenly reached over, yanked off his partner's hat and flung it back the way they'd come. He jerked to the right and came toward us with a fast, skipping walk, stopping almost in front of the Office.

His two forearms were stiff, his hands straight, one behind the other. He spoke rapidly, in staccato sentences, but he was speaking to the empty air, not to us. I couldn't catch many of his words, some of which seemed gibberish, although he seemed to be repeating "horrid." His harsh pronunciation made it sound like a crow cawing. He repeated his movements, chopping his arms. Occasionally he scooped at the ground with one hand, as if trying to pick up something dropped by the invisible person he addressed so intensely.

Except for his partner, who turned back to gather his hat, the other Shakers continued ahead, not glancing at him. The contrast between his convulsive movements and their measured pace along the path at a right angle to him was riveting. He stopped as abruptly as he'd started, and with one quick toss, he sent his own hat sailing toward Esther's feet. After a few seconds he came up the path to retrieve it, smiling warmly at her as he did so.

He looked to be eighteen or thereabouts. His dark hair was clipped Shaker style, short across the forehead and around the face, with a little length in back, but his curled across his brow and in front of his ears. He had light eyes, tanned skin, and regular features. It would be hard to avoid the word "beautiful" in describing him.

His companion came hurrying up the path, wiping his brow. His sparse blond hair was plastered to his forehead with sweat, and the sun had turned his face, blotchy with pimples, a fiery red. As he bent his abused hat brim back into shape, he greeted us. "This is Brother Elijah," Esther said.

Turning, she indicated the dark-haired youth, now standing quietly, "Brother Giles." He bowed gracefully, picking up his hat at the same time. There was nothing in his face or manner that indicated his previous behavior was anything out of the ordinary to him.

Again blotting his forehead with the back of his hand, Elijah looked up at me and burst out in a high squeak, "You're quite tall!" Then his face turned even redder and in a deeper voice, he said, "People must always say that to you." He shifted his eyes to the ground in confusion.

Remembering how my own voice had once moved up and down the register, I felt some sympathy for Elijah, although it struck me that he must be nearly of an age with Giles, and was old for a voice that wobbled. But he was young for his years, clearly subject to all the acute humiliation adolescents suffer over small things. One hand went immediately to a cheek to hide the worst of the blemishes.

Noticing his downcast expression, Giles quickly said, "Brother Elijah is one of our artists. He did the drawings for the seed packets."

"They were beautifully done," Esther added. "And the etchings were so precise that we've been able to use them over and over in the printing without losing detail."

Now Elijah was beaming, although he fluttered one hand dismissively. "As an artist, I'm nothing like Sister Hannah. Why, her drawing of 'The Blazing Tree' is *perfect*. So inspiring. She's been asked to do copies for the other communities. Then there's Sister Polly. She did a picture of the 'Gospel Union Fruit Bearing Tree.' I'm no comparison. For the seed packets, I flatter myself that I did observe the herbs closely and copied them carefully, sometimes showing where they might be found—in the woods or by water—in case people were used to picking them wild. I have to admit,

though, it was craftsman work, really. But now, the pictures
I did during Mother's Work—they were from the *heart*. The
vision I had of the Heavenly City, of God's jeweled throne!
I could only hope it came close to what I saw when I was
transported."

His pale eyes glowing, he looked up at me. "Oh, if you
could have experienced that time. I was still at the Canaan
Community then, but it was the same in all our villages. The
fervor we felt. Such an outpouring of love and of gifts of
love. We constantly exchanged small paintings, poems, accounts of the angels' visits. The music we heard. The unearthly music. Every day was exciting." With a wistful sigh,
he concluded, "Mother Ann will bless us again. It was all her
work, you know. That's why we refer to it that way. She saw
we needed our spirits uplifted, and she sent visitors from
above to us. In my prayers every night, I always ask that her
light will shine on us soon. It's been over a year now since it
ended. Why, we haven't even had a Midnight Cry for some
weeks."

Mentioning that ecstatic outburst among the Shakers,
Quincey had speculated that the elders' efforts to tamp down
some of the excesses may have been the reason for the fires.
The timing sounded exactly right. The effect of that period
must have been very great, especially on the emotional, the
susceptible, like Elijah.

It gave me a starting place for questions.

Although Giles had not spoken, he was no longer standing quietly. He constantly re-settled his hat on his head, trying for some ideal position. As well, he brushed back the
curls over his ears, first one side, then the other, his hands
going in metronomic precision. His next comment bore no
connection to what had been said. "When you record the
harvest, Sister Esther, you will be amazed at the amount of
corn we've got. We sent the last-picked ears to the kitchen
for supper."

Before she could respond, Elijah inserted, with an un-
happy grimace, "But Brother Esau says that, as there will be
much light left after we eat, we're to go back and try to finish. So we'll not have our laboring at the Meetinghouse

tonight." He glanced up at me. "We refer to our dancing services as 'laboring.' It's a pity we can't dance tonight. Really we need the practice for Sunday when we have observers. The hymns *must* be rehearsed as well. Brother Esau knows we're using some of the new ones from Mother's Work and we're not yet perfect in them."

"I'm looking for the deacon," Esther said. "I haven't seen him pass. There are several things we need to discuss. I must ask him to find lodging for Brother Michael. The Newcomers' House is filled with the additional harvest workers."

Elijah raised his almost lashless eyes. "He could have the room next to ours. Just for tonight. It was Brother Zeb's and it's empty since he didn't share with anyone. And we could show him how everything is done."

Just then, a man walking alone came into view and Esther raised a hand to him. "There is Brother Esau."

Coming up, he touched the brim of his hat, but didn't remove it. He had a formal air about him as if he were about to ascend to a pulpit and address a congregation. His hands, held together in front of him before his chest, emphasized that impression. He was lean and stiff-backed, with a fringe of white hair, tufted eyebrows to match, and a long nose. After greeting us, he inhaled with some force, as if sucking air through the length of that nose took effort. "I haven't much time at my disposal, Sister. You are not aware yet, but all the elders have been called immediately to the Central Ministry. Their duties, of course, devolve upon me." He managed to sound both self-important and martyred. "I can't recall that such a thing has ever occurred before. And just now at the harvest season when there is so much to be done. It's hard to imagine what could have arisen. I don't see how it could have anything to do with Elder Frederick's condition. *That* Jacob would have mentioned since it'd mean a vacancy in the Central Ministry. When Jacob informed me they were going, he did not even tell *me* the reason for this hasty call to New Lebanon. He was quite hurried, though." While speaking, he kept glancing crabwise out of the corner of his eyes in my direction.

Esther introduced me and explained the problem with the Newcomers' House. She mentioned Elijah's suggestion.

Esau shook his head firmly. "But he cannot stay in the Living Quarters. *The Millennial Laws* are specific on that point. Until an infant soul signs the Covenant, he or she cannot be put in with the Family. He or she must remain in the Gathering Order, then move up, after the prescribed period, the next step to the Junior Order. Really, I must speak to the Deaconess about leaving a room unoccupied in the Living Quarters when the Newcomers' House is full. Two brothers could easily have been brought up from the East Family and their room would then be vacant in just such a situation as this. Sister Thankful knows the Laws. Even at harvest, regular duties cannot be neglected. There is so much laxness. It is not as it used to be. Further calamity will descend on us as a punishment. We must adhere more strictly to—"

He interrupted himself at the sound of a horse coming fast up the wide pathway. Esau's thick eyebrows rose higher at the rider's speed. Giles said, "Why, it's Father."

Samuel Grant dismounted and looped the reins around a nearby tree, and I thought that even the way he walked seemed familiar to me. He'd changed little in the nearly twenty years since I'd seen him last. His hair had some gray, but his New Hampshire face with its pitted cheeks was as hard and stony as ever. As his eyes flicked over me, a dislike for the man was in my throat like bile. I remembered my mother using kindling rather than coal in our fireplaces.

"You're in time for the just-picked corn for supper," Giles began in a normal tone, but then his forearms jerked like a marionette's and his hands lined up precisely one in back of the other. He lunged toward his father, lightly touching him on each ear and each shoulder. He skipped in a square, repeating, "Pop, stop, hop," and that soon went into words that couldn't be followed, except for "horrid" which sounded much like "hard."

As he capered before him, Samuel Grant watched him impassively, as did the others. Perhaps one became accustomed. There was both randomness and symmetry in what Giles did, and an odd nonchalance in his manner. No contortion marred his classic features. When he finished, he spent some time readjusting his hat.

I had the impression then that his father's eyes were steadily on me, but he said nothing.

The silence was broken by the voice of a woman who came hurrying up. A stout woman, she arrived in a flurry of indignation. The brim of her flared poke bonnet trembled with it. Her chins quivered with it. Her long neckerchief was askew. It covered her upper body and came to a vee just below the waist, as Esther's did, except hers was made of silk and dyed a mulberry shade. The color unfortunately did not go well with a face florid with emotion. The frown line between her brows was so deep it might have been engraved.

She fixed her eyes accusingly on Esther and said, "Passing the Seedhouse, I saw Sister Mercy simply standing about outside. She was not doing her work. I understood she was to spend the day in the Office with you. At last she told me about the dog and said she was waiting to see if the animal would settle. She told me that permission had been granted to keep it overnight. There must be some mistake. Once fed, the animal will be difficult to drive off. Dogs are not only useless, as our rules clearly spell out, they are dirty, very dirty. They are horrid animals!"

At this point, Giles cawed out the word "horrid" three times as if mimicking her. Although she didn't look at him, her frown deepened and she seemed to swell, perhaps with outrage. The effort to keep from exploding made words impossible for her.

Esau pulled air through his nose as fast as he could. "Who gave such permission?"

Esther nodded to the woman, greeting her as Sister Thankful, before turning to Esau. Her tone was pleasant, unapologetic. "I did. I thought the elders might want to consider, just now, the advantages of having a watchdog."

Samuel Grant strode to the center of the group. He was not tall, but broad-shouldered and thick-chested. He had solid presence and an air of authority. He chopped the air with his hand. "Yes, that was wise."

His even tone disappearing, Esau almost sputtered. "That would be a transgression of—"

Grant interrupted him, "Honoring *The Millennial Laws* is important. However, they were no doubt meant to be guides for the elders, who would use their own discretion on some occasions."

Esau was breathing through his open mouth as well. "If one rule can be lightly dismissed, then any of them can. It is a very bad precedent. Elder Jacob will never countenance this."

Putting one foot on the step where Esther and I were standing, Grant said in what he perhaps meant to be a conciliatory tone, "Keeping one dog, for a good purpose, will not lead to a general flouting of all laws. Sometimes, in enclosed societies, too much is made of minor matters. I will speak to Elder Jacob myself about this. He'll agree."

If he intended to appease Esau, he'd made a very bad job of it. It was clear that Deacons made decisions on community matters, not trustees. And that peremptory waving aside of a rule could seem blasphemous to one who was a stickler for them.

Apparently, none of this crossed Samuel Grant's mind. He held out his hand to me, saying his name, waiting for me to say mine. "How do you do," I answered. "I'm Michael." He waited for my surname.

"Michael Profitt," I brought out, trying not to bare my teeth. That should be a name he'd remember. "With an *f* and two *t*'s." At that, he seemed to lose interest. He spoke to Esther, his tone as autocratic as if he were addressing a servant. "I'll be here for supper, but then I must return to New Lebanon. The matter is very grave. I'll need your help in locating some accounts, particularly any that pertain to the Maine Community."

He waited for her to precede him and disappeared into the Office.

It was as well he said nothing as he left. The standard Shaker leave-taking, urging love, might have been difficult for Esau. One couldn't be sure. His lips were pursed, but his no-color eyes were blank. Disappointment in the behavior of others was set in the long, disapproving lines that went from his nose to his chin. He was not surprised by sin. Still, his clasped hands were white-knuckled.

Chapter Eight

The moon was approaching full. There were only a few gauzy clouds. I stood looking out the window of my third-story room in the Living Quarters, and the village was a black-and-white still life. No breeze stirred the orchard. The shadows of the trees and the buildings were done in India ink. The path below me that angled by the dairy shop, the tanning shop, the Seedhouse, then toward the Trustees' Office was sketched in with a light pencil.

Yet as I turned away from the scene and resumed pacing the floor, I had to agree with Philemon. This was no City of Peace. The atmosphere pulsed as if with nearby lightning, just beyond the hills. It was quiet, however. I was sure that I was the only one awake.

Promptly at the 9:00 P.M. bell, the candles in each room had been extinguished and placed in the tall holders on the pegs beside the doors. The deaconess then moved down the hall, checking each one, collecting spent ends and replacing short tapers. Not a board creaked after that. Although the windows were open on the summer night, I couldn't hear a murmur from Elijah and Giles in the room next to mine. A long day in the fields would guarantee a sound sleep.

Following a conference with Sister Thankful, Esau assigned me to a lodging here. The two had even agreed on allowing Hallelujah an overnight stay, although watching them as they talked, I gathered that their only agreement consisted in their mutual disapproval of the idea. Whatever he'd said to her regarding the arrangements at the Newcomers' House had given a distinct lemon pucker to her mouth.

She'd walked off with an angry back. Sister Thankful's emotions seemed always on display.

As Esau guided me to my room, his face was composed. Moral homilies slid off his tongue. I wondered if he practiced them on the crows while picking corn. He said, "You will have come here hoping—nay, expecting—to find sanctuary for your spirit. A refuge from the World. But I am sorry to say that even here you'll find devotion to the Golden Calf. All Believers do not see the terrible temptation in the getting of money, for whatever good purpose. Mammon is a dazzling idol, Brother Michael, as hard to resist as that *other* craving earthly sense."

He fixed me with a ferret's stare, ready to spy out any lurking signs of lust in my heart. I quickly nodded in agreement, but he was determined to go on. "We had a brother, not long ago, who assured me that now he was in his third decade, he had put down his flesh. His very words. I felt it my duty to warn him that struggle is with us for life. He was deceiving himself. No doubt, too, he thought he was safe here. But the rules are not as rigidly enforced as they ought to be." He shook his head balefully. "Not long after, he conceived a vehement affection for a sister who tended him in an illness. They became apostates and left. You must be always on guard."

I nodded again, preferring not to know what was lurking in my heart. I was certain what was in all the corners of my mind. Suspicion. I saw motives for those fires in every one I met. Even Esau, that dry stick, seemed capable of bursting into flame.

When I asked him for writing materials, he provided them, remarking that it was wise of me to start my spiritual autobiography on the very first day. "If, in noting down each day's activity—which should *always* be done—you describe as well your daily striving for grace, you will see how to improve in your work and how to overcome stupidity of soul."

Since I was preparing a report to be sent off to Quincey, I had no doubt that, in his return comments, I'd be shown how to improve and overcome.

With that in mind, I wrote a full account, beginning with those I met. Desiring him to see all I saw, I described the dining room, the mealtime ritual, even the food. The men and women were at separate tables, each of which seated sixteen. We knelt for a silent grace and then sat in units of four, every square having its own butter, salt, pepper, cream, bread, and sugar. Then the sisters lifted from the dumb-waiter, loaded in the kitchen below, heaping platters and steaming bowls. The chicken fricassee had dumplings so light they almost floated off the sauce, the lentil loaf was creamy with cheese, the corn dripped with butter, the spinach was simmered with onion, the sliced tomatoes smelled of sun. Despite refilling my plate twice, I still found room for a heaping bowl of fresh blackberries with sweetened whipped cream.

Philemon sat across from me and he courteously introduced himself and the nearest two brothers as we sat down after prayers. One was Seth, who did the veterinary duties, a man with a glum smile, a bent back, and gnarled arthritic fingers. In his work, Crispin's and Mercy's nimble hands—not to mention their enthusiasm—must have helped. Brother Amos, who said he came originally from the Kentucky village, was near his age, but he was a blacksmith and his heavy shoulders looked powerful still. He had a thick mat of gingery gray hair on his head and some also sprouted from his ears and on his hands almost to the nail.

There was no conversation at the table since it was not allowed. However, Seth sent several speaking glances at Amos's plate, every inch of which was covered with the chicken and gravy. His own held only the lentil loaf and vegetables. When Amos refilled his, again with the chicken, he seemed to be purposely ignoring Seth.

Philemon managed to be next to me as we filed out following the sisters. It had taken me some time to locate Esther in the dining room since all the women's caps were identical, but she and an elderly woman were the last ones in their line, which we followed.

Just outside, Philemon stopped Seth, telling him about the

dog and adding, "It'd be good if you'd make sure it's healthy. Sister Esther says the animal is in the mudroom of the Seedhouse. Its presence there shouldn't be talked about until the elders have a chance to confer on whether we should keep it."

At his words, Amos came to a quick halt, raised a meaty hand, and jammed his hat down further on his head. "Dog? We'll be havin' a dog? There'll be a fuss. An almighty fuss. Same as in Kaintuck. Things goin' on good, and then somethin' upsets the haycart. Maybe only a little rock, but there's hay all over the place. People runnin' around, hotter'n anvil sparks. We shouldn't be doin' it. The women'll be jabberin' about fleas." Even his Southern drawl didn't soften the growl of his last words. "Can't *abide* fuss."

Seth answered him brusquely, "Fleas I kin take care of. And there'll be no fuss if'n we all keep our lips from flappin' like Brother Philemon says. I'll look at the dog straightaway."

Esther was walking slowly, at her older companion's pace. Philemon greeted them. Sister Hepzibah had a blackcurrant muffin of a face with plump cheeks and bright, dark eyes. Smiling warmly, she laid a fragile hand on my arm, saying, "You're new here. Welcome to our community." I told her my name and thanked her. Then she repeated her words exactly to Philemon. He showed no sign of disturbance, taking her hand gravely, saying his name, and adding, "I'm your fellow trustee, of course."

"Are you?" she replied, her brow furrowing slightly. "Let me know if I can be of any help."

Esther explained to Philemon that she'd met me earlier at the Office but, other than a murmured "More love," she didn't meet my eyes. This could have been a sign of Shaker modesty, but it made my spirits rise. They had certainly fallen when she suggested that I consider not staying and going instead to an "out family." I was aware that there was no reason for either of my reactions.

"Since all the men will be returning to the fields," Philemon went on to Esther, "I'll acquaint Brother Michael with the village. Then I have to go back to New Lebanon for the meetings with the Central Ministry regarding the problem I mentioned. If Brother Samuel and I return late, we'll try not to disturb you and Sister Hepzibah. I think it more likely that we'll stay there so we can resume our talks in the morning."

As we left, he told me, with a farewell wave to Hepzibah, "She forgets who I am because I've been gone over two weeks. But some days, she is button-bright, and we talk of our brothers and sisters who have gone ahead of us to the City of Heaven. The former office sister, named Matilda, was a particular trial for her. I could always tell when Hepzibah had a difficult day. A good many of the comments in the ledger would be written backwards." His lean face crinkled in a smile. "That's the Shaker way of swearing. Most effective. It requires such concentration that one finds the anger cools. She was competent, as is Esther, who has said she's found that she has a love of the business life. Then, too, Esther—because of her early background—is very able to meet the public, our customers, something a number of our sisters are not used to doing."

Before I could hurriedly inquire as to what that background was, Philemon let out a groan. "Being a trustee is a most responsible position. And we've been sadly let down by one of ours in a community in Alfred, Maine. The man in question, whose name is best not mentioned yet, has disappeared. There may be some explanation. It's difficult to imagine that he could have endangered his soul for the sake of mere money. You will keep this in confidence for the moment. The elders wish to tell the Family in the right way. It will affect us greatly because we, along with the other communities, must help those in Alfred. Because of his transgressions, they'll be all but destitute."

"What could he do that would bring them to that pass?"

"The titles to all property are in the names of the four trustees. One of them had died, and a new man had yet to be named. The two office sisters had no cause to doubt their brother trustee, who'd been in the community for years, and therefore they signed whatever papers he gave them. They were not Esthers. In any case, he sold a great deal of the village's outlying acreage."

Philemon brightened a little. "Luckily, that land was not fertile, so being rid of it is not so bad, especially since he got a good price." He went on gloomily, "But, of course, the community didn't get the money. He also sold some of their livestock, which was not delivered to the buyer. The worst part is this: he took out large loans from a Boston grain merchant, the pledge of security being this year's and next's seed crops, the income from which the village depended on. These loans must be paid back and they far exceed the value of the actual crops, which he'd made to appear larger than they were. Samuel Grant has been invaluable here. He is going to look over the books of the Alfred village to see what can be realized in the short term. He knows the Boston merchant and believes he can persuade him to extend the loans at reasonable interest. Brother Samuel says he understands how it could have happened since he himself had had dealings with that trustee in his own business and would have without question advanced the money. He did add that it would have only been *half* that sum. But the Shaker good name was part of the security and we must redeem it."

Writing to Quincey, I included this information. Several points occurred to me, as I was sure they would to him. Grant's older son Jared was now running his businesses, which included feed and grain. It would surely benefit the family if the Shaker hold on the seed market was weakened. Moreover, not only had Samuel Grant known that vanishing trustee, he himself was one of Hancock's. He was in an ideal position to cause financial disaster should he have that in mind.

I didn't mention my previous acquaintance with him—I was then only a boy, after all—nor did I add my impression of him. Neither did I do so when telling Quincey about Esther, saying that she was about thirty, with fair hair, light eyes, regular features, and a generous mouth. I spoke of Philemon's praise of her.

To have told him more about her would have required rational thought on my part. I wasn't capable of that where she was concerned. As a young man, I'd come back from a ball or a supper entranced with one woman or another. Many were as attractive as she was, and they'd used all the arts to make themselves more so. I'd danced with them, laughed with them, desired them. I'd stayed up for hours, head full of bright thoughts of them, as I was doing now.

This was quite different. At last, I stretched out on the bed, knowing sleep was far from me. The moon, coming through the window, made an exact rectangle of light on the floor. I can remember thinking that it must be aware it was in a Shaker village. Then, I don't how it was, perhaps I did doze off, but Esther was standing there. It was as vivid as any opium dream. She was dressed in her sober Shaker garb, her eyes on something beyond me, smiling in delighted expectation. The pink ribbons were entwined tightly in her fingers. I sat up, desperate to ask for whom she'd worn those ribbons.

Then she wasn't there. Sweat was pouring from me, although the collarless nightshirt that had been laid out for me was of the sheerest linen. I jumped up and leaned out the window for the air. I breathed in deeply and waited for my pulse to slow.

The unveiled moon was high in the sky and it must have been nearing twelve. I was about to turn and try sleep when I saw the figure in white hurrying on the path below in the dapple of shadow. At first I couldn't distinguish much. Then I could tell it was a woman, capless, long hair streaming down her back over her nightdress. The moon glinted on her hair as she emerged into the light. She stopped abruptly, looking from side to side.

Her profile was unmistakable. It was Esther. I was awake. There she was. Then she was almost running, going in the direction of the Office, but she paused again at the fork that led to the Seedhouse. Again she glanced in all directions before going ahead. I lost her in the shadow of the Seedhouse.

I grabbed my trousers and pulled them on, then fumbled under the bed for my boots. Why was she out at such an hour? I yanked on the boots, my fingers clumsy in their haste, and jammed the nightshirt into the top of my pants. Quietly as possible, testing the boards as I tiptoed, I reached the door. I held my breath lest the hinges creak as I turned the knob. Trying to avoid making noise myself, I didn't hear the footsteps coming toward my room as I edged the door open.

Chapter Nine

I stepped into a hallway flooded with light. A clear soprano rang out: "Awake, awake from your slumbers!"

It was Sister Thankful. She and Brother Esau were coming down the passage, pausing at each door to light the candles hung beside them. His hair was unruffled, and he was fully dressed down to his laced-up boots, whereas she'd only thrown her purple shawl over her nightdress. Her graying brown hair was caught up in an untidy knot at the back, loose ends straggling around her face. When they had almost reached my room, second from the end, I could see the deaconess' face. It was transformed, lit with joy. Seeing me, she sang again. "Awake from your slumbers!"

As she hurried up to me, the words rushed from her like a stream pell-mell over rocks. "I have had a visitation. From an angel. At last. Everyone but me had one during Mother's Work. It was a sign of my unworthiness, I knew. I tried harder. Harder. Doing all I could that I saw was good." Even the frown line between her brows that seemed carved into the skin was gone. She couldn't stop herself from talking, laughing. She had to tell the glad tidings over and over again. "Tonight he came to me. The sweetest music outside my door. An angel's voice. Calling to me, for all the world, like the sound of a flute. Only I heard it. At last!"

She threw back her head and sang once more. Brother Esau, behind her, his face away from the candle he held, joined in.

The door next to mine jerked open and Elijah stepped out, snapping suspenders over his nightshirt. Reaching for his candle with a trembling hand, he said, "A Midnight Cry! I must get Giles."

Even as he turned, he was singing, "The Lord of Hosts is going through the land." A good tenor, he gave the hymn a martial sound. The two deacons chorused out the words. Up and down the hall, doors were flying open and other voices rose.

Then one soared purely over them. I'd never heard anything like its beauty. "Search ye your Camps, yea read and understand; The Lord of Hosts holds the Lamps in his hand." Still singing, Giles stepped into the hall, barefoot, wearing his long white nightshirt, his dark hair shining in the candle held by Elijah behind him. He was holding Giles's boots.

Esau and Thankful turned and the two young men fell in behind him. Elijah plucked at my sleeve and I followed him. Seth, the swollen joints of his fingers waving to the music, stepped beside me. His reedy voice could hardly be heard over the lusty baritone of Amos, his sleeves rolled up over the thick muscles of his forearms. Down the winding staircase we went, everyone in white, holding candles against the darkness. Their zeal lifted their hearts. And mine. One could almost believe the Lord of Hosts was leading the way.

Aware now what Esther must have been doing—getting the word of the Midnight Cry to all the houses—I sang, too. She must have been one of the first notified. In the absence of the elders, all upper members of the hierarchy would surely be called.

Esau threw open the outer doors and there, like sentinels, stood two young men with flaming pitch-pine torches. Everyone was quiet, gathering themselves into a column of twos. Esther came running, as if blown by a wind, long hair brushed back. Concern on her face, she tugged on Thankful's sleeve, asking something. I couldn't hear the deaconess's response, only the high intoxicated sound of her words. She reached out an arm and pulled Esther next to her. Giles was now in front with Esau, followed by the two women. Behind them came four women and two men, all wearing a wide strip of scarlet cloth on their wrists. Pointing to those who had them on, Elijah stepped in beside me, whispering excitedly, "Those are the mediums. For the coming of the spirits! We're going to Mount Sinai. To the Sacred Square in the Holy Hills of Zion."

The torchbearers led the way and we marched past the darkened Girls' House and Boys' House silently. Once out of the village and some distance from them, Giles began a rousing hymn unfamiliar to me, with the rest taking up a refrain calling for "Al va lan's Trumpet" to sound. Over and over, they pleaded for his call. The strength of their faith poured from more than a hundred throats. It was impossible not to be stirred.

As we wound past the cemetery, a filmy river mist covered the ground. The unassuming tombstones, rising above it row by row, seemed mere earthly markers of the names of those who were elsewhere. Death had no dominion here. We marched upward, ever upward. The scent of pine, as heavy as incense, lay on the still air. The smoke from the tapers and torches lingered above us in white wreaths.

Entering the clearing at the top, those carrying the torches stuck them into the ground, one on either side of a low-walled square. The center contained a fountain stone, but there was no sign of water. Slowly the white-gowned community formed themselves into a circle around the area. Esau stood between Thankful and Esther in the middle of the torches; Giles and Elijah were on either side of the flaming lights; those with red cloths on the wrists were in the inner circle as well. The rest were in rows behind them. Because of my height, I could see the fountain stone and the engraved words which seemed to move in the uneven light: "War hath been declared by the God of heaven against all sin, and with the help of the Saints on earth, it shall be slain."

In a bell-like chant, Giles sang out: "Who shall ascend into the hill of the Lord? Who shall stand in his holy place?" That psalm came back to me. I was again in our Boston church, standing beside my father, one of my small hands in his coat pocket for warmth, the other in my mother's fur muff. I could feel the itch of my wool suit on my skin, my cold nose and toes. They'd swayed a little as they sang. So had I.

On this summer night, the air as soft as moonlight on my skin, surrounded by strangers, it was not the same. And yet it was. I was comforted, as I'd been then, by a sense of being in a world that made sense. Faith and hope are fragile strands but, for the Believers on that mountaintop, they were twisted into vines, binding them one to another. A resolve clenched me. I would do what I could to hold that world together for them. They were trying to be saints on earth. The odds against it were inhuman, but they *were* trying. All but one. I would find that one.

The community chanted the answer to Giles's question: "He that hath clean hands, a pure heart." At this phrase, the mediums blew out their candles and, each clutching the wrist with the red cloth, stepped over the low stone wall and walked, as if wading in a pool, to the dry fountain stone. Gravely, they began washing themselves in the invisible water. They made cups of their hands and motioned as if pouring it over one another's head.

One of them, a slender youth with an ascetic face, stepped back a little uncertainly from the others. He staggered, then went rigid. His arms dropped to his side. He seemed to have stopped breathing. With his muscles locked, he fell as stiffly backward as would a downed tree. He lay there motionless. None of the others near him took notice, but a sigh came from the group, as if they'd been holding their breath in hope and could now let go.

Abruptly, one of the women gave a wild, piercing Indian war cry. She was answered by another. The two began speaking in some unknown tongue, listening to each other, responding intensely. The other three started to whirl around and around and around, their arms thrown wide, their feet a blur beneath the white gowns. Their movements were dizzying to watch. Staring at them, I thought the earth was tilting on its axis.

A light, melodious voice, that of a young woman, rose above all in another tongue. I spun toward the torches in amazement to see who was singing. Her words were French, the accent perfect, the hymn one that must have echoed throughout the medieval cathedral in Chartres. The thickest of stone walls could not have prevented that heart's cry from reaching heaven, nor muffled the assurance that it would be heard there. I looked and looked again. To make sure, I glanced away and then back again to make sure. There was no mistaking. That joyful woman's voice came from the throat of Giles Grant.

Someone in the back began to hum quietly, then another, and soon the clearing was filled with that sound, like a rising wind. Almost all at once, the candles were extinguished by those who held them. Only the torches flared, their flames spurting and dancing as if they felt that wind. The darkness caught the eyes by surprise. The only one I could make out with certainty was Esau because of his position. He was unmoving, but the flicker of the pitch pine gave him one expression after another. Perhaps none were his.

The moon's light, as if held back by that of the candles, now came pouring down. Its brightness intensified the shadows of the encircling trees. It obscured every face. I could not see Esther, although I strained to look. She had been by Thankful, but I could no longer detect the deaconess's telltale purple shawl.

The last lovely note of the French hymn died, but the humming, an echo of an invisible world, swelled louder. It seemed to thrum upward from the ground itself, enveloping us, then spiraling to the stars, pulling them down to us. All those there swung their bodies in unison with it. The mediums whirled to it. I again had the sensation of standing on unstable ground, for the humming erased all boundaries. I was no longer an "I" but one with the others, the earth, the sky.

Then, as suddenly as lightning across a dark sky, there was the clarion call of a trumpet. The high, sweet notes reverberated across the hills, mounted to the heavens. There was no way to tell from where they came. Everyone fell immediately silent, stopped in mid-motion. Only the mediums still kept their noiseless spinning. That silvery unearthly song stopped the heart, the breath, the mind. I was part of it. While it lasted, it was all that was real.

I was not sure when it did end. I was mesmerized, the hair prickling on my arms. I not only heard the music, it tingled down my veins. A woman called out, "It is Al va lan!" Others took up her cry. "Al va lan. The angel. He has come with his trumpet." At first it was said in hushed tones, but the Believers' voices became a sea surge. "Al va lan. Al va lan. Al va lan."

All signs of order disappeared. With ecstatic cries, some began whirling alone, some together. Others embraced, weeping with joy. A few rushed to the fountain, washing themselves as the mediums had done. There was rapturous singing, clapping, dancing. Amid the tumult, Esau still knelt, eyes closed, between the torches.

I worked my way to the edges. I leaned against a tree, not sure whether that sturdy trunk was shaking or whether I was. I had been much moved, caught up in a sympathy I did not know I could feel. I closed my eyes against the moonlight, the delirium that surrounded me, trying for coherence. That yearning voice, that haunting trumpet still sounded in my ears.

After a moment, I began to return to myself. However much I might welcome such ideas, I was not ready to accept the visits of angels or the descent of spirits. It occurred to me that Giles Grant might know French, and I'd already seen he could make startling sounds. Admittedly, I was having trouble imagining that anyone, even with intense practice, could change voices. Then, the trumpet. I considered that. As a group, the Shakers didn't believe in playing musical instruments, but before joining, one might have learned to play a horn, and play it well. Yet that training couldn't have been widespread knowledge, or they wouldn't have been so overcome by the clarion call. And where did the trumpet itself come from? It certainly hadn't been brought with us.

The hard hand on my shoulder caused me to jerk upright, like cold water dashed in my face. A voice behind me said in my ear, "Do not turn." I didn't need to. I knew that voice.

It was Trapper. "Two men left New Lebanon, at two separate times. They were dressed in Shaker clothing. One was on a fast horse and would have arrived first. They both must now be in Hancock Village. I do not know their names, but they belong to this village."

It was hard to even take in his words, let alone understand them. Then the "fast horse" registered. Yes, I thought, that might be Samuel Grant on his. And then maybe Brother Jacob, or the other elder. Seeing lights, worrying about fire. That was likely.

"Only those two," he went on. "Since nightfall. The roads are watched."

"Have you been here long? Did you see anyone outside this clearing?" I asked. "In among the trees? Wandering around?"

"No."

I waited for more of a reply. At last I glanced over my shoulder. He was gone.

When I turned back, Esther was standing before me. Her loose hair was fine strands of gold, backlit by the torches. Her body was outlined beneath the thin linen nightdress. She was breathing hard, high breasts rising and falling. Her eyes were darkened with emotion, but as she lifted them to mine, I couldn't decipher what it was. She put a trembling hand on my arm.

"Brother Michael," she began, "you must—" She stopped to swallow. "You have to go with me. I need— Please."

At first I could only look at her. I couldn't get my tongue around the heart in my mouth to answer. What had to be done—what I would do—was simply clasp her in my arms, hurry her away into the deepness of the forest before she changed her mind. To kiss that mouth, to press my body into hers and never let go was just what I wanted, all I wanted. But as my lips formed the words "Yes, oh, yes," what I found myself saying was "Esther, are you *sure* that—"

She tugged on my sleeve to move me forward. "I am. I can't find her. I've searched."

I stared at her stupidly. "Who?"

"Hepzibah. For some reason I woke up tonight, and she wasn't in the room. The outer door was open. But she does

that. No matter when she wakes, she thinks it's time for services, even if it's the middle of the night. She sets off for the
Meetinghouse. But she wasn't there. No one was. The elders
were all at New Lebanon. Then I saw the lights in the Living Quarters. Sister Thankful said, or I thought she said, that
Hepzibah was with them."

"You think that she's gotten dazed in the excitement, gone
off in the woods—"

"No. I kept my eye out for her, at least when we first
came. I never saw her. More likely she's in the village. She
may have gone back to our room, but she could be confused,
walking around. She'll be so frightened. We have to go
back. You're the only one who isn't—"

She looked around without finishing the sentence and
then grasped my hand, pulling me with her.

We ran down the path, shadowed by trees, and then back
into the moonlight, exhilaration in our running. I'd never
felt more sure of my footing, despite the uneven lighting of
the path. My feet only grazed the ground. Her hand was soft,
but her grip was tight. She seemed to be going as fast as I
was. I couldn't hear her breathing or my own.

We'd just reached the cemetery when we saw them, flying toward us, small figures in white, one well ahead of the
other. For a moment, I couldn't see what I was seeing. Then,
in an open patch, I saw the face of the first. It was Mercy.
Her mouth was open, her face contorted.

She threw herself at Esther, heedless of her clumsy splint,
sobbing in her arms, trying to gasp out words. "Oh, here you
are. You're here. It was turrible. We snuck out. Cris threw a
pebble at my window. That was bad. But it's awful fer a dog.
Alone, in a strange place. We jest wanted to go tell 'im not
to worry. See if he was all right. But, oh Esther, he wurn't."
Her last words were a wail.

Crispin was still some yards away, limping crazedly, desperately toward us. I hurried forward, leaned down, and
picked him up. At first, he held himself stiffly away from my
body, looking into my face, his eyes enormous, his cheeks
tear-streaked. Moving his lips soundlessly, he clutched a
handful of my shirt, his fingers digging into my shoulder. He

threw his head from side to side, as if to shake words loose from his tongue. Not knowing what else to do, I patted his back awkwardly, saying the sort of things my father must have said to me. I don't remember my words, only that he was not to worry, it would be all right, I would see to things. His eyes on mine, his mouth almost managed to breathe an *m.* Then he relaxed a little and suddenly collapsed on my shoulder, his wet cheek against my neck.

I carried him back to where Esther was standing. She was stroking Mercy's hair, saying, "Tell me what happened. What is so terrible?"

Mercy gulped. "Hallelujah. He was just a-lyin' there. Real still. His heart beat, though. Real fast. We got him up. He threw up. He had the blind staggers, but maybe he's— Sister Ruth thinks maybe— We got her from the Nurse House. But that's when we saw— She was under the sorting bench. We only had a little candle. We didn't see before."

At this thought, her young voice began to break apart.

Esther tried to keep the alarm out of her own as she grasped the girl's arm. "Mercy, what? Who?"

Trying to swallow tears and talk at once, she brought out, "Blood. All over the back of her head. Really bad. Sister Hepzibah. She didn't move at all. An awful lot of blood, Esther. I never seen so much."

Chapter Ten

Leaving the children in Esther's care, I raced to the Seed-house. It was completely dark. There was not a sound to be heard, except for the chatter of crickets. I opened the mud room door and fumbled for the kerosene lamp I'd noticed on a hook just inside. Turning up the lamp and holding it high, I glanced quickly around. I couldn't believe it.

There was no blood on the floor. No sign there'd been any there. I knelt down. The floorboards by the workbench were damp and there was a smell of the carbolic oil used as a cleaner. That was it. There was no sign of Hallelujah, or any indication he'd been there. The room looked just as it had when I inspected it that afternoon, baskets neatly hanging on pegs, herbs on drying hooks from the ceiling, the two side workbenches uncluttered. In the flickering light, the logs beneath looked as neatly stacked as before.

Straightening up, I opened the inner door and walked through the entire Seedhouse, swinging the lamp into corners. Everything was in place. Tools were precisely set on the tables. The rose petals simmered on the iron stove, which held banked coals. Nothing had been disturbed.

I went back to the mud room, turned off the lamp, replaced it on the hook, shut the outer door, and stood there, cursing the Shakers for their tidiness. Then I saw a small light on the lower floor of the Meetinghouse.

Just as I reached it, out of breath, the doorway was filled by a tall, heavyset man, holding a candle.

"Who are you?" I asked abruptly.

"Elder Jacob," he replied, seeming as much surprised by the question as by my presence.

"I was sent by Quincey. My name is Michael." I left it at that.

He said, "All praise to Mother Ann. Philemon told earlier this evening you'd come. I knew Jasper wouldn't fail us, of course. Come inside."

He led the way to one of the small offices, set down the taper, and gestured toward the side chair. He seated himself behind the narrow desk. Since they were twins, I'd expected another Esau, all dry, skinny rectitude. The brothers were quite different. The deacon still had some thin white hair, but Jacob had grown smoothly bald. Oddly, that made him look younger, more fresh-faced. He was taller, much fleshier, what was termed a "fine figure of a man." He seemed, even now, in this dark time, to have more vitality than his brother, as if he'd gotten more of the essential energy they were forced to share in the womb.

"You've heard what happened tonight?" he asked, fatigue in his voice.

All I did was nod, waiting to hear what he'd say.

"I've just come from the Nurse House," he said, rubbing his eyes with the heels of his hands. "The two nursing sisters have cleaned and dressed Hepzibah's wound. She's still unconscious. They've done what they could for the dog. They *think* it's just sleeping. I— I can't take this in yet. Our meeting at New Lebanon had run late and I was about to go to bed when I saw some light on the horizon above Hancock. I came as fast as I could."

"You came alone?" Trapper had said there were two men, but not together.

"Yes. I saw no need to rouse anyone there. There are enough of us here and we've had some practice of late in fire-dousing." His tone held sad irony. "My horse pulled up lame outside of Hancock, but by then I could see the faint lights on the mountain and knew what it was. I hadn't thought of a Midnight Cry because we elders now discourage that practice and I still don't know why—" He didn't finish that sentence.

Leaning back wearily against the ladderback of his chair, he went on. "I took my horse to the stable. It was limping

badly then. Brother Samuel's horse was already there. He's
one of our trustees and had been with me at the meeting. I
assumed he'd seen the lights, and hurried here, and then
come to the same conclusion I had about the lights being on
the mountain not in the village. He—"

I interrupted, "Why wouldn't he arouse you before leaving?"

A crease appeared at the side of his mouth, which might
have been a wrinkle of irritation or the beginning of a wry
smile. "Samuel, because of his background, is used to being
in charge. Possibly it didn't occur to him. In any case, he evidently went immediately to his quarters above the Office by
the back way and saw nothing."

"And you saw—?"

"Sister Ruth racing to the Seedhouse with Mercy." Jacob
paused. "I pray my eyes don't meet with such a sight again
as was in the mud room when I got there. Poor Hepzibah's
head—the back of it—was crushed." The hand he brushed
over the top of his gleaming bald head trembled.

"Did you see a weapon of any kind?"

He nodded slowly. "When I knelt down beside her, I saw
a board with dark blotches on top of the wood pile beneath
the bench."

I opened my mouth to say I hadn't noticed it and I'd
looked, running the lamp along the logs. I decided to wait.

He was saying, "But then all we thought of was Hepzibah. Ruth said we had to get her to the Nurse House right
away. And Grant came running up, having by then seen our
light in the Seedhouse. The two of us carried her as gently as
we could. The children were very upset so Ruth told them
she'd take the dog and see what could be done until Seth had
a chance to look at it. I sent them back to their houses. Luckily, Sister Agatha was sleeping in the Nurse House as we
have an old brother who could slip away at any time. So she
was there to help. And Grant stayed on so he could move her
to a clean bed when they'd finished. There was a great deal
of blood, you know. A great deal."

Clearing his throat, he continued. "I went straight back to
the Seedhouse and looked to see if anything was out of

place. Nothing was. Then I put the board in the stove. And I waited to see that it was completely burned."

I jerked upright. "Why?"

He laced his fingers together on top of the desk, lifted his heavy chin. "I've decided that we'll tell the community that Sister Hepzibah, confused, had gone to the Seedhouse. Kneeling down to look at the dog, she might have raised up too quickly and hit her head on the edge of the sorting bench." He didn't meet my eyes. "Of course, that bench is smooth, well sanded. Sisters Ruth and Agatha are too good at nursing to believe that an injury with splinters in it was sustained by its edge, but they are women who can keep counsel and will do so since I asked them. Ruth was coming in to clean the Seedhouse as I left so there's no trace. Samuel had no chance to inspect the wound. Therefore, at the moment only the four of us—besides that tormented sinner who struck her—know. I'll inform Philemon."

I stared at him. Keeping my voice as calm as I could, I said, "Jasper Quincey arranged to have the roads watched by Trapper. He may have enlisted some Iroquois, as well. No matter. If Trapper says the roads were watched, they were. According to him, two men came in. You and Samuel Grant. No one left. That means there's a murderer among us. This person is very dangerous, Elder Jacob. The village should be warned of—"

He broke in. "There's no point in alarming the community at present by telling them. Hysteria might result. No, it *surely* would. You must believe me. We have to know more before such an announcement. Besides, it'd hamper your investigation. People will answer your questions more freely if they don't suspect why you're asking."

I persisted hotly. "They should at least be told that arson is the cause of the fires, so they will be alert to any suspicious sights. And they would be put on guard that way."

"I have no evidence that it is arson," Jacob replied, raising his chin even higher. "None. After the first fire—at New Lebanon—I didn't even think of it. But since then we've had six—admittedly two of them were small ones—but still *six* of them. I couldn't swallow such coincidence. We're already taking every precaution against accidental fires. And getting the dog was a very good idea on your part. We do need one."

"It's not enough," I said flatly. "Think of what happened to Hepzibah. What about having the brothers patrol the village at night?"

He shook his head decisively. "They'd have to be spread out very thin. Pairs would be impossible with our numbers. And if it's one of them, and he's determined to continue, he could then more easily set it, even pretend to have discovered it, a little too late. It'd be safest if they all kept to their rooms. Especially given what happened to Hepzibah."

Jamming my back against the chair, I tried to swallow my anger and think. Was he trying to protect someone? "You *must* tell me of any suspicion of any particular person that you have."

His face was grim. "It would be my responsibility to do so. There can be no violence in the City of Peace."

I kept my eyes on him. He didn't say he *would* tell me, only that he should. He might, but if he caught an odd expression, a stray glance, he wouldn't mention that, I was sure. I wondered why Freegift said he was worried about Elder Jacob and why he wouldn't explain that remark.

But speculation wouldn't help. Neither would any further argument. He struck me as one of those men—usually good-natured sorts—who ruled by presence and persuasion. He was not used to real disagreement. And some of his points made sense.

As if aware of my decision, he said, in an effort to soothe, "I've a great deal of faith in you, Michael. Jasper saw fit to send you. And he will be sending his advice when you tell him of the tragedy of this night. I'll tell Philemon your letter must go off immediately in the morning."

I stayed up most of the night, adding pages and pages to my previous account of the day. Before breakfast, I stopped at the Office. Philemon, who'd returned immediately from New Lebanon on hearing of Hepzibah's injury, was the only one there. He said that after the meal Jacob would tell the others that she'd had an accident and was in the Nurse

House. Seeing his pain, I had to admit that I was glad the rest of the Believers didn't yet know any version of what happened to her, let alone the truth.

Listening to their conversations on the way to the dining room, I could see how intense was the joy in the community over the events of the Midnight Cry. All seemed sure that their struggle to create heaven on earth was recognized by the citizens of heaven, who'd come to visit. They greeted each other with fervor, then launched into an account of where they'd stood when they heard the young French girl's spirit sing, what they'd felt when Al va lan's trumpet rang out. One brother named Issachar claimed he'd been cured at that instant of acute pain in his stomach. A few insisted they'd seen the angel himself floating above them in his garments of gold, playing the golden horn.

Since I certainly couldn't share their ecstatic certainty, nor rationally explain what happened, I simply nodded at whatever was said to me. All I could think of was that it would be two days before I could get any reply from Quincey. No doubt my letter was put on the train that meandered across the state, picking up people and parcels. His answer would be returned the same way.

I stood in the morning sunlight outside the Living Quarters, worried that if I took no action someone else might be hurt, and unable to see what action to take.

Chapter Eleven

I started walking. One thing I could do—that not even Jasper Quincey could, were he here—was get answers from people. My presence at the Midnight Cry had instantly made me an accepted part of the community, and since everyone in Hancock wanted to talk about last night, I'd be told everything. At great length. Of course, the hard part would be getting people to separate what they actually saw and did from what they thought they saw and did. Could they even account for their own movements, let alone those of others? Perhaps I should just let them talk.

In my letter to Quincey, I told him I was beginning with the premise that whoever struck so defenseless a woman as Hepzibah did so in a blind panic because she happened to stray into the Seedhouse. That person had gone there purposely to poison the dog and had been seen by her. My employer might shred my reasoning. But I intended to proceed. Eight people knew about Hallelujah, not counting Esther, Mercy, and Crispin. It was the movements of those eight I was most interested in.

First, I wanted to see Hepzibah. In the announcement of her injury, Esau said she was still unconscious. But on my way there, I told myself she might be awake now.

Going in to the Nurse House, I stopped short. I took in the long room. Esther was beside a bed, her back to me, pouring water from an ewer into a basin. My heart forgot to beat when I saw her. On several counts I was going to have to prepare myself before entering.

After taking two deep breaths, I marched in, murmured "More love, sister" to Esther and looked down at the bed.

Hepzibah was lying in one of the adult-sized cradles the Shakers designed for the old, her head wreathed in loose bandages. Her round unlined cheeks still had a faint pinkish tinge. Outside of an occasional flutter of the eyelashes, her face was composed, as soft as in sleep. But she was deeply unconscious.

I'd read an account by a man who'd awakened from a coma. He wrote that, deep inside, he was conscious. At the very first, finding that he couldn't control his unresponsive body, he'd felt real panic. He could hear distantly, smell faintly, feel others' touch, but he couldn't move his hand to return the touch or get the eyes to open to see. Soon that fear faded, and he felt a tree growing between his toes. He watched it leaf out with his inner eye, content to lie in its shade and dream.

I desperately hoped that was true of Hepzibah. It was hard for me to look at her. I was overcome with guilt. I should have stayed and guarded the village. Maybe I couldn't have prevented what happened, but I might have. I should have been there.

Esther sat down on the other side of the bed and we faced each other on those upright Shaker chairs. Her prim cap was again framing her face, her body enveloped in the full folds of a sober blue Shaker neckerchief and long dress. Her manner was nunlike, too, her eyes on the mending in her lap.

The room was fragrant with the mint used for disinfectant, and the thick walls of the building kept out the day's heat. Sheer linen curtains had been hung to dim the August light. Even the quiet bustle of the village was muted here. Sister Agatha moved about the room as if her feet were slippered in goosedown.

She wasn't near us but at the end of the aisle lined by beds. By her the entire wall was taken up by a built-in cabinet with forty-eight drawers, which graduated in height from top to bottom, with the larger drawers near the floor. Each was neatly labeled. She was mixing a potion on a sturdy table next to the cabinets, occasionally glancing at the elderly man in the bed to her left. When he made some dis-

turbed mewings, she slipped around the table and rocked his
bed until his small cries quieted.

My senses faithfully took in all of this but I wasn't there.
I was on that mountain road dark with moonlight, the air
thick with the earth scent of the soft moss that pushed up
under the pines. Esther was with me. She was dressed in thin
white linen, her hair loose, her body undisguised. Her hand
was tightly in mine, her eyes on mine, appealing. There was
no quiet in our running.

The coolness in the room didn't affect the fever that
heated the inside of my skin. The peacefulness of my surroundings gave me none.

I wanted Esther to speak, to say anything at all. She had a
lovely voice, clear, definite, only a trace of Boston in her
vowels. Her speech showed that she was unlikely to have
been raised on that farm she'd referred to. At last, I made a
comment on the weather, which continued fine. Nodding,
she said that it was good for the harvest and that there was a
first crop of snap beans ready for picking.

There didn't seem to be any way to get from that response
to the questions I had for her on the events of last night. I
was curious. Very curious. How had that glorious clarion
call affected her? Unlike any of the others at the Midnight
Cry, barely an hour after hearing it, she was at least collected
enough to look for Hepzibah. I blurted out, "What did you
think when you heard the trumpet?"

Her gray eyes were luminous, bright as dawn, as she
looked up. "Oh, at first—" she began eagerly. She paused,
searching for words. Then the light faded and her face
closed. She picked up her mending and took a mechanical
stitch in a torn seam. "I didn't *think*. I only felt."

Suddenly, she jabbed her needle into the shirt and burst
out, "That was the trouble. I wasn't thinking about Hepzibah. When I asked Thankful if she were with them, she
told me that they were all there, marching together to the
Holy Hills of Zion. Of course, that wasn't Thankful's
fault—she was overexcited. But I was sure that Hepzibah
must have seen the lights and joined the Cry. She never went

anywhere but to the Meetinghouse when she set off at night and I'd already looked there." Guilt edged her voice.

Dipping a cloth into rosewater, she gently dabbed it on the old woman's forehead. "The time of her awakening was odd. Usually it's well after midnight. Maybe some noise disturbed her. Since every day is Sunday to her, she's sure that when she wakes up, she should leave for services. Not that she ever dresses, but she's careful to put on her bonnet and shawl. Either I hear her looking for them or the closing of the outer door. Except once before, now that I think of it. That time, Mother Alma found her sound asleep on a spectators' bench. Last night I didn't hear her, either."

She squeezed water from the cloth and leaned back in surprise. "She *didn't* put on her outer things. Not even her cap." She finished bleakly, "They're still hanging on the hooks in our room."

"What woke you?"

Folding the cloth, she considered. "A noise. Familiar . . . but not. I thought when I heard it that it was . . . the wrong place to hear it." She shook her head. "I can't explain that."

She stroked Hepzibah's hand, her voice unsteady. "She was so kind to me when I came. Then I . . . was black inside . . . dead . . . and I wanted to stay that way." She looked at me urgently. "Do you know— Have you ever had—"

"Yes. Yes." I wanted so much to tell her that I knew, knew exactly what she meant, but all I could do was keep my eyes on hers and repeat the word.

Then, oddly, a half smile touched her mouth. "One day I woke up and I was looking forward to eating a slice of apple pie. We often have it for breakfast. Sister Bertha sweetens ours with maple syrup. It's very good. That sounds silly but I was so surprised that . . . that there was something I wanted to do." She squeezed Hepzibah's hand. "It was due to her. She was a true sister. And then so patient teaching me all that I needed to learn about the Office. If only I'd been more watchful—"

A scrabbling noise in a closet behind me stopped her and made me turn quickly. Slowly the door opened and Hallelujah's nose appeared. He gave a glad little woof and staggered toward me. There seemed nothing wrong with any individual leg but none of them worked together. He collapsed by my feet, his one upright ear still upright, and thumped his bushy yellow tail on the floor as he nuzzled my leg. Scratching his ears, I told him I was happy to see him, too. Very happy.

When I looked up, Agatha was standing beside me. She straightened her neckerchief and eyed Hallelujah with a trace of satisfaction on her thin lips. "He slept well and drank some water this morning. Praise to Mother Ann, he has no fleas. But Brother Seth needs to look at him." She transferred her glance to me, adding, "Now."

I got right up and Hallelujah tried to. He couldn't manage it. Finally, I scooped him up, murmured farewells, took one last look at Esther and then at Hepzibah, and went out.

As I neared the horse barn, Hallelujah let out several small barks and struggled in my arms. Before I could set him down, Mercy cannoned out the open door, yelping herself. The joyous reunion of girl and dog took some time but it was a pleasure to watch. While Hallelujah licked her face, she said, beaming up at me, "Brother Seth says we did right—me and Cris—gettin' him up on his legs so he could get rid of what he et."

Stooping down, since it was clear that Mercy wasn't going to stand up until she'd thoroughly petted Hallelujah, I asked, "Was it the lights from the Living Quarters that woke you and Cris?"

She shook her head. "Most times nothin'll wake *me*. But I was havin' this dream that it was hailin' and after a bit I roused enough to git up to close the window. There was Cris a-throwin' little pebbles at the glass. I went down ever so quiet and he signed to me that he thought Hallelujah must be scared and lonely. And he would be, everything smellin' so strange and not like home."

"No one saw you going to the Seedhouse? And you didn't see anybody?"

"We crept in the shadows just like playin' Injuns. Nobody coulda seen us. We're good at it. But nobody was around, not even goin' to the privy."

I stood up, smiling at her. "Were you scolded for sneaking out?"

Reluctantly, she got to her feet and considered that. "Well, I *think* so. Cris and me had to go to talk to Mother Alma this morning. On the way there, we thought mebbe we wouldn't get to work no more with Brother Seth. See, we get to do this specially. In the back of my heart, I knew that might be fair. We din't do right. But it woulda been just hard. Cris wasn't cryin' but he was wipin' his nose a lot."

Her sunbonnet thrown back on its strings, her fine hair coming untucked from under her starched cap, she glanced up at me. Shakers of all ages dressed the same and that gave the children an adult look. Not Mercy. Her face was still rounded with baby fat. Along with her fair hair and milky skin, she had eyes so light you could see through them. "We had to see Mother Alma one at a time. When you're with her, I don't know how it is, but you end up scoldin' yourself. I can't remember what she said 'zackly, except that good had come out of bad since we found Sister Hepzibah so she could get better."

Nodding with satisfaction at the thought, she glanced down at her arm, now unsplinted but still covered with a heavy cast. Her eyes widened, and she began hastily scrubbing at the stains on the plaster with her fingers. "This very morning, Sister Agatha wrapped it all up clean. I don't know how I do it. Dirt jes' jumps on me. I kin *imagine* what she'll say. Mebbe she won't see it, though."

"How did you break your arm?"

"Fell outta a tree pickin' apples. Shouldn't been doin' it. Girls ain't supposed to climb 'cuz of the skirts and all. But I did. It didn't heal right so they had to break it again. I was brave then."

"I'm sure you were."

"Well, some tears squeezed out. I couldn't help it. It hurt real bad. I didn't yowl, though, and I drank all my willow tea. Tastes ugly, but it makes you feel better. I'm gonna tell Maw when she comes to git me about how to make it in case she gets sick agin."

As I was leaving the barn, Crispin saw me and hurried

over to walk alongside. I think my height reassured him, as if being so much taller, I could see farther. He tried to match his stride to mine and I to his. I was struck by how fast he had to hobble, because of his bad leg, to keep up with my slowest stroll. I shortened my steps further. I said little; he said nothing. Our silence was companionable. After a moment, without looking at me, he reached up and took my hand.

Seth came toward us leading a horse almost Clydesdale size. Alongside him, Amos was arguing. They were too intent to greet us.

Waving a thick hand, Amos insisted. "Couldn'ta been the shoe, Ah'm tellin' you. Took it off, it wus just fine. Ah put 'em on myself not a month ago. Ah do good shoein'."

Tightening his Yankee chin, Seth retorted, "Had to be the shoe. Couldn'ta been the leg." He addressed Crispin, "Now, boy, didn't you ride this very horse out of the village and all round this mornin' to see how it went?"

Crispin nodded vigorously, his wide-brimmed hat dipping in agreement.

"Naught wrong with that left hind leg, was there?"

Crispin shook his head, equally positive.

"So I'm tellin' you, Amos," Seth said, "that not even that Brother Charles in *Kain tuck* that you're allus tellin' me about, that can pract'cally cure an animal by jes' lookin' at it, coulda made a lame horse better'n in a few hours. If Elder Jacob said it pulled up lame, then it was the shoe 'cuz it warn't the leg!"

Amos's face, red from the forge, grew redder still. The universal goodwill of the community couldn't entirely erase all disagreements.

Seth went on, running his crooked fingers gently over the animal's back. "This horse is all-round healthy. Even his droppin's are sweet. 'Course, that's 'cuz *he's* got good sense—eats only the fruits of the earth. It's the eatin' of meat that'll sicken you. Clogs the bowels. Thickens the blood. Best think on that. Why you'd make a graveyard of your stomach is more'n I kin fathom. The good Lord never intended it. And if you'd jes' recall how much better you was durin' all those years when the Central Ministry forbid the meat, you'd—"

"Better!" Amos burst out. "Ah et so many eggs Ah was afeard to open mah mouth 'cuz Ah was sure a cackle come out. And still didn't have that right filled-up feelin'. You're the one should be watchin' out. Next thing, you'll be takin' the bad spells like Brother Izzy, a-lyin on your bed moanin' half the night. What you need do is be beefin' up your bones so's—"

He stopped, as a thought occurred to him. Slowly and slyly, he brought out, "Now, Brother Seth, as Ah recollec' it's been some over a year since the Sisters started givin' us the meat again."

Seth was running his hand down the horse's foreleg and he didn't glance up as he answered, "'Bout that. For those who're fool enough to partake of it. Jes 'cuz somethin's offered don't mean you gotta eat it."

With a crafty look, Amos went on. "Now, Ah was standin' by you up there on the mountain the whole of the time and Ah catched you when we heerd the angel and you fainted."

"Didn't *faint*! Went into a trance." Seth straightened up indignantly.

"You was so wobbly-legged Ah 'bout carried you back down. Ah'm jes sayin' you heerd Al va lan."

"Nary a doubt. What in tarnation you meanin'?"

Amos took enormous pleasure in his reasoning. "If'n you sayin' that the good Lord and Mother Ann don't hold with us eatin' the meat, how come the angel comes to bless us? Which he surely did."

Openmouthed, Seth stared at Amos's triumphant expression. He drew himself up as high as his bent back allowed. "See here, Amos, you—"

His voice died away as he saw the other's expression change to one of alarm. Following Amos's eyes, he caught sight of the two women approaching us, each carrying a large basket of eggs. So did I.

The bonneted figure wearing a mulberry-tinted shawl was talking volubly to her companion. Amos muttered under his breath to me, "She'll be fussin'." He turned and strode back toward the smithy.

Seth tightened his grip on the horses' reins and said to Crispin, "Better we'd be gettin' him right smart to the barn." He muttered a farewell, Crispin brushed his hand near his heart, and they were gone.

I waited for the women. Sister Thankful hadn't appeared at breakfast, apparently an unheard of event in the community, since several had commented on it. As the two approached me, she lowered her eyes, seeming to consider that appropriate for one favored by heaven to announce the Midnight Cry. It made her look flirtatious. Even the large, sunshading Shaker bonnet couldn't contain Thankful's cheeks and chins, which jiggled over the ribbon tie. But her features were calm.

Her companion was Sister Bertha, the overseer of the kitchen, whose glazed look made it obvious that the deaconess was more than making up for her earlier quiet spell in her room. Bertha was tall and square, a block of a woman who could not only roast a cow, but looked as if she could lift it. After the meals I'd eaten, I prayed for her continued good health.

Introducing myself, I told her that. There might have been a spark of pleasure in her eyes at the compliment, but she made a slight gesture indicating that she was only doing her duty. Perhaps she thought that in praying for her I was only doing mine.

"Sister Thankful," I said, "I should like a full account of your call by the angel. I'm sure it would be inspiring to hear."

A rapt look came over her face. "I should have known early in the evening of his coming. Collecting the candles, I felt consumed by fever." She glanced sideways at Bertha, emphasizing, "*Very* different from my usual hot spells." She took a deep breath. "I must have felt Al va lan near because I cannot well recall the time before midnight. I did leave a new candle with Brother Issachar, who was poorly again. And I told Izzy—" She corrected herself quickly. "Brother Issachar, that I would mention his condition to Brother Esau.

Which I did. I remember that he hadn't yet retired and so went immediately to Issachar's room to pray with him."

She turned to Bertha, saying, "And I didn't tell you this, but it is a sign of how we have all changed since my visitation from above. The deacon told me this morning that he believed he'd been too hard on Brother Issachar in the past, lecturing him for being 'hypo,' because that night sitting there the entire time by his bedside—until I found him and told him of the angel's message—he could see the poor man truly suffered."

Shifting her filled basket from one hand to the other, Bertha remarked, "Can't recall that he was at all poorly marching up to the mountain. I was right behind him."

Without answering, Thankful turned her attention back to me, adjusting her features again to reflect the gravity of her experience. "I can remember being completely unable to sleep. I got back up and went to the kitchen for the chamomile tea—"

Bertha interrupted. "And was there not a full jar of it? The deacon said to me he could find none for Issachar last night."

"I had but the one cup!" Thankful answered indignantly. "The jug was three-quarters full. In the pantry where it always is."

With a patient nod, Bertha said, "Brothers come into the kitchen wanting something. They open the drawers and shut the eyes. You have to reach over and hand it to 'em."

Thankful resumed her faraway look. "After drinking the tea, I lay there in my room. Absolutely still. Then, at first, a long way off, but nearer and nearer, I heard Al va lan's voice. Sweet as a flute."

"Did it sound like a flute?" I asked.

She considered and answered with a protracted sigh, "Yes. And no. I cannot describe it. But I knew what he was saying to me. That *I* must rise, *I* must call the others and take them to the Holy Hills of Zion. He was guiding me the whole way. When I couldn't find Brother Esau in his room, it was the angel who nudged my memory, reminding me about Issachar. I could hear the deacon reading to him, as I lifted my hand to knock."

Thankful's remembrances of the early part of the evening may have been vague, but her recollections of all she experienced on the Holy Hill were precise. She described every tremor of emotion as she marched, knelt, sang. Every one. She almost managed to forget her self when speaking of the golden sound of the trumpet. Her self-absorption, her affectations, didn't lessen my impression of her fervor.

At last, Bertha nudged her meaningfully with her basket, saying, "The pudding for supper has to be made in time for it to set. People got to be fed, no matter what." And they went off to the kitchen.

I persisted in my interviews through the day, catching the brothers at their work as I could. Many of the older ones were in the village because their long stints in the fields in the past week had meant necessary chores had gone undone. Obviously, too, the elders felt that, after the previous night's excitement, the strict routine could be relaxed. I trudged back and forth to the Nurse House, but Hepzibah's condition was unchanged.

While I had no idea of what would interest Quincey, I heard two things that caught my attention. Whoever had been observing me from the Living Quarters had no reason to be there, and I was sure I'd seen the outline of someone by a high window when I was looking for signs of the fire at the Seedhouse. No one had complained of illness and gone to bed. Brother Issachar's "bad spell" had come on after the evening meal. Secondly, Brother Jed, who was in charge of the Boys' House, mentioned that Cris had nightmares— "sleeping-runnin' ones," he'd called them. When I asked if he'd ever left the house when that happened, he replied that he'd always heard the boy. But there was a wisp of doubt in his voice.

Writing it all up that night, I ran my fingers through my hair so often it was ink-stained black. I'd put in the smallest details. Was any of it helpful? Then, of those whose whereabouts I was most interested in, I hadn't caught all of them. Samuel Grant. Yes, I really wanted to talk to Grant, but he'd gone to New Lebanon. Elijah and Giles were in the fields. Hiking all the way there, standing there talking to them, would have looked odd indeed. And more words with Elder Jacob were needed. He was also in New Lebanon.

Pacing around the room, stopping every five minutes to look out the window, I tried to decide how soon I could get a response from Quincey about the attack on Hepzibah. Tomorrow—Saturday—was impossibly soon. On Sunday, the train didn't run. Still, I was determined to find a way tomorrow to get this report off.

In the meantime, I kept my window watch. My room overlooked the Seedhouse, and by the time the moon was high, I had a good view. A good view of nothing. No breeze even stirred the leaves of the bushes around it. But over the Berkshires there were flashes of heat lightning, like a reminder of how quickly a flame could burst out.

I tried reassuring myself. Hallelujah was in the mud room. He'd surely bark. Someone had seen me looking in those bilberry bushes by the Seedhouse. If that someone was the fire-setter, he wouldn't try tonight. No. I turned away from the window.

At last I put away my report, opening the built-in drawer where I kept my few pieces of clean linen. Seeing the envelope that still contained the money from Quincey, I wondered again why he'd given me any—let alone so much. I slipped the bulky pages in the envelope and piled my undergarments over it.

Putting away the papers didn't mean they were out of my thoughts. Restlessly, I turned on the narrow bed, sure that I'd missed something significant, something Quincey would need to know. I imagined every sort of evil that I might prevent if I only grasped the situation. I was still awake when the four o'clock rising bell clanged. At its ringing, I finally fell into a troubled sleep.

Chapter Twelve

In the morning, I felt more confidence in what I'd written. I just wanted to finish it. At the door to the Nurse House, Sister Agatha met me with troubled eyes. She said nothing, just shook her head slowly. I set out for the Meetinghouse.

The first door was open, but the room looked empty—a small shuttered space with the usual narrow writing table that served as a desk. Just as I was about to withdraw, a voice from a dark corner said, "You're very tall. You must be Brother Michael. I'm Mother Alma. I'm sorry that I haven't had an opportunity before to welcome you to the Family. Were you looking for one of the elders?"

As I entered, I could make out the seated figure of a wisp of a woman. I returned her greeting and replied that I hoped to find Elder Jacob. As my eyes adjusted to the dimness, I made out the wire-pronged wool carder in her lap and the quick movement of her fingers over it.

"He'll be here shortly. Both of the others are departing— Elder Titus for our Maine community to help there, Eldress Catherine because she must stay with her ailing parents. Jacob is just seeing them off. Would you like to wait?" She gestured to a chair on the wooden pegs near her.

As I took it down and seated myself, she said, "It must seem dark in here to you. I shield my fading eyes. I can only distinguish shapes." Most of the Shakers came from rural backgrounds and thus had little education, but this woman obviously had some.

A few rays of sunlight angled through the shafts. Sitting in front of her, I could make out her eyes, cloudy with cataracts, and her cheeks wrinkled in a series of ever-larger parentheses. Smaller ones bracketed her mouth and the longest came from the corners of her eyes. It was as if a widening smile were drawn on her face. The back of her hands were sprinkled with age spots, but her fingers were deft and delicate. She pulled the wool through the carder as gently as a mother combing a girl's hair.

Jacob had said he'd not told even the elders of the reason for my presence, so I had to avoid the direct questions I'd have liked to ask. After a moment of quiet, I remarked, "I was fortunate to have come when I did. The Midnight Cry was a moving experience."

She nodded slowly in answer. "So I heard. Those who speak of the trumpet's sweetness do so with tears in their voices."

My next words came out, unbidden. "They believe it was an angel playing it."

The eldress fixed her milky blue eyes on me, and her hands stopped their work. "But you yourself are not at all sure."

"I know of no other explanation. Does anyone here play that instrument well?"

"I'm not aware of anyone having that skill."

Leaning forward slightly, I said as much to myself as to her, "I'm not accustomed to the idea of angelic visits. In such cases, believing is seeing."

Mother Alma resumed her work. "You have to have room in the structure of your thinking for angels. As spirits, they don't take up any space." She smiled at her own fancy as she said that, and the smile filled the lines in her face exactly. "But, of course, even entertaining the idea might shake the foundation.

"Mind you, in my view, angels are not as common as butterflies, despite the many reports those in the village bring me. I've lived long and I've never seen one, even with my once reliable eyes. But when the invisible wind tosses my bonnet I do not say, 'There is no wind.'" Then she shook her head as if cross with herself. "That analogy with the wind is well worn, isn't it? With all the time I have for thinking, I should be able to come up with something fresher. But I've had no occasion to do so, never speaking with anyone who wondered if angels visited," she added, "let alone existed."

Alma raised her sightless eyes again. They saw right through me. She might as well have asked me aloud why *I* was here.

There was no lie she'd believe. I said nothing.

She ran the fine combed wool through her fingers. "But if you asked me if an angel *might* come, I'd say yes. Why would they come? Some could be messengers, as the Greek word for their name indicates." She gave a little shrug. "Others, well, perhaps angels, like butterflies, are attracted by fragrance. The scent of charity beguiles them."

All the parentheses of her face deepened. "No wonder their visits are rare."

I could say this truthfully. "At least the Believers *believe* in charity."

She was quiet for a moment and then returned to her starting point. "One must make sense of things somehow. It seems a requirement for humans. Most people just take the given explanations. But sometimes something happens, doesn't it? A tragedy. Then, for a given person, these explanations become nonsense. So the search begins."

She stopped then, but not as if waiting for an answer. Instead, she seemed to assume that, because of what had happened to me, I would agree. But she couldn't have known. I realized I wanted to tell her about the fire, my mother, my sister. I wanted to, despite the way I'd refused to think, let alone talk, about it. I was even willing to admit that I'd been unable to face it, had been too cowardly to do so, had instead escaped into opium.

As we sat there in the silence, I began to think that she did know, not the specifics, but that she understood, at least my bottled-up grief. Finally, she said slowly, "St. Paul says, 'Be ye transformed by the renewal of your mind.' That's good, but I myself would say that the renewal starts in the heart. After a tragedy, we protect ourselves from suffering, imagining we are being kind to ourselves. Instead, we become more fearful, more hardened, more separate. The protection becomes like armor, imprisoning us. We have to let the heart break. Then we can feel a true tenderness toward all. The mind opens, too."

The sound of the outer door shutting and the clump of boots in the hall saved me from an answer. Elder Jacob came in carrying a white crockery pitcher and cup. Setting them on the desk, he swept off his hat and patted his gleaming baldness with a folded handkerchief. His presence made the room seem very much smaller.

He greeted us both, adding to Alma, "The sisters were carrying jugs of switchel to the men in the fields and I told them you needed some as well. They said this pitcher had better be at least half-full by the time I reached your office with it." As he poured, the spicy-sweet smell of ginger and maple sugar filled the air. Carefully putting the cup on the desk, he took her hand and guided it there.

Thanking him, she said, "We always called this haying water, didn't we, Jacob? Working in the fields, the switchel tasted so cool on hot days."

He groaned, reaching for his hat. "Yes. And the sun is moving very slowly down the sky today. Come with me, Brother Michael, and think of some duty I must perform before going back to the harvesting."

Outside, I said, "Mother Alma has had a formidable amount of education."

"Yes, although not of the formal kind since she's a woman. Her father was a noted scholar who married when he was already up in years. Unfortunately, his wife died of childbed fever and he was left to raise Alma. He also developed cataracts in his sixties and so from the time she could barely lisp the words, Alma read the texts aloud to him. She was but in her teens when he died. Soon thereafter, she joined us, saying that she'd been taught to think and didn't know how to undo that. She understood, she told the elders, that she might be able to use that skill here."

We began walking down the path where the scarlet roses hid the fences. The new buds reached up, and the blossoming heads leaned down. Their rich color compelled the eye. The heavy August heat, like a flatiron, impressed their scent onto the air so that one breathed roses.

Jacob went on. "Esau and I were boys when she came. She was a few years older than we were. Whenever possible, we trailed about after her. Wouldn't give us a smile, though." He shook his head. "Her appearance of fragility was misleading. It still is."

His smile at his memory of the young Alma faded as he said, "You've had little enough time for thought, but has anything occurred to you regarding Hepzibah's . . . accident?"

My answer was a question. "Has anyone here shown any behavior that might lead you to think that he would react with violence?"

"One brother. But it was not at all like this." Jacob rubbed his firm-fleshed jaw. "I must tell you the circumstance so you will see that. Brother Amos came to us, something over a year ago, from our Kentucky community, where he'd been for years. It's a thriving settlement. The sisters raise silk-worms and the shawls they make from the thread sell well. They've tried to be good neighbors, but there's a serious division between them and the surrounding planters. We don't hold with slavery. It's wrong. We have Negro brothers and sisters in Pennsylvania, quite a large out family. They're strong Believers; we'd welcome them in our midst, should they decide to come. Unlike the Quakers, we've withdrawn from the World, that is to say, we don't actively help run-away slaves, but if one came to our village seeking help— well, our wagons go now and again to Pennsylvania, carrying our products, of course.

"The neighbors suspect that's what we do. Our Kentucky village is continually harassed by vandalism—barns burned, crops ruined. Stone walls have been built in an effort to stop it, but they are knocked down. One night, Brother Amos collared a local youth doing just that. As he said, he 'thumped him a good'un.'"

I raised my eyebrows. "Brother Amos is not young, but I certainly wouldn't want to be on the receiving end of one of his 'thumps.'"

"Nor I. Amos was quite repentant. He explained to the elders there that it was just that 'it were allus the *same* wall.'"

I imagined Amos's beefy face turning red under the Southern sun as, over and over again, he piled up those stones. He had all my sympathy.

Jacob continued. "The elders thought it best if he came here, out of that particular harm's way. While not a meek man, he's shown no further sign of an ungovernable temper. I can't imagine him being guilty of this kind of an act."

"It's quite different. And I believe that whoever struck Hepzibah might not be at all the sort who would normally strike out. That person had an unreasoning fear of discovery."

Jacob had the saddest smile. "You're right to choose the word 'unreasoning.' All members of our community know that even if their names were embroidered in red on their garments and they repeated it for Hepzibah as they showed her out of the Seedhouse, she'd be unlikely to remember who it was she saw there. Sister Esther is the only one she always recognizes."

I didn't reply to that. In fact, I changed the subject, remarking in a casual tone, "By the way, the horse you were riding last night is in fine fettle. I was talking to Brother Seth and Brother Amos. Neither of them can see why it should have pulled up lame."

That took all the breath out of Jacob. For a moment, his flesh seemed much less solid. He knew what I meant. If he was not delayed on the road, he himself was suspect. Then he raised a shoulder ruefully. "I can only say a rock must have lodged in the shoe for a time and later fell out."

The next hours were not useful, an overused word in Shaker conversation, but here it was true. I could find none of the people I needed to see. Even most of the kitchen sisters were gone, taking dinner to the men in the fields so they needn't stop the harvesting too long. Telling me that, Sister Bertha motioned me to a stool beneath a table filled with dozens of golden loaves of fresh-baked bread. "All you get is sandwiches. We've got the supper tonight to see to and all of tomorrow's food. No cooking on Sunday."

Using potholders, she thumped a loaf out of a pan, cut four thick slices, laid fat tomato sections on two of them,

piled on thin cucumber slices, then spread soft cheese sprinkled with herbs on the other two slices. Putting the plate in
front of me, she said, "Pie to follow. First batch of the strawberry rhubarbs are done." Then she went back to rolling out
what looked like an acre of pie dough. I ate, not caring about
the kitchen's steamy black-ovened heat.

Later in the afternoon, when I stopped by the Nurse
House, I went in quietly. I could see Esther sitting by the bed
next to the unconscious Hepzibah. She was holding her needle, but she was staring intently at the blank wall across
from her, with that exact expectant look she wore when I
imagined I saw her in my room, clutching the ribbons.
Whatever she was seeing was just what she longed for. Like
Hepzibah, only part of her was in the room. I didn't disturb
either of them.

Going back to the empty Living Quarters, I returned to
my room again to take out my pen and ink, to add Jacob's
words about Amos. I opened my drawer, thinking that I'd
finish my report tonight. Everyone, according to Jacob, including Samuel Grant, Elijah, and Giles, would be at the
evening services. Then tomorrow, Sunday or no Sunday, I'd
find a way to get it to Quincey.

As soon as I lifted the envelope from beneath my under-
clothes, I knew something was wrong. It was much too light.

It now held only the banknotes from Quincey. All my
pages were missing. I took everything from the drawer, desperately hoping the papers might have somehow slipped out.

They weren't there, nor was there any place in that uncluttered room that they might be. All my careful notes on
each person's movements at the Midnight Cry were gone.

Chapter Thirteen

Elijah's blond hair was sticking up like sprouts of straw as he watched me, intent on my movements. Taking on the role of instructor gave him an air of confidence. "Your glide is *very* good, Brother Michael. I can see you must have had lessons in the dance at some point. You do the right things with your feet, but your upper body is too stiff. Much too. You need to move generously. Think this way: you are *giving* your heart, with all your heart. And you are receiving love in return." His spread fingers again pushed up on the bowl-cut front of his hair. "Giles, hum the opening once more."

We were on the empty gleaming floor of the Meetinghouse, having hurried through Saturday supper so the two could show me some of the basic steps for the dancing service. Giles began to hum and Elijah demonstrated. His cupped hands were palms upward, just below the waist. "You see, I'm gathering gifts from the sisters in the line across from me, as we sing, ''Tis the gift to be simple.'" He raised his hands slowly until they were just below his chin. At the next line, "''Tis the gift to be free,'" he let his arms fall in graceful arcs backward as he bowed forward in thanks, his head dipping below his waist. His hair flopped down. He rose up, combing it with his fingers back into place, before resuming.

"Now I return blessings to them as we sing the third line: ''Tis the gift to come down where we ought to be.'" His praying hands were in front of his face, then he slowly lowered them palm downward until they were once again at his sides. "While we're doing the hands, we're also doing the back and forward steps. Like this." His thin body, losing all traces of gawkiness, moved to inner music. Elijah was capable of sudden transformations.

Taking out a clean handkerchief, he patted the perspiration from his face, being especially gentle around a new batch of erupting pimples on his cheek. "You'll pick it up quickly, I know. Having the dance formalized this way is much, much better. In the early days, I was told, the Believers simply leaped, whirled, and shook—each on his own. You can imagine how it *looked,* especially to World People. As if a choir were all singing different hymns! Then, too, it didn't show our union. Our togetherness. So Father Joseph Meacham devoted himself to coming up with some steps to be learned. He apparently had no experience in such things, but he wore the floorboards in his room smooth practicing. Believe me—and Giles will bear me out—there are quite a few brothers who ought to imitate Father Joseph. They *will* lift up their feet instead of gliding."

Giles was nowhere near enough to hear Elijah. He was circling down the floor by himself, in and out of the windows' perfect squares of evening sunlight. His sober coat was off, his cravat flying, his white linen sleeves billowing. He was singing the next part of the hymn, clearly and joyously, "And when we are in the place just right /We'll be in the valley of love and delight."

The Shakers said of their services that they were praying with the body. Watching Giles, I thought that was what he was doing. His soul seemed to ascend with those high-leaping steps. Yet, despite his rapt expression, the harmony of his singing, he looked to be in the wrong time, the wrong place. The surroundings were too austere for that whirling; the stiff collar and heavy boots too confining. His beauty—those dark riotous curls, those flawless features—belonged to an ancient green world. The melody itself recalled shepherds' pipes.

His eyes also on the dancer, Elijah sighed. For a naked moment, his expression was easy to read. He wore the look of aching love. Then, hastily covering up, he said, "Really, I don't know *where* he gets the energy after a long day." He continued with his air of objectivity, "And you'd think that all those twitches and pattings would wear him out. Do you know he doesn't do that when he's absorbed? Not one tic during an entire dance service. Or even when he's in the carpentry shop, turning chair legs."

I was busy adjusting my cravat. "He has true musical talent. Does he play an instrument as well?"

Elijah replied offhandedly, "He's never mentioned it. He's never even had any real voice training as far as I know."

Giles came bounding back, not the least out of breath. "I hope I didn't confuse you, Brother Michael," he said. "We do the turns sedately in place in front of the sisters. Then we repeat the first movements on the next lines." He sang in a low voice, "'When true simplicity is gained, To bow and to bend, we shan't be ashamed.' Then we circle at the end: 'To turn, to turn, 'twill be our delight /Till by turning, turning we come round right.' Like this." He ended in a slow circle. He grinned. "*Not* the way I was doing it."

"Good to hear." I grinned back. It was hard not to smile at Giles. His surface shone. I wondered about the dark interior. Did demons lurk? "You leap like an antelope, whereas I dance like a bear."

"Not at all. And with a teacher like Brother Elijah," he replied, "you'll do very well." The smile he bestowed on his friend held nothing but friendship. Deep perhaps, loving certainly, but friendship only.

It was clear that Elijah knew it. He spun on his heel. "I need to rest a bit before the others come. I find these services so intense."

Giles wandered back onto the floor, doing the steps over and over exactly, humming sweetly.

I looked at the entrance to see if anyone else had yet come. Only at mealtimes had I been able to catch the quickest glimpses of Esther. The door was open and empty so I followed Elijah to the spectators' pewlike benches. As we sat down, he said, "If the elders would only see their way clear to allow the use of just a simple instrument like the recorder, it would be so helpful for the brothers and sisters who are left-footed. I could at least tootle on it to keep them in step."

"You can play it?"

He waved a dismissive hand. "Basic notes. At the Academy we were given some elementary background in music, although my real training was, of course, in art. It was a whole new world to me. I *bloomed* there." His pale eyes, invisibly lashed, were bright with his enthusiasm.

I wondered how much musical instruction. "Which school?"

"The Boston Academy of Fine Arts. Surely you're familiar with it. It has a *fine* reputation. Normally, they take only upper level students and I was, of course, very young. But an exception was made as an experiment of sorts—to see how children develop in art. Then, too, my aunt was a patron. My teachers thought I showed real promise."

"You were raised in Boston?"

"Part of the time. When I was small we moved a great deal. My father had his . . . troubles. But my Aunt Estelle— my mother's sister—was a widow. Well-to-do. She always made a fuss over me. I *was* a pretty child." He said that defensively, as if I'd find it impossible to believe. "Eventually, she took me in and I lived with her until I was fourteen, attending the Academy. But my parents had become devout Millerites and naturally they took me away with them in 1843."

"Millerites?"

Elijah stared at me in open astonishment. "Yes. Followers of William Miller, the Adventist."

"I'm sorry. I'm not familiar with his ideas."

"You must've been in another *country* altogether!"

I thought about that and nodded. Opium transported one.

Still looking surprised, Elijah explained, "Preacher Miller was sure that Christ's Second Coming would take place in '43. So the whole group sold their possessions and gathered together to pray during the last days. In fact, all we *did* was pray. Over and over again, the Book of Revelation was read aloud. We were all sure that *we* were among those one hundred and forty-four thousand who were sealed so that we would not have to undergo the horrors of the coming Apocalpyse. The bloody hail, the burning sea, the shaking earth."

He shivered, recalling it, a child's remembered terror in his eyes. "I *did* believe we were safe, but still I could see those horse-sized locusts with their crowns of gold and lions' teeth. St. John the Divine says if they sting you with their scorpion tails you live five months in torment, gnawing your tongue off in pain. What bothered me, you see, was that even if I was safe, I was going to have to *watch*. None of us slept. In the morning we gathered on hillsides. We waited there until the darkest midnight. *Nothing* happened."

"What was the next day like?"

"People were numb. We went back inside. Everyone sat and stared at the floor. But then the error in calculation was discovered. It was October of 1844 that Christ would appear. It was a very long year. Knowing the end was coming, no one was much interested in the things of this world. Truly they didn't care whether they burnt the porridge or not. We ate it. And since they were so soon to be given robes of white, nobody washed the clothes. We talked constantly about heaven. The gates of whole pearls, the streets of transparent gold, the foundations of sapphire and topaz and emerald and amethyst. But do you know, I found that thinking about heaven was hard to do for hours at a time without one's attention straying somewhat. Which made me frantic because that might mean *I* wasn't one of the hundred and forty-four thousand."

I tried to imagine that year. Elijah looked down. I looked away, not knowing how to answer.

He sighed. "The Millerites called October of 1844 the Great Disappointment. My father wandered off. Perhaps he went out west. But my mother, along with a great many of the Millerites, joined the Shakers. It was a relief. They welcomed us and were very kind. Their Elders explained that the Second Coming of Christ had already happened. He'd come in the person of Mother Ann Lee in 1770. And," he added, "the food was so good and everything was so clean. But my mother never got over her disappointment, really, and she died of a fever."

"Did you ever think of going back to your aunt, continuing your study of art?"

"Oh, yes. But she'd remarried. By then, I had *this* face. Who'd want to look at it at breakfast?" He managed to convey both agony and petulance as he gestured toward his cheeks.

"And I could see that the Shakers might be right. They could be the ones sealed. Not that they said so." He stopped to think, his somber mood lightening. "It doesn't seem to me that they're at all sure that the Apocalypse will happen, or that there is even an eternal hell. Most of the ones I talk to hold that sinners get to come back for a second chance and we Believers return as their teachers."

I could see Elijah's problem. The Millerites' strict beliefs were spelled out, based on a literal interpretation of the Bible. The Old Testament God thundered in their ears. Now Elijah was confronted with the gentle Shakers who had only a framework. Outside of that, each Believer decided on the truth by consulting his or her inner truth. Since most of them couldn't bring themselves to rain down fire and brimstone on their fellow men, it followed that their Creator wouldn't do so either.

Elijah shook his head. "But I could see those locusts pretty clearly. So I stayed. During Mother's Work, I was so sure that we Believers were right. But when it ended, the doubts came back. I *couldn't* sleep. You can imagine, Brother Michael, how I felt when I heard the trumpet. A certain sign. We *all* heard it." Elijah was transfigured at the thought, his moods shifting once again. "My fears are gone."

He got up, straightening his back as if to demonstrate that a burden had been lifted. "Now then, I'll stand across from Giles and you can see how the sisters and brothers facing each other mirror one another's actions."

As he stepped into place on the floor, I again checked the door. No Esther. I tried to ignore my intense anticipation, pushed away impatience. I told myself that I would be satisfied with just being able to look at her now and again during the service.

Alone, Philemon came in and hurried up to me. "Brother Michael, I've thought over what you said in our talk just before supper." I'd spoken to him about the missing notes for my second report to Quincey, but we'd had only a few moments before others joined us. At my words, he'd pursed his thin lips, tightened his thin face, but now he had a curious air of relief. "Someone must have taken the pages, thinking it was your spiritual autobiography."

"You mean those writings are *not* considered private?"

"Oh, yes, of course they are," he hastened to answer. "It'd be quite wrong for anyone to look at someone else's journal, let alone remove it. But I'm sorry to say that we've had that problem before, especially during the years of Mother's Work when everyone was writing feverishly of their visions. At last several people confessed to the elders that they'd been guilty of 'peeping' at others' journals. Mother Alma said that it was an understandable sin in that they were not prompted by idle curiosity. They considered that if their brothers and sisters were being blessed by the sight of angels and heavenly streets and *they* weren't, then they were not devout enough. And they did want to know if others also wrestled with sin, as they did. As she put it, they wanted reassurance. So you see, some misguided soul probably scooped up your writings—not having a chance to really look at them on the spot—for that reason."

"Perhaps so," I answered with much doubt in my voice, "but whoever took the papers knew they belonged to me, a newcomer, and could hardly expect to find any enlightenment—or comparison—in my struggles toward grace. If anything, I would be recording my past sins."

"That could be it exactly, you see." Philemon nodded without looking at me.

"You're saying they would be reassured if I'd been extra-ordinarily . . . wicked."

Again he nodded, his eyes now on the rafters above. "This poor sinner might have hoped you'd even go into some detail on those sins. You are a very good-looking man, Brother Michael, and the person might have considered that your opportunities for certain misdeeds—" His voice trailed off. "I do believe that was the reason for the theft. You needn't be concerned that anyone took them because he or she suspected you are investigating. Do you think that, having read your notes, this person would infer that?"

"I've gone over the question in my mind, and I don't think so. I tried to be as objective as possible, wanting Quincey to draw his own conclusions. I jotted down descriptions of the events and conversations that I had with various people. An innocent person might assume that this was my everyday diary. However, if it was the guilty person who read them, my emphasis on whereabouts might seem threatening. I suppose there's no way to tell who it might have been."

"No. Sister Abigail across the hall is the one assigned to sweep and straighten your room. But anyone could have gone in and out quickly. There's not really any place of concealment in our rooms. A quick glance through drawers would take but a moment. Still, the papers may be returned, once they've been perused. We must hope so since it'll surely be difficult for you to recall all that you wish to tell Jasper." Philemon's expression was full of worry and sympathy.

"My report was detailed, but I have a good visual memory. Whatever I've seen on a page returns to me readily enough. I'll talk Sister Thankful out of a candle tonight and I'll bring the copy to you in the morning." I tried not to let my own concerns show as I added, "At least Mr. Quincey will have my first account by today. How did you send it?"

"Trapper, in his customary quiet way, was waiting for me at the Office door, asking for it. At that time, he inquired about Sister Hepzibah. I've no idea how he learned of her . . . accident. I don't know how he conveyed the letter to Boston either. He didn't take it himself since he's since then asked me again about our poor sister. He just . . . appears."

Trapper, I reasoned, would find the fastest way, but it was discouraging to think that Quincey didn't yet know the serious turn of events. And his reply, if he answered immediately, would surely take an additional couple of days to reach me. There was no point in alarming Philemon by telling him how much that worried me.

"I need to see"—as he spoke Philemon rose—"if Mother Alma would like my help coming in to the services. She enjoys the singing. Elder Jacob watches from above. Because of that vantage point, he is able to come up with some excellent suggestions on improvement." He gestured toward a small panel that I hadn't noticed built into the wall high above the floor.

I watched Philemon go, but I sat quite still, praying that Quincey was at least half as insightful as he himself thought he was.

Chapter Fourteen

As he went out, I kept my eyes on the door as if I could will Esther to appear. It took me a moment to notice that Samuel Grant was standing just inside, watching Giles and Elijah practice. He could have been glowering, but his habitual look was not one of approval.

His flinty glance then lingered on me and he ran one hand slowly down a pockmarked cheek. He came over and, without greeting, asked abruptly, "What did you say your surname was?"

"Profitt," I replied, equally shortly. "Two *t*'s." That was what I'd *said*. I don't particularly resemble my father, or so I've been told. He was not especially tall. My mother said my height came from her side of the family, but she'd often say fondly that my thick brown hair and hazel eyes were like my father's. I only remembered him as gray-haired—he was some years older than my mother—and portly. In my eyes, he was all that was substantial. In the evenings, my sister and I would sit one on each side of him on a plump couch as my mother read aloud. As the hour grew late, our heads would droop down onto his shoulders. Occasionally, he'd nudge us, saying, "Listen now, here comes a good part." No matter what else I've forgotten, the scene in Shakespeare's *Macbeth* comes vividly to mind in which the ghost of Banquo sits down at the feast and shakes his bloodied head at the friend who betrayed him. I must have been awakened to hear it many times. Betrayal by friends was uppermost in my mind when I looked at Samuel Grant.

"Large family by that name in New England," he brought out slowly. "Vermont, I think."

I shook my head. "All the Profitts I knew were in Boston. But none are left."

Grant kept looking at me moodily, his dark brows forming one line, and said, "For a moment, you reminded me a great deal of . . . someone I knew."

I kept my eyes on Giles and commented, "Your son must have been well schooled in music."

"No, he had no formal training at all. His . . . condition showed itself when he was seven. Several doctors thought it might have been a result of a brain fever. From birth on, he'd been sickly, requiring a nurse's care much of the time. They recommended that all forms of mental stimulation be avoided, so I saw to it that he spent most of the day lying quietly in a darkened room." No expression flickered over his granite face as he recounted this. "His mother was permitted to play the harpsichord softly during set times. Her youngest brother, who often visited and who played several instruments, did so as well. She had a fine voice and sang to Giles. But his learning to produce music was forbidden because the effort involved might have overexcited him."

"Was your wife French?" I asked.

He knew why I inquired since he must have been told many times about Giles's singing in that language at the Midnight Cry. But he didn't raise the point, answering, "No. She was of English descent and was born in Boston. As the boys grew older, she and they spent most of their time at our country place, although I was kept in the city by press of business."

His dark brows pulled together as if that brought up another issue—one that seemed to rankle—and he turned slightly toward me. "One must be single-minded to succeed in business. One must focus on profit. It has always amazed me the number of people who cannot grasp that. There needs to be a real change in the Shaker way of thinking. The right leader, a forward-mover, is required. Now with Elder Frederick in New Lebanon so ill, that should be uppermost in the minds of the others. Here we could do much better in seeds and herbs if that were seen as the goal and certain efficiencies put into practice. We need to specialize! Since a new seedhouse has been built at New Lebanon, a mere three miles away, we should process ours there. And at present we have sixty-nine varieties of vegetable seeds. We should instead concentrate on the best-selling ones. Then, too, if more time were spent on packaging seeds instead of, for example, tanning hides, we'd have greater profits. I'd think that leather can be bought at a reasonable price. The herb market is expanding at a great rate. Every medical school orders our herbal potions and ointments and every doctor they train prescribes them. We need to take advantage of that."

My eyes stayed resolutely on that polished floor as he spoke, and I said nothing. I was afraid he could feel my hostility radiating out from me. Even if I hadn't had strong suspicions about Grant's honesty in regard to my father's estate, and what happened to us because of the loss, I couldn't have borne his company. He carried Jasper Quincey's assumption of superiority an unpleasant step further. Quincey was impatient with what he saw as a lack of good sense in his fellows, but Grant condemned them for any failing, chief among these a failure to agree with him. But I had to keep him talking. I needed answers.

If money was the motive for the fires, then Samuel Grant had to be the one starting them. With the Shakers stumbling to produce, even for a short time, that huge seed and herb market was wide open. He knew how they made their products and who they sold them to. In terms of their business, everywhere you looked, there was Samuel Grant. He was a trustee, able to control their properties. Now he was trying to "solve" their problems in Maine, talking to the Boston bankers to extend those loans. He had everything to gain. He and his son Jared. If he wasn't here to profit personally, what *was* he doing here?

I wanted Samuel Grant to be the guilty one. Yet I could see that I wanted it too much. To truly protect these people, I had to keep an open mind. And there was something about these fires, especially those beginning small ones, that made me uneasy. It was as if I could feel an emotion surrounding the setting of them. An emotion that was building, that stayed in the air. It wasn't the coolness of greed. To explain

that to Quincey was impossible. He'd put it squarely down
to my "overheated" imagination. The only thing to do was
control my emotions.

I resumed my questions. "You didn't travel abroad?"

"We had little opportunity to do so, nor did my wife want
to. I don't think my son ever heard French spoken."

Just the way his gaze rested on his son made me sure that
the young man was a real disappointment to him. Yet if the
'condition' was a physical one, which his words indicated,
how could Giles be blamed?

As if he felt the stony weight of his father's stare at his
back, Giles's shoulders hunched, his arms upraised, shot to
the side, and his two open palms knifed the air. A litany of
sounds came from his lips but he spoke too rapidly for me to
grasp them. He yanked his body to the other side, repeating
his movements precisely. I heard then, "Gabriel, Raphael,
Israfil, Azrael." It was the names of angels, and he repeated
them in rhyming sequence, his head nodding to the verbal
music. "Uriel, Zadkiel, Michael, Gabriel, Raphael, Azrael,
Israfil." Over and over.

It was with an effort that I looked away. He seemed oblivious to watchers but it seemed rude to gawk at him. I'd find
it intolerable to be always looked at, even if approval came
with it. That wouldn't be what was directed at Giles. His behavior would be regarded by most as a deliberate—and will-
ful—violation of custom and decorum. No doubt that was
why his mother had kept him as far from any society as possible. When his symptoms first started, his parents might
have believed that he was *trying* to draw attention. Recalling
Samuel Grant's gruff treatment of me as a boy, I wondered
if punishment, perhaps severe, had been tried. Did his
mother beg and plead with him to stop his twitchings? Then
Philemon had recounted what the clergy's view of such actions were. Giles would have been subjected to harsh ha-
rangues by ministers on his failings, then terrorized by the
bell, book, and candle of the priests seeking to throw out the
devil inside him.

Did he find living in the City of Peace the "place just
right" for him? He was shielded here, and accepted, but was

this where he wanted to be? My sympathy for Giles caused my intense dislike of his father to flare again. I wanted to confront him, to tell him what a miserable excuse for a human being he was. I dug my fingernails into my palms. But he might be an arsonist—and a murderer—as well. If Grant knew who I was, my investigation was over.

Behind us I heard a prolonged inhalation of air. It had to be the deacon. Only Esau could turn breathing into a reproof to others. Without turning, Grant stood up immediately and moved off. As Esau came to stand next to the spectators' benches, he said nothing. I wondered if he were trying to decide which rule we were breaking. His white hair lay obediently in the standard haircut. His back was as upright as his stiff collar. His hands were clasped across his chest as if that were their duty and they knew it.

Then I realized the reason for his silence. He was chewing conscientiously on the mint leaves, used as breath sweeteners, that the sisters laid out by the dining room door. Swallowing, he said, "I worry, Brother Michael, that your short stay with us has given you a false impression of how we spend our days. Our usual order isn't being followed." He looked down at me. "Your hair has not yet been trimmed. And your boots, although acceptable enough until a better pair can be made, need oiling. Work some suet into the leather to keep it from cracking further. I will see that you are given some. This cannot go on. Our work schedules have not been adhered to. People are spending a great deal of time in unnecessary talk. This is due, of course, to the visitations at the Midnight Cry and the subsequent excitement."

"I find that understandable," I answered dryly.

"Ye-es." He drew out the word as if unsure. He considered and then nodded. "It was extraordinary that the angel made his presence known. He was blessing our efforts. His coming when the elders were away—and I as deacon taking their place—has not gone without notice in the community." The same satisfied smile I'd seen on Thankful's lips touched Esau's.

He went on, "It is good that you were here when this occurred. So many young men live deliciously, as the Bible says, giving no real thought to the hereafter. Perhaps you did as well."

The pause that followed these words made his statement a question. Esau was waiting for, if not a confession, at least an admission that I had sinned grievously in my former life. When I didn't respond, there was disappointment in his voice, but he tried to be encouraging. "I could see that when you asked for paper on your arrival that you intended to begin your new life properly. I've held you up to the others as an example of a brother charting the right course from the start. Many here neglect the writing down of their struggles. Thus, when a temptation arises, they forget how they avoided it in the past. They go forward and backward, without progress. Of course, you could always seek guidance from an older member of the community. Confessions should only be made to an elder, but there are others who would be happy to give counsel in the constant struggle against the flesh."

I nodded as if in thanks, since there could be no doubt that it was he I was expected to turn to. The deacon added, "On this point, since you are very new, there are some rules that you are not aware of. We do not visit in each other's rooms, except in case of illness. As I was on the staircase, I saw Brother Elijah slip into yours. No doubt he just wanted to exchange a few quiet words with you. I did not speak to him about this, considering it might be more meaningful if it came from you should he again seek you out."

Whatever Elijah had been seeking in my room, it wasn't me. He hadn't come when I was there. But I didn't offer that information.

He looked at the doorway in impatience. "Al va lan cannot have meant us to become lax because of his visit. Now our dancing service is not to start on time. The sisters are late. Although tomorrow is Sunday and they must prepare the kitchen for a day without cooking, proper planning would have ensured that all was in readiness. They cannot draw out the time with chat. I will have to speak to Elder Jacob about announcing tomorrow that we must return to order."

Esau turned on his heel, saying, "There is no help for it. It's necessary to ring the bell again to summon them." I hastily agreed with him.

Most of the brothers were now assembled and Elijah began placing them for the first hymn which called for a small circle of men, a slightly larger circle of women surrounding them, then the alternation of sexes in ever larger rings. Bustling about, he told us that he'd discussed with Elder Jacob, who would be observing from above, the effect of doing this by height so that the tallest would be in the outside round. I was directed there, glad of the arrangement, since Esther, who was above average height, surely would be in the ring just ahead of me.

As the men linked arms to practice the sideways step, Giles said, looking at his feet, "Both Elijah and I are glad you have come, Brother Michael. He even wrote a little note, beautifully illustrated, to welcome you and took it to your room. But once there, he was overcome by shyness and brought it back." Then he started his melodious hum.

The sisters hurried in, just as the bell stopped pealing. Despite the uniform dresses and the identical caps, I picked Esther out immediately. I had practice doing that, since at every meal and gathering I eyed each identical, starched Shaker cap until I picked out hers. Whenever I saw her, she was the center of my field of vision and everything else was blurred on the sides. It almost persuaded me that there was something wrong with my sight. Perhaps it was caused by the irregular hammer of my heart. It certainly brought an end to rational thinking.

We swung immediately into the quick pace of the first laboring song. While the brothers slid in one direction and the sisters in the other, we circled and sang: "By freedom invited, and music delighted, I'll skip through the room like a lamb on the green." Around and around we whirled euphorically, faster and faster. For that moment, I forgot everything but the dance. "I'll go with the music and play on the tune." The room seemed to spin instead of us. The sunlight dazzled on the gleaming floor and the glossy blue of the walls and ceiling. There was no way to go slower, but no one wanted to. Our linked arms pulled us, held us. I could see Esther as she swung past me. By now I'd picked up the refrain and I sang with my heart. "I should not have guessed it that I'd be so blessed—"

Before we could even catch our breath, Esau called out, "Next, 'Soldiers of Christ'! Form columns."

Guided by Giles, I stepped into place in a row of four brothers. The others lined up exactly behind us. The sisters matched our military rows. Esau barked, "Start on the *right* foot. Stamp out sin."

With parade ground exactness, each sang out, "The King of Kings and Lord of Hosts has blown His trumpet in our coasts/And round His standard now appears/A valiant band of volunteers." Our feet came down smartly and we wheeled and went back up the floor. "Now every soul that would do right/Is welcome to enlist and fight." On the word "right," the sound of boots stamping reverberated through the room.

Then, without a word, back into circles we went. I noted that Esther was directly ahead of me. I'd never heard the hymn that was started. The Shaker melodies were original, not influenced by those of the outside world, since they'd been isolated for more than fifty years. This one had the sway of the first song and the sharp beat of the march. "Come life, Shaker life/Come life eternal." Their rigorous practice made their voices ascend in perfect unison and their bodies move as one. I was distracted and not keeping my eye on my tutor, Giles. The brothers turned for the next line, shaking their arms, and the sisters did as well. But I was a moment too late and was facing Esther. Although her cheeks were pink from the quick steps, I was persuaded that at the sight of me, her color was higher. She looked over my head as I belatedly spun on my heel. "Shake, shake out of me, all that is carnal."

When that ended, Thankful was directly across from me and Esther, gazing neither to the left nor the right, opposite Giles. I bent down quickly, as if my bootlace needed retying. Then I straightened and slipped in on the other side of him. At the start of the hymn "'Tis the Gift to Be Simple," Esther held out her cupped fingers, offering love, and looked up.

My long arms, mirroring her action, almost touched her hands. Seeing me, her fingers trembled as she raised them. The next line was "'Tis the gift to be free," but I know she didn't sing it.

When she came up from the bow, her face was bright rose. We turned round on the next line and were again facing as the congregation sang softly: "We'll be in the valley of love and delight." My gaze could not have been more direct. Her eyes slid to the door. That she could not summon up a chilled aloof expression sent a surge of joy through me. My feet, as light as my heart, were left to their own guidance.

Just as that ended, Philemon appeared in the door. He hadn't come back from his visit upstairs and now he beckoned to Esau. After a few words together, the deacon announced that there would only be a short service tomorrow, closed to outsiders, since Elder Jacob would speak. Esther hurried to the door and went out with Philemon. The rest, slowly lining up two by two, followed. There was no sign of her when I came out. I looked in all directions, but I don't know what I would have said to her, if I could have spoken at all.

The evening air was mild, and the scents of lavender and lemon thyme from the herb garden competed with the roses. Since it was Saturday and the line before the men's bathhouse was already long, I slipped away toward the garden, grateful for a quiet moment. The dusk made everything indistinct except the high borders of shining poppies. Their satiny red petals held the sunset in yellow-centered cups. They were cultivated for their seeds, which flavored cakes and rolls, as well as providing a rich oil. The Shakers used and sold great quantities, and there were masses of the flowers. I wondered if anyone could really concentrate on their utility and not glory in that distracting beauty.

Then, in the fading light, I could see a solitary figure at the end of the plot and I almost set off in another direction. I was in no mood to talk. But I noticed it was an Indian, wearing only a headband and loincloth. The braves, as Philemon had said, slipped in and out of the village frequently, sometimes bearing items for barter. This morning I'd noticed two of them carrying a freshly killed deer tied to a pole, making their way to the kitchen. Later, they went back into the forest laden with bundles. Apparently the system worked for both sides. The Indians brought what they had, and the Shakers gave them what they needed. The braves were not given to conversation so I returned my gaze to the poppies.

When I finally looked up, he was standing silently before me. It was Trapper.

He never bothered with greetings. Holding out an envelope, he said, "From Mr. Quincey."

I took it, almost stammering. "But he could have only just got my letter to him."

His answer was brief. "I am Pequot, but I know some of the Iroquois. They have not forgotten how to ride a horse." He seemed to admit that only grudgingly. "Faster than Iron Horse that stops and starts at every crossroad." He turned. In a second, he would have been gone.

"Wait. Tomorrow I'll have another to be sent to him. Where shall we meet?"

He shook his head slightly and vanished.

If I hadn't been so eager to see Quincey's message, I'd have tried to catch him. But I hurried to the Living Quarters, lighted my candle from one in the hall, and firmly shut the door to my room. By then I was concerned. I'd expected several pages from him at least, and the envelope was very thin. I almost tore it in my haste to open it.

There was only one page. On it, there were only a few words in the same copperplate script as the initial instructions from him. The first lines read: "Continue *exactly,* but do not send letters to me. Keep notes on your person."

I shut my eyes, opened them, and read it again. It still made no sense.

Neither did the only other sentence. "If blackberries are served again, do not eat them."

Chapter Fifteen

It happened in the night. I didn't hear about it until morning, not that the darkness I rose in showed any hint of morning. Still, since it was the Sabbath, the bell rang a half hour later than during the week. It was a day to refresh the spirits, a day of rest. Only "needful work" had to be done. Until arriving here, I'd had no idea of how much of that there was on a farm. All the fowl, as well as pigs, cows, and horses, had to be fed and watered. Plus one dog. So we brothers put our work clothes on and marched to the barn, planning to change into our Sunday attire later. I hadn't any of the striped trousers that were regulation wear for the day—my legs were much too long for any they had—but I had the white shirt and a blue vest that almost fit. Before going to bed, I dutifully rubbed into my boots the greasy suet that Esau had left on my candlestand.

Sitting on the milking stool with my forehead pressed against the cow's warm flank, I was overcome by drowsiness. Most of the night, I'd lain in bed, too tired to be awake, yet too awake to sleep. There was no descent into dark oblivion—it was a "white night." My soul dwelt in dreams of Esther; my mind picked apart Quincey's terse message.

His few words stretched so many ways. He'd stressed that I was to continue *exactly,* which I took to mean that my detailed report was helpful. But if I were not to send it to *him,* then I could only assume that I was to deliver it to someone else. The implication was that Quincey was alarmed by the attack on Hepzibah and he was sending help.

I should have welcomed it since I couldn't protect all the innocent here, and I was making no headway finding the guilty one. Yet it was one thing for me to have a lack of confidence in myself; it was quite another to have my employer share it. That he had reason to, knowing my background, made it more galling. Even more unreasonably on my part, while I had to fix suspicious eyes on the Family, I did not want a stranger to do that.

When my man Friday (or was I his?) arrived, would he be bringing a written account of Quincey's ideas? I could only hope so. To merely hear them, distilled through another's memory, would be really unsatisfactory.

As for keeping the notes on my person, of course I should have done that. I could have shoved scraps of paper in my pocket until the full account could be written out. Quincey saw the danger of theft in an instant, while I had quickly become as trusting as any Shaker.

What on earth could be wrong with blackberries?

Distracted, I pulled too hard on a teat. The cow complained loudly. Crispin peered around the edge of his stall at me and I raised my head, barely managing a smile. Yesterday he'd showed me how to milk, curving his small hand in mine, letting me feel the proper squeeze on the udder. He was clearly watching me for a few minutes before beginning himself. He'd been proud of my progress and I was sorry to let him down. Now in the dim light of the kerosene lamp between our stalls, he tried to put some reassurance in his worried nod, his lips once again forming an 'm' without a sound. Hallelujah, one ear raised alertly, trotted briskly around the circle of stalls, reminding us the cows needed to be out in the pasture. He stopped and nudged me, perhaps only wanting a head scratch, but it seemed a reproach.

I'd just picked up the full bucket when Philemon arrived. He was always the first to the barn, but not this Sunday. I should have guessed the news by the slump of his shoulders. He beckoned me out to the brightening air. It had that slight crisp edge of autumn but, as well, there was a reassuring summer softness. The high clouds were already rosy. The sweet heavy smell of apples made me hungry.

Philemon's abrupt words took away the morning's glory. "Hepzibah died last night."

My shoulders sagged, too. "I'm deeply sorry. I know you mourn her."

He'd tried to shave but missed a patch on his left cheek. His eyes were red-rimmed and he fixed them on the cloudy Berkshires. "Sister Esther and I kept watch over her during the last hours. Without any liquids or nourishment, she couldn't . . . stay with us much longer, you know. As I sat there, I recalled what she'd said to me a few weeks ago. It was odd, and it touched my heart. Many years ago, when I was just out of boyhood and Hepzibah not much more than twenty, all of us were working to save the tomato crop. The field was infested with fat green worms. Hepzibah put the worms into a bucket beside her, unable to bring herself to squash them. One of the brothers, in a exasperated tone, asked, 'And what *are* you going to do with them, Sister?' She looked in her bucket, and then at him, and said, 'I'll scold them to death.' She went on with her work, but I noticed she kept eyeing the worms in some distress. When we were almost finished, I picked up her bucket and carried it off. At the time she said nothing at all, nor did she ever refer to the episode. But last month I was coming up the stairs at the Office and she was about to go into her room. Earlier she hadn't recognized me, but she stopped with her hand on the door, turned, and said, 'Thank you for taking away the tomato worms, Brother Philemon. It was very kind of you.' "

He blinked rapidly. "Do you know when she opened her eyes and looked fixedly at me last night, I thought she was going to bring that up again. She had the same intent look on her face as if there were something that had to be said before . . . we parted." He stopped and swallowed.

"What did she say?"

He fumbled in his pocket, pulling out a handful of scraps of paper. "I wrote it down so I would not forget. But she couldn't seem to finish a sentence, try as she would. Mouth too dry probably. The moment she awoke, Esther reached for the honey water by the bedside. Before the cup could be raised to her lips, Hepzibah, well, she sounded surprised, and said—" He found the piece he was looking for and handed it to me. He'd written: "A dog . . . He saw . . . I saw . . ." Philemon went on, "She turned her head as if it hurt to do it, clasped Esther's hand, saying her name. Then she settled back against the pillows and closed her eyes peacefully. A few minutes later, still holding on to Esther, she left us."

He kept looking at the distant hills. The dawn filling the sky tinted them a strawberry pink. After a bit, his voice was firmer, and with real assurance in it, he finished, "Now she is opening her eyes to the sights of heaven. When next I see Hepzibah, she'll be young again and we'll laugh about those tomato worms."

Because of the man he was, Philemon was not concentrating on laying hold of the person who hastened Hepzibah's departure. I was.

The breakfast bell sounded and he straightened his back. "As it is Sunday, the meal will be cold, but yesterday's huckleberry muffins are still a treat. Come along."

I didn't want to tell him about Quincey's note, not then. He could have shed no light on the situation and he'd have detected my discouragement. But, as we walked, I asked if there were good berry patches in the hills.

As if grateful for a cheerful subject, Philemon launched into stories of how the picking of them was always an occasion for picnics. "Especially since Jacob became an elder. He's always had a boy's spirit, looking to find pleasure in the work. We put the youngest and oldest in the wagons with the food and off we go. Everyone gets so anxious to be eating the lunch the sisters packed that we strip the patches fast. Elder Jacob goes to the children and makes them shout with laughter, showing them how empty his basket is because he's eaten so many and begging for some of theirs to fill it so Mother Alma won't scold him. He's always been able to send her off into peals, too. He'd be sorely missed if the Central Ministry appoints him as an elder in New Lebanon when Brother Frederick leaves us."

Perhaps unconsciously imitating Esau, Philemon folded his hands over his stomach. "There's some here who think holiness should have a straight face and a frowning brow, but that's wrong. It's sin that gives you a heavy heart."

"Surely Elder Jacob himself would be honored by such an advancement."

"It is truly a much-coveted honor. The Central Ministry, guided by divine inspiration, speaks to and for thousands of Believers. Of course he would accept the position. Strict obedience is a requirement of ours. Some talk against us for that, saying we're like the Papists. Still, the good of the whole must come first, and rules must be followed to that end." Philemon looked away. "He'd be but a few miles down the road. Yet, you know, he's been here since childhood and with . . . those he loves, able to see them every day. He's very close to Esau, too."

His last word caught my attention. Philemon was thinking of someone else Jacob could not bear to leave. I remembered the tender way he'd guided Alma's hand to the cup of switchel.

I was casting about for some way to get back to the ill effects of blackberries when he stopped abruptly as we were going past the Trustees' Building. "Brother Michael, I'm sorry. You asked me to look at the dates of the early fires and it went out of my mind. We should do so now. Sister Esther isn't here since she's helping prepare for the last rites, but I can guess at the month and find the right ledgers."

Inside, Philemon took down several, flipped through one, then laid it aside, still open, saying, "These are kept by dates. Very useful they can be. We've all gotten lazy with Sister Esther here and just have her find what information we need. No one but she looks at these.

"That one is the latest—it is too recent." Leaving it open, he picked up the next in the row. As he pored over that, I ran my fingers down the page of the first, filled with Esther's neat writing. I felt as if I were touching her hand and it made my breath short. All those days when I was somewhere else, unaware of her existence. It seemed impossible.

At first I couldn't focus on the words. But soon I did. She recorded everything, each morning starting a new page, although some days took up more than one. Almost always she began with an account of the weather, then entered names of visitors and sales transactions. At the end, she wrote down events in the community. Some could hardly be called notable, but they were useful. For June 30, she'd written: "A company of sisters went to Richmond swamp, along with some sisters from New Lebanon, to gather meadowsweet for tea. They had good luck, and noted the location for the deaconess. They brought back as well a quantity of strawberries, the first we have this year. Sister Thankful was very pleased because, she says, the tea is so good for treating diarrhea. She herself phrased it 'good for those unable to keep their food.' It reminded me of the time after Father's death when I was but new in service and the ladies in the parlor referred to the 'lower appendages.' It took me some time to figure out that they were talking about legs. They even referred to the piano legs in this fashion, and none found it droll."

I smiled with her. So, the loss of her father meant she'd become a maid, a position she'd probably not thought to occupy. As was usual, the prettiest girls were assigned to answering the door and waiting on visitors.

I read on eagerly, but such personal jottings were rare. It occurred to me that she only added one if she had a few lines open at the end of the day. Quickly skipping through the accounts of planting and harvesting, I was rewarded with this: "Today we had an august personage descend on us. Evert Duyckinck, editor of *The Literary World,* came to write a piece on us for his readers. He had a full head of silvery hair, a jowly chin, and an enormous front that strained his gray silk vest to its uttermost and caused him to lean back on his heels for balance. I felt as if he were staring at me through one of the professor's bug glasses, and he never stopped staring. It was as if I were in service again; such behaviors were directed at parlor maids by many who styled themselves gentlemen.

"He paid us this compliment: 'The lids of your boxes fit, your brooms sweep, your packets of herbs are approved by physicians, your brutes well cared for, and your farm and dairy products wholesome.' But he said that as if he were dismissively waving one of his soft hands at accomplishments like these. Just before leaving, he told me that in '42 an English writer of his acquaintance had visited us. 'Mr. Charles Dickens,' he announced with emphasis. Although I was not familiar with the name, I nodded. 'Now,' he went on, 'Mr. Dickens praised your farming practices, but he did add that he found the village and everything about it, "grim, grim, grim." You will forgive me for asking—it is for my readers' enlightenment, you understand—but surely *you* must find it so as well?'

"I answered, 'I have been in areas of Boston in which the air was foul, the streets filthy, the water stinking, and people so hungry they ate rotting vegetables and meat crawling with maggots. Sir, I would call *that* grim.' "

Eagerly, I turned the page, but there was no more. There were only agricultural entries, accounts of pounds of dried herbs prepared and seed packets filled until I was stopped by a phrase at the top of a page. "Remove this."

On the first line, she wrote the following: "Today is the Anniversary. My spirits are exceedingly low. I tried to overcome this by keeping at the accounts, but now I have finished. I shall allow myself the indulgence of writing out what will happen hereafter. I will imagine it as perfectly as I do when it is only in my thoughts.

"The white house at the far end of the road is just visible. As usual I will delay reaching it as long as possible to enjoy the anticipation. I am wearing my white Sunday dress, but no cap, of course, so I will look as I always did. I have plaited the pink ribbons in the sides of my hair, no longer needing to save them. After all, in the house, there is no shortage of ribbons.

"In the distance, on all sides, are the summer trees. Today, the fields on either side of me are filled with blue and purple flowers. Gentian, wild sweet William, phlox. The butterflies that dance through them, intoxicated by the phlox, are the cabbage whites. There is a border of Queen Anne's lace, and amid their foamy blossoms are the dark-winged swallowtail butterflies. The trumpet vines that drape the fences offer their delicate fragrance. The trill of the meadowlarks fills the air.

"As I near the house, I can see that it is brick that has been whitewashed. The columns beside the door are gleaming with new paint. On either side of these are huge rhododendron bushes and the pink perfection of their blooms dazzles. Being so close, it is all I can do to keep from rushing forward now, throwing open the door, spreading out my arms and"

She'd stopped here and the last words were blotted against the back of the page before as if she'd hurriedly closed the book to speak to someone who'd interrupted her.

Following this, in much larger letters, was a single sentence, written backward. That was, Philemon had said, the only form of Shaker swearing. Esther had written: "!ereh gnimoc si tnarG leumaS."

Chapter Sixteen

"Samuel Grant is coming here!" Why should Esther have been disturbed by that fact?

While Philemon continued going conscientiously through one ledger after another, I stood very still, my eyes fixed on the page in front of me. I went over what she'd written on the "Anniversary."

What day in July did that commemorate? And, by "hereafter" did Esther mean at some later point, or in another life? She recognized the house she was so bent on reaching, but was that because she had imagined it so often, or did it exist somewhere in fields bordered by summer trees? A place where she'd once been and was not simply hoping to return to but *planning* to go back to? Clearly, the person behind the doors was someone she'd known before she became a Shaker because he—whoever he was—would not be accustomed to seeing her in her cap but with ribbons in her hair. I tried not to imagine him.

Returning to my first question regarding her words on Samuel Grant, I wondered if she, too, had known him before coming to the Shakers. That was likely enough. The society of Beacon Hill was not a large group. If she'd worked for a family there some ten years ago, it would have been smaller still. She might at least have seen him coming to dinner or a party. I coupled that immediately in my mind with her remark on the behavior of gentlemen toward pretty parlor maids. No matter that that was an unfair leap in logic to assume he was one of those gentlemen. He was living alone in town, without his wife.

At last, holding out a scrap of paper, Philemon said, "I

think this is a complete list of the dates of the fires." I studied it, committing those five dates to memory, before thrusting it into my pocket, along with his note on Hepzibah's last words. He replaced each ledger precisely. As we turned to set off for breakfast, he cast a long look at Hepzibah's neglected desk.

Esther was not in the dining room. No doubt Sister Ruth had sent her firmly off to bed after the long night's wakefulness. Nor was she at the Meetinghouse, where we assembled after the meal. The dancing service would be held in the afternoon. This morning session was more in the nature of a communal meeting. We sat on the long pewlike benches, to be used later by the spectators. They were almost all filled when a man and woman, accompanied by three boys, arrived together.

I had not seen this pair before and they'd have been hard to miss. They were Viking-like in their height and fairness. He was as wide and solid as the stone barn; she was sturdy and almost as tall as he. Dressed in Shaker-made clothing, as were the towheaded children, they separated on entering. She joined the women, and he and the boys went to sit with the brothers. They must be the Krugers, the nearby out family that Esther mentioned the day I arrived.

After the opening hymn, "Farewell Earthly Glory," Elder Jacob rose, faced the congregation, and told them of Hepzibah's passing. It seemed to surprise no one. Such news would go from ear to ear with one slight breath. He referred to the cause of her death only as an "accident," giving no details.

Standing before the windows, his bald head backlit, he announced the program for the rest of the day. Following the afternoon services, we were all to meditate in our rooms or, if we preferred, as we walked quietly about the village. In the evening, Hepzibah would be laid out in the meeting room of the Living Quarters. The community could make their farewells. The sisters would serve cakes and cider. Burial would be Monday morning.

"I will read the following poem, written by one of our

brothers who has gone before us. It was much liked by Sister Hepzibah:

'I've not a word to say, nor dare I breathe complaint,
I live in God Almighty's day and call'd to be a saint,
I've plenty that is good, to eat & drink & wear:
I've decent clothes and wholesome food, enough & some to spare.
My bed is soft & sweet, my room is nice & clean,
No court on earth is kept more neat, for any King or Queen.
My brethren are my friends, my sisters kind to me,
Whoever plows or knits or spins are all at work for me.
Is this what Jesus meant, an hundredfold to give?
Then I've the whole in present time, yea every day I live.
Now this is surely gain, then where's my dreadful loss?
I shall eternal life obtain, sure as I bear my cross.'"

Then, in a conversational tone, Jacob talked about what Hepzibah was surely doing at that moment on the other side of the sky. He described the gates of translucent pearl swinging wide for her and her dazzled steps on the transparent gold of the streets. Her brothers and sisters, those already there, would be lined along those gleaming ways to greet her with great gladness, all of them dressed, as we were, in white. The Shaker-style houses behind them were white, as were the fences and the roses that draped them. The green trees beyond were filled with bright blossoms, ripe fruit, and jeweled birds. Angels, soft wings folded, would chorus as she slowly approached the shining throne of God, with Holy Mother Wisdom, Ann Lee, by His side.

Jacob made everyone see it all clearly, and the picture he painted was transcendently glorious and comfortingly familiar. The quiet in the room was absolute. Most of the Shakers had their eyes raised longingly upward. He finished by saying that, in the evening, Sister Hepzibah and Mother Ann, arms entwined, would together look down at Hancock.

The solemn hush persisted as we filed out. It hung in the air all afternoon, part of the sunlight, even seeming to quiet the bee-loud hives near the orchard. As I stared out of my window at that Sunday serenity, it was almost impossible to believe that someone here had died of violence.

Even Esau's voice was subdued as he read the Psalms while we ate our cold supper. Esther was not in her usual place; perhaps she couldn't bear the sight of Hepzibah's empty chair. Seated at the other end of the long room, she kept her head turned slightly away from me. She would be in the meeting room later and I planned on offering my sympathy to her then.

When I hurried into that room after chores, quite a few of the Shakers were already lined up, two by two, waiting to pass by the pine box at the head of the room. Before it Esther was standing, one arm around Mercy, the other around Crispin. His back was straight, even stiff, and he only moved when he shifted slightly to take his weight a little from his crooked leg. Mercy leaned toward Esther, her face with a curious light raised to hear the murmured words. I was much too far back to catch any.

Despite the somberness of the occasion and the sedateness of those assembled, there was no heaviness in the air. People greeted each other cheerily, and there was an easy sound to the conversations. Platters of seed cakes and cream cookies, each with a border of green mint leaves, were on the candlestands. Jugs of cider and cups were on a trestle table. While I can imagine that even the truest Believer is prey to midnight doubt, the simple faith that shone on their faces made it plain that they were sure that their departed sister had indeed gone to her reward.

I started to take my own place in line and then it occurred to me that if I then stepped out to catch Esther, it would be remarked on. Nor was I eager to look down on Hepzibah and feel failure wash over me. Sister Bertha was across the room, setting down another platter, and I approached her with a question in my mind.

Even the loose, flowing dress of the Shakers didn't hide her size or solidity. Her broad face was abstracted as she bit into a seed cake, chewing thoughtfully. She seemed to be tasting each ingredient separately to see if it was doing its duty.

"Try one of these," she ordered, brushing some crumbs

off her checked neckerchief. "I'm thinking a little more
anise seed might not have been amiss."

The cakes were cut into diamond shapes, each one topped
with a nut. I dutifully ate one, declaring it perfect. It was. I
had another.

"They should have been left to ripen a bit longer in the jar,
too. But there wasn't time." She held out the plate again.
"Enough nutmeg in the cream cookie?"

I didn't think I was hungry, but I finished two of them,
nodding my approval. "And," I said, "the shiny mint make
an attractive garnish."

"Useful," she corrected me. "Breath sweetener. If we dip
them in egg white and oil of peppermint and a bit of sugar,
it gets people to eat them more readily. Some brothers," she
added darkly, "walk right by the jar of fresh ones when they
leave the dining room, without taking any."

I turned slightly to keep my eye on Esther and the children. At that moment she was pouring them some strawberry cup as they helped themselves to the pastries. I
thought that Crispin's freckles looked bleached with pallor.
He signed to Mercy, who translated his question to Esther.
She bent her head, answering quietly in his ear.

Moving hurriedly to my point, I complimented Bertha.
"Even cold, your meals are delicious. I believe I ate four of
the huckleberry muffins. Has anyone ever complained about
any ill effects from any kind of berries?"

"Loose bowels?" she asked matter-of-factly. Answering
her own question, she shook her head. "No, not even that."
Noticing Thankful coming into the room just then, Bertha
inclined her head in that direction. "You might ask the deaconess. *She'd* have told me if there was a problem, and I
don't recall she ever said a word about berries. Now, very
good on herbs, she is. Worked a lot with them in New
Lebanon. Told me to be careful with the senna. Smells good,
but put it in food and it'll cause your stomach problems.
Some of her suggestions on the right ones to use are very
sound. Rosemary on the roasted mutton is quite nice."

Before I could move away, Thankful came directly up,
beaming. Because I'd shown interest in her angelic visita-

tion, as she referred to it, she now regarded me as a confidant. "Brother Michael, I *must* tell you. Al va lan came to me as I slept. It was most odd." Like her body, her voice reflected whichever emotion filled her. Now, since it was twittery excitement, she was reaching toward the higher register. It made one edgy to listen. But there was no escape. She stood in front of me, Bertha's mass was to my left and the long, jug-laden table to the right.

"I had always imagined that all angels had golden hair," the deaconess's fingers were busy adjusting the knot at the end of her silk neckerchief, "but Al va lan's was deep brown, like yours. He was also very tall and broad-shouldered like you. Just as I saw him in my mind. He was wearing—"

Her description of his robe was lost on me. Seth and Amos had moved to pour themselves some cider and the latter's bulk concealed my view of Esther. Amos's deep voice overrode the sound of Thankful's. "That's pro-gress. You cain't be livin' in the past."

Seth was shaking his head stubbornly. "What you're callin' 'pro-gress' ain't. 'Fore you got here, we sold some land to the Western Railroad people and all I heerd was how we got all this money and how we could be shippin' our seeds by rail. Warn't it wonderful! Then the next thing we had sixteen of the brethren and sisters right sick with the fever. *That* was caused by the stagnant water 'cuz the common courses were all stopped up when they're a-buildin' the railroad. A sign that was, direct from Mother Ann. We should be stickin' to the old ways, the right ways."

He took a sip and set his cup down, the better to point a gnarled finger at the scrap of paper he held. "Now, here's another point you been avoidin'.'" He was obviously gratified. "St. Paul says it, and it's as clear as sky, Amos, that you shouldn't be eatin' the meat if it offends your brother. Right thar. It's in the Epistles. To the Romans. Paul says it plump and fair. You just be readin' that right out loud for me."

Stretching out a thick arm as he held the paper in his fingers, Amos furrowed his brow and enunciated the words one by one. " 'For meat destroy not the work of God. All things indeed are pure, but it is evil for the man who eateth with of-fence.'"

Thankful raised her intense soprano so as to be heard. ". . . not a halo exactly, but a bright glow that surrounded him. He was standing at the head of the stairs in all his glory and I—"

Amos labored on slowly. " 'It is good neither to eat flesh nor to drink wine, nor any thing whereby thy brother stum-bleth, or is offended, or is made weak.' " Still looking at the paper, he took a long swallow from his cup and chewed on the drink. He held the paper out farther. As he shifted on his feet from side to side, I could see Esther's hand slipping some cookies into Crispin's long coat's pocket.

Thankful's hand stretched to a platter on the table but there was only the mint left. She nibbled delicately on a leaf as she plunged on. Her eyelashes fluttered at me. "I'm sure, Brother Michael, you, too, have had that experience that after a dream you can only remember certain—"

Bertha reached between us, snagged the empty plate, and sailed off in the direction of the kitchen. Esther picked up cups and another platter and followed with Mercy. Cris ap-peared at my side next to the trestle table. I thought he wanted to be on hand for the second round of cookies, but then his small hand found its way into mine. I squeezed it gently but didn't look down.

Amos rumbled out, "I'm a-callin' your attention to what the Apostle says here about 'all things bein' pure.' So he doesn't be seein' anythin' wrong with the *eatin'* of the meat."

"Mebbe so," Seth retorted, "but if'n your brother is of-fended—"

Esther leaned near me, setting down more cookies, and moved to the middle of the room where she stopped to ex-change a few words with a puffy-eyed Ruth, standing in the viewing line. Then she took her outside bonnet from a peg and gestured toward the children to join her. Cris let go of my hand but I could still feel the warmth of his fingers.

Just beyond them, the door opened and Esau and Samuel

Grant came in. Although walking side by side, they weren't speaking.

Then—I don't know how to explain what happened. I'd been calmly drinking cider, listening to the conversations. But at the sight of Grant, I clenched my cup so tightly that, if it hadn't been stoneware, I'd have had a handful of broken crockery. I wanted to fling myself at him, throttle him, tell him—and everyone there—that he was a betrayer, a cheat, a lecher, a fire-setter. That he'd bashed in the head of that gentle old woman who—

That was what stopped me. I had no proof that he'd killed Hepzibah. I'd no proof that he committed any of those crimes. And I'd never find the evidence of his guilt unless I stood just where I was. My legs trembled with the effort.

At that moment, Giles, who'd followed his father in, swooped down on a dish on a candlestand, plucked up three seed cakes, and began juggling them expertly. He snatched one out of the air with his teeth and, while he chewed, continuing tossing the other two in the air. Everyone in the crowded room was doing their best not to look at him or say a word.

It was Seth who broke the silence that had fallen at Giles's antics. He raised his arm, beckoning to Esau. "Now," he said triumphantly to Amos, "there's the deacon. He'll explain it to you proper."

Crispin and Mercy, now being guided toward the door by Esther, were looking in round-eyed fascination at Giles. He tossed a cake in their direction and the boy caught it, smiling hesitantly. Then all three were gone.

Swallowing hard, I turned back to Thankful. But even she had been distracted by the argument near us. All of her chins tightened as she glared at the two brothers, now joined by Esau. He was holding the paper very close to his eyes as he read. Amos wanted to get his licks in first. "What's worryin' the Apostle is if the eatin' causes the brother to stumbleth. Now supposin' Sister Bertha puts your joint of beef on our table, with the juices runnin', the skin nice and cracklin'. Everybody's mouth gets to waterin'. 'Cept one. There's one brother," he fixed an eye on Seth, "who's never gonna stumbleth. He'd rather be jawin' about it instead of chewin' it. Suppose'n he changed his mind and had a nice slice. It'd put meat on his bones."

"Jest like some people," Seth gasped out, "to be over-lookin' the part about the brother bein' offended!" He turned on his heel and joined the line before the coffin, not looking back.

Although Thankful was addressing me, her hardened face was turned in Amos's direction. "Here at Hancock, Brother Michael, we have a separate table for those who, like myself, eat only the good grains and fruits of the earth." I'd noticed that table. Brother Issachar was seated there surrounded by sisters, and one of them was Thankful. "Bertha makes every effort with the food for us. Her chestnut and rice patties are lovely. Not that they at all resemble the minced beef sort. That would be a form of lying, bearing false witness, so to speak. Her rarebit, too, is excellent since she started adding the lemon thyme I suggested. There is *no* need for any of us to be disturbed by what other Family members choose."

Esau put in sternly, "Provided, Sister Thankful, that those Family members are in no way led astray by those choices. Brother Seth brings up a point always in the forefront of my mind. We must protect those who are weaker from evil influences." He returning to his peering at the quotation.

Thankful gave him a look that said eloquently that she hadn't expected agreement from him and hadn't gotten it. It took her a few seconds to transform her face back to the reverent expression necessary when speaking of an angel. "As I was saying, he was at the top of the staircase and I was coming up to Brother Issachar's room, holding my candle." She lowered her voice, as well as her eyes. "He was speaking to me. The message was personal and important for all of us. It was necessary that I understand. But, although I was trying, I couldn't. His lips were moving, but I couldn't make out the words. Whatever do you think it could mean?" When she raised her eyes, her expression was troubled.

I was trying for some sort of answer when Bertha came up, each fist clutching a white stoneware pitcher. Elijah and

Giles were approaching the table, followed by Samuel, and Elijah hurried forward, saying, "But those are *too* heavy for you, Sister. Let me take them."

"They are a bit," she said, setting them down, however, without any trouble. "And there's more in the kitchen. You," her brisk gesture included Giles, "could help me bring them in. Take the empties with you and the cups to be washed up."

Seeing Giles heft a cup and thoughtfully balance it in his palm, Thankful shot him an alarmed look and lifted it out of his hand. "Just take two of the pitchers," she told him and began gathering the cups herself carefully. To demonstrate that he, although a deacon, was not above menial tasks, Esau picked some up as well. They all followed in Bertha's wake.

When Samuel Grant came up, I started immediately to follow Seth. Then I decided to show that I was in command of my emotions, and I stayed. He inspected the almost empty table with his usual dour look, pushing the scattered garnish on one plate into a pile, obviously thinking about something else.

Without preamble, he turned and asked Amos, "Was the silk-weaving in Kentucky profitable?"

"Waal, it took the sisters a bit to get on to doin' it the best way, then they got good. The dyin' of the thread took some figurin' cuz World People like real purty colors. Like the purply one the deaconess is wearin'. I brung that here from Kaintuck myself. Gift for the elders. It warn't long 'fore we couldn't keep enough of the shawls in the Office Store. Then we got orders from some store up east. We wuz takin' in the money. That's when the trouble started."

"What problem did you have with that?"

Amos stared at his boots gloomily. "It was a fuss. Some were sayin' that warn't right—it was worshippin' Mammon. I don't recollec' who this Mammon was, but Jesus didn't hold with him. And the way I was seein' it, Jesus whupped the money changers. Letters were flyin' to New Lebanon, and even at the Wednesday Union Meetin' everybody was talkin' about jes' that and nothin' else."

"Didn't the Central Ministry say that there was nothing

wrong with a profit, that it enabled us to give more to the poor, for example?" Samuel Grant's voice was testy.

Amos shrugged. "'Bout that time, I up and came here."

As they were speaking, the parade from the kitchen, bearing full pitchers and platters, returned. The table was again spread with refreshments. Elijah and Giles were helping themselves liberally. After putting a plate down, Esau took up his stance by Amos, about to deliver his opinion on St.Paul. He chewed on the sweets as he chewed on the words he was about to deliver.

I was going to put a cookie in my mouth to keep it shut. Just as I reached for the tray, Samuel Grant wheeled and asked me bluntly, "Elder Jacob is open to this thinking. What are your thoughts on the profit issue?"

My hand closed on the sugared leaves and I crumbled them between tightened fingers. Esau, who had also taken some, turned to hear my response. I knew my voice wasn't going to be steady and that the answer that was springing to my lips wasn't what I should say. Not at all. To give myself some time, I was about to pop the mint in my mouth.

Before I could, Esau looked at me wildly, gagging. "That's not right. That's not pep— Teaberry!" His hand flung up, knocking the leaves out of mine. "Don't eat—" he began and stopped, clutching his neck as if it were on fire. His whole body began to shake. Both the Grants, close by, grabbed for him, but he shoved them aside. He half-ran, half-staggered his way across the crowded room. Hands reached for him but, intending to or not, he pushed them all away in his mad progress for the door. Retching and coughing, he threw it open and dashed out.

I was still standing, staring as we all were. But Sister Ruth, holding her cup, rushed after him.

Chapter Seventeen

"Your premise is incorrect, Mr. Merrick." Jasper Quincey might've been glaring at me. It was hard to tell. Seated in the Krugers' sunny yellow bedroom, he had his head back to look up, so his half-glasses magnified his prominent eyes. From that angle, the usual sleepy look his heavy eyelids gave him was gone.

"You could *not* have prevented the poisoning of Deacon Esau last night. The guilt that you evidently suffer is therefore unfounded. Even if I'd been lodging in the village as you were, or indeed on the scene partaking of the refreshments in the meeting room, *I* could not have averted that. We must use *logic* to solve this problem. You're allowing emotion to overwhelm you."

I was certainly glaring at him.

When Philemon told me after breakfast that Quincey had sent a message saying that he'd arrived late the previous evening and was staying at the Krugers' home some ten miles from Hancock, there was relief mixed in with my amazement. He must have been so concerned with the attack on Hepzibah that he felt the need to bestir himself. Apparently, even he couldn't put his own comfort above such an offense. By this time, the Krugers would have given him the news of her death. At least I didn't have to do that.

I had good reason to be angry. Quincey must have been on the road from Boston ever since he'd gotten my report on the attack. He could've easily sent word ahead that he was coming. And why hadn't he communicated that simple fact in the note that Trapper had brought? Instructing me not to send on reports could only mystify me: he himself told me he never left his home. How was I to guess at his feelings? I wasn't aware he had any.

Philemon, as much surprised as I was at the news of Quincey's coming, said I was to call at the Shaker out family's house at my "earliest convenience." Setting out for the stable at a run, I saddled up Samuel Grant's horse. While all Shaker property was held in common, I'd never seen anyone but him on Lightfoot, as the thoroughbred was called. Not only was there a real satisfaction on my part in taking that horse, it proved worthy of the name. I was at the Krugers before I had a chance to tamp down my anger or contain my frustration.

Seeing my face, Freegift uncertainly waved me upstairs. I glanced into the first room. Shaker built-in cabinets filled one wall, but an enormous bed took up most of the space. Because of their size, the Krugers would need every inch of that bed. No doubt then this was the marital bedroom.

Quincey had already established himself there. He was seated at a table, obviously brought in from another room, which took up all the remaining area. He must've had to maneuver to slide behind it. When I entered, he raised his eyes from a stack of paper without moving, other than to lay aside his quill pen.

I blurted out the story of the attempt on Esau, finishing unsteadily, "A doctor from Pittsfield examined him and feels there's some chance of recovery. Thank God for that! I think that mint was meant for me. Since the theft of the notes for my next report, I should have foreseen something of the kind and . . . and taken steps."

For a long moment, Quincey looked at me without replying, placing one finger firmly on the bridge of his glasses. Then he delivered the speech reproving me for my excess emotion. His tone also implied that it was presumption on my part to imagine I could've done what he couldn't. That put my back up further but I said nothing. He pursed and unpursed his lips and asked, "What was in these stolen papers, and how did they come to be taken?"

Having to admit to my foolishness in leaving them in an unlocked drawer deflated me. Some of my indignation leaked away. I determined to remain cool and be as correct in my behavior as I could. More calmly, I told him that they were notes of my interviews on people's whereabouts during the Midnight Cry. "Philemon says they could've been filched out of curiosity—of one sort or another—but I can't shake the idea that they were taken because the guilty person suspected why I was in Hancock. It's possible that my jottings could be read as memory aids for my spiritual autobiography, but I'd guess anyone who feared discovery would be alerted."

Without any comment on my words, or any readable expression, Quincey asked, "On what basis did you choose those to be interviewed?"

I brought out my theory. "The dog was seen as a threat. Only eight people, excluding Esther and the children, knew of him."

He grunted. "You spoke to all eleven? And to anyone who might confirm their whereabouts at the time of the attack?"

At my nod, he laid aside his glasses, and said, "You will have to remove your boots."

I stared at him. "Pardon?"

He waved his hand impatiently at my slowness. "So as to avoid dirtying Mrs. Kruger's yellow coverlet. We must see if we can retrieve those interviews from your memory. Lie down on the bed, close your eyes, and try to see the people you spoke to. Include any relevant movements of their bodies, and both your immediate thoughts and later ones. Neglect nothing. I will interrupt with questions as they occur to me."

It was a long, intense recital of all I could recall of the conversations of the last three days and of the events leading up to Esau's rush from the Meetinghouse. But it was not as difficult as I'd thought when I first stretched out on the bed. The fact that I'd recorded much of what I told him was a help. Sometimes, behind my eyelids, I could see the person I spoke to and sometimes those written words sprang up as if on a chalkboard. I even managed to include the dates of all the fires.

I omitted only one thing: Esther's note to herself. It was

personal and could hardly shed light on the Shakers' problems. I did include her story of the language of the ladies in the parlor, her position there, her meeting with the editor of *The Literary World,* and her backward sentence on Samuel Grant.

Quincey broke in only rarely and then to ask me to expand on my understanding of someone's words. Early on, when I came to the encounter I'd had with Seth and Amos leading Elder Jacob's horse, I mentioned their veterinary and smithing work. Quincey growled, "You noted that about them in your first report. I *read* it." Otherwise, he sat so still I thought he'd nodded off.

When I sat up, throat parched, I was pleased and not a little proud of myself. I felt I'd presented a full account, even to recalling where people were standing in the meeting room. I laced up my boots, stood up, smoothed out my trouser legs, and moved to a chair pushed up against the cabinets across the room from Quincey. It was the only place to sit, and he would have had to crane his neck if I stood. He was silent. At last I glanced at him, impatient for comment.

Quincey simply rubbed his eyes, picked up a small brass bell, and rang it.

Freegift appeared so promptly that he might have been stationed outside the door. He almost sidled in, carrying a large tray with a stoneware pitcher, tall glasses, and a plate of sweetmeats. Placing it on the table, he stepped back and kept going backward, almost making it out of the room that way, before he was stopped by Quincey's voice.

There was no thunder in it; he spoke almost calmly, but it was a preternatural calm. All he said was, "Freegift, why have you brought glasses of that size? And why put the sherry into that pitcher?"

The servant went absolutely still, not even blinking, eyes fixed on the floor, but his words came out fast. "There is no sherry, sir. That is cold tea. Some of the imported tea you brought as a gift for Mrs. Kruger. Very nice, it is. Sweetened with honey. As well, there is candied flag root and a maple confection."

Sitting as stonily as a man in the shock of bereavement, Quincey repeated, "No sherry? It is eleven o'clock!"

Freegift gabbled out explanations. "The Krugers, being Believers, do not partake of any wines. Although they told me there is a farmer near Pittsfield, a French person, who does make an apple brandy, supposedly quite good, and I took the liberty of sending for some. Sir, I did bring up a case of the Jerez from the cellar at home. It was just that the news of Hepzibah's injury being so upsetting. Then the look on your face— And Mrs. Hingham," he glanced at me, "the cook, that is, and I had to pack so hurriedly. And we'd never had any occasion to pack at all before, so there was no system. There was such a deal of food for the hampers all about the kitchen that, in the end, I must have . . . overlooked the bottles."

His eyes sought mine desperately in hopes of an understanding audience. "We could hardly depend on an inn providing acceptable meals. So you see that she had to put up all we had, and her heart not being in it with her saying, 'Sure as you don't need onions to cry, he'll be ordering the driver to turn 'round before he's half out of Cambridge' and then—"

I missed part of what Freegift was saying because of that sentence. Maybe Quincey hadn't told me he was arriving because he wasn't sure he could force himself to arrive. I believed that.

". . . as traveling quite disordered Mr. Quincey's stomach. So eleven o'clock came and went and the sherry never crossed my mind when we were on the road. Really, these coaches—even the private ones—are not well-sprung. Although if you think of the train with all that coal dust and ash flying about—Mr. Quincey has delicate sinuses—not to mention the acute dangers of derailment, which would always be on his mind, and the jolting, and the seats not really made for a person of . . . that on the whole, the coach was no doubt the only—"

Quincey interrupted by placing his palm smartly down on the table. His voice was stoic. "Freegift." He paused for several long seconds. "Pour the tea."

When I was handed mine, I drank the whole glass at once. The tea was chilled in an icehouse and cooled my throat. I missed Quincey's expression as he sipped his. Freegift refilled my glass, brought a small plate with the sweetmeats, and disappeared.

Rolling his tongue around his mouth and swallowing one of those from the platter, Quincey's expression cleared a little. "Those are morsels of candied flag root. I must mention these to Mrs. Hingham. Since sweet flag is also known as calamus, some maintain that this is the herb mentioned in the Bible." He raised his eyes to the ceiling in disbelief. "Do not entertain that idea. It is *quite* unlikely. The Scriptural calamus must have been another aromatic, grasslike herb. Still, the American variety is an equally good digestive aid." He ate several more.

Pushing aside the empty platter, he pronounced, "Now, then, Mr. Merrick, as you can appreciate, it was the poisoning of the dog that necessitated this dreadful journey, as well as my haste."

I almost spat out the tea I was about to swallow. The dog?

With some irritation he tried to settle himself more comfortably against the chair's ladderback. "For the moment, let us limit ourselves to the discussion of that. I join you in your assumption that this poisoning was the work of the arsonist. It follows this person must be a member of the community and one of the few who knew the animal was in the village. That its death was attempted, the way it was done, and the timing provide us with information. All of that being understood—"

I cleared my throat. I had no idea what he was talking about. What I said was "It'd help me, Mr. Quincey, if you'd spell out all your inferences from these circumstances so that I'm sure mine match yours."

He managed to inject an elaborate patience into his voice. "Why would the guilty person poison the dog unless he or she planned to continue in setting the fires? One might have hoped that the previous ones could have satisfied an anger—or other emotion—that had flared inside. Too, these might have been impulsive crimes, the person being overcome with a need to set those blazes. Now, because of the deliberate, planned attempt to remove the dog, we can dismiss those possibilities. Secondly, the choice of poison indicates that the person is knowledgeable about herbs. Thirdly—"

"What was the choice of poison?' I asked bluntly.

"You must know. Surely you recall the child Mercy telling you the animal had the 'blind staggers'? And that she could feel its racing heart? Now, that alone might not have eliminated all of the likely poisons grown in the Shaker herb gardens. But you must have hit upon the berries of *Atropa belladonna* when you consider the pleasant taste and easy portability of those berries. A few could easily be slipped into a pocket. And, at this season, they would be ripening. Given all its medical uses, the Shakers get quite a few orders for the leaves, which are quite safe, so they have many of the shrubs."

"Mr. Quincey," I said in stiff exasperation, "I know nothing of the plant."

He raised his eyebrows so high that they pulled up his half-mast eyelids. "One hardly has to be a specialist. Allusions to belladonna abound in classical works. During the Parthian Wars, it was used to poison the troops of Marcus Antonius. You can't have forgotten that it was the potion Juliet uses in Shakespeare's tragedy! Belladonna," he said, as if prompting my memory. "Beautiful lady. So called because the Venetian women used it to dilate their pupils, thus making their eyes large and lovely. Perhaps you're more used to thinking of it as deadly nightshade. It is, of course, a member of the nightshade family."

I continued looking at him blankly.

He pressed down hard on his wiry hair as if that would keep in thoughts better left unsaid. "So, you didn't understand my warning about the blackberries. It'd be easy for a tablemate to mix into your serving a few of those from the belladonna bush since they are dark, shiny, and sweet. I considered that happening as only a bare possibility but worthy of mention. As few as four berries could kill."

"But why does the poisoner have to be knowledgeable about herbs to choose belladonna to give Hallelujah? All of the Shakers rotate through the Seedhouse and all, including the children, would be warned of the toxic nature of the berry."

"Because it was a *dog* that was to be poisoned. For an unknown reason, horses, cows, deer eat the plant without harm. Nightshade grows wild; many here would have known that there was no cause for concern if their animals grazed nearby. But the Shakers keep no cats or dogs—both of which will eat the berries if mixed with their food and will certainly die as a result. I assume that someone with only a rudimentary knowledge of that plant might have questioned whether it would be effective on a dog and chosen something else. Hancock's herb garden would have foxglove, for example, and possibly henbane."

Abandoning all hope of appearing to share his thinking, I asked, "What did the timing suggest to you?"

"The fact that it was done so promptly. Why not wait and see if the elders approved keeping this dog? Despite the certitude of Samuel Grant that they would see things his way, they might've shared the opinion of the deacon and deaconess. Given their other concerns, it might have taken a few days to reach the decision, but not more than that. A reasonable supposition, then, is that another fire is being planned soon. That fits with the dates you have just given. Whereas the earlier fires were widely spaced in time, the most recent ones have been only weeks apart. Therefore, I will posit that the arsonist has some event in mind that these fires will affect. Two upcoming changes that surface in the conversations you report might constitute such an event, but there are too many others that we do not and cannot know of. We needn't dwell on those two."

The only upcoming event, if it could be so termed, that I recalled mentioning was that Elder Jacob might be appointed to New Lebanon. And I didn't know what to do with that. Certainly, nothing else occurred to me. But I refused to ask him to elaborate.

"Now then, I have done what research was possible on the frame of mind of a fire-starter. As soon as Philemon described the situation to me, I sent to the *Independent* for files of all stories of arson in Boston that were investigated and eventually attributed to an individual." He let out an exasperated breath. "Unfortunately, there were few. The constables that preceded our current police seemed to have assumed that fires are always accidental and need not concern them. Our new police force is more suspicious, prompted by landlords and business owners. But your predecessors who wrote the Police News column made no effort to obtain the details that I found in your reports."

His face was impassive. "I noted that you gave information on unquestionable crimes, but you were careful, as well, to include the circumstances of all fires, even if they did not directly involve the police."

I kept my own expression neutral, although my voice might not have been even. "The public needs to be reminded of the dangers of using paraffin. Then, too, open kitchen fires and women's skirts are a hazard that they shouldn't forget. The Shakers enclose their stoves to overcome that problem."

Quincey went on without more comment. "In several cases of fires, the police were alert. A sharp-eyed officer would note a person in the usual crowd of excited onlookers who stood out because his or her reaction was extreme. One could say that this individual seemed gratified, as if the destruction were a personal act of creation. When confronted, many of these confessed, and with some willingness. Even pride. The interesting fact to me was that the guilty fell into two distinct age groups: adolescents of both sexes, and women ending their reproductive years. One woman in that category admitted starting fires when she was an adolescent, but had not done so again until recently.

"I'd term these people pyromaniacs. Fires release their inner tensions. On first listening to Philemon, I was persuaded that was the sort of individual to look for, but now we're faced with the image of a more cold-blooded person, one who plans arson for a reason. That motive we can speculate on, but cannot know. However, we can be more precise about other factors, such as opportunity, that each person on your list had."

Suddenly, he brought his hand down sharply on the table-top. "The poisoning of the deacon was unfortunate. Truly unfortunate!"

Although I was startled at his display of emotion, I considered it warranted. The fact that he hadn't reacted when I gave him the news had unsettled me. The idea of Esau lying white and still in the very room where Hepzibah died lay heavily on me.

There was indignation in his voice as well. His next words were "It doesn't add to our store of information. It doesn't clarify the motive for the fires. In terms of opportunity, it eliminates no one. We already knew the arsonist was knowledgeable about poisons. This choice merely confirms it."

"A quite unfortunate incident, particularly for the deacon. What was the poison?"

If Quincey noted my acerbic tone, he gave no sign, responding, "Because of Esau's actions after eating it, I'd think it was concentrated wintergreen oil. *Gaultheria procumbens*. It would burn his throat, hence his clutching at it. Extreme nausea follows. It affects the lungs, so the body goes into convulsions before death."

I thought about that. Possibly Esau's ability to hold his own was a good sign.

"It was shrewd to use wintergreen. Another popular name for the plant is 'teaberry' because of the beverage made from the leaves. That's an agreeable tea—for those who enjoy such things—and the herb has a number of medicinal uses, externally as a liniment. The point here is that the aroma is close enough to mint that it would get past the nose, even apparently his, and he has worked in the Seedhouse you said. Brushed on mint leaves dipped in egg white and sugar, it would go down fairly smoothly. You might have swallowed several without noticing its pungent smell."

Convulsions and death. My own. He referred to it quite matter-of-factly.

Quincey frowned. "You are not necessarily wrong in your hypothesis that you were the intended victim. While Jacob seems to have been quite discreet in not telling even the other elders, as he said, your appearance here might have alerted the poisoner. You are an unlikely convert because of your age, sex, and background. Or you might have been observed as you inspected the Seedhouse. Your room is searched for confirmation. Your notes are found. You pose a threat. A few fatal leaves are scattered on the platter near you. Perhaps even if you don't eat them, you might be warned off by the person nearest you swallowing them."

"That *is* cold-blooded."

"Yes, but this man or woman has cause to be terrified of discovery. The death of the elderly brother was not intended, I would imagine. But it happened. The rest follows from that. The original motive for the fires might elude us because it was one that we'd regard as a slight one. The motive for murder is self-preservation."

"But suppose the arsonist started from a . . . 'religious principle'; I can't think of a better term. The fires were set to call the community's attention to a straying from the spirit of their laws, for example. How then could such a person justify killing their brothers and sisters?"

The corner of his mouth quirked into what might have been a smile. "Your field of study was, I believe, history. How many holy wars were undertaken in the name of a founder who said, 'Love one another,' and 'Thou shalt not kill'? Ah, well, forgive me that easy rejoinder. I don't wish to belittle your point. We're infinitely capable of twisting our minds around to justify a deed. And, as a wise man once said, 'A surplus of virtue is more dangerous than a surplus of vice. A surplus of virtue is not subject to the constraints of conscience.'

"We can't ignore the possibility, however, that those leaves were meant for Esau. He is a staircase observer, one of those who watch as their fellows err and then mention that their misconduct was seen. But perhaps he doesn't speak of it right away. Keep in mind that Elder Jacob has kept the attack on Hepzibah quiet. If, while tending to Issachar, the deacon looked through a window and saw someone out at night, he'd only make a mental note that the person was breaking a rule. Later, he'd point out that shouldn't have been done. He'd have thought he was chiding a miscreant, not accusing a murderer."

The picture of Esau, hands clasped in righteous sorrow, doing just that sprung to my mind.

Quincey's glance at me was particularly penetrating. "Now, from your classes in logic, you'll recall the term 'supposal,' meaning a proposition that is neither affirmed nor denied, but merely put forward for remark. We will engage in supposals regarding these people."

I nodded, approving of the method, and stretched out my legs for comfort.

"We must start with the most likely, the one who had the best opportunity, the requisite knowledge, and a discernible motive. Sister Esther."

Chapter Eighteen

Iwas on my feet and halfway across the room before I
knew I was standing up, objecting at the top of my voice.
"Dismiss that idea, sir. Esther wasn't on my list for good
reason. It isn't possible to suspect her. She . . . she can't con-
ceivably be an arsonist. She's a woman! And one that could
never poison a dog. She *wanted* to keep Hallelujah. As for
striking Hepzibah, she loved the woman. You can't believe
that she—"

"*Please* sit down, Mr. Merrick. You cannot so soon have
forgotten the definition of a supposal, a term that does not
assert belief or disbelief. We must consider her. On several
occasions, Philemon spoke highly of Esther's intelligence to
you. According to your report, she's in control of her emotions. On hearing an unseen trumpet played on a mountain
she doesn't leap to the conclusion that the player must be an
angel. Now, look at the case. Were she seen out on any of the
occasions the fires were started, she need only say she was
looking for Hepzibah. Indeed, on the night the woman was
attacked, you saw her on the path before the Midnight Cry
was announced."

"But Esther *was* searching for her."

"So she told you. She might've slipped from their shared
room, intending to get rid of the dog, while *Hepzibah* was
sleeping. The old woman awakens on hearing her shut the
outer door and, confused, follows her. Unfortunately, they
meet in the Seedhouse.

"To you, Esther spoke of enjoying her work with the
herbs, and said in the past she'd kept a dog. Therefore, she
would possibly know of the canine susceptibility to bel-

ladonna. If she shows herself in favor of keeping this one, no one would believe she was guilty of poisoning it, should anyone even suspect that was what was done. While any one of those on your list might have struck the old woman in un-thinking panic, Esther *must* do so out of coolheaded self-preservation. Hepzibah always recognized *her* and was apparently capable of wondering, in the presence of others, 'My dear, what were you doing in the Seedhouse so late last night?' Speaking of Hepzibah's words, her very last ones were 'I saw . . .' She doesn't complete the sentence, but in-stead turns to Esther, which could imply that's who she did see. If it were Esther who then struck her, it was from be-hind, and the old woman wouldn't know she was the as-sailant."

I retreated back to my chair, feeling almost pushed there by his words. But they carried no weight with me. No argu-ment could convince me. I knew Esther.

He banged his palm on the table. "You are a romantic!" His tone indicated that bordered on a criminal offense. "Now, your chivalry is commendable in some ways. I sup-pose. But not if it blinds you to the fact that a woman could have committed this crime. Whether as a sex they're more moral than men, as is often stated, I do not know. However, my research shows that, in some instances, they are fire-set-ters. History shows us that they are poisoners, both of men and beasts. Surely, logic requires your agreement to this."

"Yes." I answered shortly. I didn't, however, mean that I was agreeing to the idea that *Esther* could be a suspect.

No doubt my expression reflected that. He sighed deeply. "In Robert Burton's seventeenth-century classic, *Anatomy of Melancholy,* he refers to lovesickness as a madness, one with a sudden onset. I've never had cause to dispute his analysis. And while you don't customarily hide your feel-ings, in this instance, you not only have your heart displayed on your sleeve, every word from your mouth proclaims your deep feeling. Still, with due deference to that, we can't dis-miss her as a suspect on that basis."

As much as Quincey's accusation of Esther had staggered me, these words astonished me more. I didn't know I loved

her. My narrative must make clear how completely she had
occupied my thoughts, had overtaken my feelings. Yet I repeat that I hadn't before been aware that it was love. I sat
speechless, staring at my employer.

His eyes rested on me as if I were an accident victim
badly hurt through his own carelessness, and his deliberate
tone matched that attitude. "I had occasion to speak with
Mrs. Kruger in the kitchen this morning. She spent her for-
mative years with the Shakers and is quite friendly with Sister Bertha, the kitchen overseer. They visit frequently and
exchange recipes. Mrs. Kruger was happy to speak of various sisters and brothers. I didn't need to prompt her. In the
course of our conversation, she mentioned that Esther is
well liked by the Family, yet no one can recall her speaking
of her past. She arrived, five years ago, carrying a pillowslip
with some small pieces of clean linen. That was all the property she declared when she signed the Covenant; even the
possession of a packet of pins must be listed. She signed her
Christian name only, not even adding a last initial. Without
a surname, I don't know what we could discover of her."

He raised his eyebrows at me. "Think about what we do
know. She mentions a farm, but has neither the speech nor
the manner of a rural woman. On the evidence of her journal, she was a parlor maid. While it is true that she might
learn much in such a position, she wouldn't have been assigned to greeting visitors if she hadn't already been well-
spoken. That presupposes some background.

"Now recall her statement to the effect that she felt free at
Hancock. Based on probability, she has been married, but it
is idle to speculate further on that. The domain of the con-
ceivable is too large. She may have fled from a vicious husband or a dull one. She might well consider marriage
tyranny, but without family income she would have little
choice. She could be a widow and therefore be escaping the
tyranny of poverty.

"Now, this is relevant in terms of her joining the Believers. The entire surrounding area of New York and Massachusetts is called the 'Burned-Over District' because the
fires of religious revivals have swept over it so many times

in the recent past. One begins to think that the inhabitants imbibe fervor with their mothers' milk. Many of the community's members are from this part of the northeastern seaboard.

"Yet, based on what you have told me of her and the report of her words, we could postulate that Esther's conversion to the Shakers wasn't made from religious enthusiasm but from conscious choice. The Eldress Alma is another instance of this, I gather. I find that understandable."

Quincey gazed into the middle distance. Musingly, he said, "The Shaker religion is quite interesting. An exotic sect, remarkably romantic."

I sat bolt upright. "Those are the last two adjectives I'd have chosen. Their dismissal of the importance of beauty, denial of physical love, their insistence on hard work, their drab clothing, their—"

"I am using the words in their largest sense." Quincey seemed to be making an effort to infuse a modicum of kindness into his voice, as if my slowness were a result of my "condition." "*Exotic* is defined as 'strikingly out of the ordinary, rarely met with.' Now, I know of no other Western sect that has a female messiah, a woman deity. The Shakers see Mother Ann as an embodiment of Christ. She sits on the throne of God, beside Him. That is quite different, for example, than the manner in which Roman Catholics view and venerate the Virgin Mary. One could note in passing that woman is seen as the originator of evil in Judaism, Christianity, and Islam. The Greeks blamed it on Pandora.

"As for *romantic,* that adjective can be opposed to realistic. Let us *not* limit it to describing the maudlin way men and women can regard each other. Here is what I meant. The Shakers set out to create a heaven on earth and to do all things perfectly. These are not realistic goals. Moreover, romanticism, with its emphasis on sensibility, on feeling, is set against neoclassicism, with its stress on reason, the intellect. Look at the behavior at the Midnight Cry. That was a perfect example of the Dionysian ecstasy, what scholars term a 'joyous exaltation, the inebriation of the Infinite.' At that moment the Believers were lost to themselves and in the presence of God, the most intense of feelings."

Thinking of that, I must have stirred a little on my chair because he said quite emphatically, "I am *not* digressing. I do not indulge in straying from the point. We're looking at the Shaker ethos and attempting to understand a woman like Esther. What would be the appeal of this way of life for her?"

I considered. "It does embody those values we think of as a woman's: cleanliness, order, cooperation, sharing, attention to food and to the proper upbringing of children." I paused, before adding, "But I can see why certain men of any age would find it congenial as well. Then, a number of the brothers are older. They work hard, but they'd have to do so to survive anywhere. Here they have the benefits I referred to, as well as an assurance of tender care in their declining years."

Leaning forward, he nodded, saying, "But let us not forget what could also be very attractive. Shaker theology is vague. Perhaps I should call it creative or evolving. They are open to the Eastern idea of human reincarnation. They don't rely on the Bible, despite some Believers' familiarity with it. Of course, their *Millennial Laws* are quite specific, to the point of telling the sisters how to sew on buttons, but those laws dictate behavior, not belief. Their hierarchical system is strict, but the function of elders and deacons is to lay down rules on how things ought to be done. On the other hand, thought is free; as Elijah pointed out, each individual decides on the inner truth."

When I didn't reply, he spoke briskly. "We have speculated enough on what we can know about Esther. You may now bring any arguments for her innocence that a reasonable man would take into account."

"Very well." I took a moment, trying to breathe evenly. I pushed myself to do as he asked. "She has worked very hard to expand the Shakers' herb sales. Why would she want to destroy their capacity to fill their orders?"

"I accept that. However, she may see it as a temporary disruption, necessary for long-term success. She might re-

gard her way as the only way. Samuel Grant, then, would be
a most unwelcome intrusion into her territory, especially
with his talk of wide-ranging changes. On the evidence of
her journal, she certainly did not want him as a fellow
trustee, for whatever reason. I call your attention to the fact
that the first seedhouse fire was in New Lebanon, when the
Grants were then in that village. When they came to Hancock, then the fires began there. Philemon pointed out that
many of the Shakers suspect Giles because of his bizarre actions. If some evidence, which could be manufactured by a
clever woman, soon came to light, pointing in his direction,
he'd be asked to leave. No doubt the father would accompany him. Esther is then again in charge of the situation. She
could justify her crimes as needful to protect the Shaker
herb and seed industry."

I could see that there was no point in her favor that I could
bring that he wouldn't meet with a counter interpretation. It
was a useless exercise. A vision of Esther rose before me. I
saw the softness: the fair hair, the gray eyes, the pale skin,
the full upper lip that covered her teeth at the corners. He
hadn't seen her face, heard her voice, observed her kindness
with the children, or her pain when caring for Hepzibah. If
he had, he couldn't conjure up a hard-edged woman such as
he described and call her Esther.

At that moment, I had a vivid picture of Esther following
Bertha into the kitchen and emerging with platters of cookies. One of them had been placed near me.

He stirred in his chair. "Men often endow the women they
feel inordinate affection for with the quintessential feminine
qualities: compassion, gentleness. I would call attention to
what this woman says of herself in her writings. She may
well forgive human failings, but she notes them. Her angle
of vision is acute."

I didn't respond.

Quincey ended our silence by saying, "Let us move on to
a supposal that you will find more congenial. Samuel Grant
is the guilty party. But first I must ask why you so dislike the
man. Simply his autocratic manner?"

Talking about Grant to Quincey as I lay on the bed, I'd

have said that my tone was objective. Apparently not. So I explained our history, careful to point out that my first impressions of him were made when I was a boy, that my suspicion of his cheating in regard to my dead father's share in their business wasn't based on any facts in my possession.

"Make the case against him as an arsonist."

"Profit would be the motive. If both the New Lebanon and Hancock seedhouses were destroyed when the harvest was just in, the Shakers would be hard put to fill their far-flung orders. So he'd be planning on doing just that very soon and couldn't take the chance of having a dog on the premises. He probably didn't come to the Shakers with the aim of ruining their business. He's been with them over two years. He may have only come briefly to see whether the community would accept Giles. Once on the scene, he may have recognized how very lucrative their market is. Now, Giles may have spoken to his father about dissatisfaction with his life here. If that were the case, Samuel Grant would put his plan into action and leave, planning on becoming an even richer man."

"And the son?"

Troubled, I shook my head. "Doctors don't seem able to describe Giles's condition, much less alleviate it, yet I think it belongs to their realm, rather than that of priests and ministers. Having said that, I must add that I don't know how it affects his mind."

Quincey nodded. "Let's put that aside and see Giles Grant simply as a young man, with the attendant desires, longings, hopes."

"That makes the analysis harder, not easier. With the Shakers, he's given acceptance and love. There are a few who can't manage that, but they say nothing to him. Because of his work—which he seems to enjoy—and his musical talent, he's regarded as a very useful member of the community. Where else would he find this? He's capable of deep attachments. Although he regards Elijah only as a friend, a brother, he shows real sensitivity to his feelings. Too, I'm afraid that any woman of his class would be unwilling to be Giles's wife. Under what circumstances could she learn to know him well enough to see past those external tics and flailings? She and her family would have to wonder if his condition would be passed on to any children. Once married, she'd be excluded from society. Giles must know this. Therefore, what hopes can he realistically have?"

"Then make the case that he is not realistic."

"Very well," I went on grudgingly. "Let's say that his father sees his future with clear eyes and has forced him to try the Shakers. Being young, he can't accept that this will be his present and his future. But he can't confront his father. It'd be better to be asked to leave under a cloud of suspicion than to stand up to that hard man. So he sets the New Lebanon Seedhouse on fire. Out of frustration. Philemon says that father and son came to Hancock because it was smaller, quieter. We don't know if that was the reason. Once in a new community, Giles sets more blazes. Perhaps now he's in love with the fire, the excitement it provides. He intends to continue because he sees the way he lives as dull, grinding imprisonment."

Grimacing, I threw up my hands. None of this sounded like the Giles I knew. "As for his ability to sing in French, and in a young woman's voice—" I stopped, unable to imagine how that was done.

"Yes." Quincey steepled his chunky fingers. "In his father's conversation with you in the Meetinghouse, he offered the most likely explanation. The question we can't answer is, of course, whether Giles did it consciously."

It was maddening. I hurriedly reviewed what Samuel Grant had said. All I recalled was that he'd asserted there was no way Giles could have learned the language. While I was girding up to ask Quincey what that explanation was, he asked me, "And Elijah? What would you say of him?"

I turned my thoughts that way. "He's in prison, too, but one with walls piled up stone by stone in his mind when he was young. He's trying to escape that jail of fear, terrified of the last days described in the Bible."

The corners of his mouth turned down, Quincey broke in. "You must tell Elijah to look again at Revelation 9:7. The locusts referred to are not necessarily the *size* of horses. The words in the King James Bible are these: 'And the shapes of the locusts were like unto horses prepared for battle.' Admittedly, if the locusts have teeth 'as the teeth of lions,' it is difficult to envision them as small insects."

That observation, in my view, was a definite digression, but I went on, "Elijah is imaginative, mercurial. During the fervor of the period they call Mother's Work, he was in his element. He could have been overwhelmed emotionally when it ended, I suppose, and started the fires. But poisoning—and the kind of planning required—that doesn't fit. I can well imagine him playing that trumpet—although how he got it up there I can't guess—but if it were he, his acting is as good as his playing. He seemed genuinely reassured by the idea that an angel appeared."

Quincey was silent for a moment. His ability to sit as unmoving as one of the very large lizards was noteworthy. Finally, he raised his heavy lids slightly. "I assume that all the others on your list would have the same motive, that is, preservation of the community or at least its higher principles. Therefore, I can't believe this person will stop. That would require a rethinking that would be too painful because of the two deaths. It would seem that none can be eliminated by lack of opportunity, with the possible exception of the deacon."

"But given what happened last night to Esau—"

"Mr. Merrick. We were speaking of opportunity. It is well to be thorough. You questioned this Issachar by whose bed he was reportedly praying the entire time before the assemblage on the mountain?"

I shifted on my chair in real irritation. This was another example of Quincey's checking on *my* thoroughness. Clearly whoever poisoned the dog poisoned Esau. "Yes, I did. The man was describing his constant and acute pain and it was not easy to ask whether he'd managed to doze off at all. But I did. Quite rightly, he merely stared at me for answer."

Quincey drummed his fingers on the table, saying, "I wonder if the deacon glanced out of Issachar's window that night. If he saw anyone out, did that person see the deacon?" He waved the question away.

"That leaves Thankful, Seth, Amos." Quincey's mouth quirked into what passed for a smile with him. "Amos. Now he has a nice Jesuitical turn of mind, unexpected in a blacksmith. I should like to hear one of his and Seth's exchanges, purely for the interest of it. However for these three, the original motive seems beyond reason, and therefore is beyond our understanding."

Now he wasn't smiling. "Elder Jacob. I have known him for some years. I find it impossible to imagine that he'd so underestimate me as to ask for my help, should he be guilty. Yet he's done something that puzzles me. He hasn't consulted with the Central Ministry on this problem. It's true that there was a serious fire in New Lebanon as well. He may trust no one and is therefore keeping absolutely silent. I applaud his keeping the community stable by giving the impression that Hepzibah's death was an accident. That, of course, could argue either guilt or common sense. Hysteria in a community like this would serve no purpose and would make it more difficult for us to find the answer. I wonder what approach he'll take to his brother's scrape with death. I'll talk to him this afternoon and observe his responses carefully. But, as Shakespeare noted, 'There is no art to find the mind's construction in the face.'"

Abruptly, he threw up his hands. "The timing of that trumpet player couldn't have been worse. Our murderer might see it as a sign of approval."

"I take it that you don't believe it was an angel," I said dryly.

He didn't bother to answer or look up. His eyelids had slid low again, as if all his energies were taken up in thinking and there were none left for any other purpose. After a time, he gave a minimal headshake. "I assume you didn't recognize the melody played on the trumpet."

I sat up. I hadn't thought of that. Mentally, I went back to that mountaintop. The clarity of those notes came to me, and the shining triumph of the sound. Against my will, I shivered at the memory. It seemed to me that even Quincey would have been moved, wouldn't have immediately assumed a talented mortal. But I didn't say that. "No. The arrangement eludes me. It didn't occur to me to ask if anyone knew the song, either."

"I can't see how it could help us if someone did. I was simply curious. Shaker music is original and there are quite a number of hymns and 'laboring' songs used in the dance service. There are as well short pieces sung by one member while the others rest between the dances. You'd not have heard all of these in the short time you've been here, or would not recall a given one if you had. Many new songs were apparently written during the period of Mother's Work, as they call it. They have their own system of notation so that all of them, even those uninstructed in the reading of music, can learn new ones rapidly."

He brooded a bit longer, then asked, "The boy, Crispin, is fond of the dog?"

"He's devoted to Hallelujah, and the dog to him. Why?"

"You eliminated him immediately, but I didn't. In fact, he'd be my first suspect, if I didn't tie the dog's poisoning to the fires. Crispin had opportunity. He's managed on at least one occasion to slip out of the Boys' House. He might've started the fires in his 'sleep-running' episodes, perhaps in some sort of semiconscious state. He's been badly abused. The effect of that is impossible to guess. On the night of Hepzibah's injury, he could've gone to the Seedhouse *before* awakening Mercy. Striking down the old woman is not beyond his strength. And wintergreen is a common liniment in horse barns. But if he is genuinely devoted to the dog—" He shrugged.

I just sat there. He suspected *Crispin.*

I remembered him standing beside me in the meeting room, one small hand near the platter of cookies and mint leaves, the other in mine. What kind of a bottle would oil of wintergreen be in? Could it be concealed in a pocket? But Crispin didn't, wouldn't. Not that there was any point in saying that to Quincey.

At last, he said, "I'll have to consider the next move." Almost as an afterthought, he added, "You needn't, of course, continue."

When I got my breath back, I brought out, trying to keep my voice a little steady, "You wish to dispense with my services in the investigation?"

"That is *not* what I said, sir. When you left Boston, I gave you a sum of money so that you could leave at any time. I recognized that, on arrival, you might not wish to pursue the problem here. That money is yours. It is ample. Then I hoped that there would be no threat to you. Now I am sure there is. You must decide if, being aware of the risk, you wish to go on. I'd be remiss if I didn't stress my conviction that the danger is real."

There was no hint in his voice that if I left, he felt he'd be hampered in solving the problem, no suggestion that he'd be pleased to have my help. But how could I leave my friends under the circumstances? How could I leave Crispin to his suspicions? How could I leave Esther at all?

I said, "I'll stay."

He stood up. "I should have my thoughts in order tomorrow. Please call here at this time unless I send a contrary message with Jacob."

Chapter Nineteen

Riding back into Hancock, I was boiling and Lightfoot's coat was steaming. The longer I thought of my conversation with Quincey, the more I seethed, and the faster I rode. I decided that he knew he needed me, but he wasn't going to admit it. No. That would be the straightforward thing to do, but it would put him under obligation, which he hated. It would also require that he admit he was not all sufficient in himself. Instead, he set it up so that not only would I stay, I would insist on doing so. He was just dangling evidence against Esther and Crispin in front of my nose. He couldn't honestly believe they were guilty.

I jumped from the saddle, pulled down the reins, and stalked toward the horse barn, tugging Lightfoot behind me. I was almost at the open door when the question returned. Or did Quincey believe it?

He was prepared to believe it. Of course he was. Even I couldn't keep the fog of suspicion from slipping under the tightly shut doors of my mind. Nothing could keep it out and it would poison as it spread through the village, harming the innocent. And it would spread.

The next thought kept me frozen outside the barn door, suddenly very cold. Crispin was the most vulnerable of all.

Only Quincey and I shared the theory that the other events were connected with the fires. No one in the community knew that the berries had been fed to Hallelujah and only four were aware that Hepzibah's death was no accident. In a few days, Esau's illness would be accepted as a stomach upset. But everyone in the village knew about the fires and everyone was terrified of another explosion of flames.

It was not only the loss of their long days in the fields harvesting the seeds and the lost profits. There was the wildness of fire, its uncontrollable force consuming the safe world they'd built, reminding them how fragile its wooden walls were. And every human knows the pain of the slightest touch of fire on the skin. Who imagines a hell without flames?

The Shakers were right to fear. I'd never had a dream about fire, or if I had, even my memory recoiled from it. Imagining it during the day was all the horror I needed. Tongues of fire greedily licking the walls of the house I grew up in—the sight of that was imprinted on my eyes and I hadn't seen it. I never heard the frantic cries of my mother and my sister that rang in my ears.

Pressing my eyes with my left finger and thumb, I did what I always did—and refused to think about it. The thought already on my mind was disturbing enough.

Because they didn't know Quincey's ideas on the coolheaded arsonist, the community would look at those whose behavior seemed odd. Giles had already suffered sidelong looks, but he had Elijah as a witness to his whereabouts at night. Once it was common knowledge that Crispin had slipped out alone more than once, heads would turn in his direction, whispers follow him.

The elders would have to take action, perhaps send him to another village, a very small one where he could be constantly watched, one whose seedhouse didn't serve the huge Boston market and ship from its docks. Send him away from the first home he'd found, away from Mercy, Esther, Hallelujah.

Esther was safe. Many knew she'd been out at various times looking for Hepzibah, but no one would glance at her, respected as she was. She didn't need my protection. Cris did.

Even Quincey had said that it was only our theory, a tissue of ideas, that kept him from looking sharply at the boy. The arsonist had to be found and right away.

Now I was sweating again. But standing there, I had a surprising feeling, and it was comforting, I wasn't alone in the search. There was Quincey. He'd seen things I hadn't. I didn't have to *like* him to work with him. I would do that. As I walked slowly into the barn, it occurred to me that this was the first time I hadn't felt alone in more years than I could recall.

I saw in the first stall inside a perilously small hand holding an enormous hoof up for inspection. Looking up at my arrival, Mercy gently set down the horse's leg and came forward. Over her dress, she was wearing an adult's much-creased leather blacksmith's apron that came down to her hem, and half of her fine hair had escaped from the starched cap on her head. The plaster cast on her arm was almost as black as the apron. Hallelujah came trotting out behind her, giving only a quiet wuff of welcome. He knew how to behave around horses.

She was smiling at me until her gaze fell on Lightfoot. "You musta been in an all-fired hurry," she said matter-of-factly. "I'd best walk him about a bit to cool off before givin' him water." Guiltily, I lifted off the heavy saddle and by the time I returned from putting it in the tack room, Mercy had already replaced the bridle with a rope and was leading Lightfoot in a wide circle on the grass. She barely reached the animal's shoulder. The size differential made me uneasy.

Putting out my hand for the rope, I offered, "Let me do that, Mercy. Lightfoot is a high-bred horse and spooks easily."

With an assured gesture, she waved me off with a grubby hand. "Oh, he's a bit nervy, but if you pat him nice and talk to him sweet, he comes along. And Hallelujah's a big help." Hearing his name, the dog cocked his one upright ear and looked alert, ready to do his duty, if we could just make clear to him what that was. "Has somethin' to do with his bein' a yaller dog. Always calm they are, I notice, not jumpin' and yappin'. He lays right down in the stall and the horses like that, havin' him there. Company while they eat, I s'pose. Besides, the more for me to do, the better. The boys are still harvestin' and when Brother Seth showed up at the School-house and ast for me, I was right pleased. All that readin' makes your head ache." I remembered that Shaker girls

were taught full-time in the summer, the boys in the winter.
She went on fervently, "I'm hopin' he'll need me tomorrow,
too."

"Where's Cris working?"

"He's in the fields. He's gotten good at drivin' the horses
that pull the hay wagon. He gets 'em in the right place for
the bales to be loaded. All proud of hisself settin' up there
behind those big horses. And sittin' down so much don't tire
his leg out. The nurse sisters rub it good three, four times a
week, but they say he needs a metal brace on it to get it better. And Brother Amos, he sez he kin make him a good 'un.
But Cris's got his face set dead agin it. Thinks it'd slow him
more'n he is already. They're kinda waitin' to see if he'll
come round, I guess."

I said, as if the thought just struck me, "You know, I was
talking to Brother Jeb at the Boys' House about whether Cris
had nightmares since Hepzibah was hurt." Jeb was a cheerful, round-faced youth still in his teens, barely taller than
some of his charges, who slept in the House at night. He
seemed able to keep order with humor and patience, and I'd
judged he did a better job than an older brother who might
have been irritated by the noise and exuberance around him.
"Has Cris ever said whether he gets out at night very often
when he's doing his sleep-running?"

She thought that over as she paced in the circle. "Wa'al,
he's in the bed right next to Jeb, but Jeb, he sleeps hard
sometimes, I guess. Once Cris showed me a place way down
behind the Ice House and signed that he'd woke up there and
nary an idea how he got there. Hurried right back to bed and
me was all he told about it. He wouldn't want to get Jeb in
trouble or nuthin'. But that was when he first come and he
ain't said it happens reg'lar like."

"I wish you would ask him if those nightmares trouble
him often."

She nodded, accepting my interest as friendly concern.
Then with her eyes on the ground, she said, "Elder Jacob,
when he was talkin' about heaven, he mentioned some birds,
but he didn't say nuthin' about dogs or horses bein' up there.
Do you think they go there, too?"

I dodged that for fear of saying the wrong thing. "If I were you, I'd talk to Sister Esther about that."

"I did," she answered. Her almost-blue eyes, with lashes so thin they might have been drawn with a pencil, sought mine. "She said 'zactly this: 'Everyone is happy in heaven, and all that they need to be happy is there.' So I'd have all my animal friends with me." Mercy repeated the words as she'd memorized them, in the speaker's voice. I could hear Esther's quiet reassurance. "But once I heerd the deacon say animals din't have no souls. Now, you talk like you had a fair bit of schoolin' and you'd know about the soul part."

For all I knew I was denying the arguments of whole schools of philosophy, but I replied firmly, "Animals have animal souls."

She looked up at me, her brow clearing. "They must," she agreed and stopped long enough to scratch behind Hallelujah's ears thoroughly. "Prob'ly the deacon was talkin' about people souls. Same kind of thing, I reckon. It's important 'cuz when I was listenin' to the elder yesterday, I started thinkin' about goin' to heaven myself and whether I'd like it. Didn't think so, but see, I have to go. That's where Maw must be. I been sayin' and sayin' she was comin' fer me someday, but she was right sick. And it's been a real long time. She'd have come by now if she could. I could see how much she'd like those white houses and havin' everythin' so clean and nice, with nuthin' to do but rest, and I'm glad she's there. When I tole Cris last night, he was real pleased fer her, too. More'n that, he's been worryin' that I might go off with Maw if she came here. I been tellin' him he could come, too. Maw wanted a boy. I heerd Paw tell her she couldn't do nuthin' right, only one child and that a girl. But, not knowin' Maw, Cris wasn't sure she'd take him along. It'd be hard for him here, not havin' anyone to talk fer him."

"More than that, Mercy. You're his friend and he'd miss *you* very much."

She kept walking and finally said, "He would. Mebbe not so much as he'd miss Hallelujah if the elders say he's got to go, but some. I'd miss him. I 'spect that's why I wanted him to come along if I went. He's a boy, but he's not like most, plaguin' you, tryin' to pull off your cap when no one's lookin', actin' the fool. Better'n most of the girls at make-up games, too. Goes right along. Ain't allus sayin' that 'you cain't be doin' this' and 'you cain't be doin' that' and worryin' about gettin' dirty."

Stopping, she eyed the horse critically. "I kin wipe him down now and all. You kin go about your business." With that, she marched off with Lightfoot and Hallelujah right behind her.

I was neglecting my work in the fields, but no one would know what my rotation was with the deacon in the Nurse House. That's where I headed. Esau was the one I wanted to see.

Mercy hadn't mentioned his rush from the room, but the children had left before it happened. If it was discussed in front of them, no doubt they would have been told he'd been taken ill with a stomach problem. I hoped his health would be improving, which would raise my spirits, but the question Quincey brought up regarding what he might have seen from Issachar's window was in my mind. Even if I had the opportunity, I couldn't imagine how to ask without causing him to fret about such an inquiry. I was sure that, like the rest of the community, Esau believed Hepzibah had hit her head by accident. Ailing the deacon might be, but he was an infinitely curious man.

When I went into the long shaded room, Sister Agatha was making up a bed by the door and I pointed at the deacon lying in the one across from us and raised my eyebrows in question. In an undertone, she answered, "He's some better, but he's not to be talking. His throat is red and quite raw. When Elder Jacob was here this morning, I told him that as well, but Brother Esau insisted on trying to speak to him. I know what a conscientious man the deacon is, and I'm sure that he has community matters on his mind and he'd like them seen to. But they will have to wait. Finally, I had to usher the elder out. If Brother Esau tries to talk, I'll do the same to you." Agatha had a soft voice but it had a firm edge. "Now, I noticed him stirring a bit, and you can raise him up and I'll see if he'll swallow some tea."

She went to the wall of small cabinets of butternut wood and opened a drawer, carefully counting some seeds into a porcelain bowl. I approached the bed. Esau's face was as bleached as the pillowslip, and while he'd had little spare flesh before, now it was stretched so taut that he seemed all nose. His ears stuck sadly through the thin strands of gray hair on the sides of his face. His eyes were closed, but one thin hand plucked at the sheet over his chest as if to throw it off.

I couldn't like the man, but it was painful to see him so. His wintry face had the look of Death. And that vulture Guilt gnawed at my liver.

Agatha was grinding the seeds finely with a pestle. She measured some into a cup, added liquid from a pitcher, and came up. The cup smelled of something sweetly green. Setting it on the table, she leaned near the sick man and said quietly, "Brother Esau, we're going to lift your head and I want you to try to drink a little willow tea with honey. It will soothe your throat."

He opened his eyes, looking irritated, but he glanced at her and then at me and raised a finger in agreement. I slid my right arm under his shoulders and put my left hand under his head. The bones there felt bare, without protection. Agatha held the cup to his lips with a cloth beneath his chin. It was a wise precaution. Most of the liquid dribbled from his mouth. "Try again," she ordered. This time he managed to swallow although his brows knotted in pain. "Just a bit more," she persuaded. After that, he pressed his head against my hand decisively, and I let him lie back in the pillows.

Setting the cup down, she returned to the cabinets. As soon as her back was turned, Esau's hand shot out and closed over my arm, pulling me down. I knelt beside his bed so I could hear. "Not an accident," he rasped. His eyes went to the nurse resentfully. "Wouldn't let me tell Jacob. You do it."

"I will." I mumbled the next sentence in his ear as if I were whispering prayers in case Agatha turned. It seemed better to let him talk than fret. "What makes you think so?"

He held up both hands, indicating with his thumbs and

forefingers two different sizes, emphasizing something was small and something large. It took me a minute.

"Ah. You mean the containers for the two oils are much different sizes. No one would mix them up. The peppermint was in a bigger bottle; the wintergreen in a small one."

His eyes sharpened in surprise at my knowing what oils he referred to, and he nodded with some vigor. His voice sounded as if someone had a firm grip on his throat. "Maybe not for me." His bony finger pointed at me.

"Because we were nearest?" He moved his head forward slowly in discouraged agreement.

Agatha turned slightly and glanced at us. I raised my voice, invoking Mother Ann's help in curing our brother, before whispering, "Do you have any idea why anyone would want to do that to either of us?"

His shoulders hitched slightly and his eyes roamed the room hopelessly, as if he'd turned that thought around without any conclusion. He grimaced in pain as he tried to swallow so he could speak again. His next words were barely audible. "Go. Now. Not New Lebanon. Further." He waved his left hand urgently to indicate both haste and distance. The cold, dry fingers of his right hand again clutched my wrist. "Canterbury." He seemed to relax slightly at the thought of the New Hampshire community as a haven for me.

"I'll speak to the elder today."

He held on to me, insisting on my agreement to what he'd just proposed. I added, "I'll seek his counsel on all you've said."

Esau withdrew his hand and closed his eyes as if satisfied. I stood up, raised my hand in farewell to Agatha, and left. The Infirmary's coolness made the August heat outside stupefying, but I hurried toward the offices in the Meetinghouse.

Just as I approached the door, Elder Jacob came out. After greeting me, he announced, "I am on my way to see Jasper Quincey. You've already talked?"

I fell into step beside him. "Yes. Then I stopped at the Nurse House and saw Esau." I delivered the message, observing him as I did so. Jacob's smooth, full face shrunk at my words and his likeness to his brother became obvious for a moment. He lifted one shoulder uneasily, then replied, "I can see why Esau is sure that it was deliberate. The two bottles would be impossible to mix up and only the large ones would ever be taken to the kitchen. The sisters use a fair amount of peppermint oil, especially in baking. Sister Bertha checked everything in the kitchen as soon as we realized what had happened, but there wasn't a trace of the wintergreen oil she smelled on the leaves that Esau knocked from your hand. I ask myself if it was an attempt to *poison,* that is, to cause real injury or death."

"What else could it be?"

"You know, Esau is very stern with the young brothers, lecturing them harshly on small faults. More than once I've reminded him of a few of the pranks of our youth. Perhaps remembering them, and being unable to forgive himself, despite the insignificance of them, is the reason he scolds. In any case, one of the boys might have considered that a few drops of liniment, always available in the barn, on a leaf— everyone knows Esau chews them regularly—would give *him* an unpleasant moment. Children can be thoughtlessly cruel, but whoever did it would not have realized how toxic wintergreen is. Certainly I don't remember being told myself."

"But the oil would be diluted in the liniment, wouldn't it? To cause such a reaction in Esau, it would seem the stronger essence must have been used."

He groped for his handkerchief, took off his hat, patted at the heavy sweat on his bald head, and sighed. "No doubt you're right. I've never had the intense interest others here have in herbs. I can see that I wish to believe that this is not part of the evil that is surrounding us, and that fathered the thought."

Jacob's lips were thin and straight, like his twin's. A smile almost hovered on them. "Jasper will know how much, how much exactly, was used on the leaves. I have never had a question he could not answer. He'll certainly tell me. He has the habit of telling your rather more than you asked, doesn't he? Sometimes I think he uses words as barriers rather than as bridges to another. He likes to keep life at one remove. But I cherish his friendship—it's rare. It's astonishing that he'd come, and yet it doesn't surprise me."

We were at the barn and he stopped before going in. "It's hard for me to get my mind around our problem because we elders are so isolated from the community. We spend a great deal of our time working together, not with all our brothers and sisters. As you know, we even eat in a separate room. It's necessary to maintain this distance, but one misses so much that might suggest an answer. I can see why Jacob asked for your help. You see the feelings of others, and are able to hear what is *not* being said. Tonight at the Union Meeting you will have an opportunity to put your skills to work."

"Union Meeting?" I asked.

"Odd how I forget what a short time you've been here, Michael. Once a week we hold these. Since the harvest is tiring, I felt a rest would be good for all today. The brothers and sisters sit across from each other and talk about community interests. The Central Ministry recognizes that we have no social occasions. One could hardly consider the dancing service that, and there is very little opportunity for the two groups to meet since most of the time their work is separate. The Union Meeting is an attempt to address this in a proper setting."

Now Jacob did smile. "We Believers are warned often of the 'party spirit' that would encourage too much closeness between the sexes. However, I have sat at many a Union Meeting wishing for just a half cupful of that spirit. The brothers and sisters are age-paired and most stiffly exchange remarks on how many bushels of corn were picked that day or how many jars of beets were pickled. However, at the end, the kitchen sisters bring in popcorn and taffy. There is more general talk. What I'd like to know is if there is a feeling of dis-ease throughout the village, or if only the few of us feel it. You will, of course, be observing individuals. Tell me about the atmosphere."

As he turned to go into the barn, I was thinking how likable Jacob was. He had the pleasant habit of complimenting you by stating the remark as a fact. The Bible describes another Jacob as a "smooth man." I was also wondering if his words were an effort to smooth over my suspicions of him.

Chapter Twenty

Samuel Grant's thick shoulders and broad back were directly in front of me as we marched to the Union Meeting, people falling in line in pairs after their evening chores. Philemon's wide-brimmed hat dipped toward Grant as they talked. Just ahead of them, Esther walked quietly with Agatha. Amos, beside me, was grumbling, "Ah'm tellin' you, it don't fail to happen. On Meetin' Night, ever' time, Seth's got a sick animal and so he's not goin' be comin'. Ah was there in the fields and saw that horse a-pullin' the wagon step on the scythe. Where a scythe had no call to be. Sliced its leg. That's true. Seth even had me a-lookin' at the cut. It was bad but there's no call for him to be sittin' in the barn with the fool horse. Excuse not to come, is what it is."

Scratching the back of his bristly neck in irritation, he fell into silence. I wasn't able to hear him anyway. My feelings were shouting in my ears. Barely a week ago, sitting at my desk in Boston, I'd thought every emotion was dead—except for the brief flare of anger. I'd been wrong. They'd just been asleep and now their renewed power hit me with full force. I was desperate with longing for Esther, anxious with fear for Cris, and choked with rage at the sight of Samuel Grant.

I could hear his conversation, and because I wanted the smallest piece of evidence against him, I listened. He was saying, "As you know, the work involved in tanning hides is hard for the youngest brother. Pulling the wet skins from one vat to another, hoisting them to the next floor for scraping and smoothing and then to the attic for drying is backbreaking." Philemon nodded. Almost as an afterthought, Grant added, "Even after soaking, rinsing, and leaching, animal hides have a very bad odor. It stays in your nostrils for days."

At this, it occurred to me that while Grant was now a trustee, when he first joined he must have been put on the regular work rotation. I had a vivid picture of him, straining muscles unused for years, hauling on the windlass that drew the sodden hides in a crate to the upper floor. And then there was that smell. My satisfaction at the whole idea knew no bounds.

"But," he continued, "I've discovered that we take in over three thousand dollars annually from our tanning house, as well as being able to make the leather for our shoes, harnesses, and hats. That's a substantial amount. And there's no question that the facilities here for doing the work are excellent. So I'm looking at other areas in order to see how we could increase profits by buying rather than making."

I ground my teeth. In my past association with him, I'd seen how high the cost of profits was. Philemon's answer was too low to be heard, but Grant's next point was very clear. It wasn't spoken in his usual clipped style, which gave the impression of orders being issued. He drew his words out carefully, almost as if he were trying them out to see if they would do on some future occasion. "As I pointed out to the deaconess today, it isn't engraved on tablets that we must make everything we use. It was once necessary, but no longer. Organizations age as people do; some remain vital in their thinking, some do not. Leaders who are capable of considering innovation must be chosen."

As he made that point, Grant chopped the air decisively. He expanded again at some length on the qualities needed in Shaker elders. I thought that over. Was he angling for the position? He did spend a great deal of time in New Lebanon, and he was the sort only satisfied with the highest position in any group.

By then we'd arrived at the meeting room, and Philemon seated himself across from Esther, leaning forward as he greeted her. My heart sunk. The pairings were supposed to be by age and I'd been planning on that chair. She was next to the deaconess, and there was an empty chair in the brothers' row opposite Thankful. As I hung my hat on a peg and approached, she beamed at me and made a small gesture toward it. Samuel Grant took his place across from Bertha.

As I was about to sit down, Philemon looked up and said, "But this won't do, Brother Michael. I'd be violating the spirit of the evening by drawing Sister Esther into business discussions. You sit here. I have little opportunity, in the general way, of speaking with the deaconess." So saying, he moved over one chair. I have never liked a man so much. Thankful's fleshy cheeks seemed to deflate as her smile faded.

It was the first time that I'd seen Esther since my talk with Quincey. "More love, sister," I said in greeting. She glanced up briefly, but when she returned my words, her gaze went back to the folded hands in her lap. Her calm demeanor truly disappointed me. Even though I'd been practicing that appearance myself, it seemed impossible to me that she didn't feel the force of my emotion, no matter how well hidden, and respond to it. Such an attitude on my part was beyond reason. I was conscious of that without being able to change it. I couldn't get either my mind or my heart to obey orders.

I didn't want her to look up. This way I could stare at her. Had she slept as she sat, I'd have been happy. Her dark dress, whose style dated to the eighteenth century when the Shaker elders decided that to keep up with change was vanity, gave her an old-fashioned air. The pale glow of her hair shone through her neat transparent cap. I recalled from some long-ago art lecture that the ideal of beauty in medieval times dictated ash blond hair and gray eyes. But those artists painted a woman as an icon, invariably oval-faced, narrow-lipped, the Madonna or a saint. The individual woman was not there at all. Esther could never have been the model, despite her coloring. Too much strength in her face. And the full mouth contradicted the ascetic eyes.

Quincey was, I knew, right about my feeling for her.

It occurred to me that I had to say something, for propriety's sake, or I couldn't continue looking at her. What came out was my first thought. "Sometimes my night dreams are so real that when I awaken, I'm disoriented and can't recognize my surroundings. That might be due to an unfamiliar room, but I remember that happening when I was young and slept each night in the same bed. Have you ever had that sensation?"

If she found that an odd topic of conversation, neither her words nor her face reflected it. "Oh, yes." She looked up but not at me. "In the case of a nightmare, I am certainly relieved. But when the dream springs from memory, my disappointment is awful."

So, she must visit that white house at night as well as during the day. I didn't comment, instead asking, "Do you suppose that a dream could be so powerful that one could get up and respond to what one saw in the mind, without being aware of it?"

An uneasy fear flashed across her face. "Children are given to doing that. Or so I—" She didn't finish that sentence. "At least they've been known to run from what they picture, if it terrifies them. But in dreams one often can't run, try as one will, and if in reality one *cannot* do so—"

She stopped, but she didn't have to continue. Cris was in her thinking, too. Intent, intense, I questioned, "What might he do? Relieve the fear by doing something he'd never do if fully conscious?"

She met my gaze. "He can neither run nor cry out."

What came to me was what Quincey had circled around. Cris wouldn't harm Hallelujah, as I'd said, but he could have set the fires, struck Hepzibah, poisoned Esau. Supposing he'd tried to awaken Mercy and failed and then gone to the Seedhouse alone. Finding Hepzibah leaning over the dog, he misunderstood, picked up a board— No.

I don't know if I said the word aloud. At the same moment, she shook her head, saying, "We'd have to believe there are two Crispins. The day Cris and the night Cris—two very different boys." She shook her head even more firmly. We were still looking at each other, agreeing. And so we sat, for a long moment. I couldn't look away, and she didn't.

In our silence, other conversations filled the void.

Bertha's words to Samuel Grant were clear. "So much

milk and cream we're swimmin' in it. Mind you, there's
more uses to it than you'd have thought. At first, we'd just
add the cream sauce to the dried winter vegetables like corn
and peas to plump them up. Then we found how tasty the
sauce was with all sorts—parsnips, beets, turnips, aspara-
gus. The children, the brothers, ate them right up. And
whipped cream biscuits. Still, I don't see how you could get
it to Boston without it spoilin'. But in the winter, the butter
could go on the train. And eggs, now. Plenty of those. If you
packed them in coarse rock salt, small end down, making
sure they're not touching, mind, seems to me they'd get
there fresh."

Agatha remarked to Amos, "He is better but the deacon is
not one to take illness lying down. He says he must use the
time profitably and insists on sitting up and writing. Then,
he is too modest to use the chamber pot and must pull on his
trousers and boots and go out to use the privy. I warn him
that his recovery will be postponed by . . ."

On the other side, Thankful could be heard, as she said to
Philemon, "I know the brothers say that it's helpful to have
the dog rounding up the cows, but *you* must see that it only
encourages laziness since they themselves are quite able
to . . ."

Esther and I remained still, our eyes on each other. I remember thinking that the long arch of her brows echoed the
curves of her cheekbones. The rest of the time I didn't think.
Finally, in some desperation, she looked at the wall above
me and said, "This long dry spell must be good for the haying."

I believe we stayed on that topic for some time. Nor, try
as I would, could I again catch her glance.

Near the end of the hour, Bertha bent forward to say to
Grant, "Jars of pickled lily. Now that's a thought. Doesn't
cost us at all, except for the jars. We could make more of it,
using as we do the vegetables that are good but not perfect.
Squash too big, thinnish snap beans, green pepper a bit
wrinkled, last of the carrots. Put them in cider vinegar with
the onions and herbs and they make a very nice winter rel-
ish. City folks would buy, I'm certain."

Then, because of a higher pitch and a querulous tone, Thankful's voice intruded. ". . . dog simply alone in the field, not a bird to be seen, and barking so loudly that it disturbed the peace of the *entire* village. When I pointed out the dog's behavior to Brother Seth, he actually said to me that maybe he was keeping away the demons that he could sense and we could not! As if any rational person could be persuaded that a creature of the lower orders was capable of such a thing. Seth has become fond of the animal and wishes to overlook what is clearly written down. There should be no question. The Laws say we do not keep dogs. Now *some,* who are after all newcomers, may say that we must be flexible about rules, but there are reasons for them."

Although it was Philemon she was facing, her angry glances darting down the row were clearly aimed at Samuel Grant. "As for implying that one's *age* means that one's thinking has become hardened, or that one should be disqualified for leadership, a trusteeship for example, on that ground, that is absurd."

Philemon hastened to murmur that he himself was appointed when he was in his fifties and that she must have misunderstood whoever was speaking to her. But Thankful would not be stopped. I remembered Philemon telling me that she very much wanted to be an office sister. I also recalled Samuel Grant's conspicuous lack of tact in speaking to Esau the day I arrived. I could imagine how his words to the deaconess earlier in the day might have sounded to her.

Her heavy pear-shaped face became redder, making the bristles of white hair on her chin more noticeable. She could never have been pretty, and it would have been clear to her early on how that would affect her choices in life. Now she was slipping into a genderlessness that was no kinder to her features. As she continued speaking, she dashed away a tear at the corner of her eye with the heel of her hand.

Then I was ashamed at the narrow way I judged her. I saw the well of pain that Thankful's words were drawn from. Perhaps love makes us more empathetic to all others. What Thankful's passions might drive her to, I wasn't sure of.

Her voice went up a notch. "To venture into the new and

untried is not wise. To Make Remarks," Thankful was obviously capitalizing those words, "about people's age and suggest that they are unfit to lead because they don't go for all the new fangles—" She stopped, gulping for breath.

Bertha rose and made her solid way down the aisle, turning to face the group. One of her work-roughened hands rested on Thankful's shoulder as she said comfortably, "Everyone knows that those whom an angel calls are fit to lead, Sister, in whatever capacity they are chosen for. Now, we'd best get to the kitchen before those young sisters eat all the corn they've been poppin'. We'll bring it out. There's some gingerade and just-pulled taffy, too."

She waited for Thankful, whose face was calming even as she got up. With some dignity, she straightened her neckerchief and smoothed her skirt. Lifting her chin, she turned to follow Bertha. Esther slipped behind them quickly as they went toward the door. There was a tight set to her back.

I knew she wouldn't return, and she didn't.

Chapter Twenty-one

On my way outside, I passed through the kitchen—Esther was not there, either—and stepped into the softness of the August night. The bellied moon, just past full, hung low and pale, in no hurry to climb the sky. It lighted the village without dimming the high stars. The smallest possible breeze freshened the still, warm air. Crickets chirped their satisfaction with it all.

To waste such a night on sleep was pointless, even if I believed, which I didn't, that going upstairs, putting on a nightshirt, and stretching out on the bed would end in that result. Love, as the poets had it, made you dreamy and languid, but I'd never felt more awake. I was invigorated by my thoughts of Esther. Recalling our wordless talk, as we looked at each other, I was convinced she felt exactly as I did. I couldn't be mistaken.

Exhilarated by that hope, the idea that all things were possible, I paced down the pathway, around the orchard, and back again. Admittedly, an observer would have assumed my wanderings were aimless.

There was no hurry. The Union Meeting had not yet broken up. The smell of butter-drenched popcorn drifted from the windows of the lighted room. Even after I heard the cheerful hum of voices end, the sound of the chairs being hung up, I strolled on, enjoying my idleness. In a Shaker village, that was the true guilty luxury. Besides, Quincey was no doubt working—putting his thoughts in order. He hadn't asked me to do the same, and I didn't see any way to do it.

When I found myself back at the door of the Living Quarters, I could see that the candles had been collected. The upper floors were dark. Still, I couldn't make myself go in. Wheeling about, determined to at least go past the Trustees' Building, I almost ran into Brother Jeb. Or he into me. He pulled up short, breathless, worry lines wrinkling his young forehead. He swallowed, and gasped out, "He isn't in bed again. Cris, I mean. My fault. We'll have to get some of the brothers, mount a search." With that he started to push past me.

"Wait." I caught his arm. "There might be a faster way. We'll get Hallelujah."

"Oh, do you think? I mean, is he that kind of dog? Can they all kind of sniff a trail—"

"I don't know," I answered truthfully. "But organizing people takes time, too." I did believe that. There'd be the necessity of wakening them, finding lamps and torches, sending the men in all four directions, making clear that buildings would have to be gone through.

Jeb's freckled face was bleak. "It's late. I'm thinkin' he might have gone anywhere. To the mill pond and fallen in. Don't know if he can swim, don't know where to start—"

I was pushing him back in the direction of the Boys' House, telling him to get Cris's shirt for Hallelujah to smell. "If the dog doesn't set right off, you can go back and get the brothers and I'll keep going with him. Wait here, I'll be right back."

With the image of the black waters of that deep pond in my mind, I raced toward the Seedhouse. Cris might well have gone in any direction, limping crazily in his sleep, running from the demons in his mind. And what might he do in that state? Try as I would, I couldn't stop myself from looking at each darkened building that I passed, afraid to see a bright shoot of fire, a thin column of smoke. Even as I did so, I denied every glance.

Yanking open the door of the mud room, I startled a loud bark out of Hallelujah. But that immediately turned into loud snuffles of happiness at the unexpected company. I opened the interior door of the Seedhouse to see if the dog showed any interest in going there. He would have if Cris were inside. But Hallelujah didn't even glance that way.

The window's square of moonlight hit the wall and I groped for the piece of rope hanging there on its peg. I jabbered to him as I looped it around his neck. "Hallelujah, we have to find him right away. Cris. We have to find Cris. Think."

Somehow my words caused a stirring in my mind. *Think. Where is he?* But I couldn't see how I could possibly know that. An idea stirred. Someone had said something. Something at the meeting tonight. It'd made me think of Cris. It wasn't Esther. Who was it? What was the remark? It was no use. I couldn't remember.

Hallelujah heard the urgency in my voice, but he kept hampering my efforts to put on the rope by licking my hands. Perhaps he was trying to reassure me. Once outside, he was all business, half-pulling me as we ran back to the Boys' House.

Jeb was holding a small white shirt, almost dancing with impatience. "I should go now to get the brothers, right? You take the dog and I'll—"

I snatched the shirt, kneeling down, holding it in front of the dog's nose. "Give him a chance." I thought of the noise and lights of the searchers awakening Cris if he'd fallen asleep in some building, frightening him. And then *everyone* would know that he was sometimes out at night.

Hallelujah made all the right moves. He buried his nose in the shirt, lifted it, and started making small circles near the doorstep, then widening these. He set off slowly to the south toward the round stone barn, keeping his nose very low to the ground.

Jeb kept trying to hurry ahead and I was afraid he might be leading the dog. In an effort to keep him by my side, I asked, "What woke you?"

He hung his head a little. "One of the small boys havin' a bad dream. He was right scared—said he seen a dead white face at the window and he yelled out loud. Otherwise, I'm not sure I'd've stirred all night. Sometimes I don't. Mebbe I could rig up somethin'—put a rope on my arm and Cris's?"

"You might wake up every time he turned over."

"I don't care. Least I'd know where he was. And see, it

wouldn't be good if the Elders know about him gettin' out. I
like bein' the night caretaker. The boys make you laugh with
what all they get up to, puttin' off bedtime. *And* it gets you
out of mornin' and evenin' chores. Plus a lot of that meetin'
stuff."

Brushing pale reddish hair from his brow, he asked hesitantly, "If I promise to figure somethin' out, and we find him
right off, could we kinda not mention he was out?"

Hallelujah was moving ahead fairly briskly toward the
round barn, only stopping now and then to sniff the grass. I
worried that he might be going that way because he thought
it was morning and time to milk the cows. But I only said to
Jeb, responding to his question, "*Good* idea."

Just then, the dog veered off toward the horse barn and
now didn't stop at all. It came back to me. Hallelujah was
right. That's where the boy would be. Amos had said one of
the haying wagon horses had stepped on a scythe. Cris was
the driver. He might have thought the accident was his fault.
Awake or asleep, that was on his mind. It was all I could do
now to keep from hurrying ahead of the dog, but I wanted to
be sure.

When we were almost at the door, we saw the flicker of
flame deep inside the barn reflected on the window next to
the heavy barred outer door.

I forgot entirely about the smaller side door. With shaking
hands, I shoved up the bar and threw one side of the main
door open. Jeb and I rushed in, but Hallelujah squirted
through our legs and raced ahead. We ran down the open
area between the stalls as surprised horses lifted their heads
and stared over the partitions. One, perhaps more easily startled, reared twice.

Not until we'd almost reached the end did we see that the
flame was enclosed in a kerosene lamp on the floor. Its light
showed Cris's small form curled up on the straw just outside
the last stall. Hearing the thud of our boots, he rolled over,
half-sitting, struggling fiercely to get up. Even in that dimness, I could see the terrible fear on his face.

Then Hallelujah put two front paws firmly on his chest
and licked both cheeks. Cris fell back on the straw and by

the time I knelt beside him, he had his thin arms wrapped around the dog's neck.

Jeb crouched beside me, and with as much lightness as I could muster, I said, "Cris, we were wondering where you'd got to."

Still hanging on to Hallelujah, Cris sat up and looked around as if he were wondering, too. Then he glanced round behind him. The horse in that stall, chewing hay, looked back calmly and then dipped his head for more. His right foreleg was heavily wrapped. Cris pointed at it, his mouth twisting.

"The brother who left the scythe out is to blame, not you," I said. "And Seth's taken care of that cut. Now that you've seen everything's all right, how about going back to bed?"

Cris nodded slowly. Jeb spun around in his crouch, his sturdy back to the boy, saying, "Then I'll be the horse. You climb up, close your eyes, and the next thing you know it'll be morning."

It was only as I bent down to pick up the lamp that I noticed its position. Almost hidden, tilting crazily on a pile of straw, it was inches from the horse's huge hind hoof. One twitch of the animal's leg and it would have gone flying, its glass splintering. And there was a strong smell of leaking kerosene.

Cris's eyes widened as he saw the lamp's location. I shrugged as easily as I could. "You were half-asleep or you would have remembered to hang it up. No harm done." To reassure myself that was true, I wanted to lift him, put my arms around him. Instead, I reached out and tousled his hair.

He clambered on Jeb's back. I picked up the lamp, my fingers touching the cool glass as I reached for Hallelujah's rope. I followed them out, noticing along the way that the side door was slightly ajar. No doubt that was how Cris had come in. I pulled it to and watched as he turned to wave at me. Hallelujah reached up to lick at his bare foot, dangling beside Jeb's hip. The young brother was true to his word—they galloped off.

It was only after I'd turned off the flame, replaced the

lamp, shut and barred the double door, and headed back toward the Seedhouse that the thought struck me.

The lamp's glass was cool. If Cris had turned it on soon as he arrived, it would certainly have been warm. The flame must have been lit only moments before we arrived.

That made no sense, unless Cris was feigning sleep when we hurried in. I remembered vividly his confused, frightened expression. No.

If I mentioned all this to Quincey, he'd believe Cris was pretending and that he was there to . . . No. There was no need to bring it up.

Giving Hallelujah a thorough head scratch for his good work, I shut the Seedhouse door firmly behind me.

Chapter Twenty-two

I didn't go directly back to the Living Quarters. I was hungry. Perhaps if I hadn't been, it wouldn't have happened.

I wouldn't have seen her. In other circumstances, I would have accepted what she said. Perhaps.

But that I was out at all was the result of what had happened earlier. If a small boy hadn't dreamed a face at a window and awakened Jeb; if Jeb hadn't caught me at the door and instead aroused the brothers— The conviction stays with me that it was bound to happen, no matter the circumstances, despite the odds.

In any case, I went to the orchard for a Jonathan apple. The moonlight silvered the shining leaves with a glaze, as of ice, but the smell of ripe fruit belonged to the summer night. Biting into the firm flesh of one apple, I put another in my pocket and decided to walk by the Trustees' Building. There was no reason to do it, of course. All I would see was the dark facade. At this hour, there would be no lighted candle, no possibility of even the outline of a figure by an upstairs window.

Nor was there any point in my standing there, staring at the building. It only stared blankly back at me. I'd eaten my apples. They hadn't comforted me. Flagons of wine wouldn't either. It was Esther I longed for. I just stood there.

At last, I sat down on the grass in front of the fence at the Office and pulled off my boots. The tallow that I rubbed into them at Esau's behest seemed to make them hot. At that time, there was no one to notice that I'd be straying off onto the lawn as I went back. The grass was cool and silky on the soles of my feet.

Just as I stood up, the Office door opened. I didn't move. Through a gap in the high trellis, I saw her coming out.

Esther closed the door quietly behind her and took the step down, pulling a little at the skirt of her nightgown as if it were damp and clinging too close. Her hair hung long, tangled and crimped from unbraiding. She wasn't walking like one just awakened, but she seemed rapt in her thoughts.

Just as she reached the pathway, she stopped abruptly, pulled up as short as if someone had called her name. I hadn't, and she couldn't have seen me behind the heavy-headed flowers, their deep red almost black in the shadows. She looked upward, standing still, drenched in moonlight. It gave its own color to her hair, and turned her skin ivory white.

In that heart-stopping moment, as I gazed at her, seeing nothing else, I had only one clear sense. She belonged to me, she was mine. I would have her, have that perfect beauty.

After a moment, she lifted her cupped hands as we did in the dance service. Whether she was sending love upward or catching the moon's beams was impossible to tell. When she brought them back to waist level, she stared into her palms to see what they held.

The gesture seemed to remind her of the song, and she stepped sideways onto the scrap of grass before the entryway, into the steps used in "'Tis the Gift to Be Simple." At a slow tempo, the tune itself yearns for the freedom that is the wished-for gift. A freedom from earthly desires.

As she bowed from the waist and turned, her lips framed the words I could hear in my head. She seemed to strive for perfection in each sweep of the arm, in every turn of the wrist, as if doing it just right would surely mean her prayer would be granted.

Her nightdress was loose and billowed about her as she swung. It didn't allow a glimpse of white rounded breast or hip. The hem swirled gently just above her bare feet. There was nothing in the way she moved that was meant to be sensuous.

But it was. Her body, using its own sweet reasoning, craved what her soul would deny. I couldn't have imagined anything more erotic. I was still as stone. My breath didn't stir the lightest leaf in front of me.

Impossible as it was, I felt she was aware of my presence. But she couldn't be, and it was unfair to disguise it. The only gentlemanly thing to do was leave quietly, but I wouldn't. Not without speaking to her, even if I had no notion at all of what to say.

Just as she turned round on the words "We'll be in the valley of love and delight," I walked forward, my arms outstretched, my own hands cupped.

Stiff with surprise, Esther did not drop hers as I touched them with my fingers. She only looked at me, eyes wide. The joy that I was there was unmistakable. Slowly, she moved a hand and ran her fingers down my forearm, bare beneath my rolled-up sleeve. There was wonder in her touch. When they reached the back of my hand, her arms dropped heavily to her sides, and she looked down.

"I love you." I blurted the words out.

"Michael." That was her reply. She said my name as if that were all she had to say.

I lifted my arms to hold her. My wrists were weighted with lead. There's a slowness in intense desire. With it, there's the absence of thought. But already my fingers could feel the warm skin of her beneath the cool linen, my lips the yielding soft of her mouth.

She raised her face to mine. Bending my head, I saw her eyes.

They were filled with despair. There was no mistaking it, even in that deceptive light.

Whether she would have returned my passionate kiss I don't know. I hesitated, and in that click of time she brought her hand, palm outward, to her lips. Mine pressed only against the hollow of her palm. Before my arms could close around her, she'd taken a backward step.

"Esther." I was pleading.

Her hand fell. She didn't turn away. She didn't step into my waiting arms, either.

She might have shaken her head slightly, or maybe the

small wind lifted a few tendrils of her hair, giving that impression. She was forcing out her words. "I am a Believer."

That was all she said. Turning, without a backward look, she stepped on the carved stone step and went inside.

Chapter Twenty-three

Even the crystal clarity of the dawn didn't dim my exhilaration from the night before. Yes, exhilaration. No matter what Esther had said or done, I was sure that she *felt* as I did. Love offers that supernatural sympathy. All I had to do was make her recognize and admit those feelings.

Not that I had any chance to talk to her. At breakfast, she kept her eyes relentlessly on her apple omelet. Since Quincey said he would send any instructions to Jacob rather than to Philemon, I had no excuse to go to the Office. Besides, I had something important to do before leaving for the Krugers, if that was still the plan. I wouldn't know that until the elder got back.

Last night, while I was floating on the white sea between sleep and waking, the answer—the only answer—to one troubling question came to me. I didn't need Quincey's insight on this one. I'd handle it myself. I set out to do it.

Yet, as I neared the stables, I almost persuaded myself to put it off and, as well, not bother to speak to the elder. I wanted to saddle Lightfoot and go, feel a cooling breeze on my forehead. We could race down the road bordered by unharvested green fields of corn, golden fields of wheat. His swiftness might calm me, enable me to think.

Something niggled at me, demanding my attention. Something needed to sorted out. I stopped in the middle of the path. What could it be? I stared up at the pale sky, its blue bleached by the heat. Finally, I gave up. I couldn't concentrate on the day's tasks. My head was too full of the night's music.

Yet under that, I heard the insistent pulse of urgency.

Quincey's words yesterday hadn't helped quiet it. He believed the quick attempt to poison Hallelujah meant quick action would follow. Each day's passing increased my anxiety. His arrival hadn't caused a complete shift of responsibility, either. According to him, all I was supposed to do was report to him. In fact, I now had a list of things I *wasn't* going to tell him.

Nothing that happened after the Union Meeting, I reasoned, would cast light on the problem. He already knew Cris had running nightmares. He'd known my love for Esther before I did. Describing my feelings as I watched her would cause him to glare. In terms of any conversation, she and I had said one sentence each.

I would give him an account of the meeting, but how that would help I couldn't imagine. Thankful had certainly demonstrated that she wanted to be a trustee, but Quincey was already aware of that. Samuel Grant had his one-path mind fixed, as usual, on improving profits, and that was what he'd discussed with Bertha. Amos mentioned the accident with the horse; Agatha replied to his inquiries about Esau's health. Esther and I had worried aloud about Cris. We hadn't any new insights and there was no point in mentioning what we'd actually said. In terms of what I had to contribute, there was no need to hurry to the Krugers.

Still, I hesitated by the stable door. I told myself that Quincey, in ordering his thoughts, might see what eluded me. Or he might have learned something in his talk with Jacob in the afternoon. He had to come up with something. He had to.

At last, I turned and went on the straight path. I was going to have a talk with Giles Grant.

He was in the Brethren's Shop, alone, planing off ribbons of sweet-scented maple for a chair's rocker. The room was fragrant with wood and yellow with sunshine. Motes of sawdust swirled through the shafts of light from the high windows and floated through the open door. Layers of it coated the floor and sprinkles of it lightened Giles's dark curls. Like snow, it muffled my footsteps.

Carpentry work was usually a winter task, but an exception must have been made for Giles. Leeway was allowed for the "hand-minded" members. His tranquil expression, as he concentrated, showed it a wise decision. Only when he lifted the curved slat, running sensitive fingers on the smooth wood, did he notice me.

Then there was his sunlight smile. "Come and see, Brother Michael. I like this chair. Not one wrong saw cut, not one slip of the chisel. Yesterday I decided that, instead of making the usual pile of rungs, arms, legs, and stretchers, I would treat myself to creating an entire chair. Perfectly."

I followed him over to the upended chair, watching as he fitted the bottom on tightly, precisely. "This slat still needs more sanding, but I'll put it on so you can admire the finished product." He turned the chair upright and lightly touched each of the four half-crescent pieces across the high back. "See the perfect grain in this wood? I chose each piece carefully. And it will varnish a treat. Then I'll get the sisters to weave some tapes for the seat out of the brightest colors we have. Even the angels, used to the most exquisite comfort, will enjoy this chair."

As we stepped back, it started to rock gently on its own. Perhaps our boots had caused a vibration in the floor. Giles crowed in delight. "One has come already to test it."

"I'm not surprised," I answered dryly, "since it was made by a stand-in for an angel."

"Why do you say that?"

"Giles, where did you learn to play the trumpet so wonderfully?"

His smile didn't disappear. He brushed the hair above his ear on one side and repeated the gesture exactly on the other side. Then he pulled each earlobe, as he answered, "My uncle James, my mother's brother—oh, he was a musician. A natural one. He felt sorry that I was doomed to spend my days in a darkened room, resting, with nothing to do. It started when I was eight years old or so, and it was hard. Father insisted on it, though. He was very strict. No picture books. No telling of stories. No friends in to play." Memory snuffed out Giles's smile, took away the light in his eyes.

I imagined the small boy, pleading for one small pleasure,

looking up at Samuel Grant's stone face. The image knotted my stomach.

"But Father was in town during the week. James persuaded Mother that rambles in the woods wouldn't overexcite my brain and bring on attacks. He'd hidden several instruments in a canvas case in a tree trunk."

"Let me guess. Besides the trumpet, he taught you to play the flute."

"The fife, actually. I could carry it about with me, you see, to practice when I was alone and far enough away. I still do." He walked to the wall of pegs, touching each one as if it were a talisman and singing out his litany of names as he did so: "Uriel, Zadkiel, Gabriel, Michael, Raphael, Azrael, Israfil." When he reached the peg where his jacket hung, he pulled a small silver instrument, hardly thicker than a magician's wand, from a capacious pocket. He caressed it before putting it away. Then he skipped back through the sawdust to where I was standing.

"I'm sure you play it very well."

He nodded, again sweeping his fingers through his hair on each side. "I do. Often the fife sounds shrill to rise above the drum. But it can have a sweet tone. I should think I could do the recorder, too, with a bit of practice."

"It's too bad that the elders have ruled out musical instruments. Your playing would add to the dancing service."

He lifted one shoulder, then the other. "Well, yes, maybe. But when we're all singing just right together, I think that we don't need strings or reeds or horns."

Then he looked at me in alarm, pulling each earlobe twice. "But you mustn't think I played on the mountain because I wasn't allowed to do so during services . . . or to show off. That wasn't why." His expression of concern deepened. "And 'It' didn't do it. *I* did."

"*It?* What are you talking about?"

"That's how I refer to whatever—or whoever—lives inside of me. *It* has a will of its own. Lunges at people, flings things about, mutters, screams. *It* makes me fidget until everyone begs me to stop. But I can't. Not usually. I'm not doing it. *It* is the one responsible." Pain contorted the beauty of his face as he talked.

Empathy—not pity—for Giles welled up in me. Who has not had that sense of doubleness, often described as body vs. soul, but in any case, two forces in one being that tug in different directions? We're all aware of that other voice inside that mocks, argues, sneers. Supposing that force showed itself to others? The anger people directed at Giles could reflect their fear that they might lose control, that it could also happen to them.

"That must be hard." It was all I could answer.

He picked up two of the shaving curls, entwined them, and dangled them in the air. "We've grown up together and we're like this now, I suppose. I even think *It* can do what I never could." He looked at his raised fingers in wonder, saying, "These are my hands and I tell them what to do, but they make things so quickly and so well." He gestured toward the chair. "I surprise people with what I can do. I surprise myself." He dropped the strips of wood. "Maybe I'm lucky."

It occurred to me he might indeed be lucky, in another sense. If he could blame some of his thoughts—the ones he abhorred—on that alien force, he wouldn't hate himself for them. All of us have thoughts and impulses that we'd give much to deny. Perhaps Giles could.

"But the music, now. That's *me*." He was intense, quite still, not a tic or grimace. "And I planned the Midnight Cry. I meant to do it. I wanted to help Elijah. Those dreams, which he called 'evil,' were awakening him again. He'd been so happy during Mother's Work because he'd been sure he was on the right path. But he was waking up again, so afraid, and he'd pray and pray. When I heard him, I'd get up and pray, too. It didn't seem to be helping."

"You thought another visit to the mountain would strengthen his faith and bring back his fervor."

"Exactly! He wasn't even doing any drawings, none at all. I didn't see how getting everyone up on the mountain could do any harm, and it might make Elijah himself again. That was all I had in mind. It worked, too. Why, on that note he took to your room, he'd even drawn a *tree*. He hadn't done those for a long time because he said it'd be just imitating Sister Polly and Sister Hannah. But this one, he said, grew out of his heart."

Giles stopped, skipped in a circle one way and repeated the circle in the other direction, returning to the precise spot where he'd been standing.

Without catching his breath, he went on. "And I could see how the Midnight Cry could be easily arranged. Thankful doesn't sleep well. I knew that because when I'd be up with Elijah, I'd see her slip out if I were looking out the window. If she was just visiting the privy, it was the long way round. Maybe, being a deaconess, she'd thought of some task that needed doing or perhaps she was walking about to get sleepy. So I waited for a nice night. I thought I'd just tootle on my fife outside her room and get back upstairs before she opened the door. I did, but just barely. She roused everybody at once. I forgot about the elders being gone. So instead of going off to the Meetinghouse to wake them first, she came right up to our floor. Elijah almost caught me. I just had time to jump in bed before he woke."

"You already had your trumpet hidden on the mountain."

There was a look of mischief on his face. "It's always there. I don't know where else to keep it. Sometimes I can get away long enough to go up and play it. But right then I hadn't planned on doing so. It was only when we were all full of excitement and singing that I happened to think that would be good. Elijah didn't need an actual angel."

Stopping, he looked upward. "And, suppose one of the no-nonsense angels appeared—all fortitude and justice— instead of the mercy-and-charity sort. With Elijah's luck, that's what would happen. No. All he needed was the *idea* of an angel."

"I'm curious. What melody did you play?"

Giles moved off and began whirling. The sawdust flew up around him like a cloud. "Don't know, don't know. No. No. I can't read music. I hear it. I hear it."

I waited for him to stop before asking, "How did you sing so beautifully in French, and in a woman's voice?"

He came back toward me, frowning. "I don't know. Honestly. I just opened my mouth and the hymn came out. I tried to do it again and I couldn't."

I believed him. Whatever had Samuel Grant said to me that Quincey saw as the explanation?

Giles, his light, black-lashed eyes full of worry, said, "Does Elijah have to know it was me?"

I didn't answer for a moment. Giles was thinking of his friend, but the reaction of the community is what troubled me. To them, that angelic visit was a sign of heaven's approval. Joy had been evident in every face. They would feel the loss. Most would see it as a cruel hoax. Could they forgive Giles?

I glanced around the sun-filled shop. He'd found sanctuary with the Believers. It seemed unlikely he could find it anywhere else.

Quincey would have to know, of course. No doubt he already did. Not that he told me. But he wouldn't tell anyone else, either.

Giles reached out, tapping one of my temples, then the other. He touched my right shoulder, then my left. "Please, Michael?" His voice held hope and pleading.

"I won't tell him. If anyone does, it should be you."

"I shan't." He grinned. "The angels won't mind, you know. They'll think it the hugest joke that anyone imagined I could play as well as they do."

Chapter Twenty-four

"Did I ever think of leaving?" Alma's smile widened past its familiar grooves as she repeated my question. "Hourly. Some days."

When I'd arrived, the offices were deserted. There was no sign of Jacob, nor of anyone to ask about his whereabouts. Alma's rocking chair was in the dim corner but she was not there. Not a sound came from the living quarters upstairs. The only response to my footfalls was the silence that echoed through the building. At last I put my head through the doorway of the Meetinghouse assembly room.

The blaze of sun on the wide polished floor and the glossy blue walls caused me to almost overlook Alma, seated at the end of one of the benches. She had her face lifted and her hands in her lap, the wool carder set aside next to her. The starched, see-through cap that framed her face was like a raised cup. Her stillness was absolute. As I hesitated in the doorway, she turned slightly and fixed her white, blind gaze on me.

"More love, Mother," I said hurriedly. "It's Michael. I'm sorry if I disturbed you."

Returning my greeting, she answered, "Not at all. I'm indulging myself and disobeying the orders about protecting my eyes. I need to feel the light. I store it in my spirit for gloomy days."

Picking up the carder, she felt in the bag for the rough wool. "I heard you waiting. Jacob hasn't come back from a visit to an out family nearby. Just a brief errand, he said, and mentioned you would be coming. Do sit down."

Her remark made it clear that she still hadn't been told

why I was in Hancock, let alone of my employer's arrival. Jacob said he hadn't discussed the problems with the other elders and that apparently remained true. Quincey had been puzzled about his refusal to follow this hierarchical principle embedded in the Shaker faith. *She* might be the reason. He wanted to guard her against the knowledge of the darkness in the village.

If so, I thought Jacob was making a bad mistake. Alma listened day after day as the sisters brought her their troubles. I'd want her insights into the problem. He'd said himself that Alma's apparent fragility was misleading. Porcelain can crack but it's a hard and durable substance.

Of course, he could be the guilty one, protecting himself from Alma's sharp inward eye.

Or. When Quincey speculated on this question, he'd stopped right after that "or." He knew some of Jacob's virtues and faults. I could see that the elder took pride in his ability to take care of his domain. Innocent himself, he would regard the real trouble in Hancock as a personal failure. Calling in an outsider—even a trusted one like Quincey—without permission was a distinct breach of the rules, but he might see that as preferable to being weighed in the balance and found wanting in his own eyes and those of his peers in New Lebanon. True, if his action were discovered, he would no longer be considered for the position in the Central Ministry. But I was convinced that was not what he wanted in any case. Being the spiritual leader of thousands might seem a glorious promotion to some, but Jacob would choose to be what he was—the respected patriarch of this small community.

We sat quietly while I considered this. And sat longer, not speaking. The pile of fine combed wool next to Alma mounded higher. I was content to be there, even if the peace in the room didn't calm my anxiety. Nor did it help me redirect my thoughts. The day's brightness didn't blot out my memory of the moon's light.

Once or twice, I felt that Alma's head turned toward me, as if I'd spoken aloud and she were listening. But I'd said nothing.

At last I did. I asked her about leaving. The bluntness of my question apparently didn't bother her. Alma was one of those rare people with whom one needn't edge toward a serious talk. I needed to know her answer.

"I remember one of those days clearly," she went on. "A murderous hot summer day. I was young, barely twenty." She glanced sideways at me, smiling even more. "It was much hotter in those days, Michael. All of us were in the fields, de-tasseling corn, bending each tall stalk to pull out the silk. We were hurrying to finish before the rain that must be coming, had to be coming, the answer to our daily prayer. It'd been dry for so long that the heat from all the days before hung in the air, weighing down our exhausted arms. And the threads clung to your clothes so you felt like a walking stalk yourself.

"But it was the chaff that chafed. It flew up your nose and down your sleeves and your collar. It glued to your sweat-soaked skin. It seemed half a day had passed since lunch, but the sun stuck in the sky. I could tell from my shadow it was barely two o'clock.

"All I could think of was the cool deep millpond on the other side of the village. I imagined myself walking into it, not taking off my cap and dress, just sinking deep in the water and staying until the insides of my bones turned solid again. But I didn't walk away. I finished the day. And the rains came."

"But if you had. . . . An understandable lapse, a small misdeed. They wouldn't have asked you to leave for having done that, would they?"

"No. The elders overlook a great deal before they suggest gently to rule-breakers that perhaps they aren't committed to our ways and should go. But I knew that everyone longed for that relief as much as I did. And each person reached up for the next stalk. So I did as well. That was partly it, anyway."

I waited for her to go on, but she only reached into the bag for another snarl of wool and pulled it through the sharp prongs of the carder. She was letting me decide. She'd kept the conversation light as a way of asking me if I really wanted to continue it. We were both aware that then we would be talking about the present, not the past.

Finally, because I had to know, I said, "What was the other part?"

"To allow myself to do that would have been the first step. I was afraid I wouldn't be able to turn back. I so wanted to leave, you see. For good. I was in love. He would have left with me." Her head shake said that it would have been most unwise.

The assurance of that stopped me. Perhaps she'd made peace with her long-ago decision, deciding not to regret what couldn't be changed. To probe further might cause her pain. It would be selfish of me to ask her to push past that acceptance and instead turn the wisdom of her years and her knowledge of people to bear on it again.

Nonetheless, I plunged ahead. "But . . . don't you think you would have been happy together?"

"Happy." She let the word hang in the air. "Plato said, didn't he, that happiness is perfection of the soul. My father often quoted that. But when you're young and twenty, such answers seem remote, bookish, dusty. No, it was the meaning of love that stopped me from going through the gate. Aquinas said love was the act of wishing well. That's hard, a high hurdle. I couldn't get around it even to get to the gate."

Surprised, I stared straight ahead. That sounded easy to me. I could wish all sorts of people well.

She let out her breath. "I should explain a little more about how I thought so that you can understand. Some people *need* to believe, some *want* to, and sometimes, if they're lucky, belief follows. They can see it as a sturdy lifeline or a silken thread, but most have to hold on tight. The really lucky ones, I think, are the born believers, who never doubt."

Turning to me, her eyes were fixed on my face, or so I was convinced. "He was one of those. Capital B as well as small. For him, heaven is not just a hope, but a local habitation."

I remembered Jacob standing before us—the light in back

of him—talking about Hepzibah's arrival in Paradise. It was a place more familiar to him than Boston. No one who heard him could have thought otherwise.

"But if we'd gone out into the World, it would have been otherwise. To justify that decision, he'd begin questioning in earnest. That would be indeed a fall from grace. What could I give him that would replace what I took away?" she asked. It sounded like a familiar question, echoing in her mind down the years.

I still felt that she was refusing to reconsider that original choice.

"But if," my tongue stumbled in my hurry to get the words out, "you lived together as an out family, followed all the rules otherwise?"

"Those who do that always know that they're not living *perfectly*. They must forever question their choice. And they do question it. One woman said that she'd led a good enough life, but to her it was second best. She hadn't worn the white Sunday dress."

Her hands stopped their work for once. There was a sigh, quickly suppressed, before she went on. "Mind you, there are many here in the community who have days—and nights—of doubt. But they are buoyed up by being here with their brothers and sisters in the faith. The very hardness of their choice to remain reassures them it must be the right choice."

"Did he agree with you *then,* when he was my age?" It's difficult to imagine the old as young, to see them with fresh faces, shining hair, but I was sure that Jacob couldn't have assented without a great deal of protest. He'd have envisioned a future as radiant with Alma as I saw mine with Esther.

"I don't know to what extent he agreed. We both stayed."

Astounded, I burst out, "You didn't talk about it?"

"Yes and no. I knew him so well, you see. Much of our long discussion could be carried on without words. At a glance, I could tell, on any given day, what decision he'd come to that day, knowing as well that the night might unravel it. The Bible says how hard it is to wrestle with an

angel, but one feels that at least an angel plays fair. Devils
don't. They breathe things in your ear while they clutch you,
telling you as you heave and strain that the struggle, after all,
is pointless. Even the strongest might, listening long
enough, begin to accept that persistent whisper that we are
only a handful of dust."

Her voice was even, as serene as her expression, until her
ending words. Her throat seemed to close as she said, "At
last I couldn't bear watching his fight. I announced that I
would not leave the community. His face went very white,
but he turned away without speaking."

My tone was fierce. "But why did you not at least . . . try
your lives together? Wouldn't they have taken you back?"

"Yes. At least the elders have in other cases. We have several 'apostates' as we call them who returned. One man here
in Hancock has come back twice."

There was condemnation in my voice. "I think that you
should have given him the opportunity to speak his mind."

Her response was gentle. "You think it was arrogant of me
not to. Perhaps you're right, Michael. But you must understand that, try as I might, I couldn't imagine our life after the
leaving. We couldn't live amongst World People. Out families live nearby and are therefore farmers. Such hard work.
And if the labor's done without one's brothers, it makes for
brutally long days, alone in the fields. It's not designed for a
man who enjoys society, a change of work. I imagined him
coming into the house at night, bone-weary, unable to smile,
and I'd be heart-smote at the very thought. No matter the
cause, every passing shadow that crossed his face would
darken my day."

Without needing to grope, she reached out and put her
fragile hand, as soft as the finished wool, directly on mine.
"If I wished him well, how could I wish such a life for him?
If we'd talked it over, he might have persuaded me to go.
Yes. But he could never have talked me out of that forbod-
ing vision of the future."

My hand jerked under hers, and her light touch had a
world of sympathy in it. "You want to protest that if I were
so sure it wouldn't work, then it wouldn't have. I can agree

with that premise, but I can't agree in my heart that I was wrong in my decision."

I was mule stubborn. I had to be. Rude as it was, I bit out, "You could have tried, Alma. You could have come back!"

"We could have, but we wouldn't have. If we had, the elders would have separated us, sent one to a far distant community. They would have been right to do so. But we would never have seen each other again. Not ever."

Chapter Twenty-five

If Jacob hadn't started speaking before he reached me, I wouldn't have noticed his coming. "Ah, Michael, good. You're here. I'm sorry to have kept you waiting. It took me a bit longer because I took young Mercy with me to spend time with the Kruger children for a treat."

I was seated on the top of the three marble steps that led to the brothers' entrance to the Meetinghouse, a wrist on each knee, head down. It would be more accurate to say that I was slumping, rather than sitting. My eyes were closed in an effort to block out reality; I wasn't daydreaming.

But before he arrived, I discovered that what I'd been doing for the last twelve hours was a form of dreaming. There are many kinds. Sometimes as I slide into sleep, images spring up behind my eyelids. My mind invariably begins arranging them in a narrative, as if eager to be lulled by a bedtime story. These pictures are often beautiful, often fantastic—owl-eyed cats, moving statues, feathered canoes. Occasionally, not always, an inner voice interrupts, saying, "That can't be," or "That can't happen." It pulls me back to consciousness.

Since last night, it seemed I'd been in that state, with only Esther's face imprinted on the back of my lids. Alma's quiet voice had served as my wakener. Now all I could do was hear her words sounding in my ears, resounding in my head.

Love, by any definition, comes with a set of demands. Commonly, one is that the lovers must be together, and that beyond eternity. I couldn't even see the possibility of a week with the woman I loved, under any conditions. It was clear that my salary at the newspaper wouldn't provide for the

two of us. A better-paying job might be had, but it would require we live in the city, away from any Shaker community.
As for farming, even if I had enough to rent a small holding,
I hadn't the very real skills required to raise enough to feed
us. As Alma construed it, love required far more than that.

Blinded by the joy I saw mirrored in Esther's eyes, I hadn't
caught a glimpse of the high brick wall I was heading for.
Somehow I'd thought the light caress of her fingers—that
touched my arm and my heart—was just the beginning. Her
look of despair should have told me it was the ending. She
put up her hand, stepped back, turned away. For whatever
reason, need or desire, she *was* a Believer.

For half a night and part of a day, I'd shoved that out of
my mind. Thinking of the Krugers, I was convinced we
could take that in stride. Love would conquer. That might in-
vite disbelief, but it was true. Quincey to the contrary, I'm
not sure one can separate thinking and feeling, but this time
I really had.

I stumbled backward from Alma's presence. I hope I
managed an apology for my ill-mannered remarks, but I
doubt that I did.

Jacob swept off his hat and patted his brow with the back
of his hand. His bald head was bedewed with sweat, and he
seemed distracted. His next words, however, were straightforward and rang with sincerity. The trouble was that I could
make no sense of them. "It's a fine thing you've agreed to
do, Michael, a brave one. The Iroquois are our friends, and
we wish to help them in any way we can."

At this point, he might as well have been speaking in their
language. At first, I assumed that, sunk in my own misery,
I'd not caught some key beginning sentence. He went on.
"This situation presents a problem for the Indians—a distinct danger—one worries particularly about the children.
Of course, their handling of it would not be our way, but we
must respect their beliefs. When Jasper said you would be
willing to take charge, I could see it was an ideal solution."

Now I assumed that Quincey had sent me an early message, which I hadn't received, and Jacob was referring to

their later talk together. Fortunately, I was too confused to say that, or anything else.

Then Trapper came around the side of the Meetinghouse. It was surprising that I recognized him. He was dressed as usual in a loincloth and now a heavy leather pouch dangled from it. But his forehead was encircled by a bright beaded headband and his hair was braided down his back and interwoven with feathers, some snowy, some red, some crow-black. They stood up from the crown of his head as well, making him look much taller and certainly more imposing. His face was streaked with paint of every color. So was his chest, at least that part not covered with intricate ropes of beads. By his side, he held a very long-barreled rifle.

As usual, he didn't bother with words, and there was a look in his nut-hard eyes that warned me not to bother with any either. In this conversation, that seemed the only course to take.

Jacob greeted him, and turned back to me, saying, "As Jasper asked, we will pray tonight before dinner for your success. He stressed that he wanted the prayers of the whole community." He smiled a little. "I was touched that he should make this request since I sometimes feel he is not as . . . aware spiritually as he might be. He assures me that he has the situation in hand, and you needn't be in Hancock. Selfish as it is, I wish you weren't going. Your presence is a comfort to me."

His smile was now completely gone. "But, hard as it is for me to say this, I'm sure you will be safer in the wilds than here with us. Esau continually presses me to suggest you go to another community at some distance. I cannot, of course, tell him why that is not possible, why we need you here. I'll go now to the Nurse House and tell him that you'll be away, at least for a few days. That will reassure him. The fact that you're with Trapper puts me at ease. He is a man of many talents."

All this talk of reassurance about my safety gave me no comfort. The very idea that he had to put his own mind at rest threw up alarm signals in mine. What on earth could I do that the Iroquois couldn't? From what I knew of them, if this exploit involved danger and required bravery, I'd call on them first.

With a sweeping gesture, Jacob went on, "If there is anything you need, just ask Sister Thankful. She's taken on Esau's duties for the time. Of course we're happy to lend you the dog. I don't know that Hallelujah is exactly a hunting dog. I thought that some sort of hounds did that. But, with his keen sense of smell, he can warn you if you're the one being stalked. Jasper has repeated that you will be in no danger—that you're a superb marksman."

He wished us luck and took his leave, again assuring us of their prayers. Trapper nodded gravely at him. I have no idea what I said. I know I didn't get up. Not only was I choking with rage, my legs were trembling with it.

Quincey's arrogance in making plans for others I was all too familiar with, but I'd at least trusted his intelligence. The foolishness of ordering not only me, but Trapper, away from Hancock when Quincey himself saw that the threat of another fire was imminent defied belief. How could he protect the community by himself, and from ten miles away? My anger was fueled with fear.

I was sure that he hadn't sent any message to me. If he had, he must have known he'd have gotten a loud argument. Instead, he'd calmly announced to Jacob that I'd *agreed*. And to add that I was a "superb marksman"!

The only thing I could see to do was convince Trapper of Quincey's wrongheadedness. The two of us could then go to the Krugers' and confront him. I had no idea what Trapper had been told of this lack-brained enterprise, but I had to make him see reason.

Trying to control my voice, I pointed to the rifle and asked, "Do you know how to use that?"

He ran his fingers over the thick walnut stock and then the polished silver filigree that edged the powder box above the trigger. There was respect in his touch. For once, he was willing to answer. There was even a flicker of enthusiasm on his face. "Best gun," he answered. "A Hawken. One shot all you need. Good thing. All you get, sometimes." He patted the pouch at his waist. "Plenty of powder, but no chance to load twice." His hand slid down the three-foot barrel. "Not like most guns. This one makes shot go straight." He glanced sideways at me, a sly look. "White man can do some things." He nodded in satisfaction. "I can shoot this."

"Then that's the *really* good thing, Trapper. I've never had a gun in my hands in my life." We'd certainly never had one in the house. No doubt my father had learned to shoot, but he'd died when I was young. He'd never shown any interest in hunting. Occasionally, men would be called out to kill a bear that wandered into the outskirts of Cambridge, but he spent his days in Boston at his place of business.

"Time you learn. We practice this afternoon." He gestured toward the distant, tree-crowned Berkshires. "Up there."

"What are we supposed to be hunting?"

If Trapper was surprised at my question, he didn't show it. "The cougar."

"A mountain lion? Why are *we* shooting it? Or rather why are you shooting it? I can't believe that with one afternoon's practice I could hit a fat tree, let alone a fast-moving cat."

"Could kill Indian child. Cougar will attack a brave, even. These cats, they are fierce, warlike. They don't leave when men come. They stay. It is their land. They protect it. Very hard to see, the mountain lion. Until it is too late, even for one shot."

"Why don't the *Iroquois* shoot it? Don't they have rifles?"

"A few. But they would not believe they can kill. No one see cougar for some time. This is, then, a spirit. They would not even try."

"And how do they know it is a spirit, and not a real one?"

"Medicine man have dream, vision. Best way to know anything."

My exasperation gave my voice a distinct edge. "Could you believe in an unkillable cougar?"

He nodded slowly. "Yes."

"Is that why you're dressed this way? So the Iroquois will accept you can kill it?"

Trapper drew himself up. "I am not of their tribes. I am Pequot." He spread his arm toward the southeast. It was an eloquent gesture, saying that there things were done sanely

and properly. "Who knows what Iroquois do for ceremony?"
He touched his chest with unmistakable pride. "I do it our
way, right way. My idea to paint. I come to Hancock, I am
ready to battle Spirit Cougar. Shakers see we are serious.
But this plan, Mr. Quincey thinks of. Good plan." He gestured in the direction Jacob had gone. "Even he believes.
Anyone would believe."

I sunk my head on my chest, and the brim of my hat hid
my face from Trapper. Anyone would believe. I certainly
had. There was no spirit cougar. The Iroquois didn't know
anything about this.

Whoever was setting the fires was desperately afraid of
discovery and not likely to start one, suspecting that I was
there to prevent it or that Hallelujah's bark might arouse the
village. Quincey's scheme was designed to make everyone
think the dog and I were gone for a few days. Trapper naturally assumed I knew the outline and was only asking for the
details to see if our absence was credible. Quincey had even
come up with a way to announce our departure to the community. They were going to pray for our success at dinner.

Trapper's voice intruded. "You tell anyone you can't
shoot?"

I didn't lift my head. "No. The subject never came up."

"We get dog now." He stepped back and looked at me
consideringly. Then he nodded as if he'd cast me correctly
in the drama. "Put worried look on your face. Not too much.
And we walk like warriors. They believe. We go to moun-
tains. Come back when village is dark and quiet. Good
plan."

He glanced down again at his carefully painted chest. He
knew all about the need for self-respect—and how to get his
own. There was a proper way to do things.

We marched out like warriors. Together.

Chapter Twenty-six

The anxiety in my voice was not helping. Hallelujah could sense it. He was shifting from haunch to haunch, although he should have been more comfortable than I was; his legs were a lot shorter. I was breathing words into his ear, trying to soothe him. I gave that up and instead scratched behind his stand-up ear and stroked the bristly hairs on the back of his neck. He was sitting obediently beside me. His nose was lifted and he gave an occasional sniff as if what he was smelling worried him as much as what he was hearing.

Then I tried shifting position myself by raising up and crouching down. That didn't work. It gave me leg cramps. The only remedy was to get up for a luxurious stretch. That was out of the question.

The two of us were under the spreading branches, drooping down umbrella-like, of a huge maple about ten feet from the back door of the Living Quarters. We'd been there for some time. I went back to sitting with my legs full out in front of me, slowly pulling one and then another to my chest. If I had to move quickly, it wouldn't be easy with numb legs. I jammed my trouser tops into my boots to make running easier.

Seven of us, eight counting Hallelujah, were positioned in strategic places, none far from the Seedhouse. Quincey was, of course, not cramped and crouching. He was in the kitchen of the Living Quarters. Because it was a basement room, the windows were high with a limited view, but all he had to do was make sure no one went out the back door. He was sitting in the rocker in an out-of-the-way corner. If I'd had the

placement in my command, I'd have designated the prickly
rosebushes outside the Trustees' Building for him. He'd
come up with a good plan—I couldn't think of a better
one—and he'd given Trapper a note for Philemon so he
could help make arrangements. I didn't get one, of course.

Philemon was sequestered inside the Office so that no one
leaving the building could do so unnoticed by him. Three
Iroquois were scattered about so all paths were watched.
Trapper was nearest the front entrance of the Seedhouse, although there wasn't any convenient cover close by the door.

The problem was that none of us could see much, even
with eyes accustomed to the night. The waning moon was
haloed. The stars seemed unusually far away because of
the hazy sky. There were flashes of lightning high over the
Berkshires, maybe heat lightning, or perhaps a signal of
the end of the long dry spell, but they were too distant to
help. There was certainly more moisture in the air, although it brought little cooling. The dark shirt borrowed
for me from Farmer Kruger clung to my back even though
it was two sizes too large. Beads of sweat from my forehead landed on my lashes.

If Quincey had an idea who might be going to the Seedhouse, he hadn't told anyone. Not only did I not know, I
didn't want to think about it. Trapper only knew that the first
of us who spotted anyone on the way there was to give an
owl's hoot. Twice, followed by silence, then a third time.
That was in case there was a real owl in the neighborhood.
Trapper had me rehearse the call that afternoon.

Although using the rifle wasn't part of tonight's plan, I'd
also spent quite some time practicing shooting. The actual
aiming and firing wasn't the time-consuming part of the
process: cleaning the gun thoroughly and loading it precisely were. To satisfy Trapper, I had to put the exact amount
of loose powder down the barrel, tamp that down, then drop
in the ball and tamp it just right. After each shot, the ideal
willow twig to clean the barrel had to be chosen, and enormous care had to be used not to disturb the rifling in it while
using the slender twig. All specks of powder, grime, and
even dust had to be removed from the powerful hammer that

forced the cap discharging the ball. My fingers got very sore. My shoulder ached from the recoil of the rifle.

Watching Trapper shoot, I was convinced he could cut a clover leaf at fifty yards, and I almost gave up trying. By the end of the day, however, I began to think I could do passably well. At least I was hitting stationary targets. Not that I got as much as a nod of approval or a grunt of encouragement from Trapper. But he had several of the qualities of good teachers. He regarded what he was showing me as the most important thing I would ever learn. And we were not going to stop until I did it as right as it could be done.

I didn't imagine I would ever use a gun again, but this insistence on his part kept me at it. More importantly for me, the concentration required kept my misery away and my worries at bay. Now, in this close and edgy stillness, there was nothing else to do but feel the drops of pain on my heart and the shocks of worry in my system.

That and wait for the owl call. As soon as I heard the third, I was to begin counting seconds. Quincey wanted whoever went in to be allowed to make preparations for a fire so there would be no doubt. There were, after all, some legitimate reasons that could be given for being in the Seedhouse, even in the middle of the night. Whoever went in might have prepared a plausible story. I could imagine Thankful saying she couldn't sleep, could find no chamomile tea and wanted to make some. Seth might have suddenly decided he needed a medication. Jacob could say he was worried because we were away and no one was guarding the building.

I was to allow five minutes to pass from the time I heard the signal. In the meantime, two Iroquois were to slip to the rear door and guard it. Hallelujah and I were the ones designated to rush in the front entrance.

That made sense. My size would give an attacker pause. And Hallelujah's growl should give anyone a second thought. What Quincey wanted was a complete and easy surrender. So did I.

The trouble with concentrating on listening was that one heard too much. Normally I wouldn't have noticed a bat suddenly swooping down to scoop up an insect. Now I imagined I could hear it crunch on it. Every leaf rustle impinged on my consciousness. There seemed to be whole armies of crickets. If a genuine owl's mournful "who" had sounded, I'd have passed out holding my breath for the second call.

Then the concern that had niggled at me all day, just out of reach of my consciousness, came right into my mind. The cool glass of the lamp in the horse barn and the lethal spill of kerosene beside it. The placing of that lamp in piled-up straw, so near the horse's hoof. And Cris lying beside it, fast asleep. That still didn't make sense.

I tried to think like Quincey. How could this have happened? If Cris was in some half-conscious state when he came into the barn, would he have taken the lantern down from its place by the door and gone through the ritual of lighting it? Perhaps so, out of habit. He did that every morning in one barn or another because we came down to start chores before dawn. Then, why did he not, on the same premise, hang it on the nearest peg? Every Shaker—man, woman, and child—faithfully followed that routine. Still, no one could guess what a sleepwalker might do, least of all me.

If he'd been wide awake when he arrived, why would he so foolishly place that lantern in the straw after checking on the horse? Why did he stay at all when he saw that the horse was carefully bandaged and apparently not in pain? He'd have no reason to keep watch over the animal. If Seth found him in the morning, Cris had every reason to believe he'd be cross about it.

No. In either case, that glass shouldn't have been cool if Cris were the one who lit the lamp. Hallelujah had followed the boy's track straight to the barn so he hadn't made any side excursions. He must have been there all the time that it took for Jeb to find me, for me to get the dog, return to the Boys' House, and get to the barn.

Therefore, someone else lit it.

At this point, if Quincey had been beside me, he would have interrupted with raised eyebrows and damning words.

"One more supposal. You are leaving out the possibility that the boy had been in the barn in the dark, waiting to make sure no one had noted his arrival. He'd just lit the lamp to start another fire and was about to leave when you came. So he hastily put it down and feigned a sound slumber."

It made my stomach hurt. I pulled up some loose grass as I thought. That explanation made every sense. It covered all the points.

But it was nonsense. Awake or asleep, Cris wouldn't have considered harming those horses, let alone dooming them to a horrible death. I pulled up another handful of grass. Could he have been faking? No.

Someone else lit that lantern. That person arrived shortly before us, got the lamp, walked to the very last stall with it, saw Cris, set it down so carelessly near him that it was criminal, and—

Here I stopped. I'd been visualizing that series of events and there was something wrong. I closed my eyes, remembering the scene. The lamp hadn't been dropped in a hurry. The straw around it was piled up, almost hiding it.

Someone had tried to kill Cris. Deliberately tried. By fire.

As soon as I got my breath back, I went over that idea again. No, it wasn't deliberate. The arsonist had intended to set the horse barn aflame, then saw the boy, was afraid of being recognized— No. Cris had been so fast asleep that even the clatter of Jeb's boots and mine hadn't caused him to stir until we were at the stall. The light of the lamp hadn't awakened him, either. On seeing the sleeping boy, all the intruder had to do was leave. And why start a fire in the horse barn instead of the Seedhouse? The loud panic of the kicking, neighing animals at the first flames would rouse someone. Not only would the fire be doused fairly rapidly but the chances of discovery would be greater.

On the other hand, why would anyone want to kill Cris?

He couldn't be a threat. Although he'd been out on the night of the attack on Hepzibah, he hadn't seen—

But I hadn't asked him if he had. I told Quincey I'd questioned all eleven. But not the boy. Mercy had been alone when I talked to her. Cris had been under her window, perhaps for some little time before he managed to wake her. If he saw an adult out that night, particularly one of those in the upper hierarchy—elder, trustee, deacon, deaconess—Cris wouldn't have questioned that person's presence. But whoever he saw probably was hurrying back after attacking Hepzibah. That person pretended not to see him, and Cris was making every effort not to be seen. He must have been relieved, thinking that he hadn't been. But Cris now represented a real danger. If asked, he'd recall the incident. The first opportunity to get rid of him must be taken. Last night was the first.

Now I was really sweating. I tried to relax. Tonight we were all watching. Cris would be safe. If nothing happened tonight, we would be watching tomorrow night. Would he be safe even during the day? I'd talk to Quincey. We could come up with something. I just had to persuade him of the fact that the boy's being out was understandable. *He* was not the guilty one.

Quincey hadn't sent me a note. But neither had I sent him a quick report on the events of last night. He was not aware that I'd seen Esther and Cris.

I shrugged that off. They were innocent. Their activities would not help in the solution of the problem. There was no reason to—

Suddenly Hallelujah strained forward. I clamped my hand on the back of his neck and gritted in his ear, "Don't bark!"

He didn't, but his whole body wanted to move. I gripped him tight.

Then the first owl hoot came. I swear that both the dog and I held our breath. A second call. The quiet after that was loud. Finally, the third.

Chapter Twenty-seven

The silence after the last birdcall lasted so long that I was ready to believe a spirit owl above had caught onto our signal and was mocking me. Then I heard the footsteps on the path. I knew immediately who was coming. There was no mistaking.

Hallelujah knew, too. Deep in his throat, there was a barely audible whimper, soft and longing. If I'd not had a firm grasp on the ruff of his neck, he'd have shot out from under the tree. To make sure of his silence, I quickly clamped his mouth shut with my other hand. "No!" I hissed the word at him.

No. No. I repeated the word flatly to myself in the dullness of despair.

It was Cris heading for the Seedhouse. He was definitely not sleep-running. His pace couldn't have been slower. His boots scrunched on the path; he dragged his bad leg as if it were weighted. As he passed the maple, I could see him clearly through a gap in the leaves. His shoulders slumped beneath his white nightshirt, the front half tucked into his trousers, the back half drooping down behind to his knees. Under his arm was tucked something long and rolled up. After he'd gone by, I realized it was a blanket.

We'd set up a logical framework. Whoever came tonight to the Seedhouse would have only one reason to do so. To start another fire. And Cris was on his way there.

Images and ideas jumbled in my head. Philemon's story about the blood leaking into the snow as the man lashed the legs of a lame and burdened boy. My saying to that boy we all have to be taught. So what had Cris learned in his very short life?

Fear, pain, hunger.

What could one expect from such lessons?

Driven by some dreadful need to relieve an overpowering anger, one pushed back in the blackest corner of the mind, he'd set fire—

No. He had not. Because of his background, the explanation was credible, understandable even. Still, he had *not* set those fires. There is the logic of the heart.

But what was he doing here? He was trudging openly along the path, making no attempt at concealment, carrying a blanket.

Hallelujah hadn't even wriggled in my tight two-handed grasp on his neck and muzzle, but after Cris had gone by, he once again whined gently and mournfully deep in his throat. It didn't seem to be a complaint. He simply wanted me to know how much I was asking of him in not letting him run to the boy.

The outline of the small nightshirted form was silhouetted against the dark building. He reached the door, opened it a crack, but he didn't go in. He let the blanket fall from under his arm and then stood there quietly, waiting for something, poised as if listening. He turned his head in one direction, then another. At last he leaned down, reached in, and took something from the floor of the mud room. Moving sideways a few steps, he bent over the huge rain barrel by the door, his upper body almost disappearing into it. With the dry weather, it was only half-full.

When he straightened, limping carefully, hands outstretched around a bowl, he was still huddled as miserably into himself as if he'd lost his best friend. And it came to me. That's just what Cris thought, that Hallelujah was gone. He didn't know where the dog was.

Jacob said he'd have the whole community pray for our success at dinner. But the children were fed first, separately. The hunting expedition on behalf of the Iroquois wouldn't have been announced to them.

Cris and Mercy had the responsibility of feeding and set-

tling down Hallelujah for the night. But Jacob had taken
Mercy to the Krugers'. She must have stayed there for supper, no doubt for the night. When Cris came alone before
sundown to the Seedhouse, he might have thought Seth had
Hallelujah. But after a frantic wait, he'd had to go back to
the Boys' House. Thinking the dog had run away, he'd been
afraid to ask, even if he'd thought anyone could understand
his signs. If Hallelujah was gone, even if he returned later,
it'd be a black mark. The elders' permission to keep him,
which was only provisional, would be withdrawn. They
wouldn't allow a dog for which they were responsible to
roam the countryside, perhaps chasing sheep or even killing
chickens.

Cris would have waited in bed until everyone in the Boys'
House was sound asleep, then untied the cord that connected
him to Jeb and slipped out. No doubt he thought Hallelujah
might come back and then he could be shut in the mud room
and no one would know he'd taken off.

Chris stooped over to put the water down inside, then
picked up the blanket and went in. He left the door open a
crack. He'd probably lie down very near it, thinking that the
dog would catch his scent if he came to the Seedhouse. He'd
stare at the darkness, hoping, waiting.

All I could think to do was wait myself, at least long
enough so that Quincey, when he came, could be shown to
his satisfaction that all Cris intended to do was sleep. I
hadn't been counting seconds. Perhaps by now the Iroquois
were at the back door. No one could approach the front
without my seeing them. Cris was safe in there.

But there was a problem. Soon Trapper would appear.
He'd have to assume that, for some reason, I hadn't caught
the signal. Sure that the boy was starting a fire, he couldn't
let him stay in there long. If I left the tree's covering
branches to find him to explain, I might be seen. By now,
perhaps even the Iroquois had been. Philemon, and even
Quincey, might have already left their buildings. The real
culprit could be watching from a window somewhere.
Catching even a glimpse of a moving shadow would be
enough to cause a change in plans. Quincey's carefully laid-

out plan would be off not only for tonight, but altogether.
There would be little use in trying again later if our quarry
were alerted to the fact that the Seedhouse was watched.

So there was nothing to do but wait a little longer. Trapper
knew where I was and would come to me first. He had a better chance of being unobserved than Hallelujah and I. The
longer Cris was inside, the more convinced Quincey would
be. The boy could come to no harm—

I don't know how it was, but I was up and running furiously toward the Seedhouse. Cris wasn't safe. I saw nothing
that made me think this. I just knew. I was ten feet away.

First, the sound, the sickening sound of it. Not loud. A
muffled whump.

The quiet night cracked with noise, glared with light.
Every window in the Seedhouse blazed and shattered. A
blast of heat seared my face. The explosion ripped through
the roof, sending wild sparks leaping upward. The building
shook, and the ground beneath my feet.

After that thunderclap, either I was deafened or there was
no more to hear. The hammer of my heart thrust me forward
like a ball of shot. Hallelujah was even faster, at the door before me. But it had been sucked in, stuck tight. He was leaping at it, clawing at it. I slammed into it with my shoulder,
the force of my headlong rush shoving it open.

I smashed immediately into the wall of smoke and heat. It
scalded my skin and threw me back against my will. The
breath was instantly squeezed out of my lungs with the force
of a collision. Fire needs the air, consumes it, and won't give
you a mouthful of it. Choking, gasping, I blundered forward
again. My boot heel caught on the sill of the main room or
I'd have had no idea where I was.

My eyes teared, insisting on shutting. It took all my
strength to keep them open. But it was not a dense inferno
into which I rushed. Only streamers of fire ran along the
floors, up the walls, across the rafters of the ceiling offering
a teasing bit of light. Smoke clumped solidly and then
whisked itself aside, as if to gather its strength in another
corner. Heavy tables were crazily on their sides. Some of the
thick rafters were now at angles to the ceiling.

I could make out so little that I despaired of finding him. I didn't call out; I couldn't; I was pressing my lips together too hard to hold in my breath.

Even above the fire's crackle and snap, I heard the violent clangor of the bell.

I felt Hallelujah's body against my leg. I went the way he did. It was he who found Cris. I couldn't have. The dog darted to the side. I followed, floundering through a creek of fire. I bent down, groping for the dog, and found a swallow of air. The heat in it gagged me.

Hallelujah had his mouth around a leg, tugging, tugging. I was feeling as much as seeing when my fingers found the heavy beam across the boy's chest. Squatting, I tried thrusting it up. I didn't budge it. I strained again. It might have come up an inch at best.

Then I saw Cris's eyes, blinking back the heavy tears, swimming in terror. He was frantically trying to scrabble sideways on his back, both sliding and pushing at the weight on him. I tried once more. Every muscle in my body lifted with my arms but failed to raise that too solid piece of wood. I fell to my knees, trying now to shove the wood sideways.

Heat seared up my back when I knelt. My boots were on fire, the blaze ignited and fed by the tallow I'd rubbed into them. But I felt no pain. There was no room inside me except for the agonizing need to hurry, to get Cris, to get out.

A lever, I thought, a lever. I scrambled up to grab whatever I could, stamping at the fire shooting upward from the floor, eating at my feet. It was that sudden movement, slightly backward, that saved me.

As I spun around, I saw him raising, high above his head, the table leg he held. In that instant, I thought he was rushing forward to help, even as I stared in amazement that *he* could be there. Then I knew what he intended. His face was as expressionless as a hangman's, but he was going to bring that club crashing down on me.

But it was as if he were yanked backward. The wood clattered down at my feet. He disappeared into a leaping column of fire. Above that, I glimpsed another face. It was serene, beautiful, not contorted by smoke, oblivious of the flames around it. I am sure I saw it, even with my burning eyes. Then it was gone, and so was he.

I clutched at the table leg he dropped, shoved it under the beam, and pried with all my strength. I doubt that I raised it far. Whether it was Hallelujah's frantic tugging, or whether Cris's scrabbles slid him out, I'll never know. But I pulled him up to my chest, letting his legs dangle against mine as we, with Hallelujah ahead, stumbled through the mud room, out the door, and into the blessed air.

Two lungfuls, and someone snatched Cris from me. A second whump, and I heard the building collapsing behind me. I was doused with a bucket of water, then another. I stood swaying, the fire still gnawing at my feet, at my legs. Then two strong arms encircled my chest, lifted me, swung me, and thrust me, boots-first, into the rain barrel. One can slide into unconsciousness. I pitched into it, headfirst.

Chapter Twenty-eight

I can't recall much of the next days. Except the pain. One of the doctors, nodding sagely after examining my legs and feet, said that the memory of pain fades as time passes. Later, the mind can't summon up the intensity of it. Maybe that's true. I'll see.

The first night, at the Nurse House, was not so bad. When I drifted upward from the darkness and into its light and knew where I was, there was something damp and soothing on me from the knees down. The tent of sheets over my legs didn't seem to be touching them. When Sister Ruth saw me stirring, she picked up the cup by the bedside and urged— actually, *ordered* would be more like it—that I swallow it all. I did. I didn't wake again, not completely.

I heard voices. One was, I think, Seth's. He was arguing fiercely about something, and I wanted him to be quiet, and very soon he was. Then a woman was speaking, almost whispering. She said that Cris would be fine, that he was in a nearby bed, that he would be well very soon, that I wasn't to worry, that Hallelujah was best of all, would be running around in the morning, just missing a few patches of fur, his paws might be a little sore, that was all. She said, more than once, that I had been very brave. I just lay there and listened to that voice, cool as water. It might have been Sister Ruth, but it stays in my mind that it was Esther.

The next thing, and I remember this vividly, was the sensation of being jostled, and jolted, tossed about. Anger welled up in me that I should be so treated when my feet were on fire. Couldn't they see? Why didn't they do something? It hurt so much.

I jerked open my eyes and looked directly at Freegift. He was huddled near me under some kind of canopy and there was rain all around us, but we were dry under that roof of cloth. I was stretched out beneath it on a mattress, my legs still under their separate tent. I couldn't imagine where we were and I was outraged at being pitched about. No doubt I made that harshly plain.

He blinked at me rapidly, tears in his eyes. I was aware that they were for me. I'd have taken back my words, but talking was such an effort. The skin of my face was blistered and didn't want to stretch. My lips were puffed to at least twice their size. I was straitjacketed in my narrow world of suffering and it didn't seem possible to make room for anyone or anything else. The trouble with burns is that they keep on burning.

He was pushing a high-sided bowl at me, with a reed in it, and repeating, "Please, sir, please sip this. It'll be good for you, you have to, sir."

As he held it out, his hand shook, perhaps from our rattling motion. His words ran together. "This wagon is dreadful for you, what with the weather and the ruts in the road and the horses going so fast. But really it did seem to be the only way. We'll be home soon. Everyone finally agreed with Mr. Quincey. With the doctors at the university, and the finest ones in Boston, you'll get the best care. Even Brother Seth said that just as long as they didn't put on any greasy ointments when we got back, he'd go along with your going. Said Brother Amos did a very good thing sticking your feet in the barrel. Said he'd seen a horse burned worse and what he was telling the sisters to do would work. Trapper said, too. Just what they did back at his village. Not to horses. People. Please try to take some more of this, now."

So that he'd be still, and not so worried, I drank it.

When next I awoke, Trapper was beside me. Then I knew where I was. He and I were back in the forest, in that cave, even though I could still see that we were under some cloth and the only walls the falling rain. I was reassured at the sight of him. I was not going to be in for an easy time, though, if he were with me. There was no sign of pity or sympathy on his face. His eyes were polished stones. He didn't say anything. Just raised my head, like before, and held out a cup. I knew better than to argue.

Then, what is fixed in my mind, is the molding around the edges of the ceiling, delicate carvings meant to look like draperies held by rosettes. It puzzled me for some time because I was sure that we were at Quincey's. Coming in through that wide front door with the men like pallbearers holding the board under me was hard to forget. But the molding—the whole room with its delft blue walls with white trim and Wedgwood vases filled with meadowsweet and spikes of lavender—should have been somewhere else. It *was* a soothing room. I was grateful for that molding because when those carved drapes swayed before my eyes, I knew the fever was high again.

People speak of fever dreams as if they're wild figments conjured up by the inflamed imagination, but in mine I was always back in the burning Seedhouse. Just as it had been. There was the white heat and the choking smoke. I was gasping, stumbling, holding my streaming eyes open only by an effort of will. I felt the force of fear, the stun of surprise at seeing *him* hold up that club of wood. All of it came back.

Again and again, I saw that other face, the one above the column of flames. It was fire-branded on my memory, yet I wasn't even sure if it was male or female. Its beauty was not due to the winged eyebrows, the straight nose, the shaped mouth. It was that look of peace, a serenity invulnerable to time or sorrow.

That presence, if there was one, could have had nothing to do with *him* falling over, disappearing. He must have toppled backward, over-balanced by the heaviness of the wood he held.

In my lucid moments, I was convinced I hadn't seen the face, blinded as I was by tears and smoke. Yet there was one thing. That club thumped down at my feet. It should have gone behind him if he'd fallen backward. *That* was hard to shrug out of my mind, but I did so. Thinking took too much effort.

The doctors came and went. One with a bushy beard and pince-nez irritated my raw face with his ungentle touch. After he left the room, I could hear him talking outside the door. He was saying, "febrile . . . infection . . . better to live without feet than—" He stopped as abruptly as if a hand had been clapped over his mouth. He didn't come back again.

Trapper came too often for my liking. It was he who peeled away the dead skin from my feet and legs, putting them in some sort of bath beneath the tent of sheets while he did so. I didn't watch. I didn't cry out, either, though the scraping was agonizing. It had to be done. He was causing me great pain, but I wasn't to give any sign. There was a proper way to do things. You could tell by the set of his shoulders when he came in that's what he thought. Deep down, I was sure it was vanity that kept my lips pressed together.

Freegift was always there, only disappearing to return with a tray. "This beef tea, now, Mrs. Hingham says, is very restorative." Or "A nice bit of boiled egg will do you a world of good." His face was so full of hope that I swallowed whatever it was if I could.

Quincey never came during this time. No doubt he didn't like sickrooms. Well, he might have been there on occasion, sitting beside my bed reading. That was when the molding seemed to billow like curtains in a wind though, so I'm not sure.

Not long after, I awoke one morning and the light blue draperies, the actual ones that hung over the window across from my bed, moved gently in a refreshing breeze. I was cool myself. Turning my head slightly, I saw a picture that I didn't think had been on that wall before. It was a tree with fruit that was bright red and deep green. Larger than apples, these had the shape of opening flowers and seem to spring upward, rather than weighting down the tree. It was restful, and I let my eyes follow the graceful sway of leaves and branches.

After a moment, I was aware of a movement at the open door and Philemon was standing there, watching. "Ah, Michael," he said, beaming at me, "you're awake. I hope you like the painting. Sister Hannah did it, but she says it's really a gift from Holy Mother above; that her hands were merely the instruments. She calls it 'The Tree of Life.' "

He seated himself by my bed, and pulled out a scrap of paper from his right-hand pocket. His thin white hair was brushed forward neatly, his cheeks pink were from shaving, his long coat was well brushed, and his collarless shirt was its usual spotless white. The sight of him, that familiar gesture, and on that morning, made me lightheaded with pleasure.

I remembered, on first going to the Shakers, that I'd felt frustrated anger that they wouldn't see the evil in the world. Their truest gift to me was to recognize the good.

He held up a hand as if to urge me not to speak, but he looked at me critically and carefully. "Much better. I shall make a note so that I can tell the brothers and sisters. Your eyebrows are growing back, and with that haircut, you look quite one of us."

I recalled Freegift snipping away at the frizzled ends of my hair a bit at a time for several days. I hadn't seen a mirror and didn't want one.

"But then," his long face was serious, "you always will be one of us and always in our hearts. Jasper is adamant in not allowing us to pay the doctors' fees. That wouldn't allow us to show our gratitude in any case. There is no way we can do so. Although," his smile came back, "everyone in Hancock insisted on trying by sending a gift to you. There was hardly any room in the wagon for my wares this trip. Besides the picture, there are handkerchiefs and nightshirts, all with your initials embroidered neatly. Up to the minute of my departure, Sister Bertha was adding yet another basket of fruit, jar of cider, box of cookies. Then, of course, there's a packet of notes, letters, and the children's drawings, which I've entrusted to Freegift." He glanced at his list. "Brother Giles bade me not to forget to tell you he is crafting a chair with wheels so that you can move about while you are healing. I shall bring it next visit."

Tucking the paper into his left pocket, his voice and face now somber, he went on, "There's much joy in our community that you and Brother Crispin were saved. But, as you can imagine, there is much sadness as well. I grieve that I was the one who failed the two of you. I am responsible for your suffering. It was my duty to make sure of the whereabouts of all. Quincey instructed me not to forewarn Brother Jeb that the boy might slip out, but I blame myself that I didn't tell Brother Crispin that Hallelujah was with you. It didn't occur to me. But as for," he stopped, "that anguished soul—he eluded me by going to the Seedhouse at supper time and staying hidden there until dark. No doubt he wanted to prepare so that there'd be no saving the building on this occasion. Jasper says it was paraffin, and with all the drying herbs, the chaff . . . Then the rear door was jammed shut. No doubt he intended to run out the front, letting us believe that he'd come in through the back. Trapper and the two Iroquois were still trying to batter that down when the second explosion occurred."

He shook his head and let out his breath painfully. "If you hadn't been so near the door, Crispin would have died. There were no seconds to spare. Jasper said you shouldn't have been there, that it wasn't part of his plan. And to go in as you did—you were very brave."

This time I held up my hand. I'd been needing to say this. Such words made me feel a sham. "No. To be genuinely brave requires an act of will. I ran in without thinking."

"I can't agree with you, Michael. Courage springs from the prepared heart. Yours was."

He got up. "I shan't tire you. Freegift was quite insistent about that. I'll tell all those dear to you that you'll answer their letters when you're able, shall I?"

"Please. Wish more love especially to Cris, Mercy, and—" A sudden thought came to me. "Philemon, were you at Hancock when Sister Esther came?"

"Oh, yes. In fact, I was the one who brought her. She was standing by the roadside and I stopped to ask if I could help her on her way."

"Where was this?"

He sat back down, the light of reminiscence in his eyes. "A byway off the main road to the Berkshires. Here is the odd thing about it. I was on a straight stretch of the high road, glancing down at my papers, and not attending to Chestnut. You know he is quite a sensible horse, not given to shying or quirks. But that day he veered down the lane that led to that byway. Didn't slow down or glance over his shoulder, just set right off on it as if I'd sent him in that direction. I was about to pull him up and go back when it occurred to me that I'd never visited the farms on this route. I wasn't even aware of the road being there. I still had a few barrels and bags to sell.

"But as we went on, I noticed the poor repair of the few houses and barns I passed and I couldn't see much chance of a sale. I kept on, looking for a path that would take me back. Up ahead I saw a figure, waiting. She was before the worst of all the farms I'd passed, the house roof sagging, a gaping hole in that of the barn. She stood quite still, holding a small pillowslip that I took to be a makeshift valise. Assuming she was about to visit a relative further on, I asked if she'd want me to carry her there.

"She was pale, her manner quite subdued. She thanked me politely as I helped her up, and never said another word, not even asking how far I was going or where. When I stopped to allow Chestnut a drink, I offered her some cider and gingerbread from one of our baskets. She remarked on its workmanship, turning it over and over in her hands.

"Ah, well. Soon I was telling her about Mother Ann and Hancock. I had the impression she'd heard little, if anything, about the Believers. As I neared the last crossroads, I asked if she wanted to be set down. She answered, 'I should like to see a place called the City of Peace. May I come with you there?' And so she did."

"Did she ever tell you why she was by that roadside?"

"No. As we neared Hancock, she offered that she was not a runaway wife nor an undutiful daughter. To reassure me, you know, that she'd a right to make a decision about her life. Not that we'd have asked about her past before taking her in. We don't, of course."

Rising again, he smoothed out his coat. "Sister Esther has been such a blessing for all, especially for me since she's be-

come a trustee. When we go down that road, I always give
Chestnut an extra apple for his horse sense."

"You've gone back that way?"

"Well, yes. The land thereabouts is not good. Not that
ours is the best, but we've the fertilizer and the labor,
whereas those small farmers don't. So, on my return trips,
when I haven't sold all, I call in here and there. It'd be
wasteful just to bring the wares back." Philemon picked at a
bit of lint on his sleeve. He believed that speaking of charitable acts was akin to bragging. "One family had an ailing
child so I'd take one of our elixirs, see how the lad was coming on. The mother was right grateful. Gave me a testimo-
nial that we put in the seed catalogue. Very good for
business, that is. Words from a satisfied customer, you
know." He was moving toward the door as he finished.

I raised myself up too quickly and couldn't hide the wince
of pain that caused. "Philemon, that woman must have lived
near the farm where you stopped for Esther. Did you ask her
if she knew the family who lived there?"

"I did." He hesitated and then came back. "It's not the
happiest of stories, Michael." He glanced around as if cheer
should prevail in a sickroom. "I'll tell you another time."

"I'd like to hear it now."

He reseated himself, still with a doubtful look. "Make
yourself comfortable, then. After all, the ending is that Esther is with us. And the woman was glad to hear that, not
knowing what became of her neighbor, although she said
she only spoke to her the once. I gathered that when they
came—Esther, her husband, and the little girl—it was too
plain that the man had never turned his hand to farming. But
the way he spoke made him sound a station above his neighbors and his manner showed he thought so. On the rare days
when he came to the market town, always alone, he wasn't
forthcoming, so they hesitated about offering help.

"One summer day, the farmer's wife told me, they were
on their way to church and saw Esther sitting out in front,
combing the child's hair, tying pink ribbons in it, both of
them laughing. Never saw golden curls like those, she said.
And Esther raised her hand and smiled. So she thought

kindly of her, pitied her being all alone. Blamed herself later for not going to visit, not that the poor woman had time, with a brood the size of hers.

"Then the scarlet fever struck the valley and all she could do was nurse her little ones for some months. Lost one, she did, but the rest survived.

"A year and more went by and things at that place looked worse whenever they passed, she said. Then one day, Esther hurried up to the men in the fields, asked if they'd seen her husband. Gone, he was, but he hadn't taken the horse. It wasn't long before his body surfaced in the millpond with a cord still tied around his leg. They took him to the house and the neighbor woman went along to help lay him out. She said there wasn't a sign of any children.

"They debated some about saying prayers, seeing it was bound to be self-murder. But they decided at last they would. They took him out in the back and that's when the woman saw the small grave beside the new one the men had dug. It had some field flowers on it, tied up with a bit of pink ribbon.

"She told me she heard later that the fever had carried off the child."

After Philemon had gone, I lay there remembering Esther's hands, clenching and twisting those ribbons. I thought of a small girl with shining hair.

Chapter Twenty-nine

"I cannot let Philemon take responsibility, as he seems to be doing." Quincey was standing by the lowboy, its deskbox open, at the far end of my room. He was looking sideways out the window, not at me. He was planted there as firmly as one of the elms outside. His plain frock coat, which hid any unseemly bulges, seemed to be hanging a little more loosely on him, but the jowls of his cheeks still were settled firmly on his cravat. "The fault was mine. There is no gainsaying it. To have overlooked, not one, but two, clear pointers to the truth, is inexcusable."

The trees still held his attention. "As I have always maintained, any disruption in one's schedule will cause all manner of harm. At the very least, it results in digestive upset and unsound sleep, which must affect the brain's function. Then, one oversight leads to another. Confusion worse confounded, as Milton put it. I shall *never* travel again. Orderly thinking cannot take place in unfamiliar surroundings where one is distracted by the adjustments required."

He'd used the word "inexcusable," but this sounded to me like one excuse piled on another. It was clear he was heading toward an apology, or at least edging toward one. In other circumstances, I'd certainly have let him get on with it—and enjoyed it. But I was convinced it wasn't called for here.

To stop him, I asked, "What oversights are you referring to, sir?"

He brought his palm firmly down on the top of the bureau and spun around to face me. "Hepzibah spoke the name of her attacker. And Philemon's description of her last moments showed that she was lucid."

"But . . . but all she said was, 'The dog. He saw. I saw.'"

"That was the problem. Neither of us heard what she *said*. We were both looking at what Philemon *wrote*."

Dumbfounded, I repeated, "He saw." I closed my eyes. "Esau."

"Exactly. We will not, of course, mention this to Philemon lest he also take responsibility for that. It was a natural mistake."

I protested, "Even if we'd understood what Hepzibah said, we wouldn't have accepted that. Issachar insisted that Esau was with him, praying by his bedside, the entire time."

Glumly, Quincey pressed his eyelids shut and reopened them to their usual half-mast position. "In a conversation with Bertha and Thankful, one that you reported to me in full detail, they told us he'd left Issachar's room."

"They did?"

"Recall the jug of chamomile tea that Esau reported was empty and Thankful said was half-full and in its usual place. He'd told the ailing brother that he could find none of the beverage, thus implying a search, thus explaining the fact that he was gone for some time. When you questioned Issachar, you had to tread carefully and therefore asked if he'd dozed off. If you could have phrased the question exactly, 'Did Esau leave your room?'—which would have aroused suspicion in him—no doubt he might have remembered that the deacon had done so. Perhaps not, even then. He might have regarded that errand to the kitchen as part of this concern for his condition, and thus considered that Esau was still 'with him.' Issachar was delighted that, for once, he was not being judged a hypochondriac."

"The mint leaves. Esau poisoned himself?"

"I doubt that he actually swallowed any. He need only scatter a few leaves that reeked of wintergreen on the platter so that others, finding them later, would believe that's what he ate. Simply putting one in his mouth for a few seconds would inflame the membranes, thus convincing the nurses later. He then rushed outside and spat it out. Obviously, as a

method of poisoning any given person it was woefully inef-
ficient. Anyone might have chewed on those sprigs of mint.
But, of course, he had no intention of that. The mint was
only there a few seconds. His sole purpose was to frighten
you into leaving Hancock."

He sat down heavily in the Chippendale chair by the window. The elegant splayed legs of those chairs must be quite
strong. "With you out of the way, he'd have a clear field.
Being 'confined' in the Nurse House gave him an advantage. Sister Agatha said he'd rise repeatedly—and half
dress—in order to use the privy, being 'too modest' to use
the chamber pot. On the night of the fire, he simply declared
himself recovered and told Agatha he would go to supper in
the Living Quarters. He went instead into the Seedhouse. No
one missed him since the Family thought he was in the
Nurse House. And, that being true, no one would have suspected him of starting the fire. Afterwards, he would have
joined those frantically carrying buckets to put it out."

"It was he who took my notes?"

"Undoubtedly. He must have been watching you from the
moment you arrived. In Jacob's letter requesting my help, he
said that he'd not *even* discussed the problem with the other
elders. His inclusion of that adverb gave me to understand
that he'd talked to no one. But Jacob was sorely beset, and
he wanted the advice first of someone he could trust absolutely, his birth brother. Unfortunately. Whereas Esau
couldn't have known what action I would take, when you arrived he suspected I'd sent you. Perhaps he saw you looking
at the Seedhouse. His search of your room confirmed his assumption."

Staring at the floor, he added, "You were in danger from
the very beginning."

"But why did Esau start the fires to begin with? Why?"

"This is not a supposal. I state it, although I can only base
my conclusion on what the great writers tell us of human nature. The fact that Jacob was almost certain to be appointed
to the Central Ministry was unendurable to Esau. Throughout his life, he'd been eclipsed by his twin. Jacob was

stronger, handsomer, more likable. He won, always, without being aware that his brother was competing."

He paused, shifting uncomfortably. Now the chair did creak.

I remembered Jacob saying that both he and Esau followed the lovely young Alma with their eyes. I knew which brother she loved. So must have Esau.

Quincey pushed his upper lip forward with his lower. "It is noteworthy that the classic writers link envy with fire. Hesiod says, 'bitter envy burns.' Then, of course, Livy: '*Invidiam, tamquam ignem, summa petere.*'" He cocked an eyebrow at me.

I would have thought that my Latin, learned long ago and not used for some time, would have deserted me. But I'd studied it when very young and the translation came to me. I replied, "Envy, like fire, soars upward." I was quite proud of myself.

He nodded gravely, not even quibbling with my wording. Throughout this conversation, I'd felt he'd been most careful not to puncture my self-esteem. Whether this sprang from pity for my misery or from guilt for his part in it, I couldn't tell. On the other hand, he could have given the quote in English.

His chair complained again, but he went on imperturbably. "The importance of a position in the Central Ministry, to Believers, cannot be overstated. They are remarkably democratic, as their position on women and Negroes shows. But their religion posits new revelations from heaven, coming down from above like beams of light." He gave one of his barely discernible shrugs and glanced again toward the window. "As a Deist, I myself hold that God is no longer involved in the universe He created, but they see signs of His ongoing interest. In any case, the elders in New Lebanon receive these, sometimes in the forms of visions. These men and women are consequently revered. Jacob would have been raised very high over his brother."

"That would have been hard for Esau to bear."

Quincey put a palm upward. "Setting the fires might well have delayed Jacob's appointment by the Central Ministry, either because they would have felt he was needed in Hancock or because they might begin to doubt his effectiveness. I'm inclined to think that the burning of the Seedhouse in New Lebanon was simply an accident. It may have given Esau the idea. He may have been brooding over Jacob's openness to Samuel Grant's many changes, which would have moved the Believers away from their original self-sufficiency. To him, such a move would be sinful and he could have persuaded himself that his brother was not worthy. In any case, the fires here might well have accomplished his goal. But the death of the elderly brother in the fire changed everything. Now he had to rationalize further. Perhaps he began telling himself that the entire community needed cleansing."

An exasperated sigh escaped him. "When I pressed Freegift about his earlier remark concerning his worry about Jacob, he admitted that it was, as he put it, the way Esau looked at Jacob on occasion. He saw the envy, although I doubt that Jacob ever did. Freegift is very sensitive to others' feelings. Too much so."

I was propped up on pillows and, using my elbows, inched a little higher. "But, to have known this earlier, wouldn't have made me suspect Esau. I was convinced he lacked opportunity."

Quincey heaved himself out of the chair and paced back to the window. "*I* eliminated him too quickly. And to have overlooked the remark about the tea!" He twitched at the curtains as if to adjust his view and thus soothe his spirit.

After a moment, without looking at me, he said, "We must discuss Samuel Grant. It was he who paid for my extensive searches for you and for your later care. I was enjoined to silence regarding his part until now."

"Grant?" I sat straight upward, oblivious for once of the shock of quick movement.

"Yes. He wished to make restitution to you, feeling he hadn't given you the proper share of your father's business. He'd left ample holdings with his older son Jared so he was well able to afford this. But Jared could find no trace of you. I was enlisted by the Shaker elders in New Lebanon, who were concerned about Samuel's weight of guilt. There's a reporter at the *Independent* who's familiar with the dockside area. He found you.

"Now Grant has been apprised of your identity. He wishes to settle a sum of money on you. Properly invested and carefully conserved, these funds will enable you to live as you choose. Provided, of course, you do not choose a mansion on Beacon Hill and a dissolute style of life."

I said nothing. I couldn't. Anger choked my throat. I didn't want his money now. For him to have subjected my mother to cheese parings. Kindling instead of coal. Perhaps if she'd not been using it—

Quincey's voice cut through my thoughts. "You must accept this money, Michael." I didn't notice at the time that he'd addressed me by my first name. "You will not interrupt, please, while I make my case. It's a gift, long delayed, from your father. He'd want you to have it. It is not a matter of easing Grant's conscience, although I see no reason why you should not do that."

He walked slowly to the fireplace near my bed and rested his arm on the mantel. "You must consider what the man has done for his son Giles. Confronted with the boy's condition, he consulted priests, ministers, and doctors. He followed their advice. In the end, he became convinced that all of this hadn't benefited his son, instead causing him much misery. Learning of the Shakers, he decided they could help. What does he do? He gives up his own comfortable life, his home, his work, and goes with Giles. Perhaps the man became a genuine Believer. I can't guess. But it's certain that he gave up much. Such sacrifice speaks of enormous love, not merely a sense of duty."

The image of Samuel sweating at the ropes in the Tanning House sprang to my mind. The muscles straining, the smell. When I heard him speak of that, I'd savored the picture.

Quincey spread out a palm. "I already noted to you your reporting on fires in your columns. It occurred to me that you felt the destruction of your home might have been prevented. A reporter I engaged for the purpose interviewed such former neighbors as he could find. They all testified to its quick spread, which certainly would indicate a mishap with paraffin, no doubt on a servant's part. Such an accident could have happened at any time, in any circumstances.

"Now, I gather Samuel Grant is not an easy man, not at all pleasing in his manner. Esther, given her journal entry, preferred that he remain at one remove from her. Although," he inched his eyebrows up as he considered, "her differences with him may well be philosophical. She may identify her own independence with the community's ability to produce all that they use. A way of being self-sufficient—a state she seems to prize—on a group basis." He waved a few fingers since it seemed too much trouble to move his whole hand. "My point is that you will not be swayed in this matter on such a minor consideration as Grant's likability. There's no need to give me your answer on this now."

It wasn't what I had on my mind. It was Esther. Although I didn't tell Quincey her story, it was clear to me why she so wanted to be able to care for herself. And why, after that pain and loss, she had such fear of opening her heart again.

Then I did think about Samuel Grant, although not about the money. I was being forced to revise my opinion of him. Other ideas of mine were being put in new configurations. It was taking great effort and I turned away from it. A question sprang to my mind that was easier. "How did Giles manage to sing in French and in a woman's voice?"

Quincey didn't seem surprised at my change of subject. "A speculation on my part. Grant said the boy was sickly when very young, that he had nurses much of the time. It's possible that one of them might have been French Canadian and, to lull the child, had sung the hymns of her homeland to him. During an emotional experience, such as the Midnight Cry, not only her words but the way she sang came from him as if they were his own."

This time he waved his whole hand. "As to your immediate future, you'll stay here. You may want to consider, after your convalescence, resuming your interrupted studies. Your records at Harvard show that you are capable, and they would re-admit you even though you're older. If that idea interests you, you could remain here." He gestured to show that he meant more than the room. "The west wing is empty. I don't use it."

I was incapable of reply. What confused me most was what he'd said last. Was his guilt over my injuries so great that he felt he had to make such an offer? I just lay there and looked at him.

"You needn't address that now, either. You must be tiring." He glanced at the mantel clock. "It is nearing eleven and Freegift will be bringing the sherry to my room. You yourself should take a glass of Madeira. It aids recuperation. I'll tell Freegift to bring you one." Moving toward the door, he stopped before opening it. "It'll do no harm to mention this, since you're surely aware of it. You'll be confined for a long period, if not to a bed, at least to a chair. To while away the time, it'd be useful to write a memoir of your recent experience. It'll clarify it in your thinking. It would be entirely for your own purposes. I wouldn't trouble you by reading it. However, I would recommend that you do it chronologically and not engage in bringing to bear later knowledge on any event." He had his hand on the doorknob. "It would cause me great pain to think that the words 'Had I but known' would be written down in my house."

With that, he sailed out of the room.

Chapter Thirty

When Freegift came to take away my lunch tray and I asked for the basket of letters that Philemon brought, he answered, "I'll bring it after your rest, sir." There was a surprisingly stubborn set to his mouth. He'd give in, though, if I pleaded. But as much as I wanted to hold Esther's note in my hand, even if I didn't open it just then, I wanted to know what I thought before I read it. If I had it in my hand, there'd be no resisting.

There is a languor to convalescence—quite different from the apathy of illness—but it weakens you all the same. I gave in to that. He'd just shut the door when, my way eased by the Madeira, I slid into sleep.

When I awoke, Esther was as immediately in my mind as if she'd been in the room. I began to visualize her note. The Shakers were in the habit at mealtimes of reading aloud letters from those in other communities. Hers would no doubt be of that sort, filled with news and friendly greetings. Having seen her journals, I could imagine she might include the final count on bushels from the corn harvest. But I knew she'd choose her words with care, aware that I would read above and beneath each line.

The question, for me, was whether I would accept what she wrote as the final word. My feet weren't able to carry me back to Hancock, but going on my knees was possible. I told myself that my arms were long enough, strong enough, to embrace and protect her. Without telling her that's what I was doing, of course. Room to spare for Mercy and Cris. Now, with funds from Samuel Grant, we could choose a wider life than I'd been able to envision before.

But I suspected that what I had to protect them from was me. In the back of my mind, I heard the echo of Alma's words. How hard the act of wishing well. Images sprang unwanted to my mind. Mercy sitting on that Chippendale chair in an organdy dress, her brow furrowed as she tried to remember the correct form of the irregular verbs. Cris in a stiff collar on his way to a boys' preparatory school where he could never excel at studies or at games. Esther in silk pouring tea for the ladies in the drawing room— No. Esther in a country place. No. There'd be nothing to do that she would see as useful, and the only women around her would be servants. She looked forward to her business day, but there was no place for women in offices in Boston.

The Shakers were regimented; World People had their rules as well. Any choice of a life was limited by the fact that we must live with others.

And we must die. Esther saw her village in the green hills as a way station to a city on a higher hill. If she stayed there, she knew that one day she'd walk down an eternal road of flowers, see a white house, throw open a door, bend down, and gather to her the girl with golden hair. If I persuaded her to go, how clear would the road be?

Of course, I could put on the broad-brimmed hat and the long sober coat. Every day, I'd see Esther at mealtimes; I'd go to the Office and speak to her on matters of business. At weekly Union Meetings, being age-paired, we could discuss everyday concerns. Always close, never touching. One had to truly be a Believer. I wasn't. I couldn't even imagine a heaven, let alone see the inhabitants of such a place.

Faith is a mystery. I'd been stirred by the sound of a golden trumpet. But minutes later I began to consider which of the people on the mountaintop had played it. I'd glimpsed a face in the fire. Esau disappeared. The timing was heaven-sent. But my eyes were blinded with smoke. I'd never forget it, but I could only regard it as an illusion, not a vision.

When Freegift finally brought me the basket, I decided to read the letters in order, just as they came. The top one was from Bertha. Her opening greeting, her wishes for my recovery, and her assurance of prayers were a little stilted. But

I could hear her voice in what followed: "The seedcakes are the ones you like. They'll be quite good when you get them since they improve on sitting, as do the ginger chips. I put in a bottle of blackberry syrup to go with the potions sent by the nurse sisters. They add a bit of honey to them, but that don't go far in taking away the bitter taste. I say that medicine that isn't nasty is more apt to be taken. The blackberry will do it and it is itself healthful."

A quantity of pages neatly stitched together came next. The first sentence started with "Al va lan." I didn't have to look at the signature, but I did. It was from Thankful. My resolve to go in order went out the open window. I decided I'd be stronger later and put it aside.

The uneven printing on the next sheet was so big that the few words took up half the page. "Get your feet bedder and hurry back. Hurry. I told him your coming." It was signed, "Mercy." There was an arrow directing me to the drawing of a stick figure with one ear upright. The tail was a happy curve, the dog's front legs were shorter than the back ones. Hallelujah was leaping for joy.

Alma said that when one cracks open the wall around the heart, letting it break, you feel a tenderness for all life. I was not only tender, I was sore all over.

So it took me a moment before I could pick up the very large, carefully folded envelope of paper with Esther's handwriting on the front. Inside, there were two sheets of paper. On the first, she wrote, "This letter is from Brother Crispin and me. He's fully recovered and in good health. For that, we both send you our everlasting thanks and more love than would fit in any size envelope.

"He wants me to say, right away, that school starts soon for him and he's going to learn to print so he can write you. Brother Amos has made a metal brace for his leg and he wears it *all* day. And I'm to tell you that the enclosed drawing was done by Brother Elijah, but it was done with Crispin's help. It took some time. A very patient Elijah would sketch and a very exacting Crispin would shake his head. At last, he was satisfied. I don't recognize the depiction, but he's sure you will.

"I close with my favorite line from the poem that Elder Jacob read aloud at Sister Hepzibah's services. As you may recall, it says that we, in the Family of Believers, not only look forward to the hereafter, but are content in the here and now. 'I've the whole in present time, yea every day I live.'

"I shall remember you, every day, sending prayers for your health and happiness. All of us do and will. Your Sister Esther."

I let the letter fall from my fingers and stared straight ahead. There was no need to read between the lines. She'd said it very plainly. She wouldn't leave. I'd expected that. But somehow I'd hoped. I wanted a little room left for that. I didn't see it on the page. At least I couldn't persuade myself of it. Not today, anyway.

The sunlight falling on the floor was dappled by the tree leaves, making a shifting pattern as the breeze blew. I imagined Esther sitting at her desk writing to me. Cris was surely standing at her elbow, given the 'right now' she'd put in. He'd be pointing to the brace, making writing signs, anxious that she told me everything. And she'd be nodding, smiling reassuringly at him as her pen moved over the page. But then it would have stopped as she tried to think of a way to phrase what followed. Her words seemed stilted. I'd noticed that. Was it hard for her to write them?

She was a Believer. I began to consider how she became one. When Philemon came down that little used road, she was numb, waiting. She might have been willing to go in any direction, one seeming much the same as another. When he told her of that clean and shining village, she went. And she stayed, no doubt clinging desperately to the hope that was offered. Maybe—

I'd be going back to visit. I wanted, needed, to see her, Cris, Mercy. All of them. The Shakers had become more than friends to me. They'd become my family.

Esther and I wouldn't talk. In a polite, roundabout way, I could say a few things. I would be strong and not press her. At least I hoped I would. But after all, it was the merest chance that Philemon had come by. Mere chance.

I decided to go over the letter again. Fumbling for it, I saw Elijah's drawing. Crispin's picture. I stared at it, unmoving.

There was the face, haloed by flames, untouched by them. There was the beauty of it, the peace in it. There were the winged eyebrows above eyes that now looked directly at me. It was exactly as I had seen it. So had Crispin.